I0630289

The Plains of Pluto

Imperium Volume 2, Book 2

Travis Starnes

Copyright © 2025 by Travis Starnes
All rights reserved.
No part of this publication may be reproduced, distributed, or transmitted in any form
or by any means, including photocopying, recording, or other electronic or mechanical
methods, without the prior written permission of the publisher, except as permitted by
U.S. copyright law.
The story, all names, characters, and incidents portrayed in this production are ficti-
tious. No identification with actual persons (living or deceased), places, buildings, and
products is intended or should be inferred.

Maps available at

https://tstarnes.com/book-series/imperium/

Signup to get free previews of upcoming books before they're released at

http://tstarnes.com/preview-notification-newsletter/

Contents

Chapter 1

Eastern Germania

The autumn wind bit through the fabric of Ky's cloak as he entered the large command tent, which offered little additional protection against the cold of the oncoming Germanic winter, even with the stove burning in the corner.

Not that it actually bothered him. The nanites streaming through his body were able to adjust his internal and even skin temperature to some degree, insulating him from the outside weather. He couldn't withstand long sojourns buck naked in freezing snow, but bundled up in thick furs, he would be fine.

He'd grown soft over the five-year sojourn between active wars, living in either palaces or at least comfortable longhouses. This would be his first winter back in the field, and he would have to adjust to it.

The other men gathered in the tent looked equally as grim, although they more than likely had things on their minds other than the weather outside.

"I appreciate everyone making their way here. I know our attention has been scattered the last several months, with so many crises happening simultaneously, but as we enter this new phase of the war, I wanted to get as many of our commanders and members of the alliance together as we could to discuss what the next year has in store for us."

"I'd prefer to hear about how we can turn the rout we have been under for the last six months into an advance," Bernia, the chieftain of the Anarti tribe and a member of the Germanic Alliance's ruling council, said.

"The retreat has already ended, hence the beginning of a new phase," Ky said. "The last battles cost them dearly, and we have halted them cold along the current front. The same is true of the large fleet they were sailing for Britannia. We received notice that our fleet has managed to engage and sink them, which is what has given us this moment of pause, as the Easterners pull back to lick their wounds."

"I wouldn't go so far as to call it a pause," Bomilcar said. "They continue to push both north and south, presumably looking for a place where our trenches end and they can get in behind us."

"Which is why we continue expanding," Ky replied. "Between the new trench lines being dug to the north and our river boats holding the rivers, they will find there is no way into Germania except over our trench lines. Which we have already shown them is a fatal proposition, with things as they stand now."

"But how long can things hold as they are now?" Ehtrius, the leader of the Ilergetes tribe and one of the Hispania Confederation's leaders, asked.

"I think for a while," Ky said. "Most of the line is not trench to trench, but trenches pushed behind the Wisla River, with them on the other side. There are only a few places where they are across. It's also where, for now, they are concentrating and where we are concentrating. How that will change really depends on our friends in Greece. Losing the Macedonians, the Thracians, and Thessalonians to the Easterners was a blow, and means that our lines will have to cut across Greece as well. The region does not lend itself well to large trench fortifications, which will make that area much more fluid and harder to control. Thankfully, it is also harder for large troop formations to move through that area."

"That will hurt us as well, won't it?" Lucilla asked.

"Partially. We've already started putting in rail lines. As of yet, we have not seen the Easterners use rail transport, at least not close enough that we've been able to see it. I'm not saying we should count on that, considering how quickly they seem to have copied our other advancements, but for the time being, it could be an advantage."

"There could be other problems that might keep us from holding our lines," Bomilcar said. "We are starting to see shortages of ammunition and powder. The constant defensive actions have caused us to deplete our stores a lot faster than we expected, especially since it's been along a front crossing the length of the whole continent. We've lost nearly two thousand men in the past month holding these positions. The continuous nature of trench warfare means we can't rotate units out for rest as we should."

"I know, and I have sent word to Devnum and the factories we are starting to set up in Gaul and Germania to see about increasing production. I'm hoping the large number of nitrate beds every member of the alliance has been requested to build should decrease that shortage soon."

Ky was not sure of that, however. The numbers that Sophus had projected, even with those new beds, were grim, to say the least.

"As for manpower," Ky continued. "That is one of the purposes of this meeting. I know that not every tribal leader could be here for this, but I'm hoping you will each take our request back to your councils. We have already begun passing laws allowing some levels of conscription in Britannia, and I suggest you do the same in your regions. Our need for manpower is quickly outstripping our ability to do it on a voluntary basis."

"Which is easy for people who have lived their lives in cities, living comfortably for so long," Aliverko, the chieftain of the Anglii, interjected. "My warriors complain to me of endless days in mud-filled ditches, watching their brothers fall to unseen enemies. This is not how free men fight!"

Of all the chieftains from either the Germanic Alliance or the Gallic Confederacy, Ky found Aliverko the most frustrating. The man was, at times, one of their biggest supporters, but he was also hopelessly stuck in the past. If given the choice between facing a single opponent a hundred yards away with a rifle or a knife, the man would choose a knife every time and give the other man the rifle.

"You've been to the hospital, Aliverko," Ky said. "I know you have. You've seen the injuries men who meet modern weapons fall to. You were here when we stopped the final push by the Easterners, stacking their dead in front of our trenches higher than a man could see over. I'm sure each of those men died bravely, but they still died. Is that the end you want to see for your warriors?"

Aliverko's expression remained stoic, but Ky could see him picturing the carnage that resulted from the Easterners facing trenches with barbed wire and fused artillery shells. It had been gruesome.

"The world is changing," Ky continued. "Soon, we'll be deploying weapons that will make even our current rifles seem primitive. Imagine your best warriors, charging across that field with axes and swords, when artillery shells begin falling. Each shell carries the power of fifty powder charges, exploding in a storm of metal fragments. There would be no glory in such a death, only waste."

"The Consul speaks the truth," Bomilcar added. "I've led men into combat my entire life and have spent more time on a battlefield than under a roof. I understand your men's frustrations, but they need to know that the tactics we use are to limit our losses while causing the greatest losses to the enemy. We've lost men, yes, but our casualties are nothing compared to theirs. For every Britannian or Germanic warrior who falls in those trenches, we claim ten of the enemy."

"We must adapt or perish. The TianYou Empire has already begun to learn this lesson, their latest attacks show signs of tactical evolution. They're developing their own trench networks, attempting to mirror our defensive strategies. So we will continue to change the way we fight, to stay a step ahead of them."

"At least it is nearing winter. We can use the down months to retrain the men and hopefully work some of their old ways of thinking out of them, in addition to getting more men ready for the front line," Bomilcar said.

"That's outdated thinking. The nature of trench warfare has eliminated the concept of seasonal campaigns. The fighting will continue regardless of weather, and I expect the TianYou to use winter for targeted strikes against our weaker positions."

That came as unwelcome news, especially to the seasoned commanders, nearly all of whom had come up through the ranks during the days of phalanx and shield walls, where armies provisioned off the land as they moved, and mostly held steady or even returned home during the winter months to keep from starving.

"There's also the situation in Greece, that you mentioned earlier, which will complicate your decision a little more. As you said, the lines there will be hard to adapt, and our allies here are still making the adjustment to the modern way of fighting," Modius said, gesturing to the representatives from Illyria, Epirus, and Corinth who had accompanied him up from Corinth. "But that isn't our only concern. While we have gotten a positive response from the Pannonians, who should soon be joining our effort, so far, Athens, Argos, and Sparta remain undecided. Should they join with the other polities who have joined the Easterners, the south and heart of Greece will be lost to us."

"While I would, of course, prefer those three – and I'm assuming their associated junior states – I'm more concerned with what our line must look like with the defecting states. If they had stayed with us, and if the Greeks' mission to Dacia is successful, we would have the single break between the Wisla and the Dnjester to give us a line north and south across the continent, allowing us to focus our men on the break where the two rivers do not touch, instead of stretching for a month's travel southwest through the lands of Pannonia and Illyria to the borders of Italy. Now, they can bypass our holds on the rivers and bring men straight across from Anatolia, creating a bulge in our lines the size of the Balkans. It would almost be easier just to hold the line from Dacia to Illyria and be done with it."

"And abandon those who would join you?" the representative from Corinth asked angrily.

His anger was understandable; being near the bottom of Greece near the Aegean, such a disbursement of men would mean abandoning his entire state to the Easterners.

"I said it would be easier, not that that is what we plan to do. You have joined the Western Alliance, and so we will defend you as we would any other part of the alliance. I just meant to say it makes our situation much more difficult. It also highlights where a lot of the fight will be. Considering their troop concentration, and the time it will take for them to move men through the rugged terrain of the area, I think the Easterners will, for now, concentrate their presence on the area between the Wisla and the Dniester, but once they have gotten enough resources into Greece, I can all but guarantee that is where the fighting will shift."

"So we prepare for that," Lucilla said.

"Exactly so. But it's going to take manpower and supplies. We can move a lot of supplies to Italia and ship them across the Ionian into Illyria, Epirus, and Aetolia, which should shorten our supply routes considerably. We will still have to put in rail lines to the front, but that is an easier task than bringing them down from Quadi and Antari in Southern Germania, although when time permits, we will, of course, extend those connections as well. We will need to begin training their people quickly, as they will have to make up a large part of the manpower there. But I'm not sure there are enough recruitable men in the region to protect the front that will grow there. The Easterners will have the internal lines, being the inside of the bulge, which gives them the advantage."

"I am working on that problem," Lucilla says. "I plan on stopping to talk to many of our allies who were not able to make this meeting, as I make my way back to Britannia, to encourage them to increase recruitment. Once back in Devnum, I will also continue to work on the Scandi and the Ptolemies, neither of whom has decided to join the fight yet."

"Good. For those of you here, now is the time to begin bringing in more men. The conflict will not stop over the winter, but it will slow, and we have a window to operate in, while the Easterners start to exploit their gain in Greece. That means now is the time to train new recruits, not four months from now. Go back to your people and increase your recruitment efforts. If we don't have enough men, all the technological advantage in the world will not be enough to keep the Easterners from punching through our lines and coming into Germania and Italy from Greece, which is something none of you want to contemplate."

Ky looked to the handful of representatives who had made the journey, including the Greek envoys, to ensure they were taking him seriously. Their expressions said they did.

"Good. Then let's get started."

Ky held out a hand and gently pulled Lucilla up, putting her arm inside his, leading her out of the tent while Bomilcar dealt with their guests. They knew what needed to be done and he hoped most of them would believe that it was critical that they listened and convinced their people to follow through with what was needed.

The Greeks certainly would. He could see the panic on their faces, especially the man from Corinth, who was in a terrible position if they didn't get Athens and the rest to join and at least consolidate southern Greece.

The rest ... he'd have to wait and see.

He trusted Lucilla would be able to handle them. She'd shown numerous times that she was better equipped to deal with things on the diplomatic front than he was. Until then, he had Lucilla for a few hours before she had to board a train to take her back west, and he wanted to spend as much time as he could with her.

"I want to see the front," she said as soon as they were out of the tent.

"You heard that the fighting never really ends. It's much too dangerous for you to go there."

"And it isn't for you? I've led men into battle Ky. I am not a precious doll that must be coddled."

"You did, but you weren't Empress then. You are now, and the Empire relies on you. Conchobar and Talogren are good men, but I do not think they could hold the Empire together."

"You could."

"Maybe, but without you, I don't want to."

She smiled at Ky for a moment and said, "That's sweet, and it also won't work. I want to see the front."

Ky could only shake his head. She was a stubborn woman who, once she got something in mind, could not be torn from it.

"You are supposed to be leaving in five hours and the front is three hours by horseback.

"There is a supply train scheduled to leave in ten minutes which will take roughly forty minutes to reach the front," Sophus said.

"See," she said as the AI sent the information to both of them simultaneously. "Plenty of time."

"Thank you, Sophus, that was very helpful. Fine. Let's go."

The train arrived in fifteen minutes and took forty-five minutes to get there, but that was still good timing. While mechanical clocks had become standard across the Empire and were used widely by the legions in the name of efficiency, they were not as accurate as circuit-based clocks, let alone the one available to Sophus, but it was good enough for what they were doing now."

The train itself didn't go all the way to the front, of course. It stopped outside of artillery range, since its smoke plume made it an obvious target. The enemy had begun to adapt howitzer-like cannon of their own, and plunging fire had become something of a problem, but they still predominantly used solid shot. What explosive rounds they did have used cut fuses, which were unreliable at best, and did not have the same effect on the battlefield as the Britannian impact fuse.

Still, it was better not to chance a locomotive, which was still resource-intensive and time-consuming to make. To protect people coming in from the train line, they'd built protective connected trenches leading into it, with large earthen barricades crisscrossing them, offering protection from possible shrapnel.

They led into secondary and even tertiary trenches for staging reinforcements, fallback positions, and command positions, which were themselves heavily reinforced concrete bunkers.

Not all of this was built, of course. They'd only built the first trench a month and a half prior, but the pace of the work was extraordinary.

And not just here.

This kind of work was happening across hundreds of miles. Not continuously, of course, and not all as elaborate. Trenches were needed as a counter to river crossings for most of their line, but there were some spots, like this central line starting where the Wisla River turned from its southbound path, where the trenches were incredibly extensive.

"You kept calling the work here massive, but I had no idea," Lucilla said as they made their way down the supply trench to the main command bunker that had only recently been completed.

"It is hard to truly understand unless you've seen it. Watch your step though, even with the boarding, the ground is treacherous after the last rain."

Inside the bunker, the air was still damp, but warmer. Maps and charts covered a central table, illuminated by a cluster of oil lamps. The rear wall featured narrow observation slits that offered a view of the trench network, along with a mounted spyglass, the most advanced they'd made so far, for observing the enemy trenches.

A small telegraph station was half set up against one side, although the lines for it, and to the balloons that would be launched a little to the rear, had not all been laid yet.

"You wanted to see the lines," Ky said, pointing to the observation slit. "There they are."

Lucilla approached the viewing area slowly, her mouth slightly open as she stared out of the bunker at the torn earth in front of her. Thin gray lines of trenches stretched across the landscape, dotted with clusters of soldiers huddled against the earthworks. Between them and the opposing forces, the ground was littered with unburied bodies, their shapes barely discernible in the churned-up mud.

The fact that they kept trying to send men across, to break through the lines, when they had inferior artillery and didn't have the rate of fire needed to suppress Ky's men, was a waste. Ky certainly wouldn't have made that call, but then Ky didn't know the true strength they faced.

He knew the bulk of the soldiers were from the area of the world that might have been known as China in the original timeline, but they had seen and even captured people from the Middle East, Southern and Southeastern Asia, the Steppes, and even parts of what was currently called Sardinia.

Beyond that, the TianYou were still a mystery. They did not understand who their leaders were, how they managed to copy so much technology, or how their military was structured, aside from the parts they could see in combat, which seemed to be copied from Britannia's own structure.

An explosion in the distance sent a column of dirt skyward, followed by faint cries.

Lucilla's knuckles whitened as she gripped the edge of the observation slit. "How many men die here each day?"

"Hundreds, sometimes thousands. The front lines are a constant grind. This is a war of attrition, Lucilla. Victory comes at a cost—one we're paying with blood. Most casualties are on the enemy's side of the line, since we are operating purely on the defensive at the moment, but their early attempts to copy our shells has resulted in more casualties among our men still in the trenches."

"Is there no way to end this slaughter?"

"I'm working on it. There are technologies that would end this type of war but we are a long way from those. They require innovation upon innovation, and there is no rushing them into existence. But for now, this ..." he gestured to the trenches, the carnage beyond, "... is our reality. By next year, we should at least have a new type of rifle that will increase the rate of fire of one man, so we can spread out more. But there are limits to what that can achieve. It's why we need to convince our allies to provide more reinforcements."

"You mean I need to," she said. "So we can make more bodies."

"I am not heartless, Lucilla. And we lost plenty of men when it was just swords, spears, and shields. War always takes its due. It's just easier to understand when it's personal, instead of this kind of war."

"I don't think you're heartless," she said. "but ... I'm having trouble getting my mind wrapped around this."

She was quiet for a long time, watching their men occasionally step onto a firing step, fire off a round, and step back to make room for another soldier while they reloaded. The two lines continually sniped and picked at each other.

For the most part, the rounds were ineffectual, smacking into timber or packed earth. But not every time. Men still died, stepping up at the wrong moment, catching a stray bullet, or even a ricochet through the trench.

And none of that counted the destruction of the artillery.

Ky did not press her but waited patiently. If she wanted to see this, then he would let her soak in it. Really observe it, so she understood just what they faced, and why there were no other options than this.

Finally, she turned from the viewing slit and said, "Fine. If this is what it takes, I'll find you the men to kill."

She turned and walked out of the bunker without another word, her guards falling in around her. Ky knew her anger wouldn't hold. She knew him well enough to know this wasn't what he wanted.

But still, it stung.

He'd brought this technology, these changes to their world. The rifled muskets and cannon had seemed like such advantages when fighting the Carthaginians. But now ...

"Consul?" his aide's voice broke through his thoughts.

"Right. Since we're here, let's finish the tour ourselves. I want to see how far we've gotten on the secondary trench lines."

Chapter 2

Devnum Docks

The wheels of Hortensius's hired carriage clattered to a halt on the cobblestones near Devnum's sprawling dockyards. He stepped down, his boots meeting the stone with a solid thud, only to have to hop back into the carriage almost instantly to avoid being run down by a man with a hand cart.

To say the docks were busy was an understatement. People were moving in every direction, most carrying large and heavy things. Hortensius was used to the chaos of his factories, but at least that seemed to have a structure. Ordered workstations and a place for each thing, all mostly contained inside a building.

Here, the chaos stretched in all directions and there seemed to be no sense to the madness.

Hortensius exited the carriage again, this time more carefully, looking both ways to make sure it was clear before exiting all the way. He made his way toward the administrative building, which sat back from the water, a practical structure of brick and timber.

Inside, clerks bent over their ledgers while foremen consulted charts and schedules posted on the walls. One of the clerks, a thin man with ink-stained fingers, pointed Hortensius toward the meeting room without looking up from his work.

Hortensius found Lucan already deep in discussion with his staff, standing over tables covered with technical drawings.

"My apologies for the delay," Hortensius said, stepping into the warm room, heated by a large stove in one corner. "I got tied up with a project and missed the train I'd intended to take."

Lucan smiled and shook his head. Hortensius knew his reputation, and did not take it personally.

"I'm glad you made it. Perhaps you can explain this madness to me." He jabbed a calloused finger at the blueprints. "This isn't shipbuilding, it's pure fantasy."

"I've looked those over thoroughly. The calculations are sound," Hortensius replied, moving to stand beside the table. "The displacement-to-weight ratio ..."

"Calculations?" Lucan scoffed. "I've been building ships my entire life. I get the benefit of iron ships, but when we added iron plates to wooden hulls, at least on the riverboats, we were still working with actual ships underneath those plates. This? This is a metal box that will sink faster than a stone."

"It won't. Wood or steel, water displacement will hold a sealed vessel afloat. As you've said, you've been building ships your entire life. You know that principle."

"Sealed is the key. Wood swells as it gets wet, pushes tighter into other planking. Tar and pitch seal it tight. Steel does not swell and tar and pitch will not soak into steel like it does wood."

"Which is why the Consul instructed us on these new building techniques. Specifically, the advancements in riveting. See here, and here. The overlapping plates, when properly affixed ..."

"I've seen plenty of riveted armor," Lucan cut in. "Never once did I look at a lorica segmentata and think, 'By the gods, this would make a fine boat.'"

"This is different from anything we've attempted before, true. But the principles are sound. The Consul knows what he's doing, and as you can see, many of the parts here were in the river boats, which is why he wanted us to do those first. So now we can focus on the new techniques needed for this ship."

"I don't doubt the Consul, but different is an understatement."

"I think you need to consider what we're working with. Much of it we've been using on land and have a strong understanding of. This isn't iron we're talking about, but shaped tempered high-grade steel. It'll hold up to immense strain that a wooden ship could never withstand. Second, the new riveting techniques the Consul has described should change the nature of shipbuilding completely. We've done some small-scale tests, and I can tell you, the results are amazing. These designs call for the same quality steel as the plates, heated to temperatures previously unattainable, since it can hold the heat better, and when cooled, creates a stronger bond than anything we've achieved before. Especially when paired with the new compressed air tool the Consul describes on page thirty-two."

"I saw that, but it left me a bit confused," Lucan admitted.

"I felt much the same way until we built one and started testing it. The results are … extraordinary. The steam engine forces the air into a small space giving it intense pressure, and when allowed out it escapes with incredible force. More force than a man could apply with a single hammer. It not only pushes this larger bolt into the hole making an incredibly tight fit, but it flattens the larger head, which is too large to go through the hole, tight against the metal, which is where it will stay when it cools, keeping the plates tight together. Actually, it shrinks even more as it cools, pushing the overlapping plates even tighter together."

"But does tight mean watertight?"

"Yes. We use similar riveting, although smaller rivets, on some of our steam boilers, and they hold incredibly high-pressure air. If it can hold that, it can hold water."

"As you said, a ship like this isn't the same as a boiler tank," Lucan said. "The stresses involved in seafaring …"

"Are considerable, yes," Hortensius nodded. "But we've accounted for that in the design. The plates will hold together and the metal hull will be stronger than a wooden one. This will revolutionize the way battles at sea are fought. The Consul's designs are, frankly, very impressive."

"Don't get me wrong. If the Consul says these will work, then I believe him. He hasn't led us wrong yet," Lucan said.

"My concern is these gun emplacements," one of Lucan's engineers said. "Eight guns total? Most of our ships carry thirty or more. How can we expect the same effectiveness?"

Hortensius watched as Lucan pulled out a folded telegram from his pocket, spreading it carefully on the table.

"I had the same question, and the Consul addressed it specifically. Primarily, these aren't standard cannons."

"Actually, they are much, much larger than the ones we currently mount," Hortensius added. "Larger even than the ones the legions use, because they would be too heavy to carry easily. The only other place we'll be able to deploy these cannons is the fixed positions of the coastal fortresses Admiral Valdar is building. We actually developed them for that first. That is the other benefit of the strength of these ships. A wooden-hulled ship could never support this kind of weaponry."

"But the design eliminates the gunports," the engineer said. Eight guns and they have to be manually adjusted into position as a ship is moving. It seems too complicated."

"That, too, has a benefit," Lucan said. "We know the gun ports actually weaken the hull's structural integrity, which we accepted as a necessary evil once we started building these ships. This eliminates that need ... and, with almost only the barrel exposed, the crew is protected. I will agree the rotating turret is ... complicated, and I do have my concerns about how quickly something this heavy can be turned to bring the guns into firing position."

"That is a fair concern," Hortensius said. "I've sent a message to the Consul asking about a steam-powered solution. We have enough power for propelling the ship and operating the turrets. I've already begun to develop some of my own ideas on a smaller scale, to test until I hear back from the Consul. My initial attempts tell me it's possible."

"I'm pleased to hear that," Lucan said.

"And everything else is just scaled-up versions of what we have on the river boats. The steam engines, smokestacks, powered rudders, and propeller screws, they should all be much easier to produce this time around."

"Good. So then all we have to do is wait for you to deliver the pieces and we can begin assembling our first test platform."

"How long should that take?" Hortensius asked.

"Two years. Perhaps eighteen months if everything goes perfectly, but I wouldn't count on it. Even with the Consul's directions, this is much larger than anything we have done before, and more complicated since we're outside of traditional building methods."

"I know the Admiral will try and plead for it to be faster."

"He can plead all he wants," Lucan said. "Once we have one finished, we can begin working on multiple ships simultaneously and speed things up, but until then, this will take time."

"Then I won't hold you up any longer."

Carthage

Medb put down the document she was reading and rubbed her eyes, tired of hour upon hour of sifting through minute records, trying to find any clue about what was happening in this damnable city.

Not that these documents had a chance of giving her any actual clues, filled as they were with half-truths and outright lies as every merchant and factor tried to avoid the import taxes charged by the Empire. Carthage was the biggest port with access to Oceanus, and had supplanted Kalb, which had become almost strictly a military port, sending trade either here or up the coast of Iberia to one of the ports controlled by the Hispania Alliance, to give that trade to their economy instead of that of the Empire.

Medb did not fault a little graft. She was a firm believer in catching a little and letting the rest operate more or less in the open. It kept people from hiding it as much and made it easier to keep it from obfuscating things she was trying to find.

Or that was normally the idea.

And yet, here she was, sifting through it, hoping that the rebels had tried to hide whatever they were doing inside the normal graft of business. With her agent gone, she'd had few other chances of finding anything.

She'd thought she'd been so clever when they'd first found the smuggling. They knew the rebels were getting arms and even low-grade gunpowder, so it made sense. But it had all been for nothing.

Arresting Marcellinus had, as far as she could tell, done nothing to stop them. His operation had been a distraction, nothing more. He'd just been a common, well, maybe somewhat uncommon, smuggler caught in the wrong place at the wrong time. She was happy he'd been dealt with, of course.

He'd gone beyond that acceptable level of graft and had to be dealt with, but he'd been an effective smoke screen for what the rebels were doing. Part of her wondered if they'd encouraged him, knowing he would be just that. It would have been clever, but she didn't believe in accepting anything as fact without strong evidence, and there was none to say one way or another.

Just another possible pin, unconnected, left hanging. Like all the rest. Evidence everywhere she looked, and yet not a single clue.

It was maddening.

Worse, it had been over a month since her only actual source of intelligence had been killed, and his murder was still unsolved. She knew the rebels were behind it, and the fact they could kill with such impunity irked her.

She'd pushed Claudius hard since Geral's death, to the point of vocally questioning his ability in one particularly heated moment, but she knew he'd done his best. His men had been relentless in their efforts to find the culprits, but the rebels were well entrenched and knew they were looking for them.

There was every chance they'd gone to ground and were waiting until the heat died off.

But, the longer the investigation dragged on, the more impatient she became, a state that made her a terror to those around her. The thought was a bitter one. Medb prided herself on her control, on her ability to manipulate others through intellect and strategy rather than brute force.

But when backed into a corner as she was, she'd been left with little choice.

She was saved from going around in any more mental circles by a knock at the door, which was then pushed open by one of the guards stationed at her door.

"My lady, a messenger from the gate is here. There's a man insisting he must speak with you personally. Claims it's urgent."

"And did this urgent visitor provide a name?"

"No, my lady. Says he can't discuss his business with anyone but yourself."

Some might send the man away, as visitors regularly came to the palace, asking for position or favor. Those people did not come to see her.

Although not as bad as in Britannia proper, even here, her reputation preceded her. More than preceded her. She knew there were whispers of her whisking people off the streets, throwing them into dungeons never to be seen again.

In reality, only a few people had been apprehended on her orders. Most of those arrested in the city she had no knowledge or connection to, not that it mattered to the population, or her, really.

It helped that the person in charge of security had a reputation for ruthlessness. Which meant when a person did brave that reputation and come to her, it was usually worth hearing, one way or another. If it was good information, fine. If it was a ploy, it still brought someone she should be watching into view.

Either way, it was worth it.

"Very well. Bring him in but stay within arm's reach."

The guard nodded and left, presumably to go to the gate and retrieve the caller. Five minutes later, the guard returned with a thin man whose clothes marked him as coming from the poorer section of the city.

He was a nervous man, his eyes constantly darting between Medb and the guard hovering behind him, hands clasped tightly before him.

"You claimed urgent business with me. Speak."

"I … I knew Geral, my lady. I bring a message from him."

That got Medb's attention instantly. She, however, kept the sudden interest suppressed and off her face.

"Did you now? And you've waited over a month since his death to mention this because?"

"I was afraid, my lady. The way they killed him … I thought they might be watching me, too. I have not stepped foot outside my home since his death."

"And why would they watch you?"

"Because ... because I was one of the few Geral talked to. And because of what he said the last time I saw him. He said they were starting to suspect him, that he thought he might be in danger. Said if anything happened, I should come to you. He said that he worked for you. Said he needed someone to know, in case ... but then he disappeared for weeks, and I knew. I thought they might think I was a danger, being his friend and all. As I said, Geral didn't have many friends."

"What's your name?"

"Arishan."

"Sit," Medb commanded, gesturing to a plain wooden chair opposite her desk.

Arishan hesitated, his knuckles white as he gripped the backrest before lowering himself onto it.

"Now, tell me exactly what Geral said to you. Spare no details."

Arishan swallowed hard, his Adam's apple bobbing visibly. "He came by my house, on that last day I saw him before he disappeared, looking scared. Geral never looked scared. He told me he had to check something, something about shipping. He said the lead he'd been following there was a false trail."

"We already knew about the false trail at the docks. It had nothing to do with the people Geral was investigating."

"No, my lady, that's not what he meant. He meant he'd discovered it was false and that he had finally found the real evidence. He meant the thing he was checking at the docks was something different. He said it was connected to a shipment going out that night. He said he didn't know everything, only that it was important."

"Going out?" she repeated. "Are you certain? As far as we know, the rebels have been focused on bringing supplies into the city, not sending them away."

"I'm sure, my lady. He even repeated it when he told me to take a message to you should something happen to him. That I should tell you about the shipment going out, and that he thought it was connected to what he was investigating for you."

"Did he say anything else? Who was behind the shipment? Where it was going? What was being transported?"

"No, my lady. He said he didn't have enough to be sure and needed to confirm it first. That's why he went that night. He was careful, always careful, but he said he thought someone might be watching him."

Medb didn't say anything for a moment as she grappled with the implications. Geral had been a good agent. Careful and with good reasoning. He paid attention. It had to be important if he thought this was worth him looking into, even if he thought he was being watched. If he'd stumbled onto something about outgoing shipments significant enough to get himself killed, then there was something there.

"Thank you for bringing this to my attention," she said finally. "We'll investigate the matter."

Arishan didn't look pleased with that response, however. If anything, he looked more scared.

"My lady. I fear for my life. If they knew I spoke with you …"

"I understand," she said, cutting him off. "You'll stay here in the palace for now. If your information proves useful, I can arrange work for you in Devnum, well away from any who might wish you harm."

Relief flooded Arishan's face. He began to drop into a bow, but Medb waved him off.

"Guard, escort him out. See him to suitable quarters."

As the door closed behind them, Medb drummed her fingers on the desk. Outgoing shipments. The rebels exporting something was unexpected enough, but exporting something valuable enough to kill over was something bigger. But what could they even be exporting? Groups like these imported resources, not the other way around.

Once again, she was left with more questions than answers.

Eastern Germania

Ky had heard the sound of artillery as soon as he had disembarked from the train thirty minutes before, and it had not slowed down in the time it took for his small party to guide their horses across the rocky ground to the front.

This area hadn't seen significant fighting yet. Most of the pressure from the Easterners had been in the central area between the Margus River, which would be known in later times as the Morava River, and the Wistla. The area between them was made up of a watershed of the Carpathians between the Carpathian and Sudeten mountains. They had chosen to make a stand in this area because it was the shortest land area between rivers they controlled, mostly with traditional river boats, although more of the ironclad river boats had started to show up, solidifying their hold on the Wistla and Danube and its tributaries, which together cut off both Eastern Europe and Greece from Asia.

Besides being the shortest route between the rivers with roughly sixty miles of land between them, fifteen miles of that was a very flat area that could be easily controlled by fifteen miles or so of trenches, which is where the bulk of the attacks by the Easterners had taken place.

The remainder of the land was either mountains or transition from the watershed into mountains. Land where the terrain was too steep for trenches, but also too steep for most armies to operate easily, which was almost certainly why the Easterners had focused almost entirely on that flat land between the two mountain ranges.

It had also been where they had taken huge losses. Ky had expected them to begin probing along the edges of the trench line for some time, which is why he had been pushing the engineers to build the series of reinforced concrete emplacements along the line, extending the lines of mines and barbed wire along the ridge up to the emplacements with artillery positioned with good lines of sight down the mountain and into the field below.

He just hoped it was enough to keep them from breaking through.

As they approached the main command bunker near the far southern end of the line, Bomilcar emerged from its reinforced entrance.

"Consul. Thank you for responding with such speed."

"Of course," Ky replied, dismounting smoothly and handing the reins to an aide.

"How long has this been going on?"

"Nearly six hours. They started a little north of here and have been working their way south with each wave, probing our lines, looking for a place where they can overrun it. I expect them to move into the mountains before long."

"How far up have we finished the line of defenses?"

"Almost to the summit of the closest peak, although we don't have the mines laid out nearly as far as I would like. I have a cohort stationed along the less filled-out section, but they, too, are spread out. The terrain is just too difficult for men to mass."

"Which means the enemy will face the same problem if they try to push through at that point. If they are going to continue probing, we need to finish the defensive positions all the way to the river as quickly as possible. They may decide to skip some sections and try to catch us unprepared."

"Agreed."

"Well, show me what the Easterners have tried so far," Ky said.

Bomilcar led the way into the bunker, ducking slightly under the low concrete ceiling. The space was cramped but functional, with the telegraph station taking up the bulk of the available space.

Ky moved to the observation slit and looked out past their trenches. The no-man's land in this section stretched nearly twice as wide as other sectors, the result of their gun emplacements on the mountainside forcing the enemy to dig in much further back to stay out of range. The space between the lines was littered with the consequences of the repeated assaults.

"So they've already hit the end of the line at least once?" Ky asked, seeing bodies piled up along the slope, where apparently men had tried to use the uneven ground and even large boulders that had rolled down it as cover.

That might have worked for the rifle fire from the trenches, but the artillery had the entire area well-sighted, and chunks of those larger boulders were gouged out where the explosive shells had smashed the hiding troops.

"Twice. I expect at least one more before they try the mountains themselves. Your timing was good."

"How many attacks?" Ky asked, not taking his eyes from the field.

"Four major assaults since dawn," Bomilcar answered. "They're using new tactics, sending waves in closer succession, trying to overwhelm individual sections before we can shift reinforcements."

Ky nodded. His men had fought purely defensively since the trench lines were put in place, so he hadn't gone over the various strategies used in trench warfare with his commanders, but it seemed as if the Easterners were speeding through the progression of strategies tried in past histories, during the brief stretch when trench warfare ruled, before the invention of tanks and planes reduced their usefulness.

A fresh barrage of enemy artillery fire walked across their lines, the impacts throwing dirt and debris skyward. It still looked to be mostly solid shot, with a few very underpowered explosive packed rounds mixed in. The only one that did any damage was one that exploded before it touched the ground, sending shrapnel just over the lip of the trench. The scurry of men in that section suggested some injuries may have come from that.

That, however, was clearly a lucky shot. With cut and lit fuses, it was very hard to get the timing just right.

The bombardment was clearly a prelude to an attack, maybe in hopes of getting the Britannians' heads down and lessening the fire they could send at the men coming across the open ground.

It was a poor hope. Sophus's records listed assaults where massed artillery of much higher quality than either force here could employ at the moment pounded a line for days before an attack, and caused almost no drop in the defense's effectiveness.

In all of Sophus's records, there were almost no cases where artillery itself was able to weaken a prepared position to any significant degree.

However, artillery could affect a charge of men in the open, which was shown again now as a fresh assault erupted. The sound, a cacophony of booms and cracks, was almost overwhelming. Their own artillery, positioned strategically along the line and on the mountain slopes, opened fire with a vengeance. Great gouts of earth and debris erupted amongst the advancing ranks, sending bodies and limbs flying.

The ground vibrated under his feet with each concussive wave. The howitzers, with their higher trajectory, were particularly effective, their shells arcing over the battlefield to explode amidst the enemy formations.

"They're throwing everything they have at us," Ky observed.

"It would seem so," Bomilcar confirmed. "It is ... shocking to see, every time they try this. They are not valuing the lives of their soldiers."

"As I keep saying, that is the nature of this kind of war. It is why I forbade any strategy that has us trying to break their lines. We don't have the men to waste for that, even if I were prepared to waste them. Which I am not."

"And they do? Surely they see that no men are making it through our defenses?"

"They're testing us. Each wave is a probe, a test of a different tactic, a different approach. This would be as new a form of warfare to them as it is to us, and they're trying to figure it out. Unlike the lined infantry and volley fire tactics we faced last year, they can't just copy our strategies, since we have made no attacks for them to emulate."

"And this is the best they could come up with?" Bomilcar asked, his face grim.

Ky didn't answer. There wasn't much he could say. In spite of the horrific loss of life, Ky knew it could be worse. Maybe some of their soldiers would be able to retreat and make it back to their line when the wave broke. Once newer, faster-firing small arms made it to the front, Ky knew that number would drop to almost nothing.

No one other than himself had any inkling of what a weapon like a machine gun would do in warfare such as this.

The carnage could always be worse.

Even with the artillery, the rifles they had were slow enough firing that the enemy line managed to make it to the barbed wire before being cut down or hitting the first mines they had laid out.

It ended just as every attack against his trench had ended over these last few months.

Before the first wave was completely decimated, another emerged from the distant trenches. Ky could see some slight differences in the attack, with the wave coming in staggered groups instead of all at once like the last one, probably to try and reduce the damage done by shell fire.

Whatever their strategy might have been, that was as far as it went. A general can order whatever he likes, but once the soldiers executing it come under fire, they tend to forget it and focus on their own survival, which is what happened here.

The attack faltered well before the last one as men slowed, using the bodies of their fallen comrades or shell holes for cover, trying to creep up on their lines.

It was a mistake and made them easy targets for the artillery, but Ky could understand why they'd do it. Seeing the string of dead bodies, thickest along the front of the wire line, it would be difficult to get more men to follow behind that.

The next wave, however, was different. As it advanced, it split into two distinct groups.

Half continued on the same path as the first, straight towards the waiting guns of the trench line. The other half veered south, towards the mountainside. Ky watched as the distant figures began to scale the steep incline. Even from this distance, he could see it was a difficult climb, the men scrambling over loose rock and uneven terrain.

"They're going for the mountain," he noted, stating the obvious.

Immediately, the defenders in the fortified bunkers along the slope opened fire. Ky could see small puffs of dirt and rock erupting around the climbing soldiers. There were fewer hits here than there were on the open field, but that was to be expected. Unlike the cleared, open expanses below, the mountainside was filled with boulders and small trees.

Good obstacles for men to hide behind.

Of course, that was outweighed by how much longer it took for each man to get to the Britannian line of fortifications and barbed wire, giving his own men additional chances to gun them down.

The riflemen were also not the only obstacle they had to pass.

As they got closer to the line, they encountered the edge of the much larger, although more spread out, minefield. The mines had been placed strategically, either in open paths that men would tend to gravitate to or set up in a way to trigger rockslides, and they did their job with brutal efficiency. The explosions sent cascades of rock and earth tumbling down the slope, sweeping away the men climbing up. Ky watched as enemy soldiers were buried under the sudden small avalanches. Those who weren't buried now had much more uneven terrain to clamber up, giving his riflemen more time to fire down on them. It was a grim but effective tactic, and one Bomilcar had thought of after he'd seen the mines' effectiveness along the main trench line.

Those not killed by mines or rifles were hit by the pre-sighted in artillery, which caused even more rockslides. The attack predictably faltered, with the survivors that remained turning and running back to the safety of their own lines.

The firing gradually died down, sporadic shots marking where soldiers spotted movement in the carnage-strewn field. Mostly men who'd hidden behind bodies or rocks, too afraid to make the run back to their own line. The enemy's latest attack had been decisively repulsed, leaving hundreds of bodies scattered across the killing ground and mountainside.

With no more waves appearing, the artillery fire also slowed and then stopped. The enemy trenches were dug at the cannon's far range, which meant it didn't do any good to keep firing and wasting ammunition.

That was also the reason the attacks were struggling. Confronted by the new shells, the Easterners had recoiled while they tried to figure out how to fight through them. It wouldn't be much longer until they realized that the shells, while devastating, had a much more limited effect on properly built trenches.

When they did, they'd move the trench lines up again, giving their men a much shorter distance to cross and increasing their chances of a breakthrough.

"That appears to be the last of them for now. The waste of it all … I've commanded in battles before, but this …" He gestured at the field of dead. "This is madness."

"It will only get worse."

"Worse?" Bomilcar turned from the observation slit. "How could it possibly get worse?"

"Our rifles take time to reload. Even with training, the best soldiers manage three aimed shots per minute. That leaves gaps in our firing line. The enemy can exploit those gaps if they coordinate properly. Eventually, they'll figure out the right combination of artillery bombardment and infantry tactics."

"They lost over a thousand men today trying to break through sixty yards of our line," Bomilcar countered. "Their bodies are piled three deep at the wire. No sane commander would …"

"Hortensius is working on new designs," Ky cut in. "Rifles that can fire fifteen rounds before reloading. Eventually, we will see weapons that can put out hundreds of rounds per minute. When those reach the front, crossing open ground will seem all but impossible, and yet I can tell you it can still be done by a determined enough enemy."

"Hundreds per minute?" Bomilcar's voice held disbelief. "That would turn this … into pure slaughter."

"That's the point. To make attacking so costly that the enemy won't try. Not that it will stop them, but until other technologies catch up, it is how we defend such a large area. That isn't the worst part. The worst part is that the Easterners have proven adept at copying our technology. Whatever advances we make, they'll match eventually."

A distant explosion punctuated his words. Even with the firing basically stopped for the moment, the front was never completely quiet.

"This is only the beginning," Ky continued. "The weapons will keep improving. The casualties will keep mounting. Even with the carnage you're seeing, trench lines are not impervious. And they're learning. Each attack shows more sophistication. They'll eventually figure out the right combination, and then we really will have a fight on our hands."

Chapter 3

Athens, Greece

Ramirus questioned the reasoning for holding this meeting in this particular bouleuterion with the temperatures descending as they were. He had seen such buildings in other parts of Greece, particularly northern Epirus, where the sides of the building were at least enclosed, offering more protection from the elements. But here in Athens, it had open sides that offered no such comfort. Perhaps it was to allow people to see their politicians at work, or perhaps it was because of the somewhat warmer climate of the Aegean, but he had to say he preferred the northern Greeks' choice of building styles.

This was looking to be a particularly harsh winter, and the wind coming off the ocean felt like it was cutting him to the bone as it whipped through the semicircular meeting house.

He understood it was tradition and, in moments of crisis like this, people tended to cling to such notions. But he was an old man, and he could do with a little more insulation and a little less tradition.

It could be worse. At least here, there was a roof. They could have chosen one of the open-air amphitheaters for this meeting.

The weather did not keep the Greeks away, however, and the building was packed with delegates from across southern Greece. Ramirus had already met several of them in the ongoing negotiations and recognized the Athenian and Spartan representatives with central places at the bottom of the rows of stone seats, center to all of the other men gathered there.

He also appreciated that, against tradition, they had placed a stool for him to sit on at the central spot facing the gathered men. As a younger man, Ramirus had prided himself on his ability to stand and speak for hours, defending Lucilla's father in the various political fights that were his primary battleground.

Those days were far behind him and Ramirus's knees now protested after a short walk across a room. He patted the legionary loaned to him by Modius, who had accompanied him down the difficult steps to his assigned place, sending the man back up to the top to wait for his time to leave.

He was a good boy, but Ramirus didn't need a uniformed man standing at his shoulder as he tried to negotiate with people afraid of giving away their power or sovereignty to a foreign power. Even if it meant their own safety.

Ramirus sat, looking at the men for a moment. He did not need dramatics to get their attention, but he wanted more than that. He wanted their focus, and a moment's silence had a way of doing that.

"Honored representatives," he said finally. "Things are dire, and I come before you today with no time left to argue and debate. The fears of the loss of Thessaly, Thrace, and Macedon have come true. They have joined the Eastern invaders, cutting free Greece in half. You are caught in a precarious position, by yourselves with the Eastern forces between you and the bulk of the Western Alliance. Now is the time to decide what your future will be. Now is the time to decide if this is the end of your long history."

"And you offer us what? The privilege of being crushed first? You point out that the Easterners are between us and your forces. Wouldn't that be a strong argument for the rest of the free states to follow our northern brethren and join the Easterners for our own survival, instead of siding with your lot?" the Athenian representative asked.

"We aren't in the way of either of you," one of the men Ramirus didn't recognize said. "Why should we choose either side of the conflict and put ourselves in danger? I still say our best option is to remain neutral. We have maintained our independence through worse times."

"The world has changed. Modern warfare brings destruction on a scale your ancestors never imagined. The artillery alone ..."

"We've seen the weapons," interrupted the representative of Argos. "Whether we submit to Britannia or the Easterners or even if Carthage had remained in power, the result is the same. Foreign rule."

The gathered Greeks all voiced their agreement. In some ways, Ramirus could see their point. They weren't in the direct path of the fighting, and it would be appealing to think that they could somehow hide and remain untouched while the rest of the world burned.

Appealing, but naive.

"I know you have been contacted by the Easterners, who want you to join them the same way we want you to join us. You are not being left alone. The attention is on you from all sides. The Easterners do not want to fight on two fronts and that is exactly what we want. The difference is that one side offers alliance and autonomy, while the other demands submission. Ask the refugees from Thessaly about the Eastern occupation. From what we understand, already their men are being taken from their homes and put under arms."

"And how would you be different?"

"The Western Alliance exists solely as a mutual defense," Ramirus said, using the phrase the Consul used so often. "Each member maintains complete autonomy over their internal affairs. Britannia has no interest in governing Greece. We seek only to preserve your independence against those who would strip it away entirely."

"How magnanimous of you," the Spartan representative said. "And one you will maintain right up until you bring legionaries with rifles and cannons into our cities."

"Ask the Germanic Alliance, or the Hispanians, or the Gauls if our words are so false? Those rifles and cannons we bring are not to rule your people but to preserve your ability to speak for them. The Eastern forces have already occupied three Greek states. Their people don't enjoy the luxury of debate anymore. You have sent representatives to Germania, spoken to some of our allies. You have seen for yourself that they maintain their own laws, their own customs, their own trade relationships."

"Yet you speak of weapons and warfare," the unknown representative interjected. "From where we stand, both sides seem evenly matched. Why choose either?"

Ramirus made a mental note of the man. That was twice he pushed neutrality, which if Ramirus were a suspicious man, which he was, he would conclude that it might be easier to get the Greeks to reject the West in the name of neutrality and open themselves up to invasion, rather than push the Greeks into the arms of the west.

Worse, it could work. They had compromised one of the Greeks' own, who was telling them exactly what they wanted to hear.

"That apparent balance is an illusion, and a dangerous one. The Easterners throw waves of men against our defensive lines, losing hundreds daily to our artillery. Their largest fleet in history was decimated by a far smaller force of our ships. They can't match our rate of innovation, while they struggle to copy our existing weapons, we develop new ones."

"Britannians," the compromised man said. "Always speaking of their strength while fighting from a position of weakness."

"Let me be clear; this isn't mere boasting. The death toll among the Easterners is staggering. Our iron-clad river boats control every major waterway. And this is only the beginning. The Britannian factories produce weapons that would have been unimaginable a decade ago. You have a lot to say about neutrality, but use the language of capitulation."

The Greek stood to argue but was stopped by a gesture from the Athenian.

"And what specific guarantees would the Western Alliance offer us?"

"Full participation in the Alliance Council. Complete control over your domestic affairs. Mutual defense obligations, yes, but also access to our trading networks and manufacturing techniques. We don't seek subjects - we seek partners."

"And if we remain neutral?"

"No one will remain neutral in this war."

The chamber erupted into angry shouts, delegates rising from their seats in outrage, with some even moving to leave entirely.

"We do not take kindly to threats from foreigners, Roman or otherwise," the Spartan representative said angrily.

"You mistake my meaning entirely," Ramirus said, raising his hands placatingly. "I do not threaten, merely predict. I predict the same fate that will befall your northern neighbors before this is all finished. The fate the entire continent suffered under Carthaginian rule. Complete absorption and subjugation."

"More fear-mongering from ..." the compromised man said.

"Hold your tongue," Ramirus snapped, speaking harshly for the first time. "You might speak the words of neutrality, but I hear only the Easterners when you speak."

The way the man glanced aside at his neighbors at the comment, he might as well have announced his true allegiance then. The Easterners might have picked the easiest among the Greeks to manipulate, but they also picked a fool. Ramirus could see several of the other representatives, especially the Spartan representative, look at him suspiciously, finally putting things together.

"If you choose neutrality, the Western Alliance will respect that choice. We will hold our line along Illyria and Epirus, leaving Athens and the southern states to their own devices. The Easterners, however, would offer you something completely different. In action if not in words."

He paused, letting the delegates settle back into their seats before continuing. "But consider what happened in Sarmatia after they passed through. Every small kingdom absorbed, their people conscripted, their customs erased. The Eastern forces did the same as they entered Germania, until the Western Alliance finally halted their advance. The process has already begun. The Eastern armies flood into Macedon. Their artillery positions grow closer by the day. I'm sure they would prefer that you give in to them willingly, but they will not have the luxury of waiting for that much longer, and will turn to harsher means. The time for debate grows short."

A rumble rippled through the crowd as they discussed it in hushed whispers. They knew he spoke the truth.

The Athenian representative rose. "We thank you for your words, honored ambassador. The council must discuss this matter privately."

"Of course," Ramirus said, struggling to his feet. "But do not deliberate overlong. The day approaches when Eastern forces will stand at the very steps of this chamber. When that day comes, it will be too late for choosing sides."

The legionary hurried down to assist him, but Ramirus waved him off. He'd made his case. Now it was up to the Greeks to decide their fate. As he climbed the worn steps, he could already hear heated discussion breaking out behind him. Whether they chose alliance or neutrality, war was coming to Greece. He only hoped they realized it before it was too late.

Port Vikhavn

Valdar looked over the port, which was finally bustling again after months of his fleet trapped in the harbor, unable to leave because of the enemy fleet sitting just offshore.

The activity was still all military and supply ships, since there was little commercial value in this port. But that would be changing, and not a moment too soon. He could see from where he stood that the forts were already covered in scaffolding, repairing the scars created by the numerous Easterner attempts to get through to the port.

They had held up remarkably well, although Valdar wondered if they would continue at the same level of performance once the Easterners figured out the secrets to the artillery shell like they had figured out the rifles and cannon.

His ships were also under heavy repair. They had done what they could for them, but until the Easterners' fleet had been destroyed, he had been effectively under a blockade, unable to get more than the most rudimentary supplies needed for the repairs.

That was one of the things that had his officers waiting for him in the port commander's office, in fact.

The port's command building stood on high ground overlooking the harbor. It held not only offices for the commander himself, a centurion who would soon be promoted to tribune, if his sources were correct, but also for his staff and officers, and an office for the engineer sent to oversee ship repairs.

The building was in pure chaos when he entered. Aside from all the work happening on the water and across it, this building was also undergoing renovation, as it expanded to make room for the new role this port was to have.

The commander had graciously given them use of his office for this meeting, seeing as it was the only part of the building not filled with workmen.

"Gentlemen," Valdar's entrance brought the room to attention, "be seated. We have much to discuss."

As the assembled officers settled into their chairs, Valdar continued. "We've had our first real chance to assess the damage since the defeat of the Eastern fleet. I know many of you have had a chance to tour the forts and see the wreckage still being dredged from the harbor entrance. Now that we have a moment to breathe, I'd like your thoughts on what went right and wrong with our defense."

"The forts did the job better than any of us could have predicted," Einar, the captain of the Aquila, said. "I will admit I was one who thought we would be fighting a losing battle inside this harbor the day after the enemy arrived. Instead, those forts took every cannonball the enemy had to offer and sank everything that tried to run their gauntlet. Even the enemy's biggest push only allowed a handful of ships through."

"I do wonder what the difference will be once the new artillery shells are in place," the port commander said. "How the forts will fare?"

"Considering we received our initial shipment of shells with the first supply convoy that was able to come through and the enemy has yet to copy them, I imagine well. Yes, the enemy using well-packed explosive shells could do more damage to our forts, but what we could do in return to a wooden ship is ... significant. Hell, we don't even have to be as accurate with them. An airburst above the ship would shred its sails and scour its deck."

The commander nodded, considering that. It was easy to only focus on the fire coming in when you were a landsman, instead of thinking of how that fire would look on a much more vulnerable wooden vessel.

"I think something this experience taught us was that forts alone will not hold a port. We need manpower to defend it from landings, more than just a century placed for initial security," one of the other captains said.

"It does indeed. It tells us that, wherever we build a port, it is critical that we have good relations with the locals. That's true now, more than ever. On the first boat we were able to send home, I sent a plan for the future of our naval operations, and I received a reply with today's supply shipment. This port is destined to be more than a way station. We upgraded it shortly before the blockade started so that it could handle some large-scale ship repairs, but we've still been reliant on storehouses filled with supplies shipped from home. Clearly, if they can cut off a port, those supplies would quickly dwindle, as we've seen. Which is why we are going to further extend the facilities here to make not just simple parts, but to be a full, if scaled-down, industrial base."

"We'll still need pretty significant supplies to make that work," the port commander said. "The base materials. Lumber, ore, and so on. Unprocessed lumber takes much more room than planking, meaning we'd need even more supply shipments."

"That would be true if that is where we were getting them from, but it's not. I will be meeting with Chief Ekoko soon to propose their involvement, but considering that he has already asked for something similar, I expect he will be glad to participate. In addition to end-stage production facilities here, we will send engineers to his villages to build sawmills for processing local hardwoods and mining facilities, and the supplies for growing plants like cotton and other fibrous plants for making cloth. We will not just build them but train his people to operate them. His people will then be able to sell those goods to us and use them internally to better themselves, and, in turn, buy more finished product from the small factories that we build here. The Britannian navy becomes their customer, not their master."

"That is a large project."

"It is, but it will also make this port self-sustaining. What's more, there are goods here that are in demand back home. This area has rich natural resources that the Consul has helpfully provided a general guide to finding, and it is very good land for growing crops. Working with the locals, who have the manpower to exploit these resources, we can begin sending supply shipments back home, not just receive shipments from home."

"Admiral, providing these manufacturing capabilities to the locals ... isn't that giving away our technological advantages?" Fabius, captain of the Aeolus, asked. "We know the Easterners are operating around Africa. If they were smart, they would see we have production facilities here and try to get men in to see how they work. Or at least buy the information from the locals."

"That concern was raised when I sent the proposal to Devnum. My understanding is that the Empress and Consul discussed it at length. We'll have additional praetorians stationed here, but truthfully, I'm not particularly worried."

"Why's that, sir?" asked Captain Einar.

"Because we've already shared similar capabilities with our continental allies. The basic industrial processes aren't considered critical military secrets. And this is just the beginning of our plans. The Easterners will have more to worry about than getting that information."

That got his men's attention. Considering what he'd already discussed was a fairly large expansion of the facilities here, suggesting that it was a minor part of their plans had them curious.

"We're going to establish a network of fortified ports along the African coast. Regular harbors, properly defended, within supporting distance of each other."

"With respect, Admiral," Captain Hakon interjected, "we tried that at the end of the last war. The Easterners obliterated that port completely."

"They did," Valdar acknowledged. "But that port relied solely on ships for defense. These will be different. Protected harbors with proper fortifications and emplaced cannon. And not just isolated ports, but closer to what we have here. Contact with the locals. Partnerships. Full operating concerns. I don't want just a series of way stations but a permanent presence at each harbor where we set our flag down."

The men began talking excitedly among themselves.

"To do this, we need to begin sending out patrols again, both to look for signs of any additional enemy fleets and to identify suitable locations to place fortified harbors."

"With only patrols and scouts, and not the full fleet, there are dangers," one of the schooner captains said. "It seems doubtful that the enemy fleet we destroyed will be their last one."

"I agree. Which is why you are to turn tail and run the moment you see a sign of enemy vessels. Your first priority is to ensure we receive news of a new fleet coming our way," Valdar said, and then paused, looking at the assembled captains. "Questions?"

Everyone fell silent, which was as expected. With as much work as they had ahead of them, for now, it wasn't complicated. Just extensive.

"Very well then," Valdar said, standing. "Let's get to work. Dismissed."

Agisthūs, Antari, Germania

Lucilla stepped off the train onto the platform and paused, taking a breath of the cold winter air. She'd always liked this time of year, even as a little girl, but her trip through Germania had made her appreciate it anew.

There were a great many things to love about Devnum, but the growth of industry had made the air a little heavy most days, where a deep breath such as that would lead to the taste of soot lingering at the back of your throat. Even with moving the bulk of the factories to Factorium, the city still produced enough billowing smoke into the air that it was never crisp and fresh like this.

She could see a few smokestacks here, but it wasn't the same. Factories had sprung up across the continent in the last several years as its governments caught up on some of Britannia's capacity or became hubs for raw materials, allowing Hortensius to shift more of his people to working on finished products.

Thankfully, Germania was a big place and those factories were well spread out, saving them from the thick clouds of dark smoke that settled over Devnum. She would be home soon and wanted to enjoy the fresh winter air a little bit more before she missed it again.

Chief Bernia stepped down beside her, the Antari leader's weathered face as sour as it ever was.

"I must thank you again for arranging this meeting, Chief Bernia," Lucilla said, her breath visible in the frigid air. "And for accompanying me from the front lines. It was nice not having to travel all the way from the east by myself."

"I'm happy enough to be home. And it's about time the Scandi joined the war effort. They're profiting off of our blood while they stand by claiming to be neutral is getting very old."

Lucilla tended to agree but held her tongue. The Scandi did prefer certain outcomes, which were far from available in a war such as this. Even as neutrals, they had a valuable part to play in the war, whether they knew it or not, but Lucilla needed them to be more than that. Ky had made the manpower problem clear, and Lucilla was determined to tug at every thread to find ways to solve it.

Instead, she said, "Yes, it would be good to have them join us again."

Bernia let out an uncharacteristic laugh. "Always not saying what you are thinking. That is why I'm glad you are the one handling these negotiations. You have a much better mind for diplomacy than I ever will. I gained my position simply by being the lucky bastard who survived the war with Carthage when many of my compatriots did not. I've never had that ability."

"You sound remarkably like my husband when you speak that way."

"I can only hope to be so fortunate."

Ky had worked closely with the Germanians for the last several years and more so since the war. To Lucilla, it seemed as if they approved of him even more than her own people did.

The factories weren't the only change popping up across Germania. The building they were heading toward from the train station was another. Gone were the longhouses and thatched roofs still very common at the end of the last war, replaced by stone-walled buildings with clay-fired tile roofing.

She knew the new designs went deeper than that. Wooden interior walls allowing for insulating layers of dried straw and hay between the stone and wood. Windows that had two panes of glass in them to help trap heat. Many even had pipes that pushed water through the buildings using steam engines that created pressure at central points around the city, pushing the water through the pipes the same way it did in the new ships being built, allowing water to be accessed at sinks inside.

It was one of the many things Ky and Hortensius had worked on during the interwar years, as their focus had shifted to making everyday life more comfortable and reducing the incremental workload on people. So far, it was only available in the larger cities and used in the newer buildings, which explained why so many of the older style buildings had disappeared so quickly.

Who wanted to stay in an old, damp log house having to walk to a central well once a day to gather water, when you could live in such luxury?

She felt the difference as soon as she was ushered inside the arched doorway and led to one of the main rooms used for tribal gatherings and meetings. The room was large and felt oversized considering only five men waited inside.

A tall man with broad shoulders and close-cropped blonde hair stepped away from his comrades, abruptly ending the conversation that they had been having.

"Empress Lucilla, I am Commander Hrolfson," he said curtly.

"Commander." Lucilla inclined her head. "Thank you for agreeing to this meeting."

Another new face. The political upheaval in Scandinavia had made maintaining consistent diplomatic relations challenging.

The economic growth of Gaul and Germania had lessened Scandi's more traditional power in the region, with the train lines now crisscrossing the continent making overland transportation of goods cheaper than shipping them by boat.

Their shipping was still vital, but the merchant oligarchy that had taken to ruling the Scandi were feeling the pinch from the reduced commerce and had been scrambling for more than a year to shore up their position. She had met with seven different representatives in as many months, making it difficult to form any sort of working relationship.

She found a seat at the long table in the center of the room and gestured for the rest to follow suit.

"Let us speak plainly," Lucilla began. "The situation with the Easterners grows dire. We have managed to stop their advance into Germania and hold them, but their new alliances in Greece put that all into jeopardy, giving them a new access point into the continent. We ask again for you to reforge the bonds made during the last war when we stood together to remove an oppressor and create a unified west. Join us in this war."

"Yes, let us speak plainly," Hrolfson said. "We have noted that you have been urgently pushing all of your allies to send more men to the front. While you have stopped the Eastern army, the immediacy of that need has my people concerned and has given us pause in agreeing to your request. What guarantee do we have that joining your fight will not simply drain our resources into a losing battle?"

"A losing battle? You yourself just said we stopped them cold. They are held along a line as long as the entire continent. If it wasn't …" Bernia said, slamming a fist on the table, only to stop as Lucilla raised a hand, holding it out to him.

"Your concerns are understandable, Commander, but as the chieftain says, we have shown that we can hold them and are in command of the situation. I would not call the present situation losing. Did we not follow a similar path in facing Carthage?"

"Against Carthage, you held clear advantages. Superior weapons, better tactics. Now you face an enemy with rifles that match your own, artillery that rivals yours. You will not be able to use your better technology to push past their advantage in manpower."

"Those are not fixed positions. At the start of this war, yes, their technology was more or less equal to ours, but that balance has shifted. The iron-clad riverboats we've developed give us complete control of every major waterway along the front, which is why we've been able to cut them off from moving any deeper into the continent. And our new artillery shells dwarf any kind of destructive power they can manage."

"Yet still they come."

"For now. We also cannot say unequivocally that they have the advantage in manpower. Yes, they seem willing to sacrifice men by the thousands, but that does not mean their reserves are endless. Thinking they are is driven by fear, nothing else."

"So you admit you do not know their capabilities," he said, as if none of the points she had made registered. "This could well be another Carthage."

"Or it might not be. The Carthaginians had centuries to build their empire. The Easterners are an unknown quantity."

"Precisely our point," Hrolfson said, standing. "We will not commit our people to a cause with so many uncertainties. The Easterners pose no immediate threat to our territories. For now, we will maintain our neutrality."

"Then you will profit from our ..." Bernia began, his face flushing red.

"Thank you for meeting with us," Lucilla cut in smoothly, rising from her chair. "We appreciate your time."

She inclined her head to Hrolfson and his advisors before turning to leave, Bernia following in her wake.

Bernia barely waited until they were well clear before speaking.

"Why do you humor these vultures?" he demanded. "They grow fat trading with both sides while our men die in the trenches."

"Because I've dealt with the Scandi long enough to know their ways. Pressure works, threats make them obstinate. Trust me, this conversation isn't finished."

Chapter 4

Devnum

Hortensius was bone tired as he hurried toward the main munitions factory. He was already stretched thin trying to work out the larger screw mechanism on the new ship, which was causing more issues than they had first thought it would, when he'd received an urgent message from one of his assistants. He'd left the young man to oversee the final stages of the new cartridges while he was working on the naval program.

The metal cartridges themselves were finished, along with their primed bases, and all that had been left was to determine the right load of powder. The Consul had provided guidelines, but as with anything produced, the ranges of the powder they were making varied somewhat, not just from the Consul's initial instructions, but also on a day-to-day or week-by-week basis.

So it was up to his engineers and Sorantius's people to figure out the correct loadout. As tasks go, it shouldn't have been difficult, which is why Hortensius had felt comfortable leaving it to them and going to Devnum to supervise the mechanical end of that project.

Unfortunately, as great as the telegraph was, it did not have the speed of back-and-forth communication to work out these kinds of details. So he found himself hustling back to Factorium to discuss it in person, after which he had to hop back on the train and make the reverse journey for an early morning project conference about an alteration to the screw design.

He found Sorantius and his men and Hortensius's own engineers all gathered together, waiting for him in the middle of what looked like an intense debate that stopped abruptly when he walked in.

"I'm glad you're here," Sorantius said, not even bothering to feign a smile as he glared over at Hortensius's man.

"I was just saying ..."

"Wait," Hortensius said, holding up a hand. "I don't want to come at this from the middle. You were here to discuss the new cartridge, which, the last I knew, was finished and just waiting for load specifications. Where are we on that?"

No one gathered seemed pleased with that as a starting point, since they were clearly already in the middle of a heated debate about something, but Hortensius didn't like to set himself up to be in a biased position.

"We're having issues with variations between production batches, and I believe it's mostly in the quality of the nitrate."

"That is a problem. I thought we worked out our consistency issues last year."

"We did. The problem was manageable until the production demands for more gunpowder increased. As we entered the new phase of the war, where our armies are in combat almost constantly, the demand for powder spiked. Since then, we've fallen behind almost sixty percent from what the legions are requesting."

"Sixty percent?"

That was far worse than he'd imagined. He was so stretched between so many projects that he'd had to delegate out more authority to his subordinates. He'd hoped that, in the event of a major shortfall, they would have notified him.

Clearly, that hope had been misplaced.

"Why wasn't I told?"

"Because it wasn't immediately apparent," Sorantius said. "We were still meeting the quotas, but doing so by supplementing more and more with the powder stores created over the last several years, before the fighting recommenced. Even then, we were falling behind slowly enough that the deficit took some time to be noticeable. However, once the new artillery shells were introduced, the volume of needed powder became an avalanche. To keep up with demand, which was not stopping, we began to pull nitrate early, before it reached its fullest potency. Not all at once, but it snowballed. A bit at a time until, when it became enough that failures began happening in quality assurance tests, we had built up a deficit we could not come back from."

"That is where we were when you came in," Hortensius's man said. "I appreciate that we have an issue with production schedules, but if we continue using the substandard material, we risk catastrophic failures."

"Which leaves us with an impossible choice," Sorantius continued. "We can either maintain quality and accept severe shortages, or meet quantity demands with powder that might get our soldiers killed."

He could see the dilemma. Neither option was acceptable, but he knew that Sorantius was thorough enough that, if he said those were the options available to them, then those were the options available to them.

Still, he had to try to think of alternatives.

"What about expanding the number of beds? If we double or triple the current setup …"

"We're already pushing the limits," Sorantius cut in. "The manpower requirements for managing the beds are staggering. Factor in the constant combat demands, the powder-filled shells and the fuses … No. And that's before considering the new powder formulation the Consul wants us to start working on as soon as this project is done."

"Have you looked at the numbers on total manpower needs?"

"Even if we conscripted every able-bodied person not already in the legions or essential industries, we might not meet the production targets. Even I know that is not realistic. This is an unsolvable equation, Hortensius."

Hortensius didn't say anything right away. Instead, he paced the length of the workroom, which he often did when stuck with a difficult problem. Often enough that the others knew to wait and let him pace out his thoughts.

"You're right, of course. Which leaves us with the only other option available. I'll contact the Consul today and lay out the problem for him. He may have solutions we haven't considered."

"The Consul can't conjure nitrates from thin air," one of the younger chemists muttered.

"No," Hortensius agreed, "but he's delivered what seemed impossible before. Until we hear from him, continue maximum production with what we have. Maintain quality. That's absolutely necessary, particularly for the new shells. We can't risk catastrophic failures in the field."

"And the regular powder supplies?"

"Keep pushing as hard as you can without breaking the workforce. Add in as many beds as you can with the manpower you can get now. Until the Consul delivers us a miracle, we will just have to do the best we can."

Carthage

Medb was tired, and her head hurt. It had been two weeks since the visit from Geral's friend with his last message, and progress had been achingly slow since then. Unlike the search she'd had Geral doing, looking for people when she didn't know who they were or where to find them, she knew exactly where to look. She'd thought that would at least make the search a little faster.

How wrong she'd been.

She still hadn't recruited a good agent, since the loss of Geral, who could do the leg work on this for her. She just didn't have the connections here to uncover new ones. She'd been lucky to find him in the first place, and she hadn't found another agent of his caliber since.

Which meant that she'd had to rely on a much shadier network of paid informants, who had their place, but were not great for the more detailed work. Most of those agents couldn't know who they were working for, because of how unreliable and double-crossing they could be, so she'd had to deal with them through cutouts and middlemen who were at least somewhat less shady.

It meant that her instructions to them were limited in detail, since much of it would get lost in the passing of messages, and consequently limited the detail she could get back from them.

Not that they had been completely unproductive. It had taken weeks, but a pattern was starting to show itself, from both direct observation and gossip from the seasoned hands working the docks. For months now, there had been intermittent ships coming in displaying odd behavior.

They would sail in late in the evening, empty or nearly empty, load up a shipment, and be gone before the sun rose. Carthage was a busy port, and it wasn't unusual for ships to arrive at night and leave early in the morning, but it was unusual to see the same ship do both.

For one, it made no economic sense to have a ship come in empty. Ships required men, who had to be paid and fed on the voyage, and sailing wore on the ship itself, which was one more trip closer to needing an overhaul or heavy maintenance. Which meant that any time a ship left port, it needed to bring in revenue, and a ship coming in empty would not be doing that for half its voyage.

That didn't even count the crew. Even if the ship only plied the Middle Sea, they would still be spending weeks or at least days on the water and would want more than a few hours in port before going out again.

Still, if it had only been one ship making the same kind of journey, she would have written it off as a shipmaster who'd either worked out some kind of deal to make the trip make sense or who had a set of habits she couldn't explain.

But it wasn't one ship. It was hard to tell all of the times this had happened, but those whose names her informants had provided, including one that had come into port in this time period, were all different ships.

That went beyond something explainable.

It was a pattern, and in her line of work, a pattern meant something she needed to investigate further. Which was where her current problem came to light. She'd reached the end of what her web of paid informants could do, and she needed to get more information on these ships, or place someone aboard one of them, if she could.

And that meant she needed loyal agents. The one thing she didn't have.

Which was why she'd sent for Claudius almost thirty minutes prior. She was trying not to be impatient, as he had a lot of work to do being in charge of the praetorians in the city, but she was not a woman who liked to be kept waiting.

Thankfully, a few minutes later, there was a knock on the door, followed by the praetorian being ushered in by the guards outside, who knew not to keep her waiting.

"Tribune, thank you for coming," she said as he entered, gesturing to one of the chairs across from her desk. "I trust everything in the city is quiet."

"As quiet as the city ever gets, my lady," Claudius said, standing next to the chair instead of sitting on it. "Though I suspect you didn't summon me to discuss the daily patrols."

"No. I called you because I need your help. Or rather, I need to borrow some of your men for a task. One that requires more ... discretion than their usual duties."

From Claudius's expression, it was clear he both guessed what she needed and was skeptical about it. She wasn't surprised by either. Claudius had shown he was no fool and there was only one thing the Empire's spymistress would need him for. He was also a soldier through and through, in spite of his assortment of police duties. He'd shown ability to handle intelligence gathering tasks, but he'd been vocal about his displeasure for it at every opportunity.

"As co-regent of the city, the praetorians, of course, serve at your command, but we are soldiers, not spies."

"You do yourself a disservice. You could be very good at this, I think. Besides, sometimes a soldier must act as something else to serve the Empire. Here is my issue. For the past several months, ships have been arriving in port under suspicious circumstances. They come in empty or nearly so, late in the evening. By dawn, they're gone again, loaded with cargo."

"That's unusual, but not necessarily ..."

"Different ships, Claudius. Different crews, different flags, but the same pattern. No crew stays in port more than a few hours. No shore leave, no drinking, no whoring. Just in and out, like they're afraid to be seen in daylight."

"Smugglers?"

"Perhaps, but if so, smuggling for the rebels. Geral managed to get a message to a friend just before his death that the shipping we'd been looking into wasn't the one connected to the rebels. Just another crime caught up in our investigations. He was looking into a lead that he thought was actually connected when he died. I've been using paid informants to look into it and they were able to uncover the pattern I found, but they've reached the limit of their usefulness. I need men I can trust to watch these ships when they come in."

"But ..."

"I know, and I need you to figure out a way to make it work. Paid informants are good for basic work, but they are not people I'd trust serious work to. They will serve whoever pays them the most, and will try to find new masters to bid against us. I ask them to watch specific ships or follow specific people, one of them will go to the target and offer to sell him the information. That doesn't get us what we need. I need people I can trust. Preferably people who are capable of independent thought and mostly unknown in the city."

"What exactly do you want them to do?"

"I need them to follow the cargo, see where it goes, who handles it. Without being seen. That is key. I'd rather they let the cargo go than expose themselves. But I also want to know what's going out on these ships and who's bringing it to them. Can you make that happen?"

"I can," he said, finally relenting. "Though they'll need instruction on how to do this properly. Perhaps some kind of training. I know I keep saying it, but these men are not spies."

"I understand, and we can handle that."

"Very well. I'll select the men myself. How soon do you need them?"

"As soon as possible. These ships don't keep to any schedule I can determine, but based on past patterns, we should see another within the week. And as you said, time is needed to train these men for their new jobs."

"You'll have your men in two days," Claudius promised, nodding and leaving without being dismissed.

Not that Medb minded. She didn't need the pageantry, just competent work.

Eastern Germania

For the first time in a week, the constant boom of artillery had ceased. Occasional cracks of rifle fire could be heard toward the front, but that at least didn't come with the earth shaking and concrete dust raining down on him.

It had taken the Easterners a lot longer than it should have to figure out that there was no path through the Western lines. They even tried to scale the high passes between the summits of some of the southern peaks, only to find hastily dug positions firing down on them, costing them even higher death tolls."

"So they finally stopped throwing men into the grinder," Bomilcar said, echoing Ky's thoughts. "It took them long enough."

"They had to, eventually. They clearly have as little care for life as the Carthaginians did, but no one, not even the Carthaginians, could keep feeding men into this forever. It just took them some time to accept it. They haven't given up, though."

"No. I imagine the next place they plan on trying to break us is in Greece, now that they seem to have learned their lesson."

"I concur. I wish we had better sources with the Easterners, but the people Medb and Ramirus have in Greece have reported heavy troop movements across the Dardanelles."

"I saw that in the reports. At least we have good news on that front. Ramirus did good work getting Athens and Sparta to join the alliance, which means most of the smaller states should start to fall in line, not wanting to be left on their own."

"Which leaves us with our real challenge," Ky said. "Our new front, curving along the border of Thessaly and Macedonia will greatly increase the overall size of our line. Along some of it we can pull back and continue to use rivers, but the mountains will mean we need more trench lines there than we have in place already. It will require a lot of men, plus the labor needed to get those trenches in place. I'm not sure we can do both before the Easterners attack."

"Which means Modius will have to hold them in the field until we can get the defensive works in place," Bomilcar said, his hand going to his chin, scratching absently at his beard as he thought. "The first large batch of recruits from the western allies finishes training next week, almost two cohorts worth. I know we wanted those men on the line here, but perhaps we should send them to support Modius in Greece. Help bolster whatever forces the Greeks can muster until we get proper defenses in place."

Ky considered it. They did need the men here. Even with the tempo of eastern operations dropping to almost nothing, there was still the constant trickle of casualties from stray bullets, common injuries, and disease. Trenches needed a constant flow of reinforcements to continue their effectiveness, and his line had started out thin enough. Those men were desperately needed.

Still, if the enemy got around their lines and came in behind them, it would be over all the same.

"I agree. He needs to be prepared for what this level of combat will mean, however. The on-the-ground battle with black powder rifles and explosive shells, even the primitive ones the enemy is using, firing in ranks, favors the larger forces the enemy has. He cannot meet them on their own terms."

"I'm sure he understands, but what choice do we have, we ..." Bomilcar said, and then paused as a messenger stopped in the doorway of the command bunker, saluting. "I will go and send orders to direct the new men to Greece and another telegram to Modius, letting him know what's coming at him and reminding him of your admonition."

"Good," Ky said, waving the messenger inside to hand over the telegram he was holding. "Thank you, soldier. You're dismissed."

The messenger saluted again and left.

Ky unfolded the telegram, his expression darkening as he read through its contents.

"Damn," he said to no one in particular.

He received updates from Hortensius often, sometimes good and sometimes asking for suggestions or directions on a given project. Normally, however, he did not receive any that presented an outright catastrophe, as most issues the inventor was capable of handling himself.

He could see why this one was something different and why Hortensius had sent a request for help. Finding a solution, however, was something else entirely. He had known the powder situation would get worse, with the need for fused shells taking huge amounts of powder compared to rifle cartridges, as well as the volume they were firing on a daily basis, but he hadn't expected the problem to advance this quickly.

He had read reports from Sorantius of the increasing number of nitrate beds, and thought they might close the gap in the needed production, even with the long lead time needed for their production.

"Any thoughts?" Ky subvocalized, knowing the AI would be watching and paying attention. "We need better options than nitrate beds. Preferably something where the nitrate has already been created naturally and we can just mine it."

"The limitations on available sources of nitrates remain the same as when gunpowder was first introduced. There are no significant deposits in currently controlled regions."

"Even now that we have all of Europe as allies? That has changed since we first started."

"There are some available, but even collectively, none are large enough to offset our usage. By the time of the first World War, much of the nitrate use had shifted from mined nitrate to synthetic production which is still well outside of what we will be able to achieve for a projected five to six years. There are a series of deposits in the region of Catalonia, a few in Italy, although these are scattered across numerous caves, meaning multiple mining processes that must be set up, each of

which will only produce a small amount individually. An area closer to the current front has some, although several of those are in contested regions close to the front or just on the other side, making mining difficult at best."

"What about areas outside of Europe?"

"There are several promising locations in Africa, although they are further inside the landmass, in areas where we have little to no footprint, even with Valdar's planned new ports along the western coastline. The largest concentrations lie in the Americas, with the most substantial deposits in South America, although accessing those would require circumnavigating the continent."

"Not exactly practical given our current situation," Ky replied silently.

"No. More feasible are several alternatives along eastern North America. During the original industrial revolution, they served as a major nitrate source. The region also offers additional resources, with heavy mining options and favorable shipping headwinds making transport times reasonable. If the admiral would set new ports up in good positions, there is also the option of Brazil and the Caribbean, with access to natural rubber and salt marshes, both products lacking in our current environments."

"So you're saying, if we go to the Americas, we don't just stay focused on one resource, we go all the way."

"Correct."

"That's still a significant expansion. What would we be facing if we did that? How difficult would this be?"

"The areas of greatest interest – covering nitrates and other minerals – would primarily be the Chesapeake region and extending west into the Appalachians. There the indigenous peoples are currently transitioning from the Late Archaic to Early Woodland period. Social organization consists mainly of small farming villages with some pottery production, though hunting and gathering remain prevalent. No centralized governance structures exist."

"What if we head further south, toward Brazil and the other things you discussed."

"Central America has entered the Early Intermediate period, with embryonic city-states that will eventually develop into the Mayan civi-

lization. *Brazil remains largely in the Paleolithic age, with rudimentary agriculture supplementing hunter-gatherer practices."*

"So the only organized groupings we'd have to deal with would be when we pass through Central America?"

"There would need to be little to no contact with Central America. Direct access to North America and Brazil would suffice. While native populations will certainly notice our presence, they lack the sophisticated social and military organizations we encountered in Europe and they are far less developed than what European explorers will encounter in roughly a thousand years."

"That might make it harder. We were able to use existing political structures here, forming alliances. The same will not be possible if there are no organized governments to negotiate with."

"That is true, but Valdar has shown how we can work with individual tribes, offering support in return for their assistance, allowing those tribes to grow and create governments that we can work with, while giving us longer-term facilities like the ports Valdar has built to operate out of."

"We can hope we will be as lucky this time."

"Whoever is sent will have to operate carefully, in phases. Despite the Appalachians' proximity to the coast, when viewed continentally, the practical distance is considerable. No existing infrastructure and the potential territorial conflicts with indigenous peoples will complicate operations. The most likely path to success would be to move slowly, establish relations, and use friendly populations to carve a path to the appropriate areas of the mountains."

"I agree. And I know just the person to handle this."

Chapter 5

Western Coast of Africa

Valdar stood on the beach surrounded by his men, some of whom were still unloading the longboats pulled up in the sand. The midwinter ocean breeze was biting, and he looked forward to the men getting the temporary shelters built to get away from the chill.

Around him were some of his captains, but also engineers and architects from home, legionaries for security, and even a collection of men from Chief Ekoko's tribe.

This was the spot his scouts had picked for their first new port since the war with the Easterners began, and the excitement level was high.

"This is an excellent find," he began, as the last of his men joined him. "I was assured I would be impressed, and so I am."

The peninsula's curve created a perfect natural breakwater, protecting ships from the strong ocean currents while still giving them access to the gulf to the north.

"It's an excellent location, Admiral," Captain Egil said. "With us here and the Port of Vikhavn to the north, it gives us control of the entire bay. Any ships coming around the hump of Africa and transitioning down its length will have to deal with us, one way or another."

"The beach is too exposed," the lead engineer said. "We'd need fortifications running the entire length and on the Atlantic side, not just at the harbor mouth like Vikhavn. An enemy force could land on the ocean side and march straight across."

"How many forts would we need?"

"Five, at a minimum. Two on either side of the port, one at the tip of the peninsula, and two more on the Atlantic side. It would be an enormous undertaking."

Okan, one of the sub-chieftains Ekoko had sent along, pointed across the gulf to the distant shore of the mainland.

"Those waters are too rough for your ships," he said in careful Latin, the trade language of the Empire, that his people had begun to pick up. "It is good for fishing. The land here is very rich, better than at home. Good for growing."

The man wasn't wrong. Several rivers flowed into the gulf from here, creating a lush delta that, although brown from the winter air, would be green and fertile during the summer.

Others thought so, too. Their survey told him there was a very small village in the area. A local tribe, probably fishermen.

"They'll have to be relocated," Captain Fabius said quietly, following Valdar's gaze.

"It is as it will have to be. A lot of our manpower is coming from Ekoko's tribe, and our security, and they want to expand and become something more than a handful of affiliated villages. Could we judge them, after we've done much the same? They will provide us with additional defenses, especially if we can convince them to spread south of the peninsula as well, controlling the entire mainland and giving us this protrusion for our port and ship maintenance. In return, they are far enough from home that they will rely on us to keep them supplied and in contact with their people. It will bring us back together."

"The engineers are not wrong, though. This position is not as defensible as I'd like," Egil said. "A good location strategically, but a poor one tactically."

"The range of our forts using the new shells will keep most of the enemy at bay," Valdar said. "If positioned correctly, they will have overlapping fire that will make it hard for anyone to land, although I think we will end up with three forts on the Atlantic side, and not two."

"That will require a lot of material," Fabius said.

"And the supply lines will be stretched thin," the engineer added, having been listening to them. "They will take time to build."

"Then we shouldn't delay. Begin what surveys you need and let's work out a detailed plan for the location of each fort and the port facilities. I want this started by the end of the week, using what supplies we brought with us."

"We'll need to construct temporary docks first, although with the slope of this beach, I'd like to make it something more durable and permanent once we've made some inroads."

"The permanent facilities can come later," Valdar said. "Once we've established a proper beachhead. How long for the temporary structures?"

"Three weeks, maybe four. We brought enough timber and iron for that much, at least. The permanent structures ..." The engineer shrugged. "That depends on how quickly we can establish local quarries and sawmills."

"We'll import most of what we need for now from the works Chief Ekoko is setting up near Port Vikhavn. Eventually, his people will probably set up similar works here, but that will be well outside of our timeframe and I don't want to wait. I want these forts to begin going up as soon as possible."

"I'll get started on it," the engineer said, nodding and heading to his men, who were still near the longboats, to begin giving out commands and see to bringing supplies ashore.

"Weather's turning, Admiral. Looks like a big one brewing," Captain Egil said.

Valdar studied the clouds, noting their speed and direction. The weather patterns here were different from his home waters. He'd learned on his first voyage around Africa how the winds and currents turned in a different direction here than they did north of the continent. He'd talked to the Consul about it once, who'd explained things, most of which he didn't understand.

The gist of what he got out of it was that this was just the way the world worked this far south. When the Consul said that if they went far enough, it would be cold in the summer and hot in the winter, that was where Valdar stopped listening. He could only take so much madness.

"Looks bad. Early for the season, but not unheard of."

"Should we pull back to Vikhavn?" Fabius asked.

"No need," Valdar replied. "See how the wind's running? It'll sweep up the gulf, away from us. The peninsula should give us enough protection, especially if we move the ships to the leeward side."

"Good for proving the harbor's worth, too," Egil noted. "If it can shelter ships through a hurricane, it can handle anything, although I'm not sure the temporary shelters will survive that kind of storm."

"We should talk to the engineer, then. Maybe we should start the permanent structures now and not worry about stages. Get with him and see what he thinks and, if necessary, send one of the larger ships back for another round of supplies he'll need and have the port commander there send word to acquire more, so we don't have to wait entirely on Ekoko's people."

"I'll take care of it," the man said.

Yes. This was a hell of a start.

Factorium

"These are quite detailed," Ebro said.

Sorantius nodded. His Hispania colleague had joined him four years ago and had quickly climbed up the ranks. He was quick-thinking and inventive, but sometimes had the habit of pointing out the obvious.

The stack of diagrams and instructions that had arrived earlier that morning via messenger from Germania was, as he said, very detailed. Each page was numbered at the top to identify the order they were to proceed in, and clearly laid out step-by-step instructions, along with a note that said 'the next step with guncotton.'

Straightforward. To the point. It was one of the things Sorantius appreciated about the Consul. Sorantius had had a chance to go through everything once, and now he needed to make sure Ebro was in alignment with him and understood what they needed to do.

"Indeed," Sorantius replied, flipping through the first few pages. "This is all preparation for getting the guncotton, once it's created, ready for the next step in the process, where I believe it will be turned into true powder, although the Consul has not shared those plans with me yet. It's laid out in stages. For stage one, the washing, we're going to need at least six large vats, with each able to handle roughly five hundred pounds of guncotton at a time."

"That's a lot of fresh water to carry in every day," Ebro pointed out.

"I know. We won't have to build a whole feed system, since Hortensius has already built feed lines to the various boilers for the steam engines across the city, but it will have to be greatly expanded. That's for sure."

"So, we get the water in and wash the guncotton through the vats and then redirect the water back out again. We'll also need some kind of mesh to allow the particles through, along with the residual acids and water, and keep the guncotton in. Something we can open and close to soak and then rinse it, maybe."

"The Consul anticipated that and has a mesh design on page three."

Ebro flipped to that page and said, "Yes, I spoke too soon. The vats will have to be durable and will still wear away from the acids, even diluted this way."

"Yes. Wear will become a problem and will require regular maintenance and replacement of the vats. This, however, is the easy step. The next two are much more complicated," Sorantius said, flipping aside another page, revealing large and detailed diagrams. "We're going to need Hortensius to create several of these large, steam-driven agitators. These things are massive, especially with the accompanying steam turning system to constantly rotate the inner drum with a housing where we can add soda ash into the mixture to further purify it. And then there's this one. Another large drum, this one with the added function of cutting the washed guncotton into a fine pulp, which is then passed into this stamping press to further reduce it to a fine consistency."

"Then a last wash through cloth filters," Ebro said, finishing the last document. "This is a lot of processing for one batch compared to the black powder we are currently producing. Scaling this up will be difficult. The manpower alone ..."

"I'm aware, but apparently the effectiveness of this will greatly outpace the current black powder, allowing for new types of gun designs. Or so Hortensius keeps mentioning. This isn't all, either. It seems pretty clear from where this leaves off that there are more stages for producing the gunpowder, since clearly this pulp itself, while very flammable when dried, is not going to be able to be used in weapons itself."

"So, we need an increase of water intake, passing through washing vats, through an agitator, through the stamping press, and more water for the final wash. That's it then, aside from the later stages as you mentioned."

"No, there's one more thing. We cannot just take the finished water and dump it back into the river or use it in any other processes, since it will be very acidic and saturated with particles from the washing process. The river runs to Devnum, then out to the sea, and is the primary source of the city's drinking water. The Consul points out that if the river is filled with these acids and other matter, it will make it deadly to those drinking it, which would certainly have the Empress paying us a visit."

"So, do we just store the contaminated water forever?"

"No," Sorantius said, turning to the last pages. "This is the process for purifying the water of these contaminants. We mix the water with lime, which should neutralize the acids and form into calcium salts. It will take time, but the salts will settle to the bottom of the holding tanks along with other suspended solids. Once the calcium salts have settled, the clear water can be drained from the top and put into the river, where it will be further diluted and safe to pass through the city and into the sea. As an added benefit, the salts can be repurposed as a component in fertilizer, enhancing its effectiveness and extending our current fertilizer supplies."

"So ... more infrastructure."

"Yes. Sadly, it seems impossible for us to stop the constant expansion with every new process the Consul gives us."

"Then I will get with Hortensius as soon as he returns from Devnum and begin laying out the new production facilities."

"Good. Whatever building he erects to put this in, ask him to give us extra room, as I'm sure it will be needed for the next stage, and I would like to keep from having to transfer this stuff from building to building as much as possible, considering how flammable it is."

"I'll point that out to him."

"Good man," Sorantius said, slapping the Iberian on the shoulder.

Eastern Germania

Ky silently thanked the engineers who genetically crafted him and the nanites that built his muscular system the way they did for the thousandth time since coming to this version of the past, as he finished yet another page.

He looked at the dozens of pages of detailed drawings and finely written instructions he'd finished in just the past three hours and could imagine the muscle cramps a non-enhanced person would have experienced writing all of that. Or the fatigue that would have resulted from concentrating to do it.

Ky didn't have to deal with any of that. Although not part of the original programming or interface for a tactical AI, Ky and Sophus had spent years working out ways to hack the motion assist to allow the AI to have direct control over his limbs so that it could create the documents and diagrams directly, without having to dictate to Ky and have Ky write them.

While that method had worked, even with how well Ky and Sophus interfaced and how quickly Ky could write, it did not compare to Ky being able to just hand over motor control to the computer and let it go at full speed.

It helped that the front remained quiet. Ky knew that would not last and it was only a matter of time until they were hit in Greece, but the enemy had not pulled a significant portion of their manpower from the lines facing the Western Allies in Germania, so they were either bringing people in from the east, or they had manpower elsewhere.

Either way, it was taking them time to get everything redirected into Greece for the obvious next stage of the fight.

"Consul?" one of his lictores said from outside the tent, drawing Ky's wandering mind and disconnecting Sophus from direct control of his hand.

The bad thing with tents was that there were no doors to knock on, so interruptions were always more direct and abrupt.

"Yes?"

"Captain Yrsa is here to see you."

"Good, send him in," Ky said, standing from the seat he had been in for the past three hours.

He stretched, although it was more of an instinctual thing than an actual need to relax his muscles.

"I hope it's good. I can tell you I don't like being this far from the sea."

"I appreciate your sacrifice," Ky said.

That was one thing he appreciated about Yrsa. He did not stand on deference. Empresses or dock hands were all the same to him.

"So, what was so important that you had people throw me on one of your blasted trains and rush me down here."

"I have another voyage for you."

"Really?" Yrsa said, settling onto a stool near the entrance to the tent. "Another trading run? It has been some time since the Empire fattened my purse. That last one to Sarmatia, during the last war, was quite profitable. Helped me build my fleet of ships. I could use another like it."

"Yes, although this one is different than anything you've done before. The scope is much larger, but will be potentially even more profitable, if you're willing to take the risk."

Yrsa's weathered face broke into a grin. "Risk and profit tend to go hand in hand in my experience."

"I think you should hear what I'm proposing first, before you start planning on how to spend your coin. We need a new source of nitrates for powder production. Our current supplies won't sustain the war effort much longer. I know the location of deposits, but reaching them will require a journey no one has attempted before."

"Where exactly are we talking about?"

"Far to the west, across the ocean, lies an entire continent. It's half again larger than all the Western Alliance territories and North Africa combined."

"That's impossible. Something that large, someone would have found by now."

"They haven't. Until the new navigational tools were introduced eight years ago, there would have been no way to cross that amount of water without getting lost. And since then, everyone's been a little too preoccupied for this kind of voyage, which is more costly and risky than any private merchant would be able to attempt. The place I am talking about is roughly a two-month journey, with half of that time spent out of sight of any land. That's why it remains unknown here."

"What about the Easterners? Sailing that far, I imagine I'd be getting close to their homeland. Or is this where they live?"

"No," Ky said, grabbing a piece of paper and making a rough sketch. "These continents, there are actually two of them, lie only partway to the East. One spans roughly parallel to Europe, the other to Africa, and they are connected by a narrow strip of land between them. They are called the Americas. If you were to somehow transport your ship to the far side of the Americas, you'd find yourself in the Pacific Ocean, which dwarfs the ocean that we know, which my people call the Atlantic."

"The Greek philosophers always claimed the world was vast. I had no reason to doubt them, as they tended to know what they were talking about, but the numbers were too large to truly comprehend. Seeing it laid out like this ... makes a man feel rather small."

"What we consider the 'known world' is merely a fraction of what exists. But that's precisely why this venture could be so valuable. These lands are rich in resources we desperately need, resources few here even know exist."

Ky pulled out a set of rolled maps he had drawn up and spread them across the table. The detailed cartography was unlike anything native-born cartographers could make, showing not just the eastern coastlines of North and South America, but the trade lanes and patterns of the trade winds.

"I will provide you with seven ships, fully crewed and laden with supplies, and will fill any of your own ships you wish to take in addition with more supplies. Engineers, craftsmen, farmers, and a contingent of legionaries will accompany you. Your destination lies here, in an area called the Chesapeake Bay. It is a natural harbor system larger than any you have ever seen, with multiple freshwater rivers feeding into it."

"Seven ships and all the supplies I can load is a considerable investment. You must be desperate for whatever is in those mountains."

"We are. Without these resources, our powder production will grind to a halt within eighteen months. The journey there will take roughly two months, following specific routes I will provide. I expect it will take six months at least to get to the mountains, and at least two and more likely three more months to begin mining operations, and another two for the first ships laden with nitrate to make the return voyage. That leaves a margin of error of only six months, give or take. Doable, but I would not want to cut the margin any shorter, so I plan on giving you every advantage I can."

"And we will be completely on our own out there?"

"Yes. No reinforcements, no supply lines. You will need to be entirely self-sufficient. The natives are scattered, living in small settlements across the areas you are going to, both the shoreline and in the mountains which are your ultimate destination, and the land in between. Some farm, others hunt. They are not unified, which presents both opportunities and challenges."

"So, easily conquered."

"You are not going to have the men for that. In fact, you are going to need more manpower than you can stick on a boat, which means trading with them would be simpler than fighting them. They have never seen steel tools, glass, or even horses. Simple trade goods will seem miraculous to them. Build alliances where you can. The natives know the land, the local plants, the weather patterns, and can provide the manpower you do not have. Their help will be invaluable."

"So we land, make friends, and march to these mountains then."

"I would suggest something more systematic. You will need to establish way stations between the port and the mining sites. Small settlements, trading posts, places for defense, since not everyone you encounter will be friendly. Some might grow into proper towns eventually."

"Which means settlers will follow behind me."

"I imagine that is true, eventually. Right now, with the war consuming so much manpower, we cannot spare many and there is too much need for those not directly engaged in the war. But once word spreads of opportunities in the new lands ..." Ky shrugged. "People will come. For now, focus on building relationships with the native tribes. Many will be willing to settle near your posts for trade access."

"So, establish a port, make nice with the locals, set up a chain of settlements leading to these mountains, and start mining whatever it is you need so badly."

"That is the essence of it."

"I assume these settlements and ports will belong to the Empire. Not some private venture I'll be setting up."

"The ports, settlements, and mines will all be Imperial territory," Ky confirmed. "But there's considerable profit to be made establishing trade routes between there and Britannia. The land holds vast resources beyond just nitrates. There is copper, iron, timber, and more in addition to what the natives will trade for. A shrewd merchant could build quite an enterprise."

"What should I expect from these natives? You said they were simple, without much technology."

"Stone tools, wooden clubs, spears with stone points. Some use bows. Their warfare is mainly small-scale raiding between villages. Nothing organized enough to threaten a properly fortified position. But again, fighting should be your last resort. You will be outnumbered and alone. Even though you will be better armed, fighting could end badly for you."

"And my authority to negotiate?"

"You'll have full power to make treaties and trade agreements with native tribes, within reason. Take copies of the deals Valdar has been making or the agreements we have made here on the continent as a baseline for how to make decisions. Focus on establishing trade relationships. You won't be able to secure land rights through fair purchase, as most natives there are still nomadic and do not think in that way. If they let you set up a town or village, I believe they will honor that as long as you keep your part. The Empire will honor any reasonable agreements you make."

Yrsa stood, rolling the maps carefully. "I'll begin assembling the expedition immediately. Should have everything ready to sail within the month, weather permitting."

"Good. This mission is critical, Yrsa. Without those nitrates, our powder production fails and our ability to wage this war becomes severely compromised." Ky clasped the merchant's shoulder. "You've done this for us before, and I need you to do it again. If anyone can make this work, it is you."

"I have not lost a cargo yet."

"Good man. Send word once your preparations are complete. I'll have additional maps and instructions prepared for you by then."

Chapter 6

West African Coast

'I must be insane to have the whole fleet out in this weather,' Valdar thought as the deck heaved beneath him as another massive wave crashed against the hull.

Not that he'd had a lot of choice in the matter. The schooner Tiwaz had been on one of the wide patrols that he'd set up to keep an eye out for the Eastern reinforcements to their now destroyed fleet that he'd been expecting for some time.

Communication delay was a serious problem this far away from civilization, and his victory over that fleet had been so complete that none of them had been able to flee and warn their countrymen that their attack had failed.

It was, of course, just his luck that after two months of being on alert for their ships, they'd finally found them just as the massive storm he'd predicted pushed in from the west, hammering the African coast.

And now his ships.

Rain lashed horizontally across the deck, driven by howling winds that threatened to tear the sails from their yards despite being reefed down to the bare minimum. The western coast of Africa lay somewhere to starboard, but in these conditions, they'd be lucky to spot land before running aground on it.

Valdar gripped the railing, knuckles bone-white, his oilskins plastered to him like a second skin, the salt spray stinging his eyes. Visibility was down to mere feet. It was like sailing through the end of the world. Finding his own ships was problem enough. It would be all but impossible to find the enemy.

But he didn't want them sailing past him. Once they realized the fate of their fleet, they could choose to continue north. If there were enough of them, and his scout had counted thirty sails, they could wreak havoc in the Middle Sea.

"Signal the fleet to tighten formation," Valdar ordered. "Any ship that loses sight of us in this mess will be on their own until morning."

"Signals won't carry far in this, Admiral. Half the fleet can barely see our stern lanterns as it is," his first mate said.

Valdar knew he was right. He'd brought fourteen ships with him, ten caravels and four schooners, and they were scattered across several miles of angry sea, maintaining what formation they could in the storm. The caravels were handling it better than the schooners, but even they were struggling against waves that seemed determined to swallow them whole.

"Keep her steady on this heading," he told the helmsman. "That Eastern fleet has to be close. They wouldn't risk the deeper waters in weather like this."

The words were barely out of his mouth when a flash of lightning illuminated the sea around them, and Valdar's heart nearly stopped.

"Hard to port!" he roared. "All hands brace for impact!"

The helmsman spun the wheel with desperate strength as a dark shape materialized out of the darkness directly ahead of them. The Bellona heeled over, timbers groaning as she turned. Valdar caught a glimpse of high sides and strange rigging as an Eastern caravel swept past them, so close he could have tossed a coin onto her deck.

"Beat to quarters! Gun crews to stations!" The drum took up the call as sailors scrambled to their posts. "Fire as you bear!"

It was a formality, to let everyone know the enemy was upon them. His men had been ready for combat since they left the newly dubbed Port Caolros, which was only a handful of temporary work shacks, as the construction entered the very beginning stages.

The gun crews were already in motion, as the first drum roll sounded. The Bellona's guns spoke almost as soon as the order to fire was given; the concussion of their discharge felt through the deck. Twelve explosive shells screamed across the short distance at the enemy vessel.

This was the first chance to use the new explosive shells developed by the Consul and the new cannon designed to fire them. It was why Valdar had only brought fourteen ships. These were the only ones equipped with the cannon so far, as they waited for more shipments from home.

Valdar watched as multiple impacts struck the enemy vessel along its waterline. As soon as the metal projectiles hit, a series of massive explosions lit up the night, the flashes revealing the shocking devastation as the shells detonated along the enemy hull.

It was like nothing Valdar had ever experienced.

The Eastern caravel's sides blew outward in a shower of splintered wood. Even in the heavy rain, the ship caught fire, the side facing them ripped open almost completely, now just a burning wreck illuminating the storm-tossed seas around them.

By the gods, it was something.

"More ships! Three points off the starboard bow!"

Through the curtain of rain, he could make out at least four more Eastern vessels, their high-sided bulk unmistakable even in the poor visibility. They were already turning towards the Bellona, gun ports opening along their sides.

"Helm, bring us about two points to starboard. We'll cross between them if we can, split their formation. Signal the nearest ships to form on us. Hopefully, they can see the flags. We need to concentrate our fire before they can organize themselves."

The storm raged around them as the Bellona turned to meet her opponents. Lightning cracked overhead, briefly revealing a long string of enemy ships laid out before him.

Thankfully, the enemy ships weren't the only thing the lightning showed him. The Aquila burst through a wall of rain behind the Bellona, her new cannons firing. The Eastern vessel caught in her sights never stood a chance. Multiple explosions ripped through its hull. The enemy ship split apart, vanishing beneath the waves with shocking speed.

"Maintain loose line formation!" Valdar shouted over the howling wind. "Keep enough distance to maneuver!"

His signalmen raised lanterns on the upper mast, since flags would be all but impossible to see. They were too close to the enemy, already tied up in their formation. Many of his ships would be fighting their own battles. A poor way to conduct a naval engagement, but one that Valdar would have to deal with. His men were too spread out to get into line quick enough to engage.

Trying to do it now, the Bellona and a few of the ships closest to him would be engaging the entire enemy fleet while they waited for the rest to catch up. At least it would limit how many of their ships could engage at a time.

A massive wave lifted the Bellona's bow, and as they crested it, Valdar spotted three more Eastern vessels through gaps in the rain. Their high-sided bulk made them visible despite the darkness.

"Helm, bring us between those two on the right," Valdar ordered. "Gun crews, prepare to fire both broadsides!"

The Bellona turned slowly. To his right, he could see the Aeolus engaging an enemy vessel. While his ships' new cannons were devastating, the enemy was not without their own weapons. An Eastern ship's broadside crashed into the Aeolus's rigging, sending splinters and torn canvas flying.

"Admiral!" One of the men on the railing behind him said, pointing. "The Ghaoth Álainn is taking heavy fire!"

Valdar turned to see the schooner listing badly, multiple hits visible along her hull. Captain Valerius was fighting to keep her afloat while trading fire with two Eastern vessels.

"Belay my previous command. Bring us about. We need to draw their fire from the Ghaoth Álainn."

The Bellona swung around, her guns firing as soon as its broadside pointed toward one of the enemy ships. The explosive shells smashed into the side of the enemy vessel, cracking it open like an egg.

On the other side of the enemy ships, the Seadreki appeared, firing nearly point-blank at the other ship that had targeted the Ghaoth Álainn, its cannons blazing.

A timely save, but one that put two other enemy ships very close to the Seadreki. At that close range, round shot could do a tremendous amount of damage. This intermingled, his people were able to be separated from one another and swarmed. Already, three ships had been severely damaged. None had sunk, but they were being battered from multiple angles from close-in broadsides.

"Run up the disengage signal," Valdar ordered. "Keep the lanterns lit. Put up the signal to follow the flag. I know most won't see it but put it up anyway."

The message went up to the crow's nest, followed by a one dark, one light lantern pattern. It would have been hard to see if you were at a bad angle, but almost as soon as it was up, the Seadreki and Ghaoth Álainn put their own signals up, heaving about to fall in with the flagship.

"Helm, bring us north by northeast. We'll use this wind to pull clear. Gun crews are to maintain fire on any targets that present themselves."

The men at the guns didn't even wait for the order before cannons fired again. Valdar could imagine the sheer elation of the gun captains at seeing their cannons wipe out entire ships with so little effort.

Two of the enemy ships angled hard, trying to catch the Bellona as it broke out of the melee, taking its broadsides out of the fight. Other ships had fallen in with the Bellona, and Valdar did not want to take them all back into the melee, but with the line slowly snaking away from the enemy fleet, it left them vulnerable.

"Sir, the Velox is making a run at those two Eastern ships bearing down on us," the helmsman said.

Valdar spotted the nimble schooner darting between the larger vessels, her guns blazing. Captain Bituitus was using his ship's superior handling to keep the enemy off balance, preventing them from bringing their full broadsides to bear on the withdrawing Britannian vessels.

"Clever bastard," Valdar muttered. "He's buying time for the caravels to break free."

It wasn't without risk; pulling between the two ships may have kept the enemy from putting their broadsides to work against the disengaging fleet, but it meant those same guns could rake it.

The firing was heavy, and the small schooner took a hell of a beating as it passed between the ships and limped away. Thankfully, its guns, though fewer in number, had done even more damage to the two chasing ships, leaving them reeling in the opposite direction, rudderless and out of control.

There was nothing Valdar could do about the Velox now. All he could do was defeat this fleet. Then he could worry about his injured ships.

Slowly, much too slowly, his remaining caravels fell into line. The Dumnos and the Hfran both pushed their way out of the battling fleet, their cannons firing as fast as their gun crews could reload.

They had bought a moment to escape the fight by a lucky shot. A tremendous explosion lit up the storm-darkened sky as one of Dumnos's broadsides found an enemy powder magazine. The Eastern caravel simply ceased to exist, transformed into a rapidly expanding ball of fire and debris that briefly illuminated the entire battlefield.

"Three more of our ships are visible to starboard," the first mate reported. "The Aquila, Praetor, and Hasta. All showing withdrawal signals."

That was enough. Nine of his caravels and two schooners were in line, and the Velox was safely out of the way, if hobbled. Time to finish this.

"Turn the line west and bring us to bear. All ships to fire as they will. Tear them apart."

The line snaked, slowly curving itself to the west. His gunners didn't wait for the order to fire. With more room, they could target their shots better, even through the rain, picking their victims. Behind him, other ships joined the barrage as dozens and then hundreds of shells arched into the tightly packed enemy formation.

Ships were torn apart as if made of light linen, people leaping into the violently churning sea. They tried to rally, to pull into their own line to counter the Britannians' now coordinated attacks, but it was too little too late.

Not with the new shells in action. A dozen more ships were on fire and headed toward the bottom within minutes, torn apart by Britannian guns.

That was enough for the handful of remaining Eastern vessels. They turned and tried to flee as best they could, some toward the coast with the better winds, and some toward the open ocean.

It was everyone for themselves.

"Should we pursue, Admiral?"

Valdar shook his head. "No. In this weather chasing scattered ships would be suicide. Signal all ships to form up. We need to assess damage and get our wounded to safety."

Two ships were missing, and three more heavily damaged, with lighter damage across the rest of the fleet. In return, they had sunk between twenty and twenty-five enemy vessels in near-blinding weather. Not just destroyed. Obliterated.

A good victory indeed.

Devnum

He was annoyed at being a glorified messenger. While he understood why he'd been given this task, and it had been his decision not to hand it to an underling, he still would rather not be back in Devnum. His people were good, and he'd trained them to do their jobs properly, but there were so many projects currently in the works, it was too much for the managers of each of them to coordinate between them properly.

Having looked at the notes he carried, in addition to the heavy case he'd had to keep carefully balanced and upright, he knew this was not an urgent project. Yes, it was something they had been working on for a while, but it was in no way necessary for the current war effort.

Still, the Consul had asked that they bring this sample to Hywel, the head Imperial physician, and even Sorantius was loath to disobey. The Consul, after all, was the font of all the advancements the Empire had seen in recent years, as well as its very survival, so they owed him some level of obedience.

Even from a begrudging Sorantius.

Sorantius sighed and stepped into Devnum's hospital. Although it was cold outside, it was a steady, warm temperature inside the hospital thanks to inset braziers that burned at even distances, filled with hot coals. It occurred to Sorantius that it must be someone's full-time responsibility to keep these filled with hot coals, and disposing or reheating the old coals across the entire building. He could see the benefit of keeping an even temperature to allow people to fight off their illnesses without struggling to maintain their body temperatures, but it seemed like a lot of work.

It was just one of the things that made the building unique, a standard for all of the new construction across the city and the Empire, its architecture reflecting both Roman traditions and the influence of newer construction methods promoted by Consul Ky. Walls were thick, fitted to discourage fires and help keep in the heat produced by the inset braziers, and small oil lamps were interspaced as well, keeping the hallways well-lit without needing to open windows.

"I'm looking for Imperial Physician Hywel," he said to a younger man in the simple tunic and trousers that was the uniform of everyone who worked in the hospital, perhaps to let patients know who to turn to for help.

"Go down that hallway, all the way to the end, turn left, and then all the way to the end; it's the last door on your right."

Sorantius nodded to the man then followed his directions. He passed ward after ward, seeing cots lined with wounded soldiers, women in labor, and people who had been injured in various accidents across the city. Most were in a serious state, especially the soldiers. Only the worst cases usually ended up here at the hospital, the rest were tended at front-line medical facilities. Even those in the city tended to go to the small private offices of men trained in the medical arts and practicing on their own across the city.

At last, he stopped before a door bearing a plain wooden sign reading 'Hywel, Imperial Physician.' He heard two voices from within, though he could not make out the words. Sorantius, not a man used to waiting on others and with a task given to him by the Consul, did not wait to be admitted. He knocked twice on the door and then let himself in.

Inside the room, Hywel was sitting at his desk with a slender young man, barely into adulthood, standing nervously in front of him.

Hywel looked at Sorantius, a slightly annoyed expression on his face, before turning back to the young man, ignoring the chemist.

"Try that method," Hywel said in a measured, articulate tone. "Report back if you see even a small improvement. I think you're on the right track, but remember, you aren't alone on this. Just keep at it and remember you are here to learn as much as to heal."

The young man nodded and hurried out, sparing a curious glance at Sorantius as he left the room.

Hywel exhaled and rolled his shoulders. "I used to think the training needed to become a healer was overwhelming. Every day we faced new tests by our masters in between producing poultices and doing menial tasks. We were as much servants as students. Now, these new methods from the Consul ... by the gods, I'm thankful I'm not just beginning. Our novices are breaking their brains trying to learn it all."

"I suppose so," Sorantius muttered, more an acknowledgment that he'd heard the physician than engaging.

Things had been different for all of them before the Consul's new ways of doing things. Sorantius would agree with that. But he did not long for the old ways, the fumbling about, not understanding why or how things worked. The Consul not only brought them innovations but explained those innovations.

Sorantius had no nostalgia for the past.

"What brings you here, Sorantius? If it's to explain to me again why we are low on ether for surgery, I can only say the physicians we sent to the front are the ones asking for more. If you have a problem with their request, take it up with the Consul."

"It is not about that," Sorantius said, flicking the door closed to ensure privacy. "We have increased production as you asked, but these are multi-stage chemicals, they require time to properly produce them. No, I am here about something else."

Sorantius set the case down on the desk and unfastened its brass latches, opening the hinges and revealing a series of carefully padded jars, each sealed with a wax stopper. He removed one jar and sat it on the desk, the lantern on the desk revealing a cloudy liquid inside.

"What is this?"

"A new chemical we've devised based on the Consul's instructions that he calls formaldehyde. The Consul tells me it will revolutionize how you train your young protégés. It is capable of preserving organic matter and preventing decay, although there are steps for diluting it before its use. A properly treated specimen can last months, perhaps years."

"Really," Hywel said, leaning forward, examining the liquid with newfound interest. "That would solve so many of our teaching constraints. No more rushing through dissections before the bodies rot."

"I believe that was his intent," Sorantius said, pulling a stack of papers from the case and setting them next to the jar. "The Consul provided detailed instructions for its use. Proper dilution ratios, application methods, and safety precautions. He was quite specific about the ventilation requirements."

Hywel's hand moved closer to the jar as he studied it closely, seeming to only half listen to Sorantius, transfixed by the liquid.

When his fingers moved to the wax seal, Sorantius said, "I would not open that. The fumes are quite noxious. Even a small amount can cause severe irritation to the eyes and throat."

Hywel's hand pulled back. "Chemical burns?"

That was something new that they had all come to know and hate. It was by far the most frequent injury caused in Sorantius' facilities. Even with his intense focus on the safety of his people, especially following the tank rupture seven years ago, accidents still happened.

They had learned quickly that it was possible that a simple liquid, cold to the touch, could burn a man as badly as an open flame. Worse even, since water would often not quench the burning caused by these chemicals.

"Yes, in a concentrated form like this. The documentation includes precise ratios for dilution with water before use. The Consul was quite specific about proper handling procedures."

"Fascinating." Hywel picked up the first page of instructions, reading it over as if it was the first time Sorantius had given it to him. "And this will truly prevent decay? For how long?"

"We've preserved rat specimens for three months now with no visible degradation. The tissue maintains its structure and firmness, though the color changes somewhat. However, that was a test and we threw them out at that point. I couldn't say what state the organs were in, although the Consul assures me it will keep a tissue static for some time."

"Three months ..." Hywel set down the paper, his expression thoughtful. "Do you realize what this could mean for medical training? Right now, we're forced to rush through anatomical instruction because bodies decay so quickly. Even in winter, we have perhaps a week at most before decomposition makes further study impossible."

"I'm sure that was one of the reasons the Consul asked us to develop it, although he does not often consult me on his thinking when giving us new projects."

"Still, we could preserve examples of specific injuries and diseases and show students exactly what decay looks like in its various stages or the progression of growths. Theory is all well and good, but nothing compares to seeing pathology with one's own eyes."

"There are instructions for whole body preservation as well, though that's more in your domain than mine. The chemical penetrates deep into tissue when properly administered through the blood vessels."

"Through the vessels? You mean perfusion? Like the old Egyptian embalmers with natron?"

Sorantius was familiar with the Egyptian practices. Before the Consul, they were among the foremost in creating and developing chemicals that could change the very nature of a thing. It had always fascinated him, although he had not been able to visit the place due to its being in Carthaginian hands. By the time it was free, the Consul had opened his mind to a much larger world of possibilities, and there was little reason to leave his workshop.

"Similar principle, I believe. Again, it is in the Consul's notes."

"It is interesting, though," Hywel said, sitting back and turning his attention to Sorantius directly. "Most of what the Consul gives us serves immediate military needs. This is different. Training tools aren't exactly pressing wartime priorities."

"I can explain part of that. We began work on this before the war. The Consul requested it nearly fourteen months ago, though production proved challenging."

"Really? Even with the Consul's help?"

"Even before the war, the Consul wasn't always readily available. There was so much work to be done on the continent that progress on some of our projects would stall for months, waiting for him to return."

"That is very true. But you continued working on it over this last year? And he had you bring it to us now?"

"He did. Though I suspect this timing isn't random. The Consul thinks ahead. Perhaps he sees applications beyond basic medical training."

"But he hasn't shared those plans with you directly?"

"No. As usual, he reveals only what he deems necessary for us to know at each stage. I simply make what he requests."

That's his way, isn't it? Parceling out information bit by bit, each piece precisely timed. Sometimes, I wonder if he plans these revelations years in advance."

"Given what I've seen of his other projects, I wouldn't doubt it. But, his methods have served us well enough," Sorantius said. "Will you need anything else? The production facility is running smoothly now, so supply shouldn't be an issue."

"No, I'll study these instructions thoroughly before we begin. Though I expect I'll have questions once we start implementing the preservation protocols."

"Send word to the facility if you need clarification on safety and handling. I've trained the staff in proper handling procedures. They can explain the safety requirements in detail. Otherwise, I'm afraid most of your questions will be for the Consul, and not me."

"Naturally," Hywel said, standing. "Thank you for bringing this personally. I know you'd rather be in your workshop."

Sorantius nodded, opened the door, and left, leaving Hywel to begin pouring over the notes. He could understand the enthusiasm, as he had the same reaction every time the Consul sent him new work.

If only these irritating side journeys would cease, he could actually get back to that work.

Chapter 7

Illyrian-Macedonian Border

Modius leaned against a dead, twisted juniper and surveyed the slope before them. The ground was covered in a mixture of snow and rock, alternating brown and white, making for an almost serene view, if it wasn't for what lay ahead of them out of sight.

Ahead and slightly below him, his men fanned out, scattered along a dry riverbed, with good spacing to allow them to take cover behind outcrops of stone and the small number of trees.

Part of his mind still protested seeing his men like this. At least the tightly packed rifle companies in line for volley fire were roughly reminiscent of the tightly packed shield wall he had known coming up through the ranks in the Roman army, facing off against equally tightly packed Carthaginian phalanxes.

It still made sense and felt like the proper way to fight, even if they fought at a distance, firing their rifles instead of using swords and spears. A piece of him couldn't shake the feeling that this kind of fight, each man hiding behind cover, operating almost on his own, was sheer madness.

Except he knew what happened to men in firing lines and shield walls when they went up against rifles. He'd seen it enough in the war against Carthage. Bullets were not intimidated by shields or close organization. They only respected stone and thick wood.

He agreed with the Consul's new orders for open-field battle, even if his warrior soul twinged a bit.

Besides, it was better than being stuck in one of those stinking trenches, unable to maneuver, having to live under constant fire day and night. This was at least still war and not pure carnage.

The sound of boots crunching on snow announced the approach of Renius, the tribune whose cohort Modius had taken half of for this expedition. He was a good man, although young, having been one of the later batches of recruits in the Carthaginian war. Men like him made up a large percentage of the modern officer core. They'd learned to soldier with rifle and bayonet and didn't have notions of gladius and shield to fight against, and tended to do better in this new way of war.

"Captain," Renius said, using the title Modius was still called by, even though his rank was equal to a prefect. "Scouts reported movement on that upper ridge about half an hour ago. Are we certain we want to hold below them? We will be giving them the high ground."

"True, but the slope here isn't that bad. Beyond this ridge, the ground rises more and has less cover than the riverbed. If we tried to stand there, we'd be stuck with no trees and no cover except rocks that might not provide cover for a single squad. Anyone climbing further would end up pinned by the next crest. No, this is the better ground."

A dozen or so pickets had crested that line as soon as they'd reached this point to begin probing for the enemy and confirmed that this was the most defensible piece of ground. While Modius would agree that he'd prefer the high ground, he'd take adequate cover over what elevation could be obtained here.

Besides, they were responding to the enemy's movements, which meant they were not able to determine the ground as much as they could if the enemy was coming to them.

To his right, the crew of the light howitzer unlimbered the gun behind a crumbling stone wall. Not a lot of protection, but still some, and the gun observers and a small signal team moved off to his left, to some of the highest ground on this side of the riverbed, to allow them to spot for the gun, which would be operating almost completely outside of direct line of sight from the ridge the enemy would surely be coming over.

Modius was about to order the gunners to move their limber a bit further back, to keep it from being accidentally touched off by a lucky hit, when sudden cracks of rifle fire could be heard just out of sight ahead of them. A few minutes later, his picket came racing over the ridge and down the slope, with two of the men supporting one of their comrades who was clearly injured.

The lead picket hurried to where Modius was standing and reported, "Eastern forces, sir, about four hundred strong. They've got at least one cannon with them."

Modius nodded and dismissed the man as he looked over the ground he would shortly be fighting on.

"Have two of your centuries hold the center. They are to fire as soon as the enemy is in sight and keep up the pressure. I want the enemy focused on the center," he told Renius. "Send the other two centuries along the left and right flank. Break them into squads; I don't want a grouping larger than that at any one point. Let's see if they've learned the new tactics we've been training on. Keep two squads from each flanking century in reserve in case they are needed and keep back the special teams until I signal."

Renius nodded and rushed to give orders to his centurions. Modus frowned. Even the language was changing. A contubernium was now a squad. How soon until centuries and cohorts were called something else? He would never second guess the Consul, but his conservative nature did not see the need for change simply for the sake of change.

It did not take long for the enemy to follow on the heels of his scouts. At first, it was just a handful, who halted when they met the fire of his center units, which had opened up from their cover, with aimed instead of volley fire.

Within minutes, that handful became a dark tide, flowing over the crest. They were close enough that, through his spyglass, he could make out the faces of what were probably Macedonian troops mixed with Eastern soldiers, their unusual skin tone and eyes very different from what was seen in the West. He'd met a few up close in one of the prison camps on the way to Greece last year. It was odd, seeing people so different looking from his own, much like the first time he'd met a Nubian.

The world continued to give him surprises, show him that there was more to nature than he ever knew. Of course, he would prefer if that diversity wasn't actively shooting at him now, but at least it made it easier to tell friend from foe.

The enemy tide had halted at the ridge line as they tried to find cover, many just lying on the ground trying to fire from a prone position. Not an easy task with a rifle that had to be loaded from the muzzle. It was a mistake, and not one he would have allowed his men to make, as it greatly slowed their rate of fire.

Not that he was one to not accept a gift from the enemy.

"Hold the cannon silent," he ordered, seeing the crew start to work the weapon. "Wait until they reveal their artillery position."

It took a few minutes, but from his vantage point, he could see his flanking units begin to flow around either side of the ridge line, using cover as they moved to encircle the enemy position. The enemy saw them too, and their position bulged as their line now faced not just his center, but either side along an arc until it was a semicircle.

When his men reached about a hundred and twenty passus, the enemy opened fire. Several of his men were in the open, moving to their next position when the heavy fire started, and were cut down. Most had cover, though, and began returning the fire.

"Get those wounded men back," Modius commanded. "And spread the flanking squads wider. They're still easy targets. I want more of an envelopment. Make them have to defend more ground."

Another development in the new legions. Small groups of men who did not carry rifles and were trained by the physicians for simple medical tasks, who pulled men out of the line and back to aide positions, or at least off the front line in times like this, when no aide position existed.

The enemy had the benefit of being on the interior of the battle, allowing for a tighter range of men and to quickly reinforce from one side of their line to the other without having to go all the way around.

The enemy tried to make a concerted push down the center, to split his line in two, apparently hoping they could use a charge down the slope to their advantage. His men, however, were not spooked, maintained good fire discipline and checked the attempt. The enemy was too tightly packed, allowing for most of the Britannian fire to find its mark without much difficulty.

The enemy was still slowly learning their strategy, not adjusting quickly to the shifting Britannian tactics. They only made it halfway down the slope before the men turned and ran, many not stopping when they reached their lines, continuing toward the rear, out of sight.

A dull thud between Modius's position and his men in the riverbed, followed by a geyser of dirt being thrown into the air by the impact, signaled the introduction of the enemy's cannon, which they must have finally gotten into position.

It took a minute for him to find the weapon. They had put it further back, on a higher slope, near the ridge behind the one they had put their infantry on.

Another mistake.

A direct-fire weapon needed an open field of fire. High ground was important because it allowed weapons like that a wider range of fire, and it used gravity to allow the range of the cannon to extend. Where that high ground failed was on uneven terrain such as this, where the interceding ridge with their own infantry partially blocked the depression where the riverbed was.

He couldn't be sure how many of his men the gunners could see, but he imagined the reason it landed behind his lines was because there was limited visibility. Unfortunately, it also meant they would be able to see where he'd positioned his cannon.

Still, moving his cannon would only draw their attention and putting it in the ravine with his infantry would put it under rifle fire. Better to try and take out their artillery piece altogether.

"Signal the gun crew, they may fire. Target their artillery piece," Modius told one of the runners, who dashed off toward the weapon.

No reason to expose himself with signal flags on such a small battlefield if he didn't have to. He was, after all, also in the direct line of fire of their cannon.

As if to confirm their cannon was not without teeth, another shot fired, this one still behind his front line, but much closer. Just before it hit the ground, it exploded, sending a scattering of shrapnel into his men's backs, causing a handful of casualties.

Not enough to turn the tide of battle, but Modius would not let them fire on his men unanswered.

A minute later, the Britannian gun fired, sending a shell on a high arc, coming down a dozen or so paces in front of the enemy piece. Close enough to send men scrambling, but not so close as to actually put it out of commission. Flags off to his far left went up, signaling to his gun crew the position of the shot in relation to the enemy gun.

Smartly, the enemy did not wait for ranging shots to reposition their piece. However, they stayed on the same far ridge, still without an effective line of sight on his men.

With the enemy lines solidifying, the flanks continued to press against the sides of the enemy line, spreading out more and more to get further into the enemy rear. It did put them in danger of being swept up if the enemy's flanks hinged out and came down either side of the ridge. If Modius was in their position, it would be what he would do, attempt to envelop the enemy and refuse the position.

It was their best chance at breaking the temporary stalemate between their forces.

He didn't want to give them time to consider that option. "Message to Tribune Renius to send in the special teams on the left flank. They are to go as far down the enemy flank as they can get. His flankers are to increase pressure until their assault begins."

The messenger saluted and ran off to pass the message. He'd considered having them hit in the center of the enemy line, but they'd have to get close to the enemy line to give them the Britannian's newest little surprise, so the fewer guns they had to face doing it, the better. This wasn't going to break their lines, but he wanted to keep them off balance until his cannon finished off the enemy armillary and was able to turn to their infantry, which would turn the battle.

Besides, from where he stood, it looked as if there was more cover on the very far left, enough to get within distance.

After a few minutes, he could see a small group of men working their way along a dry creek bed on the left flank. They moved carefully, just behind the flankers, waiting until they fired to move to the next set of cover.

When they reached the first enemy position, each pulled a small device from a satchel they carried slung at their sides, and in a three-step motion, pulled a strip from the end of the device, arched their arm back as if they were heaving a javelin, and threw the dart-like object they carried.

The devices sailed through the air, their nose-weighted design and fins on the back ensuring they landed point-first. As soon as they hit the ground, they exploded in geysers of rock and dust. Not as large as a shell landing, not even one of the Easterner shells, but still a notable explosion, throwing several men back from the blast. Men a little further away reeled from the shrapnel.

Another grenade landed among a group of enemy riflemen, and then another as his men continued to arm and throw grenade after grenade. It was enough to send a group of the men on that flank running, throwing their rifles to the ground as they bolted to the rear.

The grenades, the Consul's newest addition to the fight, were an ingenious weapon, not too different from the fused shells the howitzer was firing. They were only deadly in a five or ten-pace range, but men could throw them twenty or thirty yards. In a battle where everyone is using cover, it would allow them to break part of the enemy line, although Modius understood the Consul had introduced them more to be thrown into enemy trenches if his men ever had to assault one.

"Sir!" One of his aides called, drawing Modius's attention to the right flank. "Movement in the gulch."

Through his spyglass, Modius spotted that the right flank of the enemy was indeed trying to swing down, already pushing his flankers out of position even as their own left flank began to collapse. If he wasn't careful, they would end up flanking each other simultaneously, which could end in disaster.

It also sent them directly toward the howitzer, which was still firing away, chasing the enemy cannon from one position to the next.

"Send in the reserve squads and redirect two squads from the center. They are to refuse the flank at all costs. Don't let them bend past our center."

The messenger ran off, and a moment, later the fifty or so men who'd been held back, along with another twenty from the center, ran to the left flank, which had already begun to dissolve into close-quarters fighting. He didn't have enough men to put significant fire on them to stop the charge of that whole flank.

For a moment, it was a close thing as men swung with bayonet and rifle butt, rock and fist. It was impossible for him to tell right away if his men would hold or not.

"Second order to the tribune. Prepare to move the remainder of one century from the center to the left if it should collapse. But only if it collapses."

Thankfully, that did not come to pass. The extra men all came from the left, slamming into one part of the swinging enemy flank, breaking it and splitting it from contact with their own center. Just before his men enveloped the remainder of the flank, the attackers began to flee.

The danger had passed, although it had been a close thing. Renius knew his job and his men did not pursue, only stabilized the flank and returned to their firing positions, although further from the enemy than before, and allowing the medics to get in and pull the wounded from both sides back.

A huge explosion in the rear of the enemy line drew everyone's attention. His artillery piece had finally found the enemy's range, and a shell had landed almost on top of their limber. The combined explosion from the fused shell and the enemy's powder charges created a massive blast, large enough to envelop the enemy field piece, taking it out of commission and killing most of the gunners.

The grenades on the left, the failed assaults in the center and right, and now the destroyed artillery were enough for the enemy, the soldiers beginning to break and run for the rear. Those that didn't outright run, started a more controlled retreat, the outcome of the battle obvious to everyone.

"Have the men hold position. We will not pursue. Gather the wounded for travel and prepare to return to our main line," Modius said to a messenger, who saluted and ran off toward the centuries below. Once he was gone, Modius turned to one of his remaining runners. "Go back to the legion telegraph station. I want word of the battle sent to the Consul as soon as they can send it, with word that a full report will follow."

The man saluted and ran for one of the horses kept for such a situation. It was fifteen miles back to the closest station, but he wanted the Consul to know right away that the enemy had begun their probes, and it would probably be the better part of a day before he could gather his and the enemy's wounded and get his men back to their main unit.

Things on this front were heating up, and soon, one legion would not be enough to stop them.

Factorium

Hortensius wiped his hands on his apron as he paced the workshop floor, warm in spite of the cold weather outside the window thanks to the numerous foundries and machines constantly running around him.

Of all the ideas the Consul had given him recently, this one might be the most exciting Hortensius had seen yet. Working with metal, even assembling ships and weapons, while fascinating, were only extensions of the kinds of things the inventor did before the Consul's arrival.

This, however, was something completely new. He hadn't had a challenge like this since the balloon project. He looked at the water clock again. He couldn't start until ...

His thoughts were interrupted as the door creaked open, admitting a lean young man with sharp features. Septimus, one of his most promising young engineers. And the man he'd been waiting for.

"Excellent! Finally," Hortensius said, gesturing animatedly. "Come, come. I've something rather extraordinary to discuss."

He led Septimus to a large workbench where stacks of pages were set out.

"What's this about, Master Hortensius?" Septimus asked, looking at the drawings spread out across the table.

"The Consul has given us quite the challenge." Hortensius picked up one of the sketches, his enthusiasm evident in his quick movements. "We need to find something called 'petroleum' - rock oil, if you will. It's apparently seeping from the ground in certain places, although not so much in this region."

Septimus frowned. "Oil, like seed or whale oil? From rocks?"

"Yes, yes! Well, apparently, not like the oils we are used to, but it has some similarities. Flammability, the way it coats, things like that. The Consul says it exists in abundance but nearly all of it is deep in the ground in pockets and in order to reach it, we need to drill. He's provided these designs for a drill kind of like the augers used in lumber work and brace drills, although, as you'll see, it is still quite unique."

"I'm familiar with both. They are not terribly complicated, essentially a pole with a screw-like end."

"Precisely! When I first started reading about drills, that was what I thought of too. It seems that, in some locations or until we hit deep enough to reach bedrock, we can actually use something like an auger, although the Consul called it a fishtail bit. He, however, makes it clear that it is slow and ineffectual for dealing with hard stone, which is often between the surface and where this oil is located. For those instances, we need to use this."

"Ohh," he said, looking at the design Hortensius handed him. "This is ... complicated."

"I know. He calls it a two-cone bit, I guess after these two pieces here. His notes indicate that it turns in a circle on this bearing here and crushes the rock as it cuts through, instead of scraping it."

"Wouldn't that wear down these edges?"

"It would, and he notes that multiple drill bits would be needed when digging a new hole, as they will wear down. We can sharpen and refurbish them for reuse a few times before the metal is too worn down to be used again."

"It's very complex, though."

"It is, and I have found that having these detailed plans and instructions is a good step, but there is a lot of difficult work bringing something on paper into reality."

"What would we use this rock oil for?" Septimus asked, still studying the drawings.

"The Consul claims it's superior to any lubricant we currently use, although I feel that isn't the most important use. He talks about it being used as a kind of fuel and as the basis for some new types of explosives. Considering the war, I assume these two are the primary motivation for beginning work on this project."

"New explosives?" Septimus looked up sharply. "Better than our current powder?"

"He did not say. He did, however, say he believes this substance will be crucial for our continued advancement. The Easterners are matching our current technology; we need something to put us ahead again."

Septimus picked up one of the technical drawings, examining the detailed cross-sections.

"The biggest thing we have to work on is figuring out these drill heads, starting with the materials we need to use. The Consul has suggestions, but we will need to test them against actual rock to find which works the best, whether it be an alloy or hardened steel or some combination."

"I can see that. The stresses will be immense. Regular steel would shatter."

"Yes. The bits must withstand both the rotational forces and the tremendous downward pressure required to crush through rock. See these grooves along the sides? They're designed to carry the crushed rock up and out of the hole."

"Wouldn't the rock fragments be too heavy?"

"Which is why the grooves are so precisely angled. The rotation creates an upward spiral motion to evacuate the debris. Which is why something like this wasn't really possible until we got the steam engines working well, since we'll need the power they provide to both turn the drill and provide the downward force."

"When you say drilling holes, how far down are we discussing?"

"The Consul says it varies greatly by location. Could be a few hundred feet, could be thousands. That's where these come in." He indicated drawings of threaded pipe sections. "As we go deeper, we'll need to add more lengths to the drill string. They attach one to another, continuing to transfer the power downward."

"And once we actually reach this oil?"

"That's when things get truly interesting. The Consul says it's under immense pressure. When we pierce the pocket holding it, it will actually force its way up the drill shaft."

"Under its own pressure?" Septimus looked skeptical. "How is that possible?"

"Apparently, the weight of all the rock above creates this pressure over vast periods of time. The Consul explained it's similar to how water seeks its own level, but much more dramatic, and why this oil is created in the first place. In addition to the rig to hold the drill head and the drill itself, we have designs for containment systems that must be ready before we break through. Storage tanks, piping, pressure relief valves."

"This is ... a lot."

"Which is why I want you involved." Hortensius clasped the younger man's shoulder. "You've worked on several of our more complex systems, including on the river boats where we transferred power down the length of the ship. I believe you said the same thing about that project. We can do the preliminary work here, figuring out the drill head and testing it on rocks on the surface, but when it's time to erect this structure to hold and drive the drill, we'll need to move it to where the drilling needs to actually take place. The Consul provided this map, which shows exactly where we need to drill to reach this oil."

Spreading the map across the workbench, they studied the marked locations. Most were in remote areas, requiring significant logistics to transport and assemble the drilling equipment.

"We should start with the closest site, maybe something along the coast. It will be easier to transport materials and equipment by sea."

"Agreed. But first, we need to create the drill bits and test the drive mechanism." Hortensius began gathering the drawings into organized piles. "I want you to focus on the bit designs initially. I will want weekly progress reports and to know immediately if you have any problems."

"I'll get started right away," Septimus said, taking the drawings from him.

"Good man," Hortensius said, excited to see what the young engineer would actually produce.

Chapter 8

Carthage

Another body was found floating in the harbor. That made for two so far this month, along with a man stabbed in an alley, a woman whose neck was broken when she inexplicably climbed onto the roof of a small row of homes and then fell off, and another man who just disappeared with no trace anywhere.

That man had seemed promising. Valto, a man of similar means to Geral but with no connection to her previous agents. He'd indicated knowing some of the very low-level people Geral had identified for her as being involved in the rebel activity, giving him at least some sort of in with the group. He'd contacted her once since he made contact with those friends, to let her know he'd had success and should have something for her soon.

The praetorians had kept an eye out for him from afar, confirming his whereabouts and that he was still active in the poorer districts. He had returned to his home each day and was visible.

And then one day, nothing. She'd had his home under watch since his disappearance and he'd never returned to it.

Medb scowled. All this seemingly random violence, all connected by the fact that these people were all 'agents' of hers that she'd been trying to get infiltrated into the rebels that were still operating in the city. The death toll was climbing, and this didn't include the dozen more who, while still alive, had provided little more than mild gossip and secondhand rumors.

It was true, she didn't have time to properly train any of these people in intelligence gathering, since time was of the essence right now, but the same had been true of Geral and he had still managed to get deep into the conspiracy.

She'd thought she might at least stumble onto someone with a modicum of ability by now.

But no. They either allowed themselves to be sidelined or ended up dead.

She crumpled the latest report and hurled it at the wall. After a year of this, she still had no knowledge of what these people were doing.

A sharp knock interrupted her brooding.

"Enter," she said, straightening in her chair.

It wouldn't do for people to see her sulking. Claudius stepped inside, nodding to the two praetorian guards who stood outside Medb's office before closing the door behind him.

"I assume you have something," Medb said, a statement and not a question.

"I believe so. I've had men mixed among the night shift dock laborers for weeks now, and they have seen several of these unusual ships you mentioned. The ships themselves are flagged under multiple nations. Hispania, Italia, Scandi, Britannia ... even some Greek vessels. As far as I can find, there is no pattern to it."

"One or two groups working together, that I could believe, but something like this cannot be that widespread."

Claudius opened his mouth to speak but Medb continued, "Maybe Geral was wrong, and he was just seeing patterns where none exist. It would be a striking coincidence, but still, it wouldn't be the first time we've been led down false paths."

"My lady," Claudius tried again.

"I was so sure, though. Geral was quite clever, and in his note, he sounded certain this was the key. Certain enough to die for whatever he discovered."

"My Lady," Claudius said when she finally paused, "there's more. My men have noticed one peculiar thing that ties the vessels together. Every single one of these ships, regardless of flag, had crew members who spoke Egyptian."

"Egyptian? That's ... unusual. As a people, they're not generally known for their sailing prowess. Too accustomed to the calm waters of the Nile and the Middle Sea."

"Which is why it garnered my people's attention. Most merchant crews we've seen have been Scandi, regardless of the origin of the ship. There are exceptions, of course, but what's truly noteworthy is that my men found no trace of Egyptian sailors on ships that operate more normally. They appear only during these nighttime operations."

"That is notable."

"What's more, these Egyptian crew members seem to hold authority over the ships' regular crews during loading. They never leave the vessels, even during the brief periods when other crew members are granted shore leave, which is rare enough for these particular ships. So far, it's the only thing notable about these ships beyond the hours they keep. Without that, they would be odd, but otherwise innocuous. Though I confess I can think of no reason for their involvement in whatever this is."

"I can think of several reasons," Medb said darkly. "None of them good."

Factorium

Hortensius shut the heavy wooden door behind him, wanting nothing more than to flop down on his padded 'thinking' chair and close his eyes for a few minutes.

He'd spent the night on a train from the far southern tip of the country, after examining the fields that the Consul had marked for future drilling, once the mechanics for the drilling platform were all worked out. Beyond just designing it and getting it prepared, he had to make sure that the areas they wanted to build them on were actually clear. The Consul may know where this special oil was located, but he didn't know who was living there.

It was a good thing he'd checked. Several were under active farms and small villages, and one was right under where a train depot had been built to provide services for one of the more rural populations. The train station he could move. It would cost, but it was doable.

The villages were harder, and something he'd have to leave up to the Empress and her ministers.

Except for that wrinkle, the trip had been successful overall, with the exception that, as wonderful and life-changing as trains had been, sleeping on one during an overnight trip was all but impossible. The blasted thing never stopped moving or vibrating, was loud, and wasn't insulated well enough to keep you from freezing while in the cars.

All in all, not a great way to spend the night. He'd been looking forward to falling into his thinking chair and catching a few hours of rest.

That wasn't going to be an option after he walked into his office and saw a thick packet that he recognized. For a man who was busy leading the legions in a life-or-death struggle in the east, the Consul did send a lot of these packets. It never ceased to amaze him how prolific the Consul could be.

Of course, it was the new weapons that the Consul had them constantly producing and improving that enabled them to defeat Carthage and what was going to finally allow the Western Alliance to push back against the eastern threat, so he had no time to relax.

Dropping his things, Hortensius picked up the packet and broke the seal, unsurprisingly finding stacks of technical documents and drawings, each more intricate than the last.

His eyes widened slightly when he saw what it was. For more than a year, they'd been doing work that the Consul had said was leading up to a new weapon system. Even knowing that was what they were working toward, for Hortensius, it had seemed to be impossibly in the future. Something on the horizon that they would never reach.

Part of that was because the Consul hadn't shared his plan for how each step fit with the others, but Hortensius understood the reasoning for that. Even the Consul's extraordinary output had limits, and he knew the volume of instructions that he received, and that he was not the only one getting these kinds of detailed diagrams. Sorantius, Lucan, and others had equally detailed work assigned to them from the Consul, with many of the projects intertwined together, fitting like an intricate mosaic.

Seeing this, though, it was like reaching the summit of a mountain after a long climb. Not that Hortensius was one to climb very many mountains.

The Consul had mentioned, in passing at least, what the weapon would be, but that had not done it justice. It was such a far cry from the rifles they had been using since the last war. Loaded quickly from the bottom by sliding the metal-cased bullets into a long, tube-like magazine, with a lever that the soldier would have his hand through when firing. As each round fired, he would work the lever, which would automatically eject the casing from the previous round and load a new round into the firing chamber.

Where it took twenty to thirty seconds for a soldier to load one of the current rifles, pouring powder down the barrel, ramming the ball home, priming the hammer, a soldier using this could fire a round every second.

Admittedly, the magazine had limited capacity, holding what looked to be maybe seven rounds, which could quickly be expended, even the loading of those was faster. A soldier could have another seven rounds in the magazine in a matter of seconds as well. If he was reading this right, a legionnaire with this rifle could fire all seven rounds and load in seven new rounds in the time it took a current soldier to load his rifle once.

The volume of firepower would be enormous.

As would the speed at which the men went through ammunition. The Consul had warned them that they would need to have significant production of both gunpowder and the metal casings once the new weapon systems were in place, and Hortensius had begun expanding their facilities to produce more, but until this moment, it had not occurred to him just how much more they would be using.

He'd tripled the production of both after the Consul's warning, thinking he was going overboard, but he didn't question his instructions. It was clear that, instead of going overboard, he had missed the mark by several factors. They needed to seriously up production of both, to build up a stockpile of rounds to be ready when the first of the new rifles came off the line.

They had some time.

Looking at the diagrams, it was clear this would not be an easy feat.. There were going to be hurdles. The lever mechanism was complex and would take time to get the tooling right, and he was concerned about the magazine spring which pushed the bullets forward.

Just looking at the diagrams, he could see that wear would be a problem, with the spring losing tension over time. This would be the part that wore out the most, without a doubt. Well, and maybe the small pin that was used to transfer motion from the trigger to the firing mechanism.

Both were so thin that the current steel they had, even the alloys, would wear quickly. He would have to get with his gunsmiths and foundry foreman and see what thoughts they had about increasing the strength of these parts without making them unworkable for their given task, especially important in the spring which couldn't be so stiff that it lost functionality.

The Consul's notes seemed to indicate he would accept a level of failure, and they should prepare a large number of these parts to be replaced in the field. Hortensius would follow that instruction, but if he could improve on the design he would.

This would take time and it would be months if not a full year until these were in production and reached the troops.

When they did, however ... this would change the nature of warfare again.

Devnum

Lucilla hadn't realized how much she'd missed home. While it had been good to see Ky, after almost a year of separation, and she'd needed to see her people serving on the front line, and more importantly, be seen by them, this was where she belonged.

The city and country had run well in her absence. With Medb in Carthage, and Cormac with her, and Llassar in Italia working with the new government there to get through its fledgling difficulties, she'd left Talogren in command. The old warrior had been less than pleased with the honor, since he was ready to settle down, and had been happier than she'd been at her return.

After years as a bachelor, more concerned with building up his people and glory than anything else, she'd been happy to see him finally realize he could turn to a more domestic life, retire from the command he'd held for so long. It had been a hard transition for him, to be sure. The man was a warrior at heart, one of a breed who looked forward to an end in glorious combat, and had never considered living into old age.

She had also missed Titus desperately while she'd been gone. She didn't know if her father had experienced difficulty ruling when she and her brother were young, but for her, it was difficult. She understood her responsibility to her people and wanted to do everything she could for them, but in her heart, she wanted to be here, with him and Ky, just living their lives in Devnum.

Of course, her throne made that impossible.

It required sacrifices, one of which was dealing with the couple walking into the audience chamber. The pair, clearly Greek of heritage, wore more traditional Egyptian dress. She'd met with them before, and they embodied every bad trait she loathed about the Ptolemies. An unpleasant combination of constant feigned obsequiousness over a barely hidden layer of haughty superiority.

And yet, even in their current state, Egypt was a force to be recognized. The riches of the Nile made it powerful even without being as closely aligned with Britannia as some of the polities on the continent had been.

Worse, they knew they were important.

Which is why she met them in the less formal conference room, as Ky liked to call it. Still well-appointed with tapestries, fine decorations, and beautiful furniture, it was much less formal than the official audience chamber.

She'd hoped it would set them at ease, make them feel important enough, being given this more private venue, to actually listen and work with her for once.

"I trust your journey from Alexandria was without incident?" Lucilla asked, gesturing for servants to pour wine into ornate silver cups.

Arsinoe, a tall woman with sharp features, inclined her head. "The seas were favorable, Your Imperial Majesty, though the weather grew harsher as we approached your shores."

"Having just completed a journey of my own, I well understand the unpleasant nature of making such a journey, and I appreciate your coming at our request."

Diodorus, the older of the two envoys, said, "Your hospitality is most gracious, Empress."

"Hospitality is the foundation of diplomacy. Though I fear we must move beyond pleasantries to discuss graver matters. The situation on the continent has become serious, and gets closer to your own home every day. The loss of Macedon, Thessaly, and Thrace has changed the balance of power, and it is clear the war will be moving to a new front there."

"We have heard troubling reports," Arsinoe acknowledged. "But surely, with Britannia's legendary military prowess, it is a situation you can handle."

"We are not giving up and I believe we will ultimately be victorious, but we are being tested as never before. The entire continent is united, and we've committed unprecedented resources to this fight, but this new enemy is not just another Carthage. We maintain a technological edge, but they are much more advanced than your former rulers ever were. Which is why every nation that values its independence must join this fight."

Arsinoe's painted lips tightened. "Egypt has always valued its friendship with Britannia ..."

"And we also value that friendship. However, friendship is not enough. Not against this threat. I would think you, of all people, understand that after living under the heel of a foreign ruler for so long. You have prospered these last five years, regained some of your past glory. I have often commented to my husband how pleased I am that we were able to play a part in that."

"We have not forgotten," Diodorus said quickly, before Arsinoe could respond. "But internal matters require careful consideration. The timing of such commitments ..."

"If the Easterners were any closer to Egypt than they are now, they would be marching across the Sinai at this very moment. And you say there are commitments that supersede that."

"And yet, they are not. The desert is a grueling place and our men stand ready to guard our borders from any threat. Trust me when I say, we have little to fear from foreigners," Arsinoe said. "Even those who come as friends."

"It is interesting, the talk of friends and what we might fear from them. For instance, there are times when people will come to you as friends and then attempt to undermine that friendship by working with groups hostile to their new friend," Lucilla said, prompting a subtle but clumsy response from the envoys, who looked at one another. "For instance, there are times when someone who was thought to be a friend might be involved in shipping to and from rebel elements, offering them support and assistance. That is something that should be taken notice of."

Arsinoe's face tightened, the careful application of kohl around her eyes making the sudden narrowing of her eyes more pronounced. "What, exactly, are you accusing us of?"

"Nothing. You were speaking about dealing with foreigners, even those who have come to us as friends, and I wanted to agree that it is something we should *all* be aware of. It is my strongest desire that our people have close ties and work together, just as we did when Carthage held sway over your lands."

"That was a different time," Diodorus interjected.

"And yet, here we are, facing a new enemy with seemingly massive reservoirs of manpower, bent on enslaving everyone under their boot. So ... is it that much different? I think it does us good to discuss how things used to be and how they could easily end up being that way again. In order to avoid misunderstandings that could endanger the friendship we all hold so dear."

"It seems to me you want to hold your assistance over our heads forever. That does not make us your vassals, nor require us to jump to your every call," Arsinoe said.

"I would never claim either. Let me speak plainly. I remember well how your people lived under Carthaginian rule. Do you? How many Egyptian ships were allowed in your own harbors? How many of your nobles could travel without Carthaginian escorts?

How many decisions could your leaders make without consulting their masters?"

"We are well aware of our history."

"Are you? Because it seems to me your people have forgotten. Forgotten when you were closed off from the rest of the world, taken over by Carthaginians who saw themselves as gods. Your religious leaders were put in chains. Your grain was fed to Carthaginian armies while your own people went hungry. I remember those times clearly."

"That was before," Diodorus tried again.

"Before Britannia intervened. Before we spent blood and treasure to free your lands. Before you could sit here as equals, rather than supplicants begging for scraps of authority from your masters."

"You overstep," Arsinoe snapped, rising halfway from her chair. "Egypt is sovereign ..."

"Because we made it so," Lucilla's voice cracked like a whip. "Because our legions fought and died to break Carthaginian power. Because we chose to restore your independence rather than claim Egypt for ourselves."

Diodorus placed a restraining hand on Arsinoe's arm. "Your Majesty, while we appreciate Britannia's past support ..."

"Do you? Then explain to me why you are so reluctant to support us in terms, now that we come to you for help. We were there in your hour of need. Where are you in ours?"

She paused, giving both of them a serious look. One that would send her own people cowering in fear. Diodorus, for his part, looked at least worried about the turn the meeting was taking. It was Arsinoe that concerned Lucilla the most.

She was not here out of happenstance. Niece to the current Ptolemaic king, who liked to style himself as pharaoh of a new dynasty, she was hostile and arrogant as ever. Lucilla had tried to play it coy, but Arsinoe was immune to diplomatic niceties. She believed the world owed her something because her family once ruled a major empire, without realizing they no longer did so.

Egypt may be in resurgence, but they did not have the power they once had. It was time for her, and her uncle, to realize that.

"Let me be direct. Egypt must choose its path. Will you join the Western Alliance and contribute meaningfully to this war effort, or will you stand aside and watch as the Eastern Empire marches to your border? If you choose the latter, know that Britannian legions will not come to you a second time. A bitten hand does not offer aid twice."

"You dare ..." Arsinoe began.

"I do dare. The world is at war, and it is time your people realized it. I give you two weeks to contact your uncle and provide your answer. Not to negotiate, not to deliberate, to answer. Will you join the Western Alliance? Yes or no? Your contribution need not match ours in scale, but it must exist."

Arsinoe's face flushed beneath her makeup. "Who are you to make such demands? Egypt is not some minor province to be ordered about by Britannia. We are the heirs to thousands of years of civilization, while your empire is barely old enough to walk!"

"Your empire would not exist without us," Lucilla replied. "The world has changed. The old ways of playing both sides, of careful neutrality, they no longer serve. The Easterners will not stop at Greece. You are fools if you do not see that."

"Perhaps we do not fear them as you do," Arsinoe shot back. "Perhaps we see opportunity where you see only threat. There are other powers in this world besides Britannia."

Diodorus raised his hands. "Please, let us not speak in haste. Surely we can find common ground ..."

"No," Arsinoe cut him off. "I will not sit here and be lectured like a child. You freed us from Carthage? We freed ourselves! Your assistance merely hastened the inevitable."

"Is that what you tell yourself?" Lucilla asked. "That you would have somehow thrown off their chains without our legions? Without our ships? Without our blood?"

"We did not ask for your intervention!"

"No. You were too busy collaborating with your masters to ask for anything."

Diodorus tried again. "Your Imperial Majesty, perhaps if we took some time to discuss terms ..."

"The time for discussion is past," Lucilla said. "Two weeks. That is all the time you have to decide whether Egypt stands with the West or against it."

Diodorus grabbed Arsinoe's arm as she started to rise. "We should consider carefully before speaking further."

"Yes," Lucilla agreed. "You should. Two weeks. I suggest you use them wisely."

"This is outrageous!" Arsinoe wrenched her arm free. "We will not be bullied or threatened. Egypt is not your vassal!"

"No. You are our ally. Or you were. Now you must decide if you wish to remain so."

"And if we decide otherwise?"

"Then you will learn the difference between friend and foe. I suggest you consider carefully which you wish Britannia to be."

"Consider this," Arsinoe snarled. "Perhaps we already have."

She stormed from the room, Diodorus hurrying after her with a hasty bow. As the door closed behind them, Lucilla flopped back in her seat.

That could have gone better.

Chapter 9

Carthage

The city was quiet as the day turned to evening. Winter in Africa was a far cry from how it was in Ériu, but even without the thickly packed snow, the pace was slower this time of year.

Without harvests to sell, most of the markets were a far cry from the bustling centers of commerce they were in midsummer. People still came to the city to sell and trade wares, but as the end of winter neared, most stayed home, limiting their need for food and supplies as much as possible as what they squirreled away all year dwindled.

This decrease in the daily ebb of population had the side effect of sending most of the rebels into hiding. With a smaller overall populace and fewer people on the streets, it was difficult for them to blend in as easily, naturally curtailing their activity.

While this was good for the overall safety and well-being of the city, it was a temporary fix at best. Worse, when the rebels were less active, it made the people Medb used to try and get information on them easier to spot, and it was harder to keep tabs on what activity they did have.

Which was why she was on this tour of the city.

Not that she thought she was going to find something that Claudius's men missed. She just wanted to publicly remind them that she was still here, and they were not forgotten.

A juvenile response to their lack of success, but she was running light on choices.

She was a little surprised when Claudius and a few praetorians turned out of a side street and veered toward them, matching pace.

"The tour going well?" he asked casually as he waved their guards back as they continued to walk, giving them a little space for privacy.

"It is. You seem to have things well in hand."

"Only on the surface. Maintaining this level of control is costly, both in manpower and gold. The rebels may be quiet, but they haven't gone away. Just last week, we lost two men to an ambush."

"Things are as they must be. I assume you are here now, however, because you have something for me."

"I do, my lady. We've managed to examine some of the suspicious crates."

She didn't need him to elaborate on what he meant by suspicious crates. She also wasn't happy to hear this news.

"You risked alerting the smugglers? I thought I made it clear we couldn't risk spooking them before we understood the full scope of their operation."

"You did, and we did not alert them. My men have been … strategically clumsy over the past week. A dropped crate here, a wedged container there, all in full view of the crew, who never leave their cargo unattended. Nothing that would raise suspicion beyond normal port mishaps. They only caught glimpses of the contents, and the watchers were too focused on berating the stupid worker to notice them peeking at the contents."

"Clever. And what did they see?"

"The crates contained powder, not the low-grade stuff we sell on the open market or that we've found in the hands of rebels. The same stuff used by the legions, in their original shipping pouches."

"You're certain?"

"Absolutely. And that's not all. We found rifled muskets. We couldn't look to see the maker's mark, but this type is only produced in Factorium and not sold. The worst, though, were several cases of the new fused artillery shells as well. The ones with the new shape."

"What?" Medb said, stopping cold, an unusual display of acknowledgement from her.

"Which is why I wanted to talk to you right away. I can't help but wonder how the Ptolemies acquired them. We aren't talking about just a few. It was several cases packed with the weapons."

"While the Egyptian connection is clear enough, it doesn't necessarily mean the Ptolemies are the source. There are other possibilities to consider."

"What? We would have heard of raids on military depots or armories."

"Those would not be the only places to acquire those items. Equipment can be lost in combat zones, collected later and sold, or shipments might be getting skimmed during production and transport. The gods know, we've had enough officials inside our own government arrested for corruption. There are many hands involved in moving weapons from factory to frontline."

"With respect, I find it unlikely that Hortensius would allow such theft from his facilities," Claudius objected. "The man guards his innovations like a mother hen with her chicks."

"True enough," Medb conceded. "But Hortensius can't watch every worker, every cart, every warehouse. The supply chain has grown complex as production has increased."

"Which is my point, my lady. The level of coordination needed to get equipment at its source, or to put together the network to gather scavenged supplies in this quantity, is beyond a normal smuggling operation. That isn't even considering the shipping involved with it."

"I agree, which leads us to a more pressing question. Why go to such lengths? What purpose do these particular weapons serve?" she said, starting to walk again as she began to get her thoughts back into some sense of order.

"It's not for here. I think Carthage is only a waystation in whatever's happening. We've seen no evidence of rebels using the rifles or shells. Some of the captured insurgents had Britannian powder, yes, but nothing approaching this level of sophistication."

"Precisely. If their aim was simply arming local malcontents, there are far more practical options. Basic firearms, traditional weapons, items that wouldn't draw immediate attention."

"But a smuggling operation like this makes little sense from a pure profit perspective. The quantity is too small to be worth the risk and the quality is enough to bring unwanted eyes. There would be cheaper ways to make a coin."

"Unless what we're seeing is merely the visible portion of a much larger enterprise."

"My lady?"

"We may have only intercepted a fraction of the total shipments. Other crates could contain conventional weapons or valuable goods meant for rebel forces or black market sale, to offset their costs, and explain the funding of the rebels. As you said, this could be just a stop along their journey. Your own men report that most of these crates don't remain in Carthage. They're transferred to other vessels and shipped elsewhere. The question is, where?"

"The Egyptian connection seems clear enough, but ..."

"Proving it is another matter entirely," Medb said. "Particularly given the likelihood of high-level involvement. We've already seen how corruption can infiltrate even the most trusted institutions."

"We're making progress on getting someone aboard one of these ships, and we've secured a schooner to track vessels leaving port."

"Good. As always, I appreciate that you think ahead, though I expect our quarry will take precautions against being followed."

"The captain is experienced in such matters. He'll maintain distance and use multiple vessels to relay positions. His name was on the list you gave me from Ramirus."

"Excellent." Medb's approval was genuine. "You're on the right track and doing good work. Stay on them, and hopefully they will do something soon that will finally give us more answers than questions."

"Yes, my lady."

He bowed and left quickly, the two men who'd accompanied him breaking off and following him while Medb's own guard closed ranks to finish their tour.

Claudius was doing well, anticipating what she would have done, even when he still had questions as to why.

Now, she only had to hope that they finally had found a break in the network before whatever these people were doing came to fruition.

Factorium

Sorantius entered the main workroom of the munitions factory, the familiar bouquet of chemicals and soot hitting him as he did. He had been out checking on their latest shipments headed to the front, mostly ether and other medical supplies, and hoped that time had been enough for his people to make progress on setting up for the latest tests.

While he wanted to be there for the actual first run of all new chemicals, his time was much too valuable to spend setting up the apparatus needed to take care of it.

Thankfully, he had trained his assistants well and they were busy meticulously cleaning glassware and setting up the specialized equipment needed for the day's experiment. On the table, brass clamps held thick glass containers steady, including the new mercury-filled thermometer that replaced the older version the Consul had introduced several years previously. It was a delicate instrument that would hopefully allow them more precise control of the volatile reaction they were about to create.

Or at least that was what the Consul had promised.

"Where are we?" he asked as he walked behind the busily working men, who all jumped in surprise at his voice.

One of the chemists straightened, wiping his hands on a clean rag before answering. "The nitrocellulose is ready. We've double-checked it and made sure it was a well-washed batch. We've also confirmed the ether-alcohol mixture is at the required ratio, three parts ether to one part alcohol, by weight."

Sorantius picked up a glass beaker, tilting it to examine the pale liquid within. The faint, sharp smell of the mixture filled his nose as he gave a short nod.

"Good. Any problems?"

"None, sir. The mixture matches the Consul's specifications exactly."

Satisfied, Sorantius moved to the opposite side of the table, where a large copper basin sat atop a reinforced stand. A small valve near the bottom connected to a water pipe, ready to be used to adjust the temperature as needed, while a burner rested beneath it. Sorantius crouched slightly, running his hand along the base of the setup, noting the heavy insulation.

"Sir," another assistant said hesitantly from behind him. "While the water has been preheated to just below the minimum range, we're unsure if we'll be able to maintain a constant temperature throughout the entire process."

Sorantius straightened and gestured toward the thermometer resting on the table. He picked it up and held it between his fingers, the slim column of mercury flowing as he turned it.

"That is why the Consul had us develop this. It should allow us to monitor the temperature with precision. The bath must remain between forty-five and fifty degrees on the Consul's measurement scale, no higher. If the mercury rises beyond the top marker here," he said, pointing to the etched lines on the glass. "The reaction will accelerate uncontrollably. That's why one of you was assigned to always watch the line and alert us if it does. We can add cool water if it rises too high or increase the flame if it drops too low."

"Yes, sir," the assistant replied, nodding and checking the new device attached to the tub.

Sorantius, sweeping his gaze over the table one last time, turned back to his team and said, "Alright. Let's begin."

The assistants moved quickly, one uncorking a sealed jar of nitrocellulose while another brought the ether-alcohol mixture closer to the table. The first assistant began adding the nitrocellulose slowly, using a wooden scoop to transfer it into the waiting solvent. Each scoop was small, and the process was deliberate; too much at once could destabilize the reaction.

As the nitrocellulose was introduced, two other chemists began stirring the mixture with long-handled paddles, also moving slowly. Numerous accidents over the years had taught all of them the dangers of not treating these chemicals cautiously.

Sorantius leaned in, watching the pale strands of nitrocellulose swirl and dissolve into the clear liquid, creating a faintly cloudy appearance. He adjusted one of his assistant's arms, nudging it up to correct the angle of the man's paddle, which wasn't properly scraping the bottom of the container evenly.

"Temperature?" he called out without looking up.

"Forty-seven degrees," the assistant with the thermometer replied.

"Good. Keep it there."

He watched, moving around the table, as the chemicals in the container were carefully mixed. Even though he knew from the Consul's notes what was going to happen, it was amazing to see the way it thickened gradually as more nitrocellulose was added. If he was adding a solid like flour or dirt into liquid, he would understand, but adding a liquid and having that reaction was another amazing thing the Consul had delivered.

"Slow your additions," he ordered the first assistant as he saw some of the tell-tale signs the instructions had said to watch for. "We're approaching the critical point."

The assistant obeyed, reducing the size of each scoop and waiting longer between additions. The others continued to stir, sweat beading on their brows despite the cool draft seeping through the windows. Sorantius occasionally adjusted the angle of the paddles or added small splashes of solvent to ensure the viscosity remained consistent.

"Temperature?" he asked again.

"Fifty degrees," the assistant said, glancing nervously at the thermometer. He turned the valve to release a trickle of cool water into the bath, lowering the temperature to forty-nine.

Sorantius frowned at the man, who paled slightly. The man should not have waited for him to say something to make the adjustment.

That was someone he would have to keep a closer eye on in the future.

Giving the man one last forceful glare, he refocused his attention on the thickening mixture. Its consistency had shifted dramatically in the past few minutes, becoming gelatinous and opaque. He reached out with a gloved hand, touching the surface with the edge of a stirring rod. The resistance was faint, but growing.

"It's thinner than I expected," one of the assistants commented hesitantly, peering over the edge of the container.

"We've followed the instructions precisely," Sorantius said. "Continue."

The assistants exchanged uncertain glances but resumed their work. The mixture thickened further, the paddles meeting greater resistance with each pass. Sorantius adjusted the stirring speed once more, hoping they had it right. Temperatures and measurements were one thing, but when the notes talked about rates of combination and other handling, things became less precise.

Another costly lesson learned over time.

Suddenly, the mixture began to change rapidly, solidifying at an accelerated pace. The paddles moved sluggishly now, and one assistant grunted with effort as he tried to keep his motion even.

"Stop stirring!" Sorantius barked. "Remove it from the water bath immediately."

The assistants scrambled to comply, lifting the container carefully and placing it on a nearby flat surface lined with clean parchment.

The man who'd been by the thermometer said, "The temperature hit the upper limit just before it started to thicken."

Sorantius frowned, but his expression quickly shifted to one of calculation rather than frustration. He'd been watching it as closely as the others, and had been the one deciding the changes that were made. It was as he'd worried; human action was the uncontrollable variable.

He just hoped it wasn't enough to ruin the experiment completely.

"That explains the acceleration," he said, gesturing for the assistants to spread the gelatinous mass out for examination. "The reaction likely sped up due to the temperature reaching the threshold."

The mass was more solid than he had anticipated, but it matched the descriptions provided by the Consul closely enough. Sorantius ran his gloved fingers over the surface, noting its texture and flexibility.

"Unexpected," he muttered, "but not unworkable."

One of the assistants leaned closer, studying the material with wide eyes.

"It's … remarkable," he said. "The consistency, it could be shaped or formed easily."

A stupid statement, as that was one of the things the Consul's instructions had indicated. The man had read it, so he shouldn't be surprised when it was as the Consul predicted. He straightened, gesturing for the assistant whose only job was to document every detail of the process for their own records and to send to the Consul.

"Record everything," he instructed. "From the exact measurements to the unexpected deviations. We'll refine this further, but for now, begin drying it. Once it's stable, we'll cut it into grains for testing."

As the assistants moved to obey, Sorantius allowed himself a small, satisfied smile.

Another successful development to report to the Consul.

Devnum

Lucilla stood at the threshold of the Imperial Forum, trying to calm her nerves. This was a moment her father had never been forced into, even when Carthage was on their doorstep. She hadn't even contemplated it as a possibility until Ky brought it up, and she had fought him over the proposal for weeks.

But with every point countered, it became more and more clear that he was right. She had tried to forestall it by convincing either the Egyptians or the Scandi to see the light and join them.

And she had failed.

Yes, they had added some of the Greek states to their ranks, but that had made things worse, not better, as the curved front following the borders of their new allies nearly doubled the front lines. In return, they didn't have enough men to pad out their existing lines properly, let alone man the new ones.

Not that she had ever considered turning the Greeks away. Aside from it being the right thing to do, adding more land, men, and resources to the enemy would have made things even worse for them.

That all made sense when she'd worked with her advisers and Senator Taenaris to work out the details on what she was about to propose. Now that she was on the very literal threshold of taking that step, however, it seemed a much less smart decision.

And yet, the decision was made. There was no choice but to move forward.

As she crossed into the chamber, Lucilla could feel the eyes of the assembled senators boring into her. She did not address the senators often. The last time had been to announce the beginning of a new war. Her presence was guaranteed to put the assembled men on edge.

"Esteemed senators," Lucilla began as she took her place in the center of the chamber, with everyone looking down on her. "I stand before you today burdened by an urgent duty concerning the future of our Empire. The situation grows increasingly dire."

She paused, letting the words settle in.

"The forces amassed by the Easterners are staggering. Our Western Alliance, already stretched perilously thin, has expanded again, reaching out to embrace Greece, the center of our civilization. But doing so has a cost. In Africa, Admiral Valdar has begun spearheading efforts to fortify new ports along Africa's coast to protect our homeland from new attempts of an Eastern invasion from the sea. But doing so has a cost."

Again, she paused.

"To protect our civilization and our lives, that cost must be paid. And it must be paid now. That is why I am bringing before you new legislation to drastically increase the size of our legions with the conscription of seventy-five thousand able-bodied men between the ages of twenty and forty."

The chamber erupted into discordant shouts as senators sprang to their feet, yelling in opposition, cutting off what she had planned to say next.

"Madam Empress!" Senator Bredei from the Caledonian contingent said, his face reddening with indignation. "Have you lost your mind? Our farms are already short-staffed with all of the volunteers who have already joined the legions. We cannot bear more!"

"And what of our industry?" one of the Roman senators added. "We cannot simply pluck men from their livelihoods without consequences! How will we clothe and feed these recruits? Who will build the weapons rolling out of Factorium? The last request from Hortensius to this body asking for more funds indicated how direly short-staffed his factories are."

"Senators," she said, her voice carrying over theirs with an air of authority she had learned nearly from birth. "I would not ask this if it were not *necessary*. We have not made this decision lightly, and we are aware of the burden it will place on our people and have carve-outs to ensure the Empire may continue. Men involved in critical industries will not be drafted. We will focus on those who work in non-essential sectors, those whose absence will not endanger our food supply or production capabilities."

Any hope that would placate them was instantly rebuffed. The backlash was immediate and fierce.

"You underestimate how interconnected our industries are! If we start taking away from agriculture or textiles ..."

"Of course, I understand how interconnected they are. Our lead industrialists and sector leaders will take part in discussions to determine where these conscripts will come from. We are not walking into this blindly."

"How do you propose to manage such a selective process?" came another objection from across the room.

"We'll have chaos on our hands!" yelled yet another voice.

"What chaos will we have if we lose? What is your wealth worth if we fall?" she said. "Because the Easterners will not wait for us to find a solution every man here will agree to. They will not slow their assaults on us because you do not want to pay more for your dinner. They are coming. That is a fact. We have held them so far, but only just, and our numbers are being depleted every day, faster than we can recruit new volunteers. We will reach a point where we are no longer able to defend the Alliance's border. When that point comes, there will not be time to make a decision. The moment will have passed."

"We cannot ignore this threat while hoping others will come to our aid, our allies falter as well! Egypt has refused the call. Scandi has refused the call. The friends we do have look to us. We assembled this alliance. We called for this war. If we dither now, how long until they start seeing capitulation as their only chance for survival?"

"Your Majesty, we have never resorted to conscription before," Senator Uticensis, a Roman and usually one of her supporters, said. "Our volunteer legions have served us well through countless conflicts. Perhaps if we doubled the legionaries' pay, we would see more men willingly take up arms."

"This is not like wars we have fought before. We cheered when the Consul added new weapons, allowing us to kill Carthaginians by the thousands. I cheered along with you, because at the time, we desperately needed that to survive, but those decisions have now come back at us. We now face the same weapons, turned on us. War is more brutal and deadly now than it ever was, and we no longer fight for an island, a few thousand men here and there. We fight for a continent. That is why simply counting on volunteers won't work. The current combined legions of the Western Alliance number barely a hundred thousand men, spread thin across twice the length of Sarmatia and Greece. Even with our Greek allies contributing another thirty thousand, it is not enough."

"Increased pay might bring in five thousand new volunteers, perhaps ten thousand at most," she continued. "But we need seventy-five thousand to maintain our defensive positions and have any hope of mounting counter-offensives. Without reinforcing Greece, the Eastern armies will simply roll through those territories and outflank our entire defensive line."

Senator Bredei jabbed a finger toward her. "Why is this all on us? You speak about how bloody this war is, why must the blood be solely Britannic?"

"This is not only on us. Our allies in Germania, Hispania, Italia, Greece, and Gaul are already preparing similar measures. They recognize the danger as much as we do, and are preparing to conscript the same number of men, or even more. Germania has committed to conscripting a hundred thousand men. Gaul to matching our seventy-five thousand. We are not the only ones paying the costs due for freedom. I have spent the past three months in personal negotiations with every allied leader. They face the same challenges we do. This is not Britannia acting alone, but part of a coordinated response across the Western Alliance."

"You would turn us into another Carthage!" Senator Brandubh of the Ulaid delegation said. "They built their empire on the backs of conscripted slaves, forcing men to die for causes not their own. Is that what we're to become?"

"That is unfair, Senator. Carthage treated its conscripts as disposable tools, marching them to death without training or proper equipment. Our conscripted soldiers will receive the same thorough training, the same quality weapons, and the same opportunities for advancement as any volunteer, and they will be fighting in defense of our country, not to expand an empire built on cruelty. It is why we must do this now, and not bicker and argue. It will take months to get every conscripted man trained and ready to fight. We do not have time to debate this."

"This is unacceptable!" Senator Kaeso shouted. "If you persist with this madness, we will block all military funding requests that come before this body. We will have no god-king like the Carthaginians."

He stood up and angrily stormed toward the exit of the forum, more than half of the gathered senators stood and followed him out.

Lucilla fumed as she watched them go. Why must it always be this way? Shortsighted men unable to see the picture beyond their own coin purses and fears.

When only a handful remained, mostly those like Taenaris who had helped craft the proposal, she said, "This is foolishness. You need to convince your colleagues to return and support this measure or prepare yourselves to learn Eastern tongues and bow to Eastern masters. If we do not do this, we ... will ... lose!"

Chapter 10

Devnum

"You're here very early," Lucan's voice came from behind him.

Hortensius stood and turned from the small furnace that he'd been adjusting, looking up to see the shipbuilder standing a few steps away, looking tired. Which was to be expected, considering the sun was just now making its way over the horizon, washing out the torchlight the manufacturer had been operating under just a little bit before.

"Lucan! I'm glad you're up," he said, walking over to stacks of metal sheeting that had been delivered late the previous evening. "Come take a look at this."

The shipwright joined him and looked over the silver-colored metal stacked up almost to his knees.

"I'm not sure what I'm supposed to be looking at."

"See these color differences? And if you run your hand along this section, can you feel the texture differences?"

"I ... yes, I think so," he said, following Hortensius's suggestion and running his hand over the plate.

"I was concerned with the uniformity of the metal composition. Most of the metal we've made to date has been much smaller than these plates, and I was concerned we'd get some variations in the composition while rolling these sheets out. I'd hoped we'd compensated for it, but clearly, we did not do a good enough job."

"Do we need to wait and refine the process further?"

"We do need to refine it and see if we can get a more standardized product, but no, I don't want to hold up production any longer than we need to. While they are not quite up to specifications, they are close. We just need to account for it in the riveting process. The metal itself should still stand up to the stresses once the vessel is assembled, and function properly."

"So we're ready to begin then?"

"Yes, but I do wish we'd had time to establish more permanent facilities. These portable furnaces we brought will do the job for now, but they cannot hold enough fuel reserves to operate unattended for long. And I am concerned that that might cause the temperature to dip and fluctuate a bit."

"We discussed this. The need to get a larger, permanent furnace out here would also require reinforcing the docks to adjust for the weight, which we don't have time to do. We do have men working on it and we should be able to start installing something permanent in the next six months, but you said we could make do with the portable ones for now."

"We can. We can," Hortensius confirmed. "Like the plates, we just have to make adjustments for that. It will make the work harder and slower than I'd like, but yes, faster than if we waited."

"As the Consul said, war waits for no man. I guess that applies to processes as well."

"True enough. Still, it complicates matters," Hortensius said, and then gestured to a stack of smaller metal sections off to the side. "I've selected those for our initial tests. The Consul's notes warn of several variables affecting the riveting process that his instructions would be unable to account for and that we'd need to experiment before settling on the best method."

"Did he say what sort of variables?"

"Metal expansion and contraction, primarily. The heating and cooling process causes minute changes in the steel's structure, and can be affected both by the temperatures and humidity, as well as salt content in the air. If we don't account for it properly, we risk compromising the integrity of the entire ship."

"And here I thought the caravels were too complicated to construct quickly."

"Oh, we're just getting started. You need to look at the later plans, for after the hull is assembled," Hortensius said with a wry smile. He clapped his hands, calling out to the gathered workers. "Right then, let's begin our first attempt!"

Men who'd been standing around waiting for the go-ahead for more than an hour sprang into action, some going to the furnace while others lifted up the plates, putting them between large holders Hortensius had installed earlier that morning.

While they had done some testing of the riveting process back in Factorium, the Consul's warnings had prompted Hortensius to leave the bulk of it for testing here, so he could see the actual challenges they faced. Hortensius watched intently as the first heated rivet was hammered into place, examining it closely as the workers stepped away, moving to the next section to be riveted. After less than a minute, however, he called a halt to the process.

"Stop! Everyone, halt the work!"

"Problem?" Lucan asked.

"Yes. See this rivet head on the back end. It isn't flush with the metal as it cools. There's a gap, which means we didn't get it closed tightly together. The rivets are supposed to contract as they cool, with the smashed tail of the rivet pulling in and locking the plates in place. That force of the metal cooling is what causes it to lock into place. The force of smashing it into place should also cause the shank of the rivet to expand slightly, filling the entire hole. That isn't happening here."

"But this didn't happen in your factory tests, right?"

"No. You," he said, pointing at one of the workers. "Show me how you put in the rivet."

The man nodded and hopped to his assignment, going to the furnace and dropping one of the pre-made rivets into the glowing coals. The metal quickly heated and, once it was glowing cherry-red, he extracted it with long-handled tongs and carried it to the pre-drilled hole in the test plates. He carefully positioned the rivet through the aligned holes and then shifted the tongs to maintain pressure on the rivet head while drawing his hammer. Once positioned, he began striking the open end of the rivet, deforming the shaft. After several hard strokes, he stepped back, making room for Hortensius to look at it closely.

The manufacturer took the man's tongs and nudged the still hot, but not glowing, bolt. To his dismay, it rattled slightly.

"Damn."

"Problem?"

Hortensius didn't answer right away, still staring at the offending rivet, his brow frowned in concentration.

"Yes. A serious problem," he finally replied. "The rivet is cooling too quickly before it's properly hammered into place. It's not much, mind you, but enough to prevent the head from deforming completely. This means it's not applying sufficient clamping force, and the shaft isn't molding properly into the hole."

Lucan leaned in, squinting at the rivet. "Which means?"

"It means the plates will have some wiggle room, and they won't be watertight."

"Ohh."

The inventor looked at the bolt for another moment before he turned to the gathered workers, who were waiting expectantly for further instructions.

"Right, we need to reorganize. We'll work in teams of three. One to heat the rivets, one to position, and one to hammer," he said before pointing to a burly man with a hammer. "I want you to strike as soon as the rivet's in position. Don't hesitate. It's important your end of the rivet is hit while it is still at its hottest. And you, hold it in place tightly. You'll feel some force when the hammer strikes, so brace yourself."

When the men all nodded their understanding, Hortensius stepped back and gestured for them to proceed. Again a rivet was put into place, although much faster than the previous attempt. When they finished, he waved them off and inspected the result.

"Better," he muttered, "but still not quite there. We're still losing too much time between heating and positioning."

After staring at the metal for a moment, thinking he moved over to a small worktable that had been set up and pulled sheets of paper out of a satchel he'd set there. For several minutes, he flipped through the pages of diagrams and instructions, sometimes doubling back to reread a section. Finally, nodding to himself, he looked around the dock until he found one of the metal buckets his factories had been producing for several years sitting upside down so it wouldn't collect water.

Retrieving it and a thick leather apron next to the furnace, he walked over to the man at the furnace.

"When the rivet's ready, I want you to toss it carefully at the bucket that man will be holding. It's important you don't miss," he said, before turning to the indicated man, holding out the bucket and thick apron. "Put this on, it should offer some protection. I want you to catch the rivet in this bucket, fish it out and slot it into position as quickly as you can."

"Is this safe?" Lucan asked.

"Less safe than I would like, but the damp air is helping the bolt cool off faster. This will be an even bigger problem when they are several more steps away, working on the frame well across from the dock. I can't think of a way to get the rivet to the positioner faster than throwing it, and the Consul's notes indicate this is one strategy that can be used."

Lucan seemed unsure, but stepped back. The team looked equally uncertain, especially the man tasked with catching the rivets, but they followed their orders.

The furnace worker heated the rivet until it glowed cherry-red, then quickly tossed it across, where it made a thunk sound as it landed in the metal bucket. The positioner fished it out, moving with haste to place it in the pre-drilled hole, followed by the hammerer smashing the rivet into position.

The entire ordeal lasted only seconds.

Once again, Hortensius moved close to the rivet to check it. To his relief, the rivet had cooled in place, held firmly by the surrounding metal.

"Excellent! This looks promising. Let's do a few more to be certain."

The team worked diligently, assembling more sections of the test frame. Hortensius watched silently, following behind them. After they'd completed a sizeable portion, he called for a halt.

Carefully, he inspected each rivet, checking for any signs of weakness or improper seating. To his satisfaction, they all appeared to be holding strong.

"This is good work," he announced. "I believe we're ready to begin assembling the test frame in earnest. We'll need to assemble a larger section to truly gauge its watertightness, but this is a promising start."

He took Lucan by the arm and led him to the worktable.

"Let's go ahead and begin assembling the test frame. Once we get the first few spans done all the way around, we can lower it into the water and check it for watertightness. If this works as the Consul says, we should be good to continue. I will send some more men to you, since I think I just tripled the men it will take to build it. While you do that, I'll need to return to the workshop and see what I can do to increase the metal sheet production."

"You have a lot more faith in this than I have," Lucan said, still looking at the riveted sheets wearily.

"The Consul hasn't steered us wrong yet. I know this goes against everything you've ever worked on, but the idea behind it is sound, I think."

"I hope so. I really do."

Carthage

It was late, and Medb was not pleased to be summoned in the middle of the night like some kind of hired hand. The only reason she hadn't immediately sent the messenger back with harsh words for his master was that the request had come from Claudius.

The praetorian had been all but silent for the past two weeks following their discovery of the contents of the crates. She'd even heard that he'd left the city for several days. She didn't need him to report to her regularly, as he had earned enough trust for her to allow him somewhat of a free hand, but the silence had started to become concerning.

Although not as much as silence followed by a sudden summons.

She arrived with her small guard detachment at the prescribed warehouse and was surprised to see nearly twenty praetorians gathered around, waiting. More unusual than that was the pair climbing the warehouse with rifles slung over their backs.

She didn't see Claudius right away, not until he stepped out of a darkened spot next to the warehouse. All of the men had dark cloaks draped over them, making them particularly hard to see.

"What is all this?" she asked when she reached him.

"My lady, thank you for coming. I know it is late. The surveillance operation you ordered bore fruit tonight. As you instructed, we maintained surveillance on the merchant ships involved in the smuggling, following them offshore when they left port. Most went on to other ports or headed back to Britannia, but three did not. I believe these three ships came in empty and left full, suggesting Carthage is being used as some kind of transshipment point. Those ships sailed a day to the east, where they met other ships out of sight of any harbor, near dusk. The ships got close enough to use rope and gangplank between them. We were not able to get close enough to see specifics without being noticed, but I believe they were transferring cargo."

"That is interesting, but it does not explain tonight," Medb pointed out.

"This will. Two of the ships were from the remaining Greek cities that have yet to declare to one side or another, and the last was Egyptian. More notably, the previous day the Egyptian ship had delivered a new set of Ptolemaic envoys and, after their mid-ocean meeting, they sailed back here. One of the men who disembarked from that ship was, in fact, one of those new envoys. They must not have completely unloaded or they exchanged cargo because he came to a warehouse one building over with crates that came off that ship tonight. He is, in fact, still inside."

"By himself?"

"No. Several members from other questionable ships currently in port entered the same warehouse around the same time, along with several men we've been monitoring for connections with the rebels here in the city. If we are ever going to find a link between them, something solid like you were asking for, this is the moment to get it."

"How many are inside, in total? What kind of guards or combatants?"

"Twenty at most, with about half being muscle they brought with them. I didn't see firearms on any of them, but they could have hidden them inside the crates or otherwise concealed them. The streets are mostly empty and I have more men on a perimeter around the building. We control all access points to this block."

Medb considered the situation. The intelligence gathered by Claudius was too valuable to ignore. This could be the break they needed to unravel the network of support for the Carthaginian rebels and figure out what this smuggling operation was really about. It wasn't without risk, however. A poorly executed raid could alert their contacts and drive them further underground.

Ultimately, though, they had been operating in the dark for too long. They needed answers, and they needed them now.

"Very well. Proceed."

Claudius inclined his head in acknowledgment, then turned to face his men. He had clearly worked the details out with his men ahead of time, ready if he got the go-ahead he wanted, because a single hand gesture was enough to send all the men gathered there into motion, running to predetermined positions.

The precision of it was impressive. Within a minute, the building was surrounded and the one man left outside as some kind of guard was hauled down by one of the praetorians who moved on him with an impressive lack of noise, slashing the man's throat before he could get a sound off.

Claudius had broken his men into three teams assembled at two different entry points, the main door and a side entrance, with additional men on the roof to cover the streets should any manage to escape. Each entrance had men stacked up at them, looking to him and waiting for the signal to enter.

"My lady, you should wait here," Claudius said when he realized she and her guards were following behind him.

"I will be behind you. Don't worry, I will stay out of your way," she said, her tone making it clear this wasn't up for debate.

Claudius frowned but did not argue. Instead, he raised his hand, holding it aloft for a moment, before bringing it down in a sharp, quick motion.

Chaos ensued.

The main and side doors splintered inward with a thunderous crash as the praetorians burst through. Shouts of alarm and confusion followed from inside as the smugglers found themselves suddenly under attack.

Medb and her guards, who kept themselves between her and the ensuing combat, slipped inside behind the initial wave of soldiers, where her guards pushed her under cover behind a stack of crates. It was a good spot. She could see the fight without being in the direct line of fire.

Well, mostly not in the line of fire.

The warehouse was a cavernous space, filled with towering shelves and scattered crates.

"By order of the governor, you are all under arrest. Surrender now!" Claudius's voice boomed.

His words were met with a hail of gunfire. Muzzle flashes lit up the gloom as several of the smugglers holding muskets opened fire. Even a few arcuballista bolts flew through the intervening space, suggesting how haphazardly they were armed. The praetorians responded in kind, with the benefit of their superior weapons.

Medb ducked lower as bullets whizzed overhead, splintering wood and ricocheting off metal.

Near the center of the warehouse, she spotted the Ptolemaic trade representative that she'd met roughly a week before when he'd come to the city and introduced himself to Cormac. The man's eyes were wide with panic as he fumbled for something at his waist. He did not get a chance to pull whatever weapon he was carrying, as a nearby praetorian saw the action as well and lifted his rifle. The Ptolemaic representative jerked backward, a red stain blossoming on his chest as he crumpled to the ground, dead before he hit the floor.

The firefight intensified as the remaining armed men were pushed further back into a corner of the warehouse by the better-armed and trained praetorians. It was getting hard to see anything as the building grew hazy with gun smoke.

In a matter of minutes, the gunfire tapered off and then ended.

"Clear on the left!" a voice called out.

"Right side secure!" another responded.

Medb emerged cautiously from her cover, surveying the aftermath. The warehouse floor was littered with spent cartridges, splintered wood, and bodies.

"We've secured the building, my lady. Seven survivors in custody. The rest …" He gestured to the bodies scattered across the floor.

"And your men?"

"Two wounded, nothing serious. We caught them by surprise."

"Good work," Medb said, her eyes roaming the warehouse. "Now, let's see what our friends were so eager to protect."

She moved purposefully toward a cluster of crates that had been at the center of the smugglers' defensive efforts. Praetorians were already prying them open, revealing their contents.

Medb peered inside the first crate. It was full of muskets, and not the rifles she'd hoped for.

Claudius joined her, his expression equally puzzled. "None of this is protected ordnance. Nothing like what we saw before."

Medb's mind raced, trying to piece together the implications. "Most likely intended for the rebels, considering how they were armed. The other shipments must not have been intended for here, and either never left ships or simply transferred from ship to ship. They probably wouldn't want any of it in any warehouses here, in case they were searched. Still, arming the rebels is a serious matter, and perhaps they know where the more concerning shipments went."

As she continued her examination, a praetorian approached, holding a small, ornate box. "My lady, we found this on the Ptolemaic envoy's body."

Medb took the box, turning it over in her hands. It was finely crafted, with intricate designs etched into its surface. She opened it carefully, revealing a collection of sealed documents bearing official-looking seals.

"Well, well. It seems our late friend was carrying some rather interesting correspondence."

As she read, she couldn't keep the annoyed look off her face.

"My lady?"

"It's either just numbers or in code. Clearly, something the recipients would know, but meaningless to us. Find me one of the rebels that were here, so we can ask them."

"I'm sorry, my lady, the rebels fought to the last. The only men remaining are sailors who threw down their weapons once the last of the rebels fell."

"Well, then let's see what they know."

Claudius nodded, gesturing to his men who dragged forward the seven survivors, all looking worse for wear. Some sported fresh cuts and bruises. Two even had quick bandages for bullet wounds that were not, at the moment, life-threatening. All had a look that men who'd transferred in from the trenches in the east called shell shock.

A term apparently originating with the Consul.

Medb circled the group like a predator sizing up its prey.

"Gentlemen," she said after circling them twice, building them up. "I trust you understand the gravity of your situation. Smuggling prohibited weapons. Consorting with rebels. These are serious offenses."

One of the men, a fat sailor with a beard, spat at her feet.

"We ain't telling you nothing, bitch," he said in Egyptian, one of the many languages she spoke.

Medb smiled at him, cocking her head to the side. Then, without warning, she lashed out, her fist connecting with the man's jaw. He crumpled to the ground, groaning.

"I suggest you reconsider your approach," she said calmly. "Now, who wants to start talking?"

Some of the prisoners exchanged nervous glances, but the rest kept their defiant exteriors.

Medb sighed dramatically. "Very well. Claudius, pick one."

The praetorian hesitated for a moment, then grabbed one of the men, shoving him to his knees in front of Medb.

"Last chance. Tell me about your operation. Where are these shipments coming from? Where are they going?"

"To the hells with you," he said, following his older comrades' example, spitting at her feet.

"Wrong answer," she said, and nodded at him.

The praetorian behind him looked to Claudius, who nodded in turn. Medb frowned at the lack of obedience, but at least he carried out his orders. With a swift motion, the soldier brought a dagger across the man's throat, sending a torrent of blood across the floor.

Medb stepped to the side to avoid the spray and frowned at the men, circling the group and stopping in front of the youngest of them, a scrawny lad barely out of his teens.

The boy's eyes widened in terror. "Please, I don't know anything! I'm just a deckhand!"

"Wrong answer," she said, looking up at another praetorian.

"Wait!" One of the other prisoners, an older man with graying hair, said. "Leave the boy alone. I'll talk."

"A wise decision. Start with where these shipments were bound."

The man swallowed hard, trying to ignore the looks of the other prisoners. "Syria and Judea. That's all I know, I swear. We'd meet ships out at sea, transfer the cargo. They never told us exactly where it went after that."

"And who received the cargo?"

"Easterners. Strange-looking men. It's impossible to miss them."

Medb nodded, processing the information. "What is Egypt's role in all this?"

The man hesitated. "I ... I don't know much. Just rumors."

"Tell me," Medb insisted, her voice dangerously low.

"There's been talk of changes coming. Something big. But I don't know details, I swear!"

Medb studied him for a moment, then turned to Claudius. "Take them away. Quietly. We can't risk alerting the Ptolemaic representatives in the city. Keep them locked up. No one is to talk to them without my order."

"Also, the surveillance is over. They will figure out we captured some of their men soon, so I want to bite into this operation before they do. I want you to seize any of the suspicious ships known to be part of this smuggling operation that enter the harbor. Detain all sailors for questioning and have the ships thoroughly searched. Leave no plank unturned."

Claudius nodded grimly. "It will be done, my lady. But what of the Ptolemaic envoys still in the city? They're bound to notice when their ships start disappearing."

Medb's lips curved into a predatory smile. "Let them notice. I will send a message to the Empress now, and she can decide how far we take this."

As Claudius moved to carry out her orders, Medb found herself concerned. The pieces finally all came together for her, and she thought she knew what was going on.

And it wasn't good.

Chapter 11

Port Caolros

Admiral Valdar wished he could have stayed on his ship. At least his quarters there, cramped as they were, had a comfortable chair for him to sit on. The temporary commander's office, which he had taken over, was in a nearby temporary shelter until the buildings of the port itself were in place.

Which wouldn't happen until the four forts on the peninsula were finished.

Priorities being what they were, they could not waste resources on simple pleasures when there were so many critical things to do that even the building he was in was slipshod. He understood that, but there were times, like today, when he was forced to go over pages of reports from supply ships, scout ships, construction teams, and an endless list of others, where he almost wanted to order a retreat to his cabin.

Or at least order his chair unbolted and brought to him.

Still, it would not do to have his men thinking the admiral had gone soft. So he had to forbear and deal with the poorly assembled wooden atrocity masquerading as a seat.

Valdar scribbled another quick note to address the supply chain issues with the quartermaster. The recent storms had taken their toll, delaying shipments and hampering construction, and the engineers were using that as the reason things were falling behind.

Well, that might not be fair. He knew the men were working hard. While some things they could get from inland, most of the produced metal parts had to come to them aboard ships. It was his job to light a fire under the posteriors of those captains not keeping to their schedule.

Not that it was all bad news. At least their scout ships had reported no sign of Eastern vessels in the vicinity.

As Valdar set down his pen and was about to stretch to prepare himself to address the next batch, the door to his office burst open without warning, slamming hard against its backstop to rebound and almost hit Doctor Phelan in the face as he rushed in. The man looked to be in a state, his face ashen and his normally impeccable appearance disheveled.

"By the gods, man," Valdar said in surprise, rising to his feet.

Doctor Phelan, seeming to realize how sudden his appearance was and the breach of protocol, bowed slightly and said, "My deepest apologies for the intrusion, Admiral. I wouldn't have barged in like this if the situation wasn't a matter of utmost urgency."

"What situation?"

"Sir, we have a rapidly spreading illness among the men stationed here. It started with just a few cases, nothing out of the ordinary, mind you, which is why it has surprised us like it has. We thought it was just exhaustion from the construction work, maybe a touch of fever. But this morning three men who seemed to be on the mend suddenly took a turn for the worse. They ... they didn't make it, sir."

"From what appeared to be a simple fever?"

"They didn't die of the fever alone. The Consul's lessons have taught us that fevers are just a symptom of the body fighting off an infection of some kind, although it can be fatal if it gets high enough. It's why we weren't alarmed. It's how quickly the fevers went from minor to life-threatening that is concerning. It's unlike anything I've seen before, Admiral. High fevers that spike without warning, severe muscle aches that leave the men writhing in agony, and a type of respiratory distress that makes it appear as if they're drowning on dry land."

"How many are affected now?"

"That's the truly terrifying part, sir. It's spreading like wildfire. One of the things I'm here to request is the need to convert one of the newly constructed barracks into a makeshift infirmary. Even that, I fear, will not be enough. The illness seems highly contagious, but we can't figure out how it's transmitting so quickly. Men who've had no direct contact with the sick are falling ill."

As if on cue, there was a commotion outside. The door burst open again, and two burly construction supervisors stumbled in, supporting a third man between them. The sick worker's face was flushed with fever, his breath coming in ragged gasps.

"Doctor!" one of the supervisors called out, panic evident in his voice. "Segestes just collapsed on the job site. He was fine an hour ago!"

Phelan rushed to examine the stricken man, putting his hand to the man's neck, feeling his forehead, and lifting his eyelids to look into the man's drooping and unresponsive eyes.

"It's the same symptoms. Take him to the infirmary immediately," the doctor confirmed, before turning back to Valdar as the men left. "Admiral, I fear we're on the brink of a full-blown epidemic. Our current facilities simply cannot handle this volume. If we don't act quickly …"

"Have you seen anything like this before, Doctor? Anything similar?"

Phelan shook his head. "Nothing quite like this. The fever pattern is reminiscent of some ailments in Egypt and Nubia I've read about, but the speed of onset and the respiratory symptoms; it's baffling."

"Should we begin quarantining them?"

"We are in the process of doing that, but I fear it will be woefully inadequate. We've isolated the sick as best we can, but with new cases popping up seemingly at random across the camp, it's like trying to plug a sieve with our fingers."

"What do you need from me, Doctor? I have to rely on your judgment on this."

"We need more supplies, for one. We are quickly running out of what we have. Especially the distilled alcohol from Factorium, along with some of the more traditional herbal remedies, such as willow bark and the rest that we've been using to reduce fever and pain. One of Chief Ekoko's men mentioned several plants they use that have worked well for combating a similar disease they have seen. I wanted to try some of that as well."

"Make me a list," Valdar ordered. "Everything you need, the remedies from Port Vikhavn, other medicines, bandages, extra cots, whatever it takes. And be liberal with your estimates. I want us prepared for the worst."

Phelan took a pen and piece of paper off the desk and hurriedly scribbled down his requirements as Valdar moved to stick his head out of the door.

"You," he barked, seeing an aide walking nearby. "Fetch me Captain Einar of the Aquila and then get all of the engineers you can find and the praetorian commander. Be quick about it!"

By the time the doctor finished writing, the grizzled captain had arrived sweating, having clearly run all the way from his ship.

"Captain," Valdar said without preamble or apology for the urgency of the summons, handing the doctor's list to him. "I need you to make an emergency run to Port Vikhavn. We have a medical crisis on our hands. These are the supplies we need. Impress upon the port commander the gravity of our situation. If they give you any trouble, you have my authority to requisition whatever is necessary."

"This is ... a substantial request, Admiral."

"I'm aware," Valdar said, offering no explanation.

"Understood, sir. We'll set sail within the hour."

As the captain turned to leave, Valdar called after him, "And Einar? Make it clear to your crew, no shore leave, no unnecessary contact in Vikhavn. Let none of your men disembark unless absolutely necessary. Whatever is happening here, we don't know how it spreads or how contagious it is."

The expression on Einar's face showed more concern than he had seen on the man in the midst of battle. Valdar didn't blame him. Cannonballs they could understand but this, this was something much more frightening.

To his credit, however, the captain simply snapped a salute and hurried out without another word.

A few minutes later, most of the engineers and the newly assigned port commander were ushered into the quickly crowding office.

"I apologize for the hastiness of the summons, but the good doctor has just informed me that we are facing a new crisis. I'm sure you've noticed an upswing in the number of men being put on sick call over the last few days. It appears an unknown illness is spreading rapidly through our ranks, and the doctor believes that it is on the verge of sweeping through everyone stationed here, which is why, effective immediately, I'm placing Port Caolros and all ships under quarantine."

The proclamation sent a shock through the assembled men. While Valdar was sure that they had noted that more of their men were sick than normal, people in their position tended to be hyper-focused on the task they had at hand, missing obvious details outside their purview.

Valdar certainly had missed it himself.

"To what extent are we shutting down the port?" the praetorian commander asked.

It was the right question and showed he'd been through some of the newer training Faenius had been putting his men through, as the Consul put more focus on the control of disease in their cities and legion camps.

"Full isolation," Valdar said. "No one disembarks at this port. Messenger ships are not to make landfall at unaffected ports. Any contact, if it happens, must be hands-off and at signaling distance. I need you to enforce this strictly, Lucius. Lives depend on it."

The commander nodded grimly. "Understood, Admiral. I'll see to it personally."

"How will this quarantine impact our ongoing construction?" Valdar asked the lead engineer.

"It'll slow us down considerably, sir. We rely on regular supply shipments and rotating work crews."

"Is there any way we can still stay close to the schedule? I'm aware this makes it difficult, but it is imperative this port is functional before midsummer, and letting the outbreak run rampant will slow us down even more."

"We could potentially reorganize our work schedules, focusing on projects that require fewer men in close proximity, and save the rest for when the outbreak is hopefully over. If this does not go on into the summer, then we should still make your deadline."

Valdar nodded. "Good. Very good. Work out the details and bring me a revised plan by tomorrow morning."

"I believe I will be dispatching one of the caravels to the hospital in Devnum," Valdar then said to the doctor. "I need you to write up as detailed a report as possible on what we're dealing with here. Aside from it being information they can use in their studies, I believe we will need as many eyes looking at our situation as possible."

"A wise move. I'll start immediately. I think I must stress again my concern about the spread of this disease until we can determine its cause."

"I understood that, Doctor. We are taking this *very* seriously, with as many precautions as possible, but the work on the port must also go on. There is a balance we must reach between protecting our people from this disease and protecting them from the Eastern warships that are sure to arrive eventually. After you finish your report, I need you to work with these gentlemen to establish isolation areas for new cases."

"We'll start planning out options for him," the engineer said.

"Good. We'll maintain essential work, but safety is our priority. I want daily reports on new cases, progression patterns, and the effectiveness of our containment measures. Get to it, gentlemen. Time and tide wait for no man."

Devnum

Lucilla stood at the entrance of the grand banquet hall, her posture impeccable, smiling at each guest as they entered. The soft strains of Roman music gave a calm, welcoming background to the whole affair. The group performing in the corner was one of many artisans she helped sponsor and maintain throughout the city, as part of her civic responsibility as Empress.

She had not held many of these events during the early days of the Empire, but in the interwar years, she had found them useful tools in her diplomacy with their new allies. Although she'd been somewhat distracted through the winter and into the spring, it was time to start using them again.

Some of her advisors suggested it was a waste and that she would be seen as a spendthrift by the populace, what with everyone in the Empire sacrificing as the war dragged on. She understood that, but she also knew she needed to try everything she could to get the Scandi and Egyptians to come fully into the fold.

Especially the Egyptians. They had a sizable population and a wealth that could change the nature of things in Greece, where the situation was growing increasingly fraught.

Which was why she stood by the entrance to the hall now, greeting each of the delegations and why she had mentally rehearsed the nuances of each culture's customs.

Events like these were all about impression rather than substance.

The first to arrive were the representatives of the Mpongo tribe, the allies made by Valdar near Port Vikhavn. At first, she hadn't paid much attention to them, except what she read in the admiral's dispatches, but the tribe was clearly wanting to step onto a larger stage. Aside from sending two envoys to the city to deal directly with the Empire, they were sending more and more men to help man the ports Valdar was building, saving the Empire the expense of diverting more manpower to provide security, and to the support of Valdar's plan.

With that level of help, she'd had little choice but to invite them, bringing them onto a larger stage for the first time.

Lucilla inclined her head respectfully, her hands outstretched in welcome. "Eyenga, Lombe, I am glad you were able to come. I hope your first week in our city has been pleasant."

Lombe, the spokesman for the pair, was resplendent in traditional, adorned garb that had clearly been altered and influenced by Britannian fashion, although the style was more that of everyday clothing worn by sailors and soldiers rather than the upper crust of Britannian society. She was sure that would change quickly. The envoys seemed almost uncanny in their ability to adapt to new cultures and take advantage of them.

She wished she was as good as they were at that. The pair even spoke Latin better than many of their Gaulic or Germanic allies, although with an unusual accent that she had not heard before meeting them. Lombe gripped Lucilla's hands warmly while his partner Eyenga stood slightly behind him, her hands clasped in front of her.

"Empress, your city is quite the marvel. We have barely begun to explore it, and already, my eyes cannot eat anymore. Although I have heard tell of Factorium, your manufacturing city. I am quite eager to see that."

Lucilla guided them into the hall. "Then I will have to make time to show you there myself. It is … an experience."

After a little more cordial chit-chat, the Mpongo envoys moved into the banquet hall, clearly enjoying themselves as more diplomats arrived. She had invited all of their allies from the Western alliance, in addition to the Scandi and Egyptians. She hoped it would allow for their allied diplomats to help her in persuading those two polities to join the alliance. Since her own efforts so far had not gone well.

The Egyptian envoys, Arsinoe and Diodorus, were, of course, the last to arrive. A petty diplomatic ploy, but one that fit them well. Lucilla contained her feelings about the pair, managing to keep her diplomatic smile in place in spite of the underlying tension she could feel from them.

Once everyone had arrived, Lucilla made her way to the head of the main table. As she took her seat, servants began to bring out the first course, a series of small dishes representing the cuisines of each represented culture. She had worked with her cooks to ensure everything was just right.

She noted with satisfaction the looks of pleasant surprise, especially at the large game bird that had come with their Mpongo friends, who had been kind enough to instruct her cooks on how to prepare it.

As the meal progressed, Lucilla rose periodically to circulate among the guests. With allies, she discussed how things were going at home, how the conscriptions were going with their people, and the state of the war. While some would consider those poor topics of conversation while dining, she found settings like this helped to loosen men's tongues and get them to talk where they might otherwise be more reserved.

Of course, that was not true in all circumstances.

"Arsinoe, Diodorus," she said as she approached the Egyptians. "I hope you're finding the evening enjoyable."

"It is very pleasant," Arsinoe said, in much the same way someone would describe meeting an onerous relative.

"Have you given any more thought to our last conversation?"

"We have conveyed our position, Empress Lucilla. Egypt's interests are our primary concern."

Lucilla was about to respond when she noticed a commotion near the entrance. A man in Egyptian dress, who she recognized as one of the envoys' aides, had rushed in and was making his way directly to the pair. Reaching them, he bent low, whispering urgently into Arsinoe's ear.

The change in Arsinoe's demeanor was immediate and striking. A look of genuine concern replaced her previous mask of indifference and annoyance. Diodorus leaned in, listening intently and his face wore the same expression.

Lucilla watched, her diplomatic smile never wavering. She knew better than to try and eavesdrop on their conversation. Their relationship was already tense, no need to add a violation of privacy on top of it. Still, she couldn't help but wonder what could have caused such a reaction.

Before she could formulate a tactful inquiry or find a clue as to what was happening, the envoys stood abruptly.

"If you'll excuse us," Arsinoe said, not waiting for a response as they quickly left the banquet, the aide following in their wake.

The sudden departure of the Egyptians did not go unnoticed, sending ripples of confusion through the banquet hall. The music faltered, then stopped entirely as guests turned to one another, murmuring.

"What's happening?" a Gallic diplomat asked, rising from his seat to peer towards the entrance.

Lucilla maintained her composure, though internally, she was as perplexed as her guests. She watched as several delegates stood, craning their necks to catch a glimpse of the retreating Egyptians.

Before Lucilla could respond, however, the Scandi, too, rose and started toward the exit.

"My friends," she said, intercepting them. "Why are you leaving so soon?"

"There are some things we need to attend to," one of the men said, looking to where the Egyptians had gone.

"Is there something I can help with?"

"I'm afraid not," he said. "If you'll excuse us."

If the Egyptians' sudden departure had caused consternation, the Scandi following after caused mild panic.

Or at least worry.

The room erupted into a flurry of activity. Delegates began calling for their own aides, dispatching them with hurried whispers, no doubt to gather information or send word to their respective governments that things were not as close to being finalized as their Britannian allies had let on.

She needed to regain control of the situation.

"My esteemed guests, may I have your attention, please?"

The chatter subsided as she raised her voice to speak over the crowd. All eyes turned to her.

"I understand that the sudden departure of our Egyptian and Scandi colleagues has caused some concern. While the situation is unusual, I assure you that there is no cause for alarm. As you all know, diplomacy is a complex dance. Neither of our departed friends are part of our alliance, yet. While I know we all hope to add them to our number, and I believe it is still very possible, their departure does not change the fundamental nature of our relationships or our shared goals."

She paused, letting that sink in, making eye contact with several of the assembled representatives.

"Building strong alliances takes time. It requires patience, understanding, and a willingness to navigate unexpected developments. What we've witnessed tonight is simply part of that process. Also, I, for one, hate to let something like this ruin an otherwise pleasant evening. So I propose a toast. To you, my friends and allies. To unity and perseverance. To the strength of our alliance and the promise of a brighter future for all of our nations."

The delegates raised their glasses, seeming to have calmed down somewhat, to varying degrees. As they drank, Lucilla could see the tension in the room beginning to dissipate.

Before she could say anything else, one of her aides approached, a folded paper in hand.

"Empress," he said quietly, "an urgent telegram for you."

Lucilla nodded, maintaining her smile for the benefit of the watching delegates.

"If you'll excuse me for just a moment," she said to the room at large. "Please, continue enjoying your meal. I shall return shortly."

She stepped away from the table, turning slightly to obscure the telegram from view as she unfolded it. Her eyes scanned the message quickly.

As she read, Lucilla felt a chill run down her spine. Medb's breakdown of the situation in Carthage, the Egyptian part in it, and the former queen's suspicions about what that meant were very concerning. Worse, she agreed with Medb's conclusion. It not only explained what was happening in Carthage, but the timing of this revelation and the Egyptians' abrupt departure from the banquet could not be coincidental.

She would have to check if any Egyptians in Kalb had sent a message through the telegraph system, allowing them to beat Medb's message by a matter of minutes, but the end result was the same.

Lucilla folded the telegram, tucking it away. She took a deep breath, composing herself before turning back to face her guests.

"My friends," she announced, keeping her tone calm and light. "I apologize, but I must take my leave to attend to an urgent matter. Please, stay and enjoy your meals. I assure you that I will speak with each of you individually in the coming days to address any questions or concerns you may have."

She gestured to the musicians, who had been waiting silently since the commotion began. The music could barely be heard over the cacophony of noise from her guests, but there wasn't much she could do about that. With a subtle nod, she summoned a messenger to her side.

"Gather my inner circle," she instructed in a low voice. "Do it quickly."

Chapter 12

Factorium

Hortensius hurried onto the shooting range they had set up behind one of the factories on the west side of town. He'd scheduled this test two days ago, but a sudden emergency with the ship test platform had required him to make a quick run to Devnum.

How foolish he'd been when he'd thought the telegraph lines going up meant less back-and-forth travel for him. Yes, it was partially his fault, as he liked to keep his hands in all of the projects and the new ship design may be the most complex thing they'd worked on yet, but it was exhausting to shuttle back and forth so many times each week.

Worse, this trip had been made all that much more stressful when the Empress had heard he was in the city and required him to stop by the palace so she could make sure he knew how important it was to her that the new rifles were ready now. He'd known that, of course, but apparently, new things were happening and she wanted to light a fire under his posterior to get him moving.

"Master Hortensius, we should be ready to begin," the range officer, Rufus, reported as soon as he'd arrived, gesturing to where a soldier stood holding one of the new rifles.

Although he'd seen the weapon many times, it still struck him as odd after so many years with their current standard-issue weapon. The lever on the bottom and much shorter length made it look almost toy-like compared to the long, graceful lines of the old rifle.

"Once we complete these tests, I want the production lines to start setting up so we can begin scaling. We need these shipping out within a few weeks," he said to one of his assistants, who nodded as he passed by heading to the soldier.

"They've shown you what to do?" he asked.

"Yes. Work the lever fully back and then forward until it locks in place to load a new round."

"Yes. Watch out for this feed port here. It will shoot the previous casing out to make room for the next one. The casing will be hot, so don't put your hand in the way of it or have it pointed at your face when you work the lever."

"I understand."

"Good man," Hortensius said and stepped back, looking to the range officer. "You may begin when ready."

The praetorian they had selected for the test shouldered the weapon, aligning the rear sight with the front blade. He took several slow breaths, calming himself as he steadied the weapon, pointing it at the paper target affixed to a hay bale downrange.

"Fire when ready," Rufus commanded.

The rifle cracked, a sharper, higher-pitched sound than what Hortensius was used to with the old rifle. Hortensius reached out and was handed a brass spyglass by an assistant, allowing him to see downrange. There was a clear hole in the paper. About two finger spans left of the center of the target.

Hortensius said, handing the spyglass back and clapping his hands together. "Excellent! Just excellent. We'll need to make a series of shots to be sure, but it seems the accuracy is still very good, even with the shorter barrel. Please fire again."

There had been some contention among his men during the development of the rifle, with many thinking the shorter barrel would decrease the accuracy over time, in spite of the Consul's notes.

Hortensius, for one, had not doubted it.

The praetorian made a small adjustment to the rear sight and then worked the lever, the action sliding smoothly as it ejected the spent casing and chambered the next round. The man, who'd been serious so far, actually smiled as he did so.

Hortensius wasn't surprised. If he'd seen combat, then he would know firsthand how needing a few seconds to reload versus thirty seconds at best would be a game changer.

The man raised the rifle and fired again. This one hit even closer to the center. A single finger width away. A few more, and he would be satisfied with the accuracy of the weapon, which was the main point of the test.

They could repeatedly try the lever, pressure test the barrel, the feed mechanism, and nearly every other part of the rifle in the factory, but only actually having the weapon fired by an expert would tell them if it was accurate or not.

"One more," he ordered.

The soldier nodded and began to pull the lever back. Instead of going all the way back, sending the spent casing flying out of the rifle, there was a metallic snap sound, with the lever short of being fully opened. The soldier tried working the lever back and forth, but it remained stuck, unable to be pulled all the way back.

"The cartridge is jammed, sir. I can't extract it."

Hortensius's earlier elation evaporated. He'd expected a lot of things, but their tests on the lever had been thorough, and they hadn't encountered jamming problems. Hurrying forward, he took the rifle from the man and examined the partially open action. The brass cartridge had somehow twisted sideways, wedging itself between the carrier block and chamber wall.

"Take a break over there. We'll call you when we're ready," Hortensius told the gathered soldiers and range master before turning to his aides. "Disassemble this rifle immediately. I want every component laid out and inspected thoroughly."

As the testing team carefully took apart the rifle, Hortensius paced back and forth, watching over their shoulders. They had spent the most time with the weapon, so they were, of course, the right choice to disassemble it. But familiarity sometimes bred a kind of blindness. An inability, or maybe even unwillingness, to see problems in a person's own work.

So, he remained vigilant as they worked. Still, even knowing that, he was concerned. The Consul's instructions had been clear, and he'd been so certain they had ironed out all the kinks in the design.

When they finished, he looked over the table where each component of the rifle had been carefully arranged.

"Check the firing pin first. Look for any signs of burrs or misalignment. Then, move on to the extractor and ejector. I want every measurement compared against the specifications."

For the next hour, Hortensius watched as his team meticulously inspected each component. They used calipers to verify the length, width, and thickness of each part. They ran their fingers along edges to feel for imperfections and held parts up to the light to check for hairline cracks.

And with each part they examined, they found everything was as it should be. Nothing out of specs or broken. Nothing bowed, bent, or twisted. Everything seemed to be in order, yet the rifle had still jammed.

"Maybe the problem was in assembly. Let's reassemble it, but I want you to do it slowly. I want every step double-checked against these drawings and confirmed to be accurate and not out of alignment before we move on to the next one."

The team worked methodically, cleaning each part thoroughly and applying oils as needed before putting the rifle back together. Hortensius supervised closely, watching to make sure every component was seated properly and aligned correctly.

When they finished, it looked the same as it had before they disassembled it. He was somewhat bothered by the fact that they hadn't found any reason for the jamming. He had hoped that it had been simply assembled wrong, and putting it back together fixed the issue, but he knew that was wishful thinking.

Something like this was going to be more than just an assembly error.

Once the rifle was ready, Hortensius waved the range officer and praetorian back, handing the soldier the rifle.

"Please try again," he said.

The soldier stepped into the firing position and looked back to him for confirmation. When Hortensius gave him a nod, the man worked the lever, pulling in a round, lifted the rifle, and took aim.

Crack! The first shot rang out cleanly.

"Work the lever and fire again," Hortensius said when the man lowered the weapon.

He chambered another round and fired again without issue.

"Perhaps it was just a temporary misalignment," Hortensius said back to his aides. "Once more, if you please."

The soldier nodded and worked the lever again. As if to purposefully prove Hortensius wrong, the familiar metallic scraping noise sounded again when he attempted to chamber a new round, with the lever refusing to close.

"Pluto take it all," Hortensius muttered. "Clear the round out and try again."

Over the next half hour, the man continued to test the weapon. Maddeningly, the results of the stubborn repetition were wildly inconsistent. Sometimes, the weapon would fire three or four rounds flawlessly before jamming. Other times, it would jam on the second shot.

"This makes no sense," he said when he finally called a halt to the attempts. "Why is it so inconsistent? If it were a simple mechanical flaw, we'd see the same problem every time."

He turned to his lead engineer. "I want you to make some modifications. Increase the tension on the extractor spring slightly. And let's take a closer look at the feeding mechanism. There might be a minor misalignment we're missing."

They had checked that the last time they disassembled the rifle, and everything matched the Consul's notes, but none of his men were going to argue with him. They simply nodded and set to work, not only increasing tension on the extractor spring but also taking a fine file to the ejector, smoothing out any potential rough spots that might be causing the cartridges to snag.

"Alright, let's try again," Hortensius said once the modifications were complete.

The testing process began anew. Initially, there seemed to be some improvement with a longer span of time between jams, once managing eight rounds in succession before jamming.

"Ha! I think we've cracked it," Hortensius exclaimed, allowing himself a moment of optimism. "If it keeps on like this, we'll know we're on the right track."

His elation was short-lived. The very next round jammed. And the one after that. And the one after that. The longer they fired, the clearer it became that there was no consistent pattern to when the weapon would fail.

"This doesn't make any sense," Hortensius muttered.

Hours passed as they assembled and reassembled the rifle. His team had gone through countless iterations of modifications and testing, but the core problem remained. Sometimes, the rifle would fire flawlessly for several rounds, other times, it would jam almost immediately.

As Hortensius stared at the disassembled rifle as his men worked, a new thought struck him.

"What if it's not the rifle at all?"

"My lord?" One of the engineers asked.

"Bring me samples from different batches of ammunition. I want to compare them."

When Rufus returned with several boxes of cartridges, Hortensius immediately set about examining them. He measured the dimensions of cartridges from different batches, weighed them, and even cut a few open to inspect the powder inside.

"Look here," he said, holding up two cartridges side by side. "The crimping on these is ever so slightly different."

"Our tests showed variations like that had little effect on its being fired," an engineer said.

"I know. Still, I want you to go get a handful of rounds from different batches. I want to keep careful track of which rounds from which batch are being fired."

His men followed his orders, and in fifteen minutes, they began a new series of tests, this time carefully tracking which batch of ammunition was being used in the rifle. As the results came in, a pattern began to emerge.

"It's the cartridges," Hortensius announced, both relieved and frustrated. "The percentage of jams is consistent within each batch of ammunition but varies between batches. While that probably means the rifle mechanism is sound, we will have to redo these tests once we get our cartridge manufacturing process sorted out. Right now, I want you to head to the munitions line immediately. Inspect every step of the cartridge production, look for any variations in the crimping process, powder measuring, or case forming. Let's figure out where the problem is originating."

It was going to take them time to sort out the problem. The Empress was not going to be happy about this delay.

Maleth

It was a shame he had to stay cramped in his offices on such a beautiful day. Over the last five years, he'd served all across the Empire, from Britannia, where it seemed to rain constantly, to Germania, in the winter, as an aide to one of the commanders helping build the Germanic Alliance a legion of their own.

All of that made him appreciate his current position even more. The island of Maleth was small compared to many in the Middle Sea, but its location made it much more important than its size would indicate, sitting in the waters between Sicilia and North Africa. Much of the trade in the region passed through, or at least near, his port.

It was a coveted position, and Rolfus knew many of the officers in the legions envied him the assignment. For Rolfus, though, it was the view that made it.

He'd grown up in a small village south of Rome, on the western coast of Italia, so the views here reminded him of the views from his home. He would never regret signing up for the legions near the end of the last war and helping push the Carthaginians out of his homeland, but he regretted having to leave that place.

Still, he was a professional now, and he had a job to do. He couldn't stare out the window all day, and his aide was waiting for him to respond.

"I don't understand why Talticus didn't take care of this when he had the port," he said, finishing the thought he'd started earlier, before being distracted by the stunning view.

"He felt the expense and effort would be more than the improvement achieved by dredging the harbor would bring."

"What you mean is he knew he was retiring, and he didn't want to deal with it, so he left it for the next poor bastard who got this assignment. Namely me."

The man smiled, but didn't reply. He'd been at this port through three commanders and was much too smart to badmouth any of them.

At least not where the current commander could hear it.

"Very well, I ..." Rolfus started to say and then paused as something in the harbor drew his attention. "That's odd. We don't often see such a large Egyptian fleet here."

The aide rose and joined him at the window. A dozen ships bearing the sign of the Ptolemaic kingdom were coming into port. While they did get trade fleets in, usually, there were a handful or maybe ten ships in total. Twelve was a very large number. Large enough that Rolfus would have thought someone would have sent him word that such a large contingent was coming.

Even if they were not unloading and just stopping in, that many sailors pouring into the port would cause all kinds of havoc.

"Vercassixtos," Rolfus called out.

After a beat, the door opened and the praetorian who'd been standing outside his door entered.

"See about getting some more men down to the docks. Twelve ships just pulled in, and it's going to get very busy down there."

"Yes, Centurion," the man said, saluting.

'Gauls,' he thought wryly as the praetorian left. Every last one he'd met seemed to be born with a stick up their butt. They couldn't even say yes without it sounding like they were giving a blood oath.

He spared the ships one last look, noting how high they rode in the water, and then pushed it out of his mind. He had the dredging project to get started, and Vercassixtos was man enough to make sure the guards on the docks had everything they needed.

For the next twenty minutes, he went over the general plan for the dredging. They couldn't close the harbor entirely, so it would have to be done in sections. They'd start with the western half first, although he was sure he'd be getting messages of complaint from shipmasters and probably some logistics minister back in Kalb or

Britannia, since it would undoubtedly slow how much cargo could move through the port.

Still, if they wanted to replace him, they could go ahead and do it. If they wanted to ignore it until ships started grounding on the debris on the seabed under the docks, they could do that and see what happened then.

"Get those to the port master, and make sure to have a copy made and sent to Kalb. I want them to have it on record so I at least can say 'I told you what I was going to do' when they start yelling."

"A good precaution," the aide said, again with that smile, as he stood to leave.

Before the man could take a step, however, both were frozen in place by the report of rifle fire from outside the window. It was followed, almost instantly, by shouts and screams erupting from the direction of the docks. Rolfus rushed to the window, wondering what the fool Egyptians had done to cause gunfire.

He expected a brawl or something of the like down the hill at the docks. What he saw, instead, were swarms of armed men pouring from the Egyptian ships, overwhelming the unprepared dock guards in a matter of moments and shooting anyone in sight.

As he watched, the guards on the docks were completely overwhelmed. These men had been in the port a long time and were more accustomed to maintaining order than repelling invasions. They had in no way been prepared for this.

Neither had Rolfus.

"By all the gods," Rolfus mumbled, frozen in place.

The shock didn't last long. Rolfus had seen time in combat and fought against Carthaginian hordes. And he knew his duty.

"Go. Run and order the alarm sounded! Ring every bell in the city! And get a message to the harbor fort; I want those Egyptian ships blasted out of the water! Also, run up the signal flags. Any ships in the harbor need to flee. Tell them to make for Kalb or any other safe port. Tell them what's happening! Vercassixtos!"

The aide ran through the door, almost colliding with the praetorian who finally looked something other than prim and proper. Although, Rolfus wasn't sure shock was what he wanted to see on his chief praetorian's face. Outside the window, the invaders had already pushed beyond the docks, swarming into the nearby buildings. In the harbor, the Egyptian vessels had opened fire on the other ships, catching them completely off guard.

"Assemble your men and any other soldiers you can find. Don't let them engage piecemeal, we need a coordinated defense. Set up positions around the market square. Once we have sufficient numbers, we'll push towards the docks."

The praetorian nodded, not bothering with a salute as he ran out the door to begin putting together a defense of the city.

As Rolfus moved to follow him, the deep boom of larger cannon fire caused him to stop. The fort commander was a good man and hadn't waited for the orders to fire. Plumes of water erupted around the Egyptian ships as the gunners found their range.

Not that it was going to matter. The floating Trojan horses had already done their jobs and filled his city with hostile soldiers.

Part of him wanted to ask why? Why was this happening? Why were the Egyptians attacking them and killing his people? Not that it mattered. His duty was clear. Maleth was a key strategic point, vital to Britannian control of the central Mediterranean. Its loss would be catastrophic.

A thunderous explosion rocked the building, causing Rolfus to stumble. One of the Egyptian ships had taken a direct hit from the fort. It listed heavily, flames engulfing its deck.

Rolfus gave the harbor one last look before racing out of the building and down the winding streets toward the market square. The sounds of battle grew louder the closer he got to the harbor. As he rounded the final corner, he saw Vercassixtos had done his job, as dozens of men were already in the square with more coming by the minute. The ones already there were dragging furniture and carts to form makeshift barricades on the only thoroughfare that led to the harbor.

"Get that cannon into position!" Vercassixtos bellowed, pointing to a small fieldpiece being wheeled up by a group of soldiers. "I want a clear line of fire down the main road!"

Good man. He'd even thought to get the one small field piece they had. It was tiny by comparison to the ones in the fort, meant to be mobile enough to be pulled along with fast-riding cavalry.

However, it was also all they had. Rolfus knew he'd only be able to pull a hundred or so men at best, and not many more rifles than that to arm civilians, so they'd need every advantage they could get.

Rolfus climbed atop an overturned wagon to be able to see more clearly down the hill toward the docks. What he saw was not good. More Egyptian ships were coming into the port, disgorging fresh waves of soldiers onto the pier. The harbor fort was still fighting valiantly, its guns blasting away at the Egyptian ships, several of which were on fire with pillars of smoke rising from them. It also wasn't going to be enough. This port was meant to be protected by fleets, keeping invaders from ever getting this far, and was geared toward commerce, not combat. It was never meant to repel such an overwhelming force.

And overwhelming was the right word. He counted nearly thirty enemy ships now crowding the harbor. The fort's guns couldn't sink them fast enough. Even worse, he could see Egyptian troops swarming toward the fort itself, cannon fire from their ships providing covering fire as the soldiers attempted to breach the gates.

"We've assembled all the men we could find," Vercassixtos said.

Rolfus jumped down from his perch. "We hold this position at all costs. Get those barricades finished and make sure every man has plenty of ammunition. I want sharpshooters in the upper windows of those buildings."

They did the best they could with the time they had. Already, he could see the Egyptians pushing toward the city center where they were waiting. He started conscripting every able-bodied civilian he could find, and had a decent barricade going when the enemy got to them and finally realized there was still a resistance in the city.

"Here they come!" someone shouted.

A wave of Egyptian troops appeared at the bottom of the street, advancing quickly toward them. Rolfus raised his sword.

"Hold your fire!" he commanded. "Wait for my signal!"

He knew the fashion lately was independent fire, what with the trenches and all, but Rolfus had been in enough fights to know the effect of well-timed volley fire. He needed to break this wave, and that was the way to do it.

He waited until the Egyptians were barely a hundred yards away before yelling, "Fire!"

The crash of massed rifle fire was deafening. Billows of smoke blocked his view for a moment, filling the market square, but not so much that he couldn't see the entire front rank of the Egyptians go down as they were hit by the wall of lead.

He wasn't done yet.

"Cannon! Fire canister!"

The field piece belched flame, sending a load of metal balls scything through the Egyptians. Return fire began to pepper the Britannian positions, bullets whining past Rolfus's head and thudding into the barricades. A few of his people went down, but the difference in the death toll was massive, and they had only held their resistance for a few minutes before the attack crumbled.

"They're pulling back!" someone shouted triumphantly.

Rolfus allowed himself a grim smile as he watched the Egyptians retreat.

"Don't just cheer! Resupply and tend to the wounded. They'll be back, and in greater numbers."

The problem was that this time, they'd come up the main street toward the market and governmental center. Next time, they would be smart and come at them through alleys and side streets. They'd fill the houses overlooking the market and rain death down on them.

They couldn't remain here.

"We can't stay on the defensive," Rolfus decided. "We need to push them back, buy time for reinforcements to arrive."

His second-in-command, a grizzled veteran named Gaius, nodded in agreement. "What's the plan, sir?"

Rolfus outlined his strategy. They would advance in leapfrog fashion, one group providing covering fire while the other moved forward. It was a risky maneuver, especially given their limited numbers, but staying put would only result in them being overwhelmed.

"We move in five minutes," Rolfus told Vercassixtos. "They'll pin us in the next time they attack. Prepare the men to press forward. We'll go house to house, using the buildings for cover."

Vercassixtos looked grim, but he seemed to understand the reasoning behind the plan.

It took a few minutes to get everyone organized, and then they began to advance cautiously. As soon as they got one street in, he found exactly what he'd predicted; small groups of Egyptians in the alleyways, already coming for them. His men darted from cover to cover, while their comrades laid down suppressing fire as they pushed toward the docks. Again, he'd caught the Egyptians off guard, and the men in this second, more spread-out attack, began to fall back.

That was where his luck ended. His fear had been that this would turn into house-to-house fighting, and that was exactly what happened. Every building became a fortress, every street a killing ground. The cannon proved less useful in such close quarters, meaning it was limited to the central street while the praetorians and legionaries held to the buildings on either side.

They made slow but steady progress, pushing the Egyptians back toward the docks. But the cost was high. His men were being whittled down, losing a handful with every street they took. And always, there seemed to be more Egyptian soldiers coming up the hill toward them.

Things turned even worse when the guns of the harbor fort, which had provided a kind of background music to the fighting, suddenly fell silent. He knew what that meant. The fort had fallen, and soon, there would be a lot more Egyptians available to attack them.

He didn't even need to wait long. They had only made it another block when a large wave of Egyptian troops, likely those who had just taken the fort, surged into the street coming toward them, pouring into the side alleys and houses.

His men started to fall much more quickly and they were now in real danger of being overrun.

"Fall back!" Rolfus shouted. "Back to the market square!"

But it was too late. The sheer weight of the enemy numbers was overwhelming. Rolfus watched in horror as his cannon was overrun, its crew abandoning the gun and fleeing for their lives.

The retreat quickly turned into a rout. Rolfus and what remained of his command fell back through the city, taking whatever cover they could find. But it was a losing battle. Every time they tried to make a stand, fresh waves of Egyptian troops would flank them, forcing them to withdraw or be surrounded.

Finally, they found themselves pushed back to the government buildings. The ornate columns and stone walls provided some cover, and the wide steps leading up to the main entrance gave them a height advantage.

Not that it would be enough.

The Egyptians advanced cautiously, wary after the losses they had suffered. But they had numbers on their side, and worse, they had captured Britannian weapons. Specifically, the cannon that had been abandoned earlier.

"Take cover!" he yelled, just as the gun belched fire.

Canister shot ripped into the building. His men screamed and fell, shredded by the hail of metal. Rolfus himself was even hit, with a piece of shrapnel slicing across his cheek. He ignored it.

"Return fire!" he ordered, raising his own rifle.

But it was hopeless. Their ammunition was nearly spent, and for every Egyptian they felled, five more seemed to take his place while his men fell one by one, not to be replaced.

He leaned out to take another shot when a bullet struck his shoulder, spinning him around. He lay on the ground, dazed for a moment, staring into Vercassixtos's dead eyes, a neat hole in his forehead.

It was over. They had fought bravely, but only a handful of them remained, and most of those were wounded like he was. To continue would only result in more needless deaths.

"We surrender!" he shouted, his voice hoarse. "We surrender!"

His few remaining men echoed the cry, one finding a cloth to wave. Still, another two men died before the gunfire gradually died away. As Egyptian soldiers swarmed up the steps, Rolfus looked out over the city he had failed to defend. Smoke rose from dozens of buildings, and the streets were littered with bodies. In the harbor, he could see more ships arriving, bearing the standard of the Ptolemaic kingdom.

The island had fallen. He just hoped one of the ships managed to get away to sound the alarm before another port could be ambushed like his.

Chapter 13

Devnum

Lucilla walked with purpose, her head up and her face set like stone, as she crossed the courtyard and started up the steps toward the Imperial Forum. Ministers and others with business inside the palace complex moved out of her way when they saw her, and not simply out of deference.

She ignored them. She was there on a mission and the flood of telegraph messages routed through the port of Kalb had made it all the more imperative.

Not that there still weren't obstacles. One, in fact, was hustling down the steps to intercept her even as she neared the entrance to the seat of the Imperial Senate.

"Empress, I implore you to reconsider," Taenaris said, as worked up as she'd ever seen him. "This will make it even harder for us to get your bill through and it could alienate many of our supporters. They are still on edge from your last performance. This is a bad idea."

Lucilla didn't even slow down. "Bad ideas are all we have left."

She left him to follow in her wake. She knew he meant well, and he was an excellent politician, but he was as short-sighted as his colleagues. They'd grown complacent over the years of peace and had forgotten that inaction was the death of a people.

She could almost feel the tension as she entered the chamber and made her way to the open central floor. Senators huddled in small groups, having hushed but agitated conversations. As they should be. She knew that news of the attacks hadn't stayed secret. Word was already spreading through the city like wildfire.

Taking her place, Lucilla paused to allow the groups to break up and the men to take their seats. Most did so quickly, probably eager to find out what exactly happened and what she was going to do about it. Others were less prompt.

Petty shows of independence for men who had forgotten how they got their positions and to whom they owed their allegiance.

"Honored senators of the Britannic Empire, by now, I am certain you have heard about the treachery of the Ptolemies and their cowardly attacks on our ports. I wish I could tell you that we saw this coming or that we were prepared for this, but I cannot."

This was clearly not what the men had hoped she would say, as several gave their comrades side-eyed glances of worry.

"I can tell you that it could have been worse. While I cannot divulge all of the intelligence we are working with, we managed to raid a meeting between smugglers and high-level Egyptian officials several weeks ago that seems to have forced their plan into action early. Yes, the coordinated attacks on Maleth, Cyprus, and the trading outposts on the border of Egyptian territory were terrible and costly, but they have not crippled us. Our major ports and military outposts in the region remain safe and still able to prosecute the war. That being said, I think it is time this body considers its role in allowing these events to happen. The Ptolemies are opportunists. They did not join us in the fight against Carthage until they were certain we were going to win, and they would not have joined either side now if they weren't equally certain. We gave them that certainty. The endless debating and hesitation, instead of doing what we had to do, showed how *weak* we were and made them believe that we were not willing to do everything we could to stop this invasion."

A murmur of discontent rippled through the chamber at the accusation, but Lucilla ignored it and pressed on. "That weakness, and the defections it allowed, has caused the situation to become even more dire than it was when I spoke to you a month ago, begging for you to do what you *knew* we had to do. With Egypt and Greece now fully aligned with the Easterners, our manpower problem has become even more untenable and our strategic position has been severely compromised. Instead of being stopped near the borders of Sarmatia, the enemy now has multiple avenues for invasion. They are able to use Greece as a springboard into the continent and Egypt as their gateway to the Middle Sea. Instead of having to fight on one front, long as it is, we now must fight on three."

At least several of the senators had the good sense to shift uncomfortably, looking nervous at their role in the failure of the Empire to protect itself.

"I want to make the current military situation very clear. Our forces are stretched thin having to fight on multiple fronts across two continents. Eastern fleets persistently attempt to push northward along the African coast. They are testing us at every turn. We cannot afford to remain complacent in the face of such aggression. If we fail to act today, it will not be me who brings you tyranny, but the Easterners who will bring chains, swords, and fire to our lands. Our way of life, our freedoms, everything we have built and cherished, stands on the precipice of destruction. The only thing that will stop them is to sign the act of conscription and allow us to start getting the manpower we desperately need into the legions in time to stop this."

They had to know where she was going with her speech, but it wasn't until she named the conscription law that they reacted, with almost half the senators yelling in protest.

"We will never agree to this kind of law!" one shouted, his face red with anger. "It goes against everything we stand for!"

"You will agree to this," she said, speaking over him and the other shouting men. "You will agree to it because it is what you have to do. You will do it because it is your duty to your people and your Empire. I will not stand by while you neglect that duty. So I give you this one chance. Pass the necessary emergency measure, or I will dissolve this senate and appoint new representatives who grasp the severity of the crisis we face."

The chamber erupted in outrage. Senators leaped to their feet, shouting accusations and protests.

"Tyrant! You would destroy the very thing you claim to protect!"

She let them yell and vent. She'd known how that would go over, and she didn't care. This was what had to happen if she was going to ensure the Empire continued to stand. So she faced them, unmoved and impassive.

When their shouts finally began to fade, she said, "I say again, you have this one chance. Next time I come before this body, you will either willingly sign this law, or I will show you the steel of my resolve. The choice is yours, senators."

Eastern Germania

"Why bother? They haven't moved in days," a voice behind Gundomar said as he peered through a narrow firing slit in the earthen wall of the trench.

While the man was right in that the Easterners had been very quiet recently, except for the occasional exchange of rifle fire to make sure everyone kept their heads down, the attitude was very wrong.

This was the hardest problem with this new form of warfare. When they were marching from pitched battle to pitched battle, the men were always *doing* something. Active. It at least gave them something to focus on, even if it was coming up with new complaints about how much they had to march each day.

In the trenches, there were long days of nothing happening, just sitting in one spot, waiting for the enemy to do something. It bred complacency, which was as dangerous as any rifle bullet.

"Which doesn't mean you won't see any action today. Or tomorrow. So keep your wits about you, because when they come running, you're going to want to be ready."

As if on cue, a rifle crack split the air. A legionnaire, a fresh-faced recruit barely old enough to shave, ducked as a bullet whistled overhead.

"Gods!" Cassius exclaimed, his face pale. "That was close!"

Two soldiers who'd been standing near a firing step nearby quickly rose up and returned fire before hopping back down. There was no way of knowing where the transgressing bullet had come from, so their fire had been generally in the direction of the enemy trench. It, in turn, caused a few more bullets to come their way again, each much too high to be a threat.

This was the way of it, men shooting blindly back and forth, hoping to get lucky and not wanting to stay visible for long enough to become a target.

Mostly, it gave them something to do and to talk about to break the tedium.

"Can't hit the broad side of a barn, can you?" one of the men teased, elbowing the other in the ribs.

"Like you're any better. At least I hit the logs in front of their trench. Your shot went way over."

They went back and forth like this for several minutes until one of the younger men near them, a replacement who'd joined a few weeks prior, yelped. For a moment, they all thought something had happened, although the boy had been sitting on the ground, so it was unlikely that shrapnel or a bullet could have gotten him.

They figured out what the boy was screaming about when a large rat scurried between his feet, disappearing into a gap in the trenchwork. The young soldier's face flushed red as the veterans around him burst into laughter.

"Scared of a little rat, boy?" one of the optios chuckled. "Wait till you see what the enemy's got in store for us."

Gundomar could appreciate a little humor and camaraderie among the men, but all of them had taken their eyes off the observation slits. He'd just opened his mouth to reprimand them for their inattention when the world exploded.

The first shell hit maybe a hundred paces away, straight in the trench, showering them with dirt and splinters. He was looking in that direction when the shell exploded, and he saw a soldier, he couldn't tell who, literally torn apart by the force of the explosion before the concussive force threw Gundomar sideways, slamming him against the trench wall.

For a moment, all he could hear was a high-pitched ringing. The world was covered in a sea of dust, making it impossible to see anything. His senses returned slowly, including hearing the screams of his men.

Gundomar pushed himself up, his vision blurry and unfocused. He blinked hard, trying to clear the grit from his eyes.

"Incoming!" someone shouted.

Another explosion rocked the trench, a little further out, on the ground behind the trench this time. Gundomar felt the heat of the blast, fire and concussive force washed over the trench, causing all of the men still standing to duck.

"Take cover!" Gundomar bellowed, stumbling forward, grabbing soldiers and pushing them towards whatever shelter they could find. "Get down!"

The air was thick with dust and smoke, making it hard to breathe. Gundomar coughed violently, tasting copper in his mouth. He wiped his face, his hand coming away streaked with blood, whether his own or someone else's, he couldn't tell.

"Medic!" The cry came from further down the line. "We need a medic here!"

Gundomar turned to see a legionnaire crawling towards him, one leg missing and the other a mangled mess of flesh and bone, leaving a trail of blood in his wake.

"Mama," he whimpered, his face ashen. "Oh gods! Mama! Please, someone!"

Before Gundomar could reach him, another shell landed nearby, on the rim of the trench a dozen paces away. The explosion threw up a shower of dirt and debris, momentarily obscuring his view. When the dust settled, Aulus lay motionless, half-buried under a collapsed section of the trench.

Other men had been closer, and he could see hands sticking out of the logs, rock, and dirt rearranged by the explosion.

"Dig them out! There are men trapped under there!"

"We're coming for you!" one of the soldiers shouted encouragingly as they dug. "Hold on, lads! We'll get you out!"

The shelling continued unabated. As bad as it was each time a shell landed close by, Gundomar noticed that despite the intensity of the barrage, many of the shells were overshooting their position. Their aim was off. The shells that did hit were deadly, unlike anything he had been close to before, much more like their own new shells, but most seemed to explode where no one was. A small mercy nonetheless.

However they got these new shells, Gundomar knew this wasn't their whole plan. An assault would follow the shelling. They'd tried it with much less devastating rounds, and they'd try it here. Shaking off his daze, he grabbed a stunned soldier by the shoulders, physically turning him around and pushing him towards the firing step.

"On your feet!" Gundomar roared as he started getting more men into place. "Man your positions! They'll be coming soon!"

He moved down the line, repeating his orders and physically manhandling soldiers into place when necessary. Slowly, training began to overcome panic. Soldiers moved with purpose, taking up defensive positions or working to reinforce damaged sections of the trench. Even with the terror and excitement, Gundomar allowed himself a moment of pride in his men's resilience.

Now they needed fire of their own.

He hurried down the trench to make a call to headquarters for counter-battery fire, only to pull up short as he found the small telegraph station a twisted wreck of splintered wood and tangled wire. Without it, they had no way to call for support. There was no way command didn't know about the barrage, not with all the large-scale explosions, but it was still his job to report.

Gundomar's eyes fell on Pavo, a wiry young legionnaire who, although he had only been with them for six months, had earned the respect and even affection of the older veterans. He grabbed the young soldier as he was about to run by and pulled him to a stop.

"I need you to run a message back to command," he said, scribbling a hasty note on a scrap of paper. "We need immediate counter-battery fire on the enemy positions. Our location is being shelled with new more powerful explosives, and we expect an infantry assault to follow."

He pressed the paper into Pavo's trembling hands.

"You run like Cerberus is at your heels, boy. The lives of every man in this trench depend on you getting this message through. Do you understand?"

Pavo nodded. "Yes, Centurion!"

"Then go!"

Gundomar gave him a push towards the communication trench to get him going. As Pavo disappeared around the bend, Gundomar hurried back to his men.

The bombardment slackened as he got back, which meant they would be coming any time. They had played this game in the trenches enough times for him to know what was about to happen. The enemy was trying to soften them up before an attack, hoping to catch them with their heads down, hiding.

Pulling out a spyglass, he peeked through an observation slit. As if summoned by his thoughts, dark figures began to emerge from the trenches and into No Man's Land. He had to give it to them, they were doing it better than they had before, when they made a mad rush across open ground. This time, they were advancing in coordinated waves, using the craters as cover.

"Here they come!" Gundomar bellowed. "Steady now! Wait for my order!"

He watched as the first wave of Eastern infantry drew closer. Behind them, more soldiers poured out of their trenches, a seemingly endless tide of men.

A whistling overhead caught Gundomar's attention. He looked up, expecting to see more enemy shells, but instead saw Alliance shells exploding harmlessly behind the enemy lines.

It hit well short of the enemy batteries. Not a single one got close to the enemy guns. The counter-battery fire was completely ineffectual.

He couldn't focus on that now. The enemy was in effective range, where most of his boys would hit what they were aiming at. He just needed to wait until enough of them popped up and made a run for the next series of shell holes.

"Ready!" he shouted.

Rifles rose to shoulders, barrels pointing over the lip of the trench. Gundomar waited and watched.

"Fire!"

The sound was deafening as dozens of rifles discharged simultaneously. The first wave of attackers stumbled and fell back, having run into a wall of lead. That wasn't going to stop them.

Even as he watched, more men came out of the trench, scrambling over the bodies of their fallen comrades.

Worse, the volley had broken them up. They were much more spread out. Now, rate of fire was what mattered.

"Reload!" Gundomar ordered. "Fire at will!"

Men worked to reload their weapons as quickly as possible. They made a good showing of it. Most were trained and had been fighting for a while, and they had spent time drilling on firing quickly with the new boys, over the last few months, to make sure they were ready for a moment like this.

His men did a damn fine job, most firing every twenty to thirty seconds, loading and firing, loading and firing. Gundomar was next to one of the younger boys, trying to keep him going and calm, since they had a tendency to panic. All too often, they would load three or four bullets into the rifle before firing, leading to explosions and mishaps. The one closest to him, though, was doing a good job.

Gundomar was about to tell him that when, without warning, the soldier's head snapped back, a spray of blood erupting from his forehead as he dropped to the ground, eyes staring sightlessly at the sky.

Gundomar swallowed hard, pushing down the bile that rose in his throat. The boy was barely old enough to shave, and the centurion felt a moment of fury for his death. Not that there was time for grief. He grabbed the boy's loaded rifle and stepped up onto a shooting platform, firing a shot and seeing a man in the distance fall before hopping back down.

It wasn't his place to fire a gun. Stray shots were dropping his men now in ones and twos, and he knew his job was to stay in the trench, making sure everyone was firing and doing what they were supposed to do, but he wanted to just get one, to avenge the boy's death.

The Eastern soldiers kept coming, wave after relentless wave. For every one that fell, two more seemed to take his place. The men were fighting bravely, reloading and firing with impressive speed, but it wasn't going to be enough. They were getting closer, and their numbers seemed endless.

Suddenly, the whistle of incoming shells changed. It was lower, closer. Gundomar's first thought was that the enemy was shelling along the front even though their own men were in the way, but as the first shells landed, he realized with a jolt that it was Alliance artillery.

Explosions erupted across No Man's Land, much closer to the Western Alliance trenches than before. Eastern soldiers were caught in the blasts, their bodies thrown like leaves in a storm. The advance faltered as men sought cover in shell holes, desperate to escape the deadly barrage.

"That's it!" Gundomar shouted, his voice hoarse from yelling and the acrid smoke. "Keep firing! Give them hell!"

A cheer went up from his men as they witnessed the devastation wrought by their artillery. But Gundomar knew better than to celebrate too soon. The enemy had pushed through an artillery barrage before. Their guns couldn't cover all of No Man's Land and the enemy soldiers were a lot closer than the last time they'd tried a charge like this.

He was proven right minutes later when the Easterners began pushing forward again, some running flat out and others moving from cover to cover. They were going to get to his lines, his rifles and the artillery be damned.

"Grenades!" he bellowed. "Bayonets! Prepare for close combat!"

Men scrambled to comply, reaching for the fin-shaped grenades at their belts. This was the part he always worried about. There had been a few times when a man had pulled the strap on his grenade only to be shot before he could throw it, killing several of his comrades.

Thankfully, that didn't happen this time. Nearly all of the grenades landed among the advancing troops, and all made it out of the trenches. Explosions ripped along their ranks, as more of the enemy were cut down.

And yet, on they came.

Gundomar pulled his gladius, glad that the standard equipment still left officers with a sword, for when things got tight. The men had their rifles and bayonets, good weapons for hand-to-hand, but they were too cumbersome for officers, whose job it was to lead, and not shoot at the enemy. He had the dropped rifle from earlier, but the boy's bayonet was still on his body, and there wasn't enough time to go for it.

The first Eastern soldier vaulted into the trench, landing heavily on the muddy ground a few steps away. Gundomar didn't hesitate. He lunged forward, driving his gladius into the man's back before he had a chance to recover from his leap.

More enemy soldiers followed after him, pouring into the trench, engaging in brutal hand-to-hand combat with Gundomar's men. The narrow confines of the trench made it difficult to maneuver, and the fighting quickly devolved into a chaotic melee.

It was violent and brutal, and if his men were at full fighting force, they could have beaten this group easily. But they weren't. The artillery barrage they suffered had weakened them, with a lot of his people in the open when those first shells hit, and the rest shaken by the new experience.

Gundomar grabbed a loaded rifle dropped by one of the men next to him and fired point-blank into an advancing enemy soldier, then swung the butt of the rifle to catch another in the face. The impact sent the man reeling back, blood streaming from his broken nose.

All around him, his men were fighting for their lives. The young legionnaire who'd nearly wet himself earlier at the sight of a rat, was now battling like a demon possessed. He'd lost his rifle somewhere in the chaos and was wielding his entrenching tool like an axe, bringing it down with brutal force on any enemy soldier who came within his reach.

For a moment, things seemed to be at a stalemate. He was losing too many men, but the enemy assault was slowing, thanks to the artillery.

A commotion from further down the trench behind him drew Gundomar's attention. For a moment, he feared that somehow a fresh wave of enemy soldiers had managed to make it into the trench and were pushing to take this whole section, until he saw the cut of their pants and tunics. It was a wave of reinforcements, charging up from the rear from the communication trenches, led by Pavo, the lad he'd sent with the message earlier.

The quick-thinking boy had brought men back with him. The reinforcements slammed into the Eastern soldiers' flank, catching them by surprise.

His men rallied at his cry, finding new strength. With the reinforcements bolstering their numbers, they began to slowly but surely drive the enemy back. The fighting was still fierce, but the tide had turned.

It only took a few minutes for the last of the Eastern soldiers to be driven out of the trench or cut down where they stood. Those who could were scrambling back over the top of the trench, fleeing toward their own lines.

They had won, but the cost was high. Men lay sprawled in grotesque positions all along the trench. They died in a hundred ways, torn apart, burned, stabbed, and shot, some laying where they fell, killed instantly, others curled up, having died in agony, clutching at their wounds.

The enemy's attack had been repulsed, but at a terrible cost. The enemy had copied their new shells and maybe even the cannon. Which meant they were on even footing again.

The war was going to last a very, very long time.

Chapter 14

Port Caolros

The sickly-sweet stench of diseased sweat permeated the makeshift hospital wing. It was overwhelming. He made this trip every day, even with the quarantine in place, because he had to.

It was no different than standing on the main deck in the heat of combat, with shells smashing all around him, directing the battle. Danger took second place to duty.

The ward, a hastily erected structure of wood and canvas, was crammed with cots. Row after row of them. Men lay under thin blankets, their faces soaked in sweat, their breathing labored. He paused at the first row. A young sailor, eyes half-closed, twitched as he fought off a cough that threatened to overpower him. The sailor clutched a tattered scrap of cloth against his mouth. His neighbor on the adjacent cot fared little better, moaning through a fever that had left him delirious.

An orderly hurried forward with a bucket of water and set it on the plank flooring, refilling a small clay cup for him.

He recognized one of the older sailors, a man who served on the Bellona since the last war. He remembered the man's booming laugh and jovial manner. Now the skin on his face sagged and he lay curled on his side, his breathing shallow and ragged.

"Admiral," he said in a weak voice, trying to push himself up.

Valdar put his hand on the man's shoulder and gently pushed him back down. "No, don't strain yourself. You need to get better. We're going to need you soon."

"I'll be ready, Admiral. At your order."

In spite of himself, the man's eyes closed and he shuddered slightly as he lapsed back into unconsciousness. Valdar patted his shoulder and then stepped back, looking around before heading to the tent entrance where Doctor Phelan had just entered.

"Just the man I was looking to see. It looks worse," Valdar said, indicating the increase in the number of pads and cots from yesterday.

"It is. It's still spreading faster than we can contain it. I believe almost fifteen percent of the port's workforce is showing some level of symptoms now. That's double what it was two weeks ago."

"Are they all still sick? Is no one recovering?"

"Some pull through. Others do not. We're losing about three in ten, but half of those who contract it are no longer fit to work even when the worst of the symptoms abate. Long-term difficulty breathing, lingering weakness, swollen bellies and faces, dropsy, even some levels of madness. The range of long-term effects has been as wide as the people it affects, and many of them have been in some form debilitating."

"And nothing's working to slow it? Losing half of my workforce is not something we can recover from."

"Most of what we've tried has little effect, and we're left with just trying to keep them comfortable, controlling the worst of the fever with constant bathing, and easing the coughing where we can. The only thing that looks to have any effect is the tree bark the Mpongo healers recommended to us, but even that seems to work only a fraction of the time."

"But it is working?"

"Yes, to be clear, it isn't a cure, but it does seem to help with the symptoms when we can get it."

"If it works, then I will get you more. I'll ..." Valdar started to say when a young man came running into the tent, out of breath. "Easy, sailor."

"Ad... admiral," he said, trying to get enough air to talk. "An urgent dispatch from the capital."

Valdar took the folded note and opened it. The words hit him like a physical punch in the gut.

Admiral Valdar,

Ptolemaic forces have seized Maleth and several other ports along the Middle Sea. Their ships now raid our merchant vessels with impunity. You are required to return north immediately and make sail for the Middle Sea to end their piracy and retake the occupied ports.

-Her Imperial Majesty, Flavia Lucilla Germanicus, Empress of the Britannic Empire, Supreme Governor of Rome, Protector of the Realm

"You," he said, pointing at one of the guards. "Find the port commander and any captains you can, and have them meet at the commander's office. Send messages to any ships in the harbor, but they need to hurry. I want everyone there in twenty minutes."

As the man ran off, Valdar finished his assessment of the men in the hospital tent, but his mind was no longer on it. He couldn't believe the Egyptians would turncoat and support the Easterners, after everything the Empire had done to free them from the Carthaginians.

Maybe something had happened to push them that way, Valdar didn't know. His focus had been here, expanding the reach of the Empire south to protect it from incursion before the enemy ever got to Britannia's home water, and he was out of touch with things in the Middle Sea.

Not that any scenario Valdar could think of explained their treachery.

But, he couldn't just go now to get things moving, even though he wanted to. Getting all of the men he'd need to talk to together would take some time. Besides, he owed it to the injured men to finish his tour.

When that time was up, however, he practically sprinted to the commander's office, which was, in fact, a tent, one of many temporary structures still being used. With so much of the labor force ill and the forts still their main focus, the rest of the port would have to wait to be finished.

Most of his captains were there, minus the dozen that were out on patrol and Captain Einar, who was on his second trip back to Port Vikhavn for more supplies.

Valdar didn't wait for the men in port but not yet there to join them.

"The Ptolemaic Empire has betrayed us," Valdar said as soon as he was inside the tent, holding up the dispatch. "They've seized Maleth and other ports along the Middle Sea. Her Imperial Majesty commands us north immediately to address this threat."

The room erupted in exclamations of shock and anger.

"Those treacherous bastards," Bituitus spat. "While we fought the Easterners, they plotted against us."

"We should burn their harbors and ports," another said.

"I couldn't agree more," Valdar said. "And the Empress has ordered us to do just that. Well, to retake control of the Middle Sea from them, at least. But, we have a lot of things up in the air here, and we need to put this house in order before I sail off with the bulk of our fleet. This illness continues to spread through Port Caolros, construction remains incomplete on critical fortifications and dock facilities, and I doubt the fleet we sank will be the last we will face. The Easterners certainly haven't given up trying to come at us from this direction."

He let out a sigh and grabbed a stool, pulling it over to the head of the table where the men sat. Some of his vitriol from reading the news had abated now that he started talking. For an old sea hound like him, logistics was life and it had a way of settling him.

"I am going to take two-thirds of the fleet with me, and leave the remaining third here at Port Caolros, although you will have the duty to cover Port Vikhavn as well. Since I am leaving this section of the fleet, Captain Einar will have overall command while I am gone. I will have written orders for him when he returns, explaining everything I'm going to say here. We are going to split the ships remaining here into two squadrons. One will be responsible for providing direct support and protection of the two ports, but especially this one. Port Vikhavn can mostly protect itself with its fort, at least until we respond, but Port Caolros remains vulnerable until its fortifications are completed."

Because even signal flags had their limitations for a large enough fleet, taking time to travel the length of a battle line, his fleet was divided into three sections, one commanded by him directly and the other two commanded by his most senior captains. Which made it the natural dividing line when deciding what ships to leave behind.

"The other squadron will be responsible for patrolling the sea lanes out as far as reasonable to catch any Eastern ships trying to sail north."

"Admiral, with respect, if the Easterners strike with anything like the size of force they've used in the past, there's little either squadron can do to stop them," Captain Cruidne said.

"You're right, the risk is real," Valdar acknowledged. "But orders are orders. Also, consider the alternative. If Egypt controls the Middle Sea, they'll weaken the supply lines and our ability to reinforce our armies in Greece, to say nothing of what it does to the economy of not just the Empire, but all of the Western Alliance countries. It also puts us in a very precarious position."

"What of the sick?" Captain Dag asked. "A lot of us have crews down with the illness. I'm not sure any ship in the fleet can maintain a full crew."

"We'll consolidate healthy crews onto the ships remaining here. The ships sailing north will be very shorthanded, but we can bring on new men in Kalb before sailing into battle. It'll lower our efficiency, but I don't want to put you up against possibly terrible odds and leave you shorthanded at the same time."

All of the captains remaining behind looked visibly relieved at this news.

"Do your best to protect the port and what we are building here, but do not let yourselves be caught. I hate to say the men here in the port would have to be left on their own, but we need to maintain a mobile presence in the region, and I don't want the ships remaining behind to throw their lives away in an all-or-nothing defense. If it looks like you'll be overwhelmed, load up everyone you can and sail for Vikhavn. Harass the enemy fleet and keep eyes on it, but the survival of the fleets here is the paramount concern. We can rebuild the port, if need be. Any questions?"

Although there were sure to be a few before he sailed, he'd given the captains a lot to think about, and they all still looked stunned by the news he'd dropped on them.

He straightened, meeting each captain's eyes in turn. "Good. I know this is difficult, and we're going to have to face some difficult choices in the next few days, but we serve the Empire, and our duty is clear. Dismissed."

Devnum

Hywel was frustrated.

It wasn't an unusual state for him, and he knew many of his juniors found him difficult to work with, but this time, it felt different. Normally, he was frustrated because people wouldn't listen or were taking too long.

He wasn't, however, normally frustrated by a lack in his own ability. Even before meeting the Consul and gaining access to all the knowledge he had to share, Hywel had been supremely confident in his own ability.

Yes, he knew many of his 'revelations' in the past were incorrect, made by the misunderstanding of how sickness worked. But he'd been so good at what he did, and got his position now because of his ability to change to meet the needs at the moment and his confidence in his abilities.

Rarely did he find himself stumped, without even a guess as to what the problem was. Except that was exactly where he found himself now.

After receiving word of the illness plaguing Valdar's fleet, he'd ordered some of the sick sent here for observation and care, hoping the experience they'd had over the last few years with major outbreaks of disease and the Consul's guidance would help identify the cause of the illness.

The physician who'd gone with the fleet, a man named Phelan whom Hywel remembered training here but didn't have much connection to, had at first been resistant to sending the sick, fearing a new outbreak, even after Hywel's insistence that they had become quite good at containing the spread of diseases in the hospital.

Now that they were here, however, he was second-guessing his decision. Not because it had caused some kind of new outbreak, but because he had been stymied by this disease in ways he hadn't been before.

He had just started to make his rounds of the quarantined section, set aside from the men in the hospital, and they were much the same as they had been at his last visit the day before, minus a few empty cots from sailors who had not survived the night.

He paused at the bedside of a particularly ill sailor, noting the man's jaundiced skin and labored breathing.

"How long has he been like this?" Hywel asked the attending nurse.

"Since yesterday evening, Doctor. His fever spiked during the night, and the chills started shortly after."

Hywel nodded, picking up the clipboard attached to the bed. An interesting invention from the Consul. Not as direct in its applications as some of the other technology he had introduced, but it did make keeping the pages of paperwork that had become part of the medical profession easier to keep track of.

Hywel had been resistant at first, but there was something to being able to quickly see the history of a given patient, what had been tried on them, and all the variables of their case without having to remember anything.

This man's notes were not good. Nor was the next, a man who'd been suffering from severe chills and profuse sweating for the better part of a day but had been otherwise only slightly ill when he'd arrived.

The progression of the disease was concerning. Worse was how varied the symptoms were. High fevers, respiratory distress, skin discoloration all came with the disease, but not in any recognizable pattern. Some patients exhibited all of these, while others showed only a few. It was a puzzle.

The junior physician, who'd been standing at his elbow while he looked over the records, asked, "Doctor Hywel, have you found any treatments that seem to be working?"

"Unfortunately, no. The best we can do for now is try to manage their symptoms and hope they pull through. We have tried several of the Consul's cures, but nothing seems to alter the course of the disease itself."

The man's face fell, although Hywel was fairly certain the man had known what he was going to say. Even men who were more learned sometimes let hope overrode their better judgment.

Something had been bothering him for the last few days, however. Seeing the head nurse of this section enter the ward, Hywel waved her over.

"I need a detailed log of all staff illnesses for any who've worked in this section or been in contact with those who've worked in here in the past few months. Not just since the sailors arrived. And gather any reports from visiting physicians or apothecaries who may have treated the staff."

The nurse looked puzzled. "All staff illnesses, sir? Even before the sailors came?"

"Yes. I want to rule out any possibility of a milder form of the same disease circulating among the staff. We need to be thorough."

This was where the Consul's insistence on constant note-taking would come to some use. As the nurse hurried off to retrieve the records, Hywel couldn't shake the feeling that he'd seen something like this before. Not exactly the same, but similar enough to niggle at his memory.

They'd had an outbreak six months ago that had given them a lot of trouble in spite of the Consul's emphasis on hygiene, and a year ago, one that had managed to escape their quarantine ward even when the staff that worked there were also quarantined.

He remembered the panicked notes from his staff and the difficulty in getting enough people in to properly work with the sick. They'd had to send out to Londinium to borrow some of the people sent there to help combat it.

He hadn't had any calls like that this time, and it bothered him, considering how rampant the disease was at Port Caolros.

When the nurse returned with a stack of infirmary logs, Hywel thanked her and began to review them carefully, paying close attention to the dates of onset and the descriptions of symptoms. He cross-referenced the staff illness logs with the timeline of the sailors' arrival and the onset of their symptoms.

He probably could have had one of his staff do this work, but he wanted to be sure before he acted on it. However, after an hour of carefully going over every record, he'd found no correlation between the staff illnesses and the sailors' disease. Several staff members had experienced short bouts of fever and coughs, but these were scattered throughout the past months and didn't cluster after the sailors' arrival. More importantly, none of the staff illnesses matched the specific symptoms of the disease affecting the sailors.

Finding the nurse again, he asked, "What about other patients in the hospital? Were any admitted around the same time as the sailors? Have there been any recent visitors who reported feeling unwell?"

"No, Doctor. Other than these men, things have been fairly slow since winter ended and none of those who have come in have presented with similar symptoms. We've had a slight increase in cases of breathing problems, but nothing that is out of the ordinary with what we saw last year. There haven't been any major outbreaks in months."

Hywel nodded. That was what he thought, but he wanted to double-check to make sure. These men had been here for almost two weeks now, which should have been enough time for secondary infections to manifest if the disease were contagious.

"So it's not spreading person-to-person. If it were, we would have seen secondary infections by now, especially among the caregivers."

"That's good news, isn't it?"

"In a way, yes," Hywel agreed, realizing he had been talking out loud. "But it also means we're dealing with something more complex. If it's not contagious in the usual sense, then the illness must be linked to something specific to the region or the men who were stationed there. It could be food, water, or some environmental condition. Perhaps they were exposed to a toxin at the port. Were any provisions brought from the sailors' ships?"

"I don't know, Doctor."

"Go check, please. If so, I would like them brought here so we can examine them."

As the nurse went to check on the provisions, Hywel continued to ponder the situation. The lack of person-to-person transmission ruled out many common diseases, but it also made the source of the illness more elusive.

When the nurse returned, she brought a small sack of provisions that remained from the voyage that had delivered the men.

One of the things Sorantius had been working on for months had been chemicals to detect some known toxins. Although originally intended for non-consumables, mostly rock and metal to help with sickness that was a problem in some Caledonian mine where some of the smelting plants were releasing toxins into the air, they were able to be used with other things.

It wouldn't rule out all toxins, but it could rule out some. The nurse, however, did not return back to her duties after handing it off.

Instead, she said, "Doctor, I've been thinking about what the sailors told us when they first arrived. They kept mentioning how humid it was at the port. Some of them talked about 'bad air' making them sick."

Hywel raised an eyebrow. "Bad air?"

"Yes, they described stagnant water and a heavy, oppressive atmosphere. I know it's an old idea, but I thought it might be worth mentioning."

"I appreciate you trying to think wider, and while the environment may indeed play a role, I don't think it's as simple as 'bad air' causing the disease." He paused, choosing his words carefully. "Based on the Consul's notes, we know that disease is primarily transmitted through the small 'germs' he has described to us, not simply through atmospheric conditions. Better yet, everything we have been able to study has suggested the Consul is right. But, you might actually have a good thought. The humid climate and stagnant water the sailors described could certainly provide an ideal breeding ground for these germs. We know they breed better in warm, moist conditions. It's how those germs get into people's systems that I'm more concerned with. What's transmitting it. I would say that it was not easily transmitted from person to person, but the doctor in Port Caolros keeps highlighting how quickly the disease is spreading, which does make me think it's something there that's causing it."

The nurse looked thoughtful. "Something in the environment?"

"Yes. Whether it's in the food, the water, or carried by some local insect or animal, the source of this illness seems to be localized to that area. The challenge now is to identify what that source might be. I'll have to send a note to the doctors there to get us more information about that, and see if we can't isolate the cases. See if there are any local plants or animals that might carry disease or perhaps something in the water supply."

The nurse nodded and headed back to her patients. He appreciated her thinking and willingness to express her thoughts. It's what he wanted of all of his personnel, even when he thought they were wrong.

Now, he just had to get some answers to his questions.

Chapter 15

Lucilla set aside another report detailing Egyptian raids on Britannian merchant vessels. They were getting bolder by the day. Kalb had started to send out patrols to slow some of the bleeding, but most of the experienced captains were with Valdar, and until he arrived, the bulk of their warships were escorting convoys to the front in Italia and up into Greece to help supply the lines being built there.

She knew he was hurrying, but the bleeding needed to stop if they were going to get things under control. With the sudden adoption of the new shells by the Easterners, almost certainly made possible thanks to the smuggling operation uncovered by Medb, they needed those supplies on the front more than ever.

Ky had already started moving much of their logistics to the rail lines stretching from Gaul all the way to Greece and the Far East, but it was much slower than sending ships full of supplies, which they had been doing.

Worse, bottlenecks had already started to happen, which would further slow down the amount of supplies that could get to the front. The carry-on effects of this were going to be felt far and wide.

She pulled out another sheaf of paper to write yet another message to Valdar to urge him on when something caught her attention. At first, it was at the edge of her consciousness, and it took a moment for her to work out what it was. It was like the normal sounds of the city, people going about their day doing the work that kept the city working, but angrier. Sharper. The volume was also growing steadily until she discerned the shouts mixed with the general din of noise.

Frowning, Lucilla rose from her desk and walked to the window to look out at the streets below. What she saw made her breath catch. A mass of people pressed against the palace gates and stretched down the thoroughfare into the distance, spilling over into every one of the surrounding streets. Here and there people were carrying banners, crude cloth signs with hastily painted slogans condemning conscription. Others took more active means to show their displeasure, hurling stones over the gates. For now, it was just in the direction of the palace, clattering harmlessly in the courtyard, but here and there the projectiles started hitting guards.

She could see more people arriving every moment, causing the sea of humanity to surge forward and crash against the gate like a relentless tide.

"Cynwrig!" she called to her guard. "Send men to reinforce the gates and ensure every entrance is double guarded. And send for Commander Faenius immediately."

He nodded and hurried to carry out his orders.

What bothered her was that there hadn't been any sign of this the day before. Usually, these kinds of things built over days, with smaller groups, the core of those upset over whatever had the masses riled up, yelling for change, and then the number of people increasing steadily as more learned about whatever the outrage was.

Rarely did unrest happen all at once like this. Not without help. It wasn't hard to figure out where that help had come from. The proposed conscription law had not been made public and she was certain the news of them didn't come from her people.

Senators, on the other hand, had every reason to release news of it, especially after she'd threatened them with dissolution if they failed to pass the measure.

A merchant in rich clothing climbed atop an overturned cart and started yelling. She couldn't hear what he was saying, but a moment later the crowd began to chant, 'Our sons, not your soldiers!' It wasn't hard to work out what he'd said.

She was amazed by the scale and coordination of this. They had gone to extreme lengths to make this happen, and it wasn't their concern for the youth of Britannia that drove them. Of that she was certain. It wasn't even about their positions in the senate.

This was about money and power.

When choosing senators, each of the leaders of the three polities had picked men of status because they needed their support in creating the Empire. For a time, that had worked, but many of these men had grown fat and rich, finding ways of taking what they knew and creating policies they could turn to their advantage.

Some remained dedicated servants, to be sure. But enough were more concerned about their own coin purses, or the continued support of wealthy patrons, than the future of the Empire, that they were willing to send a mob against the palace rather than agree to something that could cost them money in the short term.

They'd rather see the Empire fall than their profits decline.

The mob continued to grow as she watched, with more groups arriving from side streets and pouring around the sides of the palace complex, swelling the crowd's numbers.

"Their lands, their fights!" came a new chant from multiple points in the crowd.

Again, this felt more coordinated than spontaneous.

"Your Highness, these are being distributed throughout the city," Commander Faenius said, walking into her office without preamble and thrusting several printed pamphlets toward her.

It confirmed what she'd feared. The pamphlets painted a nightmarish vision of her conscription proposal, claiming that all young men would be seized immediately from their homes and thrust into service, that entire families would be drafted, that Britannia was transforming into a military dictatorship under her rule.

Worse, she knew some people would believe it. Carthage had essentially done that in the last war, and enough of those from the continent who'd escaped their service had migrated into Rome and told their story that it had become common knowledge.

There had even been a few plays on the topic, children torn from their families and the harrowing journey they'd been forced to endure to get back home. She'd seen a few of them and they were well done, but it kept this very thing in the popular consciousness.

Primed the people's fears.

"This is deliberate misrepresentation," she said, furious. "How many of these are circulating?"

"Thousands, at least. They appeared overnight. Your Highness, the situation out there is deteriorating quickly. While the majority remains non-violent, certain elements are becoming more aggressive. We've identified several agitators we believe are fueling the situation."

"Do they have any connection to senators?"

"I don't know, but we can look into it."

"Do it. I want to know who, specifically, is pushing this. We also need to find out how they're managing to print and distribute this many pamphlets so quickly without our knowledge."

"Private printing presses," Faenius replied. "They've been springing up across the city, primarily producing entertainment, printing plays and stories quickly enough to be very cheap for the people. We should have been monitoring them more closely."

"Or controlling them entirely," Lucilla said, although she also knew that wasn't practical.

Now that people had access to printing, and more people were becoming literate, they all wanted some kind of printed text, both for the enjoyment of it and as a status symbol.

Faenius nodded slightly before getting back on task. "Your Highness, with your permission, I can deploy the praetorians to disperse this mob before it gets further out of hand. If we allow this to continue unchecked, it will escalate to riots and looting. A swift show of force now could prevent that."

"No. That's exactly what they want, Faenius. The senators are hoping we'll crack down violently, both on private commerce and on these protesters. They want me to react like a tyrant so they can use it against me. Probably to force me to give in to their demands, although I'm sure if we act rashly enough, a few might have higher aspirations."

She doubted any of the senators would believe they could make themselves Emperor using public support, but what men thought they could do and the reality of the situation was often not the same thing.

"With respect, Your Highness, peaceful dispersal may not be possible at this point. The crowd is starting to get very worked up and the agitators among them are deliberately trying to provoke violence. We should at least prepare for the likelihood that force will be necessary."

"I understand your concerns, but we have to find a way to make it work without resorting to violence. If we lose public support, everything becomes exponentially more difficult. No serious injuries, Commander. You may contain and control the crowd, but I want no clubs swinging unless absolutely necessary for defense."

Faenius was clearly not happy with this command. "And if they refuse to disperse?"

"Then corral them and wait them out, although even in that case, I want the primary agitators brought in for questioning. Quietly, if possible. Once this immediate crisis passes, I want surveillance maintained on the printing operations we identify as having produced these pamphlets. We need to know which senators are behind this so we can watch for similar moves in the future."

"It would be simpler to shut them down entirely," Faenius said.

"I know, but Ramirus once said something to me when I complained about leaving a known dissident in place, instead of arresting him. It is better to know about the enemy and keep tabs on them, than force them underground and have no idea what they're doing. I think that's the case here."

Faenius looked like he didn't buy that entirely, but saluted and said, "As you command, Your Highness. I'll see to it personally."

Lucilla returned to the window, watching the crowd below continue to swell. She should have anticipated this move. They'd been too quiet after her threat. She'd known they'd do something, but she hadn't considered this, and it was the obvious move for them.

Self-recriminations, though, would get her nowhere. Now she needed to figure out her countermove and shut this nonsense down once and for all.

Carthage

The audience chamber had half a dozen people in it when Medb walked past the guards and into the room. It looked to be mostly local officials, but she did recognize the captain of the Britannian warship currently docked in the harbor, which suggested this was more than just one of the regular meetings that were needed to keep a city the size of Carthage running.

She also didn't have time for it to continue.

"Leave us," she said curtly as soon as she approached the group.

The warship captain, a man she didn't know well, looked a little perplexed as men often did in situations like this, but the locals knew her well, bowing and taking their leave as ordered. The captain gave a glance at Cormac, still obviously confused, but was at least smart enough to take the hint and followed the other men out of the room without questioning the command.

Cormac was used to her work persona.

As the last of them filed out, he turned to her and said, "If this is about cargo into the city, I've already taken steps to address that. I know a few supplies from Italia and Greece are running low, but I've spoken with the main shipping factor and made sure he will have resupplies here before any run out. I did have to guarantee him more protection after that last raid off the coast of Sicilia, though. I've spoken to Niall, and he has assured me that Kalb will increase patrols from here to the mainland, and I've convinced the factor to change the routing of the goods he brings in. And yes, I've considered the drop in volume from goods having to cross the continent by train rather than go around by ship, but we will just have to deal with that. Commander Niall is even looking into building up one of the smaller ports on the southeastern side of

Hispania to help expand capacity. It'll allow for more ships to pass through while still being close enough for Kalb to protect."

"I'm pleased that you have a handle on everything, but that is not why I'm here."

"Then what is it?"

"I've been summoned back to Devnum,"

Cormac's face fell slightly as he asked, "Why?"

"The Empress didn't say, but it likely pertains to Egypt's sudden betrayal."

"You don't think … I mean, the senate isn't looking for someone to blame, are they? They can't possibly place it on you?"

"I doubt it, or if they are, I doubt it will be very successful. I did my duty and uncovered the Egyptian treachery before it happened. It's hard to say if I found it just before they launched their attacks, or if my discovery of their actions forced them to launch their plans early, but either way, if there's blame to be had, it doesn't rest on me."

"I'm not sure facts and what people choose to believe, or at least where they choose to place the blame, are always in agreement," Cormac pointed out. "But still, this is a terrible time to recall you. Egyptian troops could move westward any day now, threatening our holdings in North Africa."

"I'm well aware of the situation."

"I know you are, but several trading stations on the outskirts of Egypt have already fallen. It's clear they're planning to march this way. We can't just leave the city to some junior commander. The moment we shift our forces to counter Egypt, the rebels inside Carthage will see an opportunity to strike. We'll have another internal crisis on our hands! This is a terrible time for us to return home."

"You misunderstand, Cormac. You're not going anywhere. Only I am."

"What? Why?"

"Because our responsibilities are different. We were sent here for me to uncover suspected rebel activity, which admittedly has been sidetracked by finding out that the Egyptian's actions were also going through Carthage, and you were sent to replace the previous governor and get the city under control. What happened with the Egyptians takes precedence and is pulling me away from my previous assignment, but your responsibilities remain. You need to keep Carthage from descending into chaos. That includes dealing with Egyptian forces in the east and continuing my work to root out the remaining rebels in the city, which will hopefully be weaker now that they aren't being supplied by the Egyptians."

"Hunting down people isn't my strength. I'm a soldier, not a spy."

"You've faced tougher assignments, Cormac. What you dealt with in Hispania at the end of the last war wasn't so different. I have faith in your ability to handle it, though I won't pretend it will be easy."

"I suppose you're right, and you have been training Claudius, so I suppose he can ..."

"I'm taking Claudius with me," Medb said, feeling a little bad at having to pull the rug out from under Cormac's feet twice in the same conversation.

"You can't be serious! You're leaving me critically short-handed when I need reliable officers the most!"

"I know it's not ideal for you, but Claudius has proven quite good at the intelligence side of things. He's smart, observant, and adaptable. Traits not easily found in most soldiers. I believe a lot of the issues with the Egyptians, at least with the smuggling end of what they were doing, originated in Devnum, and I will need him to track those down, especially once I leave."

"Once you leave? What do you mean? You won't be staying in Devnum either?"

This was the part of the conversation Medb had been dreading the most. Ever since finding out what the Egyptians were up to, Medb had been considering that her focus the last year and a half had been in the wrong place. She'd let herself get drawn into minutiae instead of keeping an eye on the bigger picture as Ramirus had taught her. The message from the Empress was simply the prodding she needed to correct that error.

However, she knew Cormac wouldn't be pleased. He had become very protective of her and had a tendency to go overboard when he thought someone was putting her in danger.

Even when that someone was her.

"I don't know yet. That's how bad our intelligence is right now. I'm not even sure where to start with something like this. All I know is that we've been behind in intelligence since the war began. We know too little about the Easterners and we've been completely reactive for too long. I intend to change that."

"If you mean going east, then I forbid it. No one who has gone east has ever returned, and I'm not going to allow you to go charging off recklessly ..."

"Forbid?" she asked coolly.

She knew he meant well, but there were times when his more ... traditional tendencies showed themselves, and she had to remind him that she wasn't born some helpless girl. She might not be a queen any longer, but the list of people allowed to tell her what to do was very small, and he was not on it.

"A poor choice of words."

"Indeed. I appreciate your worry, but please give me more credit than that. I won't promise this won't take me to the east, but I do not go 'charging off recklessly.' What I will do is follow leads wherever they take me. I promise not to leave you completely alone in Carthage. I've already sent a message to the Empress that you need additional help here with me gone."

"Of course, you're right. I know you're smart enough not to put yourself in danger. I just ... I'll miss you."

Medb gave him a warm smile and stepped closer, putting her arms around him.

"And I'll miss you, too. I promise not to do anything so reckless that I won't be able to come home to you."

"Good," he said, leaning down and kissing her.

"You know," she said, breaking the kiss. "If you wanted me to stay, you should have led with this. It's much more convincing."

Cormac just shook his head and kissed her again.

Chapter 16

Southern Wistla River

Leodgar walked along the iron top deck of the Isarna, enjoying a few minutes of calm night air. These iron ships were a miracle and he'd shown dozens of times over the last eight months just how powerful they were, but being inside of one was a little like being inside of a closed furnace.

They were cramped, hot, and everything inside of it felt like it was covered in a layer of coal dust from the constantly burning boilers powering the entire thing.

Fresh air had truly become a luxury at this point.

Worse, the opportunities to take these small escapes out of the ship were few and far between, as most of the time the enemy was never far away, trying to find a way across the river. It was only after weeks of relative quiet on the opposite bank that he felt safe enough for these short sojourns, and then only in the evening when the moon was overcast like tonight.

And only for a few short minutes.

Leodgar closed his eyes and listened to the water lapping against the armored plating and the sounds made by the small number of Britannian legionaries on patrol on their side of the river.

In another time and place it would be almost peaceful.

With one last deep breath of fresh air, Leodgar turned and went back to the top hatch of the ship, descending back into the armored confines of the vessel.

Most of the men were in hammocks stretched along the gun deck. It wasn't luxurious living, but men had an uncanny knack for becoming accustomed to all sorts of accommodations.

Just outside of the ship's pilot house, from where the ship was commanded and steered, he found Appius already waiting for him.

The man looked a little green.

The youngest of his officers, he knew how he would have felt in the young man's place. It was going to be his first time in command of a watch, which was a big moment in any young officer's career. Even though they were battling a war, it didn't take away the duty to train the next generation of leaders in the legion, especially in the navy, which had not existed a decade ago.

"Sir," Appius said, standing at attention when he noticed Leodgar.

"Stand easy," he said, patting the young man's arm. "Are you ready for your first watch?"

"Yes, sir. I ... Yes, sir."

Leodgar smiled again. "You'll do fine. The opposite bank has been quiet all day. We haven't even seen a picket today. Which doesn't mean they aren't over there. Quiet and safe are two very different things. You can't let your guard down."

"No, Sir. I mean, Yes, Sir."

"You're not alone on this stretch. There's a century spread over this mile on the friendly side of the river doing some reconnaissance. Not enough to fight, but they will be keeping an eye on the opposite side. Part of your job tonight is to be in regular communication with their pickets. I'm not expecting them to see anything, but protocols must be maintained, and it will be good practice for both of you."

"Yes, Sir."

"Good. We'll stay with a skeleton watch tonight. Keep the gun crews ..."

Leodgar's next words were swallowed up by a thunderous explosion, the blast close enough to make the ironclad's armor plates shudder. More shells exploded seconds later, causing both men to grip the low ceiling to brace themselves as the ship began to shake more violently.

"Battle stations!" Leodgar bellowed, already running into the pilot house. "Every man to his gun!"

Pushing a sailor out of the way, Leodgar pressed himself up against the observation slit, trying to see what was out there in spite of the overcast night. He could have kicked himself, walking along the top of the boat, oblivious to the Easterners setting up on the opposite bank.

There. The telltale flashes of enemy artillery and rifles on the eastern bank.

"Opposite shore. Cannon fire two points aft of the midline. Have gunners spread fire across the entire section of the bank and signal the infantry on the shore to bring up units."

The crew scrambled to carry out their orders, although the delay in his cannons opening fire felt like an eternity. Part of his brain defended them, since most had been settling down for the night and everyone was caught off guard by the attack, but he did not like giving the Easterners free rein in attacking his ship.

A tremendous impact rocked the Isarna. He'd been looking down that side of the ship when it went off, and saw the shell explode as it hit the water, billowing out into a fireball. It wasn't solid shot like they'd faced before. These were explosive shells, just like the ones they'd started using.

They'd been hit by the concussive force and shrapnel, not a shell itself. The explosion seemed a little weaker than the shells they were using, but not by much. The armored plates on this ship were thick, but he worried that they would not be strong enough to deflect a direct hit by one of those shells.

His cannon finally opened fire, and explosions of their own began tearing up the opposite shore. Except for brief illumination when a shell exploded, however, he had no idea how accurate his fire was or where, exactly, the enemy cannon was firing from.

It wasn't direct fire, which had to mean they'd somehow also copied the howitzer design, allowing angled fire which gave their cannons some added protection.

Another shell exploded off the port bow, closer this time. The enemy gunners were finding their range.

"Signal the shore battery!" he ordered. "We need illumination! And tell them to launch one of the damn observation balloons."

Moments later, a distinctive whump sound came from the western bank. The firing sound was much different to a cannon, but distinctive enough that he could hear it over all the noise. A bright light exploded above the river, slowly drifting down, casting harsh white light over the river. The illumination revealed a nightmarish scene; dozens of small boats packed with Eastern troops were already on the water, while more waited at the far bank.

Everyone on the opposite bank froze at the sudden light. They may have seen the artillery in action, but this was new. He'd made sure his men knew enough about it not to freeze, since the light did not last long, but it must have been a surprise when the shoreline lit up like midday.

It had shocked him the first time he'd seen it demonstrated.

"All guns, target those boats!" Leodgar commanded. "Priority to the closest craft!"

The Isarna's rifled cannon roared in response. The first shot caught a boat packed with soldiers square in the center, the explosion ripping it in half and throwing men, and parts of men, into the water for dozens of paces in every direction.

More cannon fire followed as the gun crews found their targets. Shell after shell slammed into the approaching boats. Some missed, sending up towering geysers of water, but others found their marks. The river began filling with debris and bodies.

Another shell struck close by, sending water cascading over the iron deck. Leodgar ignored it, trying to focus on something new in the water. A group of boats were coming out very close together, but not pushing hard toward their position. They were moving slowly, staying a little off the shoreline.

It took him a moment to make out the thing they were dragging between them. Some kind of wooden structure, like logs lashed together, with some kind of planking lashed to their tops. He'd never seen the likes of it before, but its function was obvious.

It was some kind of portable bridge they could put in place to get men across the river quickly. A clever design, and also a sign that there were a lot more men on the other shore than he thought if their plan was to storm across once the bridges were laid down.

"They're trying to bridge the river," he called out. "New priority targets, sink those log rafts! Make sure to signal the men on the shore."

His gunners adjusted their aim, blasting away at the makeshift bridges. He wished the infantry had more than a single cannon. The rifles were nice, but even with the flares, visibility wasn't great and they didn't have enough men to mass fire. What was going to win this battle were high explosives, and he could only get half his tubes into the battle.

One shell found its mark, blasting timber and bodies skyward. But there were more coming, and in the intermittent flashes of artillery fire, he could see dozens of small boats weaving between the larger pontoons.

"Sir!" A sailor pointed through the observation slit. "Look!"

In the darkness, several boats had slipped dangerously close. Grappling hooks sailed upward, clanging against the iron hull. Ropes were pulled taut as the enemy prepared to climb them.

They were well under the angle his guns could reach.

"Repel boarders!" Leodgar shouted.

His men started to toss grenades out the gun ports, which forced most of the boats back, but one had men already halfway up the side, trying to get up quickly. If they had any kind of explosive on them, they could do serious damage to his ship.

One of his crewmen, a particularly brave man who he'd have to single out for recognition if he survived, popped up out of one of the top hatches and sprinted across the deck. The sailor slashed through one rope, then another, sending the climbers into the water. The other two ropes that were still attached went slack as men fell off the sides and into the water.

The crewman had come prepared and reached to his belt, producing one of the fin-stabilized grenades, yanking the safety strap free and hurled it into the water where the men had fallen.

The explosion sent a column of water and pieces of men raining down against the ship's hull.

"Tell that man ..." he began, and then the world erupted in flame and thunder.

Leodgar was picked up by the force and hurled into the opposing wall, bouncing off the wood and metal interior before slamming into the deck, his head cracking against the metal. For a moment, everything was blurry and he could barely focus on anything but the copper taste in his mouth.

Looking up, he realized he could see clouds and the occasional star. Actual stars. It took another beat for his brain to recognize the massive hole torn in the pilot house roof.

Around him, several of the men he'd been standing with lay motionless, dead, including poor Appius, who was staring at him with lifeless eyes, a gigantic gash in the side of his head.

Leodgar shook his head to clear it, and the sight of the young officer, before pushing himself off the deck. Blood ran down his face, and his left arm hung useless.

"Damage report!" He said, trying to maintain his balance as the deck pitched beneath him.

"Five dead here, sir," someone called out. "Steering mechanism's damaged!"

"Get damage control parties moving," Leodgar ordered, pressing a hand to his bleeding scalp. "And keep those guns firing!"

"Sir, we're taking on water below. That last hit opened up the hull."

"Open the starboard ports and start bailing," Leodgar commanded. "Get the carpenter's mate down there. We patch what we can but keep those guns firing."

Moving back to the observation slit, he watched more boats push forward across the river. The water between the river banks had become a hellscape of fire, smoke, and bodies.

They were going to be swamped soon.

"Reload with canister!" Leodgar ordered.

Enemy artillery continued to pound their position. A shell burst directly overhead, showering shrapnel down through the open roof, killing a sailor right behind him.

The enemy fire rate had slowed, but his guns were now completely occupied with the boats trying to board them, giving the enemy gunners free rein.

He was considering if they should abandon the ship and burn it, try to escape to the shore, when fresh explosions began to walk across the eastern shore, hammering the enemy guns and men still trying to launch boats.

Several of the explosions were deeper inland, away from the shore. They must have hit an enemy gun and its limber directly, as an explosion rippled into a much larger explosion that seemed to cascade down a line. It was as if some great beast had burned a line down the fields behind the shoreline, sending flames streaking into the sky.

The enemy had set up their guns and powder stores too close together, allowing them to be caught in a kind of cascade.

Running to the other side and looking out the opposite observation slit, he saw multiple Britannian field pieces opening up, along with maybe a hundred rifles.

The reinforcements had arrived.

He could even see that one of the observation balloons was up, which explained how they were hitting those enemy pieces so accurately.

The combined firepower of the ironclad and shore artillery converged on the enemy positions. Through the smoke, Leodgar could see muzzle flashes and watched as they became fewer and more sporadic.

The enemy was still sending a few boats into the water, but with their cannons gone and the massive explosion in their rear, the fight had been taken out of them. Another few minutes and what boats were still left in the water turned around and tried to retreat. The crude bridge pieces had been thoroughly shattered, leaving broken timbers and bodies floating downstream.

Leodgar watched through the observation slit as the enemy withdrew into the darkness. The eastern bank, briefly illuminated by shell fire, showed the aftermath: broken artillery pieces, cratered ground, and far too many still forms lying where they had fallen.

"Cease fire. Keep the men at their guns, but everyone else is to help with the repair efforts. Signal the shore that we are damaged and have dead and wounded."

A sailor approached, medical kit in hand. "Sir, let me see to that arm ..."

Leodgar waved him off with his good hand. "See to the critically wounded first. I can wait."

The sailor hesitated, then nodded and hurried off. Leodgar looked up, out the open hole in the roof of the pilot house.

They'd repulsed the attack. Barely, but they'd survived.

Devnum

The crowd gathered in front of the Palace Complex was the largest they'd had in the week, filling every possible space around the palace.

The big difference was that this one had been planned. In the week that the senators had continued to sic mobs on the palace and work up the people with their ridiculous lies, she hadn't been sitting idly by.

Yes, she should have seen this coming and blocked it, but she had been in politics her entire life and knew how the game was played.

Which was why they'd done more than just inform the masses that a major speech by the Empress was coming. She'd had her people construct a raised platform just inside the palace grounds that stood higher than the wall to ensure that every man sitting in that section could see the crowd, and that the crowd could see them. She'd invited, with praetorians to escort some of the more reticent people, members of both Imperial and Roman senates, along with government officials and regional officials from here in Rome as well as Caledonia and Ulaid. She'd also made sure to include all of the visiting dignitaries in the city.

All of that was for a reason, but it was also a smoke screen to make sure every Imperial Senator was there and sitting in places of honor at the very front.

She would not allow any of these men to hide from what was coming.

They'd erected a second stage at an angle from the one filled with senators, but this one was just a platform from which she could speak. Ky had described the way they used to be able to project their voices through devices like the earpiece she wore so that they could be heard over a large area, and she wished she'd had one of those now.

She'd been trained to project her voice well and knew at least those in the area around the palace square would hear her. They'd also handed out copies of the speech to men set to go around town and repeat it, but it would be nice for everyone to hear her at the same time.

She spared one last glance at the senators, several of whom had smug looks on their faces, no doubt thinking they had gotten the upper hand and this was, in fact, a public backing down for her to give in to their demands and give them what they wanted.

Foolish men.

"People of Britannia, I have heard your cries for justice for the youth of our Empire and for fair treatment. I have heard you, and I understand. My own husband stands on the front lines fighting this war with your sons, brothers, and husbands just as he did six years ago against the Carthaginians. I know the weight this war has placed upon your shoulders. I've seen the empty chairs at dinner tables, the shops struggling to stay open, the fields left fallow as our young men march off to distant battlefields. Which is why I stand before you today. I have struggled with the decisions I have been forced to make for the good of every citizen of our Empire. I have cried as a mother over a son for each man we have lost, which is why I feel it is right that I lay the case of our Empire before you myself. You, the people of Britannia, should know what we face so you can fully understand the decisions made on your behalf. This is your right as citizens. I know that by now, many of you have heard that Egypt – once our ally – has betrayed us. They have thrown their lot in with the Eastern forces, the very enemy that seeks to crush our way of life beneath their heel."

A murmur rippled through the crowd. They had, of course, heard of this. It had been the talk of the town ever since the word broke. But hearing about it second-hand and from your leader were two very different things.

"It's true, this was a shock to everyone in the Empire, but we will meet this challenge as we've met every challenge we have faced before. Doing so ... surviving this betrayal, will not come easily. It is going to require hard decisions for us to deal with this. I also know that by now, many of you have heard rumors of conscription. Again, this is true. What isn't true is some of the information you have heard surrounding the acts of conscription we are in the process of drawing up. I implore you, before you let fear or anger cloud your judgment, listen to what I have to say. Let me make the case to you, the people of Britannia, on why we had to come to this hard decision."

There was another sweep of unsettling sounds from the crowd, although it was more muted than Lucilla had expected. Maybe they weren't prepared for her to address the issue so directly.

"Our forces, while they still hold the line in Eastern Germania, are being pressed hard. They fight bravely, but with the addition of much of Greece and Egypt to the Easterners' already significant numbers, we have again found ourselves greatly outnumbered. Worse, these Easterners have found ways to copy even our newest technology, which has taken from us the very advantage that allowed us to defeat the larger Carthaginian forces in the last war. Egyptian pirates now strike at our bases in the Middle Sea and raid our ships, limiting the supplies available to our men in the field. These challenges have cost us dearly, but we have not backed down, because they have made it clear now, and in their allying with the Carthaginians in the last war, that they will accept nothing short of total domination of every town and village ... until they have subjugated us like the Carthaginians of old. I will not stand by and allow the rise of a new Carthage, no matter where they come from. I tell you this not to scare you, but for you to understand the difficulties we face. For you to understand what has driven us to the point of asking what we have to ask. Without more soldiers to hold the line, all of the will in the world will not stop them. Without the manpower we need, manpower we are not achieving through volunteers alone, all we have built, all we have sacrificed for, will crumble. I have walked the trenches of Germania. I have seen the brutal reality of this war with my own eyes, and I tell you now, we cannot afford the luxury of complacency!"

The crowd grew quieter. That was the one thing the senators had made sure to leave out of their pamphlets. They didn't want the people to really know the stakes we were facing.

"So yes, we are asking to be entrusted with your sons and husbands, brothers and fathers, to ensure that every one of us has a future. We ask this, but we are not Carthage. We do not hurl bodies at our enemy until one side breaks, and we do not spend lives needlessly or foolishly. We are Britannia! Our strength has always lain in the quality of our soldiers, not merely their quantity. Every man called to serve will receive the same rigorous training that has made our legions the envy of the world. And we will not discriminate. No one will fight while others live in safety. The son of a senator will march alongside the son of a baker. And for those who serve, I give you my solemn vow, your families will be cared for, your livelihoods protected. I ask you, how many of your neighbors, your friends, have already volunteered? How many families are already missing fathers, sons, and brothers? This is not about forcing you to fight, it's about sharing the burden equally, so that no one family, no one community, bears too much of the cost. To those of you who have served before, I ask you to speak to your neighbors, your friends. Help them understand what is at stake. Remind them of the oaths their fathers and grandfathers took, the sacrifices they made so that we might stand here today, free and prosperous."

She paused dramatically, looking over to the senators.

"I know you have heard that we intend all sorts of atrocities, that we would ask for your sons while forgetting who we are and what we stand for. Those are lies. Some among our leadership would have us bury our heads in the sand, pretending the storm will pass us by if we simply ignore it. They sit in their villas, counting their coin, while our brave men and women bleed on distant shores. To those men, who claim to speak for the people while lining their own pockets, I say this. Stand with us now or stand aside. The time for half-measures and compromise is over. If you cannot find the courage to do what must be done, then you reveal yourselves as cowards who would let Britannia burn, just to protect your own fortunes. People of Britannia, I call on you now to make your voices heard. Demand accountability from your leaders. Refuse to let complacency and greed destroy everything we have built. And know this, if the senate will not act, then I will. I will enact whatever emergency measures are necessary to ensure our survival, even if it means overriding their authority."

The crowd got very silent at that. This was the point that had a lot of people up in arms. When presented starkly, it could look like despotism. Again, maybe they didn't think she would address it so directly. Either way, she knew she had the crowd's attention. Even the men in the senate, sitting with the other dignitaries, were silent, waiting to hear what she had to say.

"That, however, is not the path I wish to take. I want to pass a law to ensure the conscription is fair and that everyone pays the cost for the lives we lead, instead of leaving the fighting to the poorest members of society while the rich sit on their piles of wealth, profiting from men dying. We are strongest when we stand together, not as senators and citizens, not as rich and poor, but as Britannians. Our history is one of endurance, of rising to meet every challenge that fate has thrown our way. And we are not alone in this. Every other people on the continent, all of our allies, are enacting similar laws and mobilizing their people in the defense of the west. We do not stand alone, but we cannot stay safe on our island while others send their children to fight for us. As we stand with our neighbors here, so should we stand with our neighbors across the channel."

That got a response. The senators might have felt smug in riling up the mob, but they'd forgotten that the mob was still the mob. They might be easily angered, but they were still on their own side, worried about their own self-interests. Senators forgot that anger at their enemies was not the same as support for them. People clapped and a few shouted support or agreement with what she'd said. She knew they were at a tipping point. That they could be made to do the right thing, if it were presented as the best option for them and their families.

"So I ask you now, will you stand with me? Will you fight, not just for your own families, but for every family in Britannia? Will you show the world, once again, that we are a people who cannot be broken, who will not be cowed, who will face every threat and emerge victorious?"

A roar went up from the crowd.

"Then let us move forward as one! Let us show our enemies, and those who would doubt us, that Britannia's strength lies not in our walls or our weapons, but in the unbreakable spirit of our people. Together, we will weather this storm. Together, we will secure a future for our children and our children's children. Together, we will write the next glorious chapter in the history of Britannia!"

As the crowd's cheers reached a fever pitch, Lucilla stepped back from the podium. She knew this was just a moment, and people's whims were fickle, but already she had her people out on the streets, making this same pitch on every major corner in the city and sending word to the other major cities in the Empire. Telling them what they faced and laying it out for them, in more detail, what she was prepared to offer the people who were conscripted and those who stayed home.

She just hoped she could keep the momentum going.

Chapter 17

Medb was happy to finally get off the train. With the exception of two short boat rides, she had been on one for the past five days, traveling up from Kalb to the coast of Gaul and then from Londinium up to Devnum.

While it was a miracle they could travel so fast, since a trip like that would have taken a month or two at best in the old days, it wasn't particularly pleasant.

Of course, she could have taken a boat, which would have taken maybe a day less, but she'd wanted to stop and talk to a few people on the continent along the way, as she tried to work out her plans for once she left the capital again.

What she hadn't expected was the squad of praetorians on the platform that snapped to attention when she and Claudius stepped off the train.

"What is this about?" she asked the optio in charge of the squad.

She had gotten a sense the Empress was displeased with her from her message demanding that she return to the capital, but she hadn't thought it was clapped-in-irons-level displeasure.

"There have been disturbances in the city, my lady. Things have calmed, somewhat, but we were ordered to ensure your safe arrival at the palace."

"Disturbances?"

"Over the new conscription laws. There were protests over them, although that has turned into anger at some of the ... better-offs avoiding service to the Empire. The worst of it has settled, but the Empress wanted to make sure you didn't have any problems."

Medb frowned at that. She'd been so focused on what was happening to the south, that she hadn't realized things were getting out of hand in Britain.

Another sign that she'd been in Carthage too long, and had lost the handle on what was happening in the Empire as a whole.

"Lead on," Medb said, gesturing off the platform.

With her escort in tow, Medb made her way toward the Imperial Palace. After a few minutes of walking, it became clear the upheaval had been a little worse than the praetorian had made it out to be. Here and there, buildings showed damage from the unrest and a few had been gutted by fire.

The Empress was also clearly still doing damage control, with men on most major street corners, reading aloud from some kind of proclamation, surrounded by citizens.

It did seem to be working, as none of the crowds seemed particularly ready to riot.

The biggest sign of what seemed to be recent violence was in the wealthier districts close to the palace. The damage looked more extensive, or at least more recent, to several of the homes in that section, including a home she knew belonged to one of the Imperial senators. It must have been burned recently, as the shell of what had once been a fairly impressive home was still smoking, with brigades of men throwing water buckets on it.

"What happened there?" she asked one of her escorts.

"It is the home of one of the senators. The people's anger over conscription has turned to anger over some elements of the city not doing their part to support the war effort. Word spread that his son was stationed in Ulaid instead of serving with his unit. A mob stormed it last night, took what they could carry away, and burned it down. The senator was not home, thankfully."

"Thankfully," Medb repeated, but she wondered how word of that got to the common people.

Senators were normally much better at hiding that kind of thing.

When they reached the palace, Medb turned to Claudius and said, "Go ahead to my offices and start deciding who you want for your investigations. I want names by the time I get there after talking to the Empress. I'm not sure when I'll be leaving, but I'd like your investigation to be up and running in the next day or two."

Claudius saluted and turned to walk toward a separate section of buildings where her offices were located while she left her escort behind and was led by a servant to the Empress's private study.

She found the Empress at her desk, reading some kind of report. Although their relationship had been rocky in those early days of the Empire, when Medb had been a glorified prisoner, since her ... adjustment in attitude, she had found Lucilla to be a fairly reasonable monarch.

Which is why the displeased look on her face was a little concerning.

"You have some explaining to do," she said as soon as the door closed. "How did Egyptian ships manage to seize multiple ports without warning? Where were your intelligence networks?"

"I did warn you, as soon as we had a hint of their involvement. These weren't some random criminals; this was an organized attempt supported by a government that had spent the last two hundred years keeping itself alive under Carthaginian rule. They knew what they were doing. My agent died uncovering the link between the shipments in Carthage. That is how closely they guarded their secrets."

"Not good enough. Maleth. Cyprus. Our trading outposts. All lost because we didn't see this coming."

"Because we uncovered them. They were set up to react as soon as they were discovered. Had we not found the shipments, they would still be our 'allies' siphoning off whatever technology they could while secretly helping the Easterners. We didn't get attacked because we missed the signs, we got attacked because we uncovered them."

"How did they get their hands on our newer weapons? They aren't part of the alliance, and so were limited to only much older weapon sales," Lucilla asked, her tone much less accusatory than when Medb had first walked in.

"I'm not sure yet, but it is troubling. We've looked at the weapon shipment we captured, and they are pristine. No wear from transportation or battle. Most still packed with grease and protection, exactly how it comes out of our own factories."

"You're suggesting these came out of our own factories?"

"I am. Everything I've seen suggests they didn't come from leaks in our supply lines. I think they were diverted before they even reached any of the armories. Probably before they were tallied on the quartermaster's rolls."

"Something worth looking at. Although, even if they were getting weapons, it doesn't explain how they managed to duplicate them so quickly."

"Something else I've been concerned about. Even the Carthaginians, with all their resources, never managed to copy any of the weapons we created. The only firearms they ever used were the cannons sold to them by the Easterners. And yet, somehow, the Easterners have been able to get production versions in the field in a few months?"

"Yes. Although reports from the front indicate their accuracy remains inconsistent."

"If they get a chance to copy more of our designs, they'll improve."

"Which we need to prevent from happening. Have you identified which factory the shipments went missing from?"

"Not yet, but we will soon. I have Claudius putting together a team right now and they should start the investigation before I leave, so I can make sure they're on the right track."

"What do you mean 'leave'?"

"I'm heading to the front, specifically to the prisoner camps, to start questioning prisoners and try to learn more about who we're fighting."

"Absolutely not. If we have some kind of leak in our development, that is our priority. We cannot defeat them if they keep up with us on our technology and we need your expertise to root out these traitors."

"Claudius can handle that investigation. I've spent the last year training him on intelligence and he was deeply involved in uncovering the current smuggling. He knows what to look for, who to watch, how to build a network of informants. I agree this is important, but I think our lack of information on the Easterners is our weakest point. Besides, we don't know for sure if the smuggling is directly connected to the Easterners. Yes, they got their hands on the end product, but that doesn't guarantee that the people selling the goods knew who they were selling it to. It could be simple corruption; merchants selling to whoever pays the highest."

"A point, although I find it unlikely, but we've had this lack of knowledge about the Easterners ever since the last war. Why is it so urgent you go now?"

"Because for the first time, we have access to actual Eastern soldiers and officers, not just their proxies. Men who know not just about the capabilities of their army, but who can give us some real sense about who the Tian-You are. The smuggling is a problem, yes, but it is not the only place we're blind."

"You believe the prisoners will reveal such information?"

"Some will. They're soldiers, not fanatics. They have families, homes, and lives they want to return to. Some will talk simply to improve their living conditions. Others will let things slip without realizing it. A few might even decide their loyalty to their empire isn't worth dying for."

Lucilla was quiet for a full minute as she considered Medb's proposal.

Finally, she nodded slowly. "You're right. I apologize for my earlier harshness. The Egyptian betrayal ... it has everyone on edge. It wasn't your fault."

"I appreciate that."

"But I want regular reports, both from you and Claudius. If either investigation reveals immediate threats ..."

"You'll know as soon as possible."

"When do you leave?"

"Tomorrow, if possible. Day after at the latest. The sooner I begin questioning prisoners, the better."

"Very well," Lucilla said.

Middle Sea, Southeast of Sicilia

Valdar squinted against the early summer sun, the spray stinging his face. They'd been in the Middle Sea for almost a week, and the hunting had been good.

It helped that the Easterners didn't seem to have much in the way of ships in this region. The only thing they'd found were Ptolemaic ships, mostly Britannian-built merchant designs mixed with some attempts to copy the better Britannian warships.

They were generally smaller than the Easterner ships he'd faced in the south and less sturdily constructed. This, coupled with the fact that Egyptians had never been the best sailors, made their ships easy pickings.

Thankfully, the shells now being used by the Eastern forces on land, the ones copied from the Britannian designs, had not made it to these ships yet. Every Ptolemaic ship was still using round shot. While that could be deadly, it took a great many more cannonballs to sink one of his ships than explosive shells, which meant their attempts to fight back did not last long.

They'd tried, though.

The first few days, the hunting had been good, with the Ptolemaic ships trying to take his small fleet head-on.

None of those fights had gone well for them.

After that, the hunting had gotten slimmer. They'd heard from some fishing ships off the coast of Italia that the Egyptians were now sailing in small convoys, presumably hoping that more guns would keep them safe.

They clearly hadn't been paying attention to what happened in these same waters during the last war.

"Sir," one of his officers said, running up and skidding to a stop, saluting. "Scouts report they've spotted the convoy we were told about, and the direction suggests it's heading for Maleth."

"Probably trying to slip in relief supplies now that we have the island under blockade. Order the scouts to chase the convoy this way but to keep their distance. I don't want the Egyptians to decide to turn and fight just yet," Valdar said, pulling out a spyglass and examining their position.

Waving to a signalman, he ordered, "Signal the fleet to position behind that northwest promontory, with the exception of the Aquila and Seadreki. I want those two further down. Positioning is at their discretion, but I want them far enough away to be out of sight, but close enough to be able to hear the guns when the fight starts and to come in as a blocking force. I want the convoy to be caught between us. When we launch the attack, I want all of the schooners to fan out behind us and come around in crescent formation, spread out south of the convoy. They are not to engage directly in the fighting. Their job is to grab any ship that tries to run south. If those ships strike their sails, fine, otherwise, sink them."

The signalman saluted and ran off to deliver the orders. It took a few minutes for everything to be delivered, but his captains were good and had been in enough fleet engagements to know what he expected of them. He could see the first ships beginning to peel away to their assigned positions before the last signal was even sent.

Most of them moved close to the coastline, where the terrain to the east jutted out, helping to block them from view as the convoy passed. The only exceptions were the Aquila and Seadreki. They made sail and disappeared to the west.

Time seemed to drag on as they waited. Naval combat was slow combat, and a lack of patience had forced many a captain to make a mistake and end their sailing days early.

"Signals from the scout ships, Admiral," called his flag lieutenant. "Enemy convoy maintaining course and we should see them soon."

"Good," Valdar said, pacing the quarterdeck, counting the minutes as the distance between his fleet and the convoy closed.

Finally, he saw them. Tiny dots at first, but quickly growing large enough to see details as the Ptolemaic ships drew closer. He'd dealt with Egyptian captains many times over the years, and he'd never been overly impressed by their ability behind the wheel.

They didn't change his opinion now.

Their formation was tight. Too tight. Any kind of scattering would require coordination, with the outer layer peeling off first and the inner ships being forced to wait for them. It would make them vulnerable when the trap closed.

Their escorts were also spread out, two in front, two in back.

Good for anti-piracy work when you had singles and pairs to worry about, but they were now at war with a major power.

"Ready the gun crews."

His officers relayed the commands to his gun crews and those of the other ships. Their captains would have been watching, but he wanted to make sure everyone was ready. While this would be an easier fight than the ones he'd had over the last year and a half, it wasn't just the fight.

This was to be a message.

Below decks, gun crews worked quietly as the convoy drew closer.

When the lead Ptolemaic escort was less than half a mile off the coast and parallel to their position, Valdar raised his telescope one final time. He could see their crews clearly now, sailors moving on deck and soldiers stationed along the rails with rifles.

Again, the right thing to do if they were facing pirates.

"Signal the flanking ships," he commanded. "Prepare to emerge."

As the convoy ships passed, flags snapped up the Bellona's rigging. In the distance, answering pennants appeared briefly along the coastline.

"Helm, bring us about." Valdar's voice was steady. "Gun crews stand ready."

The Bellona swung gracefully from her hiding place, her sister ships falling in line. The Ptolemaic convoy spotted them immediately. Valdar could see the sudden flurry of activity on their decks as men began to panic and shout orders.

"Too late," he muttered, before yelling, "Open fire!"

The Bellona's guns roared. The range was short and they'd had a lot of time to work out firing solutions thanks to the Egyptians sailing in a very straight path. Shells arced across the water, bursting into flames and shards of metal as they struck the Ptolemaic warship's hull. The explosions ripped through the vessel's wooden sides as one, then two, then three hit, tearing a hole in the side of the ship.

His guns didn't all fire at once. The fire from the cannons was staggered, something they'd worked out after the last engagement against the Easterners. They'd found that when they fired all the shots at once, they would more or less hit at the same time, with the explosions of the ones that hit an instant before the later shells came in actually setting off the later shells before they hit the boats.

True, the explosion would still be close enough to do damage, but they found that when they staggered the fire of a broadside into two groups, separating them by a second or so, the second set of shells would either also impact the ship instead of going off prematurely or, sometimes, they would get lucky and the round would go through the hole created by the first shell and explode deeper inside the target.

This didn't seem to be as true against harder to penetrate stone targets like forts, but it was very true against wooden ships.

And they got lucky.

That is exactly what happened this time. A shell punched through a hole opened in the side of the lead Egyptian ship, disappearing past the open planking before impacting and exploding. A beat later, there was a thunderous blast as the ship's powder magazine exploded and sent burning timber high into the morning sky.

The shock wave rolled across the water. One of the merchant ships, sailing too close to the escort, caught fire as blazing debris rained down across its deck. Panic erupted through the convoy as ships tried to turn, only to spot the Britannian vessels emerging from both flanks.

"Second volley!" Valdar commanded. "Target the next escort!"

Again, the guns thundered, and again, they found their mark, hitting the second escort ship in the rear of the convoy. They weren't so lucky as to hit the powder magazine twice in a row, but several shells did impact near the ship's waterline, tearing splintered holes that let the seawater rush in. It didn't take long for the crew to start scrambling over the sides, jumping into the sea.

The remaining two Ptolemaic escorts tried to put themselves between Valdar's ships and their charges, who had begun to scatter, apparently trying to break west for Maleth and safety.

They were going to be very surprised when Valdar's other warships came into view and they realized they were trapped.

"Helm, three points to starboard," Valdar commanded. "Gun crews, prepare to fire on my mark."

He had no use for the warships, but he wanted to capture as many of the merchantmen as possible. The Ptolemaic warships turned and finally managed to get off a response to the earlier Britannian volleys, but their shots went wide, splashing harmlessly into the water. Black powder smoke drifted across the waves as the more ineffective round shot sailed past.

"Signal the schooners; tell them to focus on cutting off escape routes. Don't waste ammunition on crippled vessels. Any ships that break out, they are to force them to strike or sink them."

The lighter, faster schooners continued on as his caravels turned to engage the warships, swinging around the small fleet to keep them moving toward the anvil in Valdar's hammer and anvil, blocking them from fleeing south.

Some, apparently, smelled a trap and tried to turn and beat the schooners, while a few others looked as if they wanted to head for the shoreline of Sicilia, maybe to beach and run inland.

Or maybe they were just panicking. Either way, it was complete chaos with ships much too close together, even if they coordinated their maneuvers. Which they didn't. Three of the vessels collided, their yards becoming entangled.

The Bellona's guns thundered again, joined by the rest of the battle line. Shells slammed into the escorts, who managed to stay afloat in spite of it. Some of the rounds went past the escort, hitting into the tangled merchant ships, tearing several apart and sending flames racing up the rigging of another.

His men reloaded and targeted one of the remaining escorts. It was trying in vain to maintain some kind of protective block for the merchants, but its positioning was poor, especially once the merchants started to scatter.

Two of his schooners were currently chasing down the ships trying to make landfall, bow guns hitting the ships in the rear. One struck its sails, pulling the cloth down and dragging it to a halt.

The other tried to make it in spite of the warning shots and was quickly headed to the bottom.

Valdar noted what was happening but kept his eyes on the warship.

"Fire as you bear!"

The Bellona's guns roared in sequence. The first shells struck the warship's bow, blasting holes below the waterline. The second set of shells hit amidships, destroying gun positions and sending splinters scything through the Egyptian gun crews.

Two more shells and the ship was both sinking and burning.

Which was the moment the Aquila and Seadreki made their appearance, causing even more panic among the merchantmen, if such was possible. Several of the ships began to throw cargo overboard, desperately trying to lighten their ships. Barrels and crates bobbed in the growing debris field.

One of the merchant captains showed more cunning than his fellows, turning between two of the ships currently burning down to the waterline, using the smoke from his burning comrades as cover.

Valdar smiled grimly at the attempt. He had to applaud it.

"Clever, but not clever enough. Signal Seadreki, I want bracketing fire through that smoke screen. Drive them out."

Their two ships began to fire shells blindly into the smoke. The resulting flashes of explosions told them that something had been hit. The ship came drifting out of the smoke a moment later, clearly out of control with its main mast hanging loose, hit by a lucky shot, or unlucky from their point of view.

Seeing one of the merchant ships who had struck their sails being left alone, for the moment, several more dropped their sails sending the cloth crashing to the deck and immobilizing themselves. A few even raised white flags to make their surrender very clear.

"Signal one of the schooners to take possession of that surrender," Valdar ordered, then turned to his first officer. "Target the vessel to their starboard. They seem less inclined to wisdom."

Orders were passed and his guns roared again. Three shells punched through the merchant's wooden hull just above the waterline. Secondary explosions ripped through the ship's hold as the shells detonated, flames and smoke pouring out of the holes.

The rest of his schooners were chasing down merchantmen, raking them with fire until they struck their sails. It had become a chaotic mix of ships, however, and Valdar was starting to have difficulty keeping track of the position of all of the ships.

He was attempting to do just that when a junior officer ran up and drew his attention to off the port side. A flash of movement caught his attention. Valdar turned to find the final Ptolemaic escort, which he'd honestly thought was sunk, coming through the smoke, directly at the Bellona, apparently planning on ramming them.

It was a confusing decision, as most of the merchants had already struck and the other warships were below the waves, while he still had a dozen ships on the water. Even if they were successful and took down the Bellona, did they think they would stop this attack?

Or was it worth it to spend their lives trying to take one ship with them? Not that they were going to be successful.

Puffs of smoke erupted from its deck as riflemen tried to strike out at them in vain, although the range was long for them.

"Have half the guns loaded with canister, the rest targeting the hull with explosive shells. Fire at the gun captain's discretion."

It was a bit of overkill. If he was going to sink them, there was no need to rake the deck with shot, but he wanted the message sent loud and clear, to those who survived the battle, of what happened to those that stood against Britannia.

His guns fired again, this time in full broadside. The combined effect of grapeshot and explosive shells was devastating at such close range. The grapeshot scythed through the Egyptian soldiers on deck while shells tore massive holes in the ship's hull. The escort's charge faltered as its bow began to settle into the water.

That took the fight out of the rest of the ships, the last ships striking their sails and running up white flags. The battle was over. The waters around them were littered with floating debris and burning wreckage. Only half the merchant ships had survived.

"Signal all ships," Valdar commanded. "Begin rescue operations for survivors. I want prisoners segregated by ship and rank. Officers are to be brought to the Bellona and have the lowest ranked officer brought to me. Also, have damage control parties inspect each captured vessel. I want to know which can be salvaged and which need to be scuttled. And get teams searching those holds, I want a full accounting of their cargo."

"Aye-aye, sir," his first officer replied, already moving to relay the orders.

Valdar watched as boats were lowered to begin collecting prisoners from the water. The morning's work had been productive. They'd eliminated another Ptolemaic escort squadron and captured several merchants with their cargo intact. More importantly, they'd demonstrated that the Middle Sea remained Britannia's domain, regardless of Egypt's betrayal.

Valdar checked his own ship's damage, which was minimal, with only one round shot striking his hull. It cracked some wood planking higher up that would need to be fixed, but other than that, they were untouched.

One of the schooners had a little damage, but it also was fairly minor and could be fixed in a few hours without the need to drydock.

By the time he finished the survey of the damage to his ships, two of his soldiers escorted an older-looking Ptolemaic officer onto the quarterdeck. He looked like the old sea dogs that could be found on most ships at sea. A man with decades of experience but without the connections to rise above the gun decks.

The man's uniform was soaked; he'd clearly spent some time in the sea before he'd been fished out. Blood trickled from a cut above his eye that had yet to be patched.

"Your name?" Valdar asked in rusty Greek.

"Kemeni."

"What was your position?"

"Commanded the gun deck on the Nebet."

"By right of combat and the laws of war, your ships are now property of the Britannian Empire. While your fellow officers will be questioned, then transported to prisoner camps, you are the lucky man that gets to avoid that fate."

"I know nothing to tell you and wouldn't if I could."

"You misunderstand. I don't want information from you. I want you to lead all of the non-enlisted, who will be put ashore on the African coast. No weapons and no cargo, just the clothes on your back and a few provisions. If you are lucky enough to make it back to Alexandria, I have a message for you to deliver."

"What message?"

"I want your leaders, and anyone else you see, to know that every captain we see under an Egyptian flag will suffer the same fate as those here today. I will not allow a single Egyptian ship to remain afloat in the Middle Sea. Tell your leaders this is what they wrought by choosing to throw their lot in with the Eastern hordes. Tell them that their choice has consequences."

"You will witness the whole of the consequences."

The next hour passed in organized chaos as prisoners were processed and distributed among the Britannian vessels, with those being taken to a prison camp to be hauled back to Kalb on one of the caravels while two of the schooners would be dispatched to drop off the rest in Africa as promised. Valdar supervised from the quarterdeck, dispatching orders as needed. When a midshipman reported the preliminary inspection of the captured merchants complete, he nodded.

"Very well. Begin scuttling the damaged vessels. I want nothing left that could not be salvaged."

The midshipman hesitated. "Sir, two of the merchants still have substantial cargo in their holds."

"Can they be safely sailed to port?"

"No, Sir. The hull damage is too severe."

"Then sink them. Better their cargo feeds the fish than supplies our enemies."

Valdar watched as demolition crews went to work on the crippled ships. They worked methodically, setting charges below the waterline where they would do the most damage. One by one, the vessels disappeared beneath the waves in a cascade of bubbles and debris.

Kemeni observed the destruction, his expression unreadable. "You sink good ships like they're worthless."

"Ships are tools, nothing more. These tools were used against us. Now they'll decay on the seafloor where they can do no further harm."

The last merchant ship slipped beneath the surface with a final gurgle. Valdar turned to the Egyptian.

"Remember this day, gun commander. Remember what happens when you challenge Britannian control of these waters. Your Eastern allies may have matched our weapons on land, but the sea remains our domain."

"For now, perhaps." Kemeni's voice carried a note of warning. "But the world changes. The old powers fade. New ones rise."

"Then let them rise on land. The waves belong to Britannia, as they always have." Valdar signaled to the marines. "Take him below. See that he and his gun crews are ready for transfer when we make landfall."

As the Egyptian was led away, Valdar's first officer approached. "Sir, preliminary count shows three hundred twelve prisoners. Forty-eight officers, including ship captains."

"Separate the officers by vessel. I want to know exactly who commanded what. And check their papers against our intelligence reports. Some of these men may have been involved in earlier raids on our shipping."

"Aye, sir. What about the civilian merchants we found aboard?"

"Keep them isolated from the military prisoners. Once we verify they're truly civilians, we'll decide their fate." Valdar frowned. "Though any merchant willingly carrying military cargo to our enemies forfeits the protections of civilian status."

The officer nodded and moved off to implement the orders. Valdar returned his attention to the debris-strewn waters. The morning's work had been productive, but it was only the beginning. Egypt's betrayal had opened a new front in an already complex war. Their ships would need to be hunted down and destroyed, their ports blockaded, their trade strangled.

It would be a long campaign, but necessary. The Eastern Empire had to learn that challenging Britannia at sea carried a steep price. Every ship they lost, every cargo seized, every crew captured would reinforce that lesson.

Valdar allowed himself a grim smile. They had chosen this path. Now, they would walk it to its bitter end.

"Signal the fleet," he ordered. "Make for the African coast. I want these prisoners offloaded before nightfall." The signalman raised his flags, and the Britannian vessels began forming up for the journey south. Behind them, the last traces of the morning's battle disappeared beneath the waves, leaving only scattered debris to mark where a Ptolemaic convoy had sailed its final voyage.

Chapter 18

Devnum

For the third time in a short few months, Lucilla made her way into the Imperial Forum in hopes of finally getting the conscription laws passed and the men in training. She couldn't help but still be angry at most of these men, who'd cost them valuable time they did not have.

As it was, with the time needed for the training, it would be winter before most of these men made it onto the battlefield. Until then, the stakes on the front would get even higher, and goals like retaking the islands invaded by the Egyptians would have to remain only a plan, the people living there forced to endure living under the yoke again.

At least her work to counter the senators' plan to stop conscription altogether had been successful. The changes in the kinship of the men inside were immediately obvious and striking.

Senator Alypius, who had led the opposition against her conscription law, sat isolated on the far edge of the Roman section. His former allies, Kaeso, Bredei, and the others who had stormed out during her last address, now kept their distance from him and each other, scattered in ones and twos across the benches.

For now, the coalition they'd managed to assemble over this issue was broken. She wasn't naïve enough to think they would be permanently cowed, of course, but they wouldn't be causing her problems today.

Lucilla took her position at the central lectern, setting a stack of papers on it, while allowing her gaze to sweep across the senators.

Her slow, deliberate stare made it very clear to them who was in charge here.

"Honored Senators, we gather once again to address the defense of our Empire. As before, the burden of conscription weighs heavily on my heart. Heavier than that, however, is the knowledge of how certain members of this body chose to manipulate our citizens rather than lead them. How they valued their personal interests above the security of our nation."

Lucilla paused, turning specifically toward Alypius. "Senator, you claimed conscription would destroy our economy. You said it would tear families apart. But when you secretly funded pamphlets spreading lies about the scope of service requirements, did you consider how *your deception* might tear our society apart? And you, Senator Kaeso. Your dramatic exit from our last session was well-choreographed. As was your subsequent meeting with the merchant guilds, where you suggested I planned to seize their assets to fund the war effort. A creative fiction, but one that served only to incite panic. Many of you tried to work behind the scenes, spreading lies and fear among the people, all in defense of your own purses. I don't know if you hoped these actions would go unnoticed, expected that your self-serving moves would stay hidden in the background, but *they did not.* We have spoken to many of the people you hoped to influence. The evidence of your machinations has come to light, and they have failed. Your efforts to turn the mob against me revealed your true nature to our citizens. They saw not defenders of their interests, but manipulators serving their own ambitions. While you hid in your villas, I stood before them. While you whispered lies, I spoke the truth."

She paused again, staring hard at the offending senators, many of whom looked worried about what would happen now that their treachery was exposed.

"And yet, I will not impose on you the same consequences some of you wanted for me. I will not call for your ouster, for your public pillorying, for your head on the block. I am happy to accept the public shame you have earned as consequence enough. Before you think I am sparing you out of some feminine weakness, which more than one of you accused me of, I want to make something very clear. My focus has always been on protecting the Empire, and I will never let personal vindication outweigh the duty placed upon me. For what is coming, I require a unified senate, not one fractured by internal dissension. I also know many would use my taking rightful payment for your betrayals as another sign of tyranny. So, in the name of the unity I need to ensure the Empire fights on and remains free, I absolve you of your ill deeds."

She stopped again, placed both hands on the lectern's edge to ensure she had their full attention.

"But understand this; your previous influence is spent. There will not be a second instance of my magnanimity. If any of you turn on your duty again, you will find yourself a shorter man than you are today. And before you think you can succeed next time where you failed this time, and that the profit is worth putting your neck to the block, let me highlight something for you. Your trust is squandered and cannot be easily regained. Those who opposed conscription to protect their wealth have been exposed, and the people have seen you for what you were. Allies you once counted on will now look at you with concern and doubt."

Stabbing a finger out at the men, she added, "And your own legacy will be put on the line. While the conscription will be fair and equitably applied, there will be one exception. At least one eligible member of every family of someone holding a position in the imperial government will be required to serve. Your sons will serve alongside common citizens, and any injustice you have planned will affect not those who you see as beneath you, but *your own blood*. I have my family on the front lines. Senator Taenaris's son was wounded several months ago along the Wistla. Senator Brandubh and Senator Rotri have family members currently in the trenches. And Senator Domhnall lost his brother in one of the early skirmishes against the Eastern invaders. Each of these men has supported their kin, who stepped up and heeded the call to service to the Empire. It is now time for the rest of you to do the same."

Lucilla placed her hand on the stack of papers she'd set on the lectern.

"Before we proceed to the vote, I have something to share. This declaration arrived this morning, signed by over three thousand citizens of Devnum, organized by Master Ercán. Many of you know him from his large glass works on the north end of town. What you may not know is that he lost two of his sons over the last year! One in a fight near the Wisla at the beginning of the war and another in Greece just a few months ago. Let me read you their words."

Lifting the paper up, she began, "We, the citizens of the Britannic Empire, recognizing the dire threat we face, stand united in the defense of our homes, our families, and our future. We did not surrender to the Carthaginians and we will not surrender now. We urge our leaders to take the actions necessary to ensure our survival and that our way of life continues. We acknowledge that all who live under the banner of the Empire share in its fortunes, and thus, all must bear their share of its burdens. Because of this, we declare our full support for the Conscription Act as proposed by Her Imperial Majesty, Empress Lucilla, and repudiate any attempts to stop these efforts in the name of profit or position. Furthermore, we affirm that no single class, nor any privileged few, should be exempt from the duty of defending Britannia. We accept that our sons, our brothers, and our fathers must take up arms to protect our homelands and wish for the burden to be shared by all. We ask that the sons of senators and merchants stand with the sons of factory workers and stable hands. We sign this declaration not as separate peoples of Rome, Caledonia, and Ulaid, but as one Empire, united in its purpose. Let all who oppose this measure be remembered as those who would have Britannia fall."

She set the declaration down and added, "The signatures include Master Naso, who lost his eldest in the defense of port Vikhavn, the widow of Tribune Gartnait, who fell in the trenches facing the Eastern hordes, and Shipwright Lucan, whose son was on Maleth when it fell."

Senator Kaeso raised his hand. "Your Majesty, if I might …"

"You may not," she said, pulling the bulk of the pages from her stack. "This is a list of every Britannian family that has lost someone in the current war. This only includes Britannians, and not those of our allies. This also isn't every person lost, just the families that have lost someone. Would you care to guess how many names appear on these pages?"

She looked from man to man, waiting for an answer. Not one said a word.

"Over twenty-one thousand. And do you know how many of those names belong to senatorial families?" She let the question hang. "Two. Only two of your number have known this sacrifice, and they are among the bill's supporters. Those who yelled loudest about tyranny and the suffering caused by conscription are all among families who have given nothing."

"Your Majesty," Senator Alypius stood. "I've always supported the principle of conscription. My concerns were merely about implementation ..."

"Really? I have here a pamphlet that I know you paid to have produced. It seems pretty clear that 'Conscription represents nothing less than Imperial slavery, a violation of citizens and the beginning of tyranny.' Are you suggesting this means something other than the words say? Do you have some clever spin to put on it that changes its very clear and plain meaning?"

Alypius sank back into his seat, his face reddening as the other senators edged further away from him.

"I thought not. Now, to the bill. You have all read it several times and clearly know what is in it, so I see no point in going over its provisions again. I will say that of all the members of the Western Alliance, we will be the last to enact this provision. All of our allies have already put nearly identical measures in place. Maybe it is because they are closer to the danger and, therefore, unable to stick their heads in the sand like you have, or maybe it's simply because they are more well-reasoned than our venerable leadership. Either way, I will not have Britannia lead from behind. If we want to continue being Primate of the West, then we must earn that right. So does anyone object to skipping the reading of the bill and moving directly to a vote?"

None of the men had a counter to that.

"I hoped not. Those in favor of the Conscription Act, raise your hands."

Hands rose across the chamber, first from her supporters, then from the uncertain middle, and finally, with obvious reluctance, from those who had opposed her most strongly. Even Alypius, after a moment's hesitation, raised his hand.

"The vote is recorded as unanimous. My office will provide detailed implementation guidelines by day's end," she said, gathering her papers before pausing as she turned to leave the chambers. "And senators, remember this moment. Remember how close you came to choosing personal interest over that of the Empire. *I* certainly will."

Factorium

He had not worked this hard in a long time, not since he was marching with the legions, before he became a praetorian. He had probably lost a good one and a half libra and put on twice as much of that in muscle. Claudius shook his head after pushing the crate into place, wiping the sweat from his brow, his calloused hands rough against his skin. Claudius gave a small smirk.

Even his hands had changed.

The summer heat bore down on the train yard outside of the factory warehouse, making the air inside thick and stifling. The large fans powered by the steam engines helped, but it was still stifling.

He adjusted his ill-fitting worker's uniform, missing his much preferred praetorian uniform.

He had been here for over a week, watching the rail yard and warehouses that all of the smuggled goods he'd traced had come through. He'd tried the docks first, but the shipments had been widely scattered, with each seeming to come from a different berth in Devnum with no pattern to be found among the teams who loaded them.

Which led him to go one step back, following the path of goods from the factory to their holding warehouse, where they were shipped from.

It had not taken long to start noticing some suspicious activity. Every day a dozen trains were loaded and moved to Devnum, and aboard half of them crates were added that had not been on the manifests his team had been given. He assumed that the other half had the same additions, and he just had not been around when the unaccounted crates were added.

Worse, he had seen enough of these crates put into train cars at the last moment to recognize they each had the same 'slight damage' to the outside of the crate in the same spot. The kind of thing most workers would just accept and move on without a thought, since it seemed every crate got dinged up in some way. But once he saw the pattern of how identical the 'damage' was, he could not unsee it.

Today was no different. They had just loaded the last crates and were about to close the door to this train car when several workers showed up with three crates to be added at the last moment. Crates not on the list he had seen and all with the same damaged spot.

As one of the workers dropped off a crate and went to head back to the warehouse, Claudius asked, "Sorry, I was just checking the manifest to make sure we had everything, and I can't find these crates listed. I just wanted to make sure I wasn't screwing anything up and didn't have an old manifest or anything."

"No, what you've got is probably right. They're always screwing this stuff up and the manager's having to send stuff the plant foreman missed. You know how it is."

"Yeah. I guess it's like that everywhere. Thanks."

The man nodded, friendly enough, and headed back into the factory. Claudius doubted that he personally was up to anything. He had been keeping an eye on who was bringing these crates, and it was different men every time.

Which left him going another step up the line.

"Excuse me, sir," Claudius said, bowing his head slightly to the foreman. "I'm having trouble with the manifests. Those unmarked crates, they're not on my list."

"They wouldn't be. Those are the manager's business, and he makes up the manifests, so it's the same either way. Just do what you're told and load them up."

"But I don't want to …"

"Look, I get it, and I appreciate that you're being thorough. Things move fast around here and sometimes the manager calls down last-minute additions. They don't always make it to the paperwork."

"Is that … common? I mean, I don't want to cause any trouble, but it seems like there have been a few of these unmarked crates on every train."

"It's fine," he said, starting to get exasperated. "The boss knows what he's doing. Just focus on your assigned tasks, alright?"

Nodding, Claudius thanked the foreman and walked away. His instincts told him the foreman wasn't actually behind it either. If he was, he wouldn't name someone Claudius could go check with and if the manager was behind it and the foreman was in the know, he wouldn't have thrown his boss under the train carriage so quickly.

He seemed like a guy just trying to get his job done without anyone bothering him. Which was the grease that made all empires go.

Walking past his work area where his coworkers were starting to load the next train car, Claudius continued on to the edge of the train yard, where a trio of praetorians stood guard, since this was a controlled facility.

He could see the men loading the train car looking at him strangely using their peripheral vision, probably wondering what trouble he was about to get himself into. Not that it mattered. He had seen what he needed to see, so the masquerade was no longer needed.

"You," he said to the optio who commanded this shift's detachment, one of the men who was in the know that he was here investigating. "Gather more men and secure the exits. No workers leave until I give the word. You two, come with me."

If his coworkers had been confused by why he had walked off the job, they must have been very puzzled at why two praetorians were now following behind him at a respectful distance. Claudius had let his helpful worker guise slip and was now walking how he normally did, back straight, head held high.

Like someone in charge.

He looked over and saw the two men he had worked with all week staring at him. Both looked away, making themselves very focused on the task at hand.

They knew authority when they saw it.

The manager, a portly man with thinning hair, looked up as they entered his office.

"What's the meaning of this?" he demanded, rising from his chair as the praetorians let themselves in without knocking or notice and then remarking when he saw that they had a man between them, dressed like a common worker. "What has this man done?"

Obviously, he didn't know that Claudius had been working at the rail yard. This was not the kind of man who got to know his people. He sat in his office, lording over them, the ruler of his very small kingdom.

"This is Tribune Claudius Marcellus Paulus. He has questions for you," one of the guards said.

The man might be a terrible manager and a small despot, but he was clearly not a fool. The color drained from his face as realization dawned. His mouth opened and closed several times before he managed to speak.

"Tribune? I ... I don't understand. What's going on?"

Feigning confusion. They always went with that first.

"I think you know exactly what's going on. Extra crates are being shipped out of your rail yard that appear on no official manifest, and it all appears to be at your order," Claudius said.

A statement, not a question.

"Extra crates? I'm not sure what you mean. We're moving so much material these days, supporting the war effort. It's impossible to keep track of every ..."

"Don't insult my intelligence," Claudius interrupted. "These crates have been added to shipments for days, always at the last minute, always marked in the same way. Probably to make it easier to identify them on the other end."

Sweat beaded on the manager's brow. "There must be some misunderstanding. Perhaps the foreman ..."

"Has made it very clear this is common at this rail yard and that he was instructed that these were being added directly on your order."

"Now see here, I don't know what you're implying, but we're doing our part for the Empire, working around the clock to meet demands. If there have been some … administrative oversights, I assure you it's nothing more than that."

Claudius didn't respond immediately. Instead, he turned to one of the praetorian guards.

"Go fetch Master Hortensius. Tell him it's urgent."

"Be reasonable," the manager said, sitting back in his chair nervously. "He's a busy man. Surely that's not necessary. I'm more than capable of sorting out any discrepancies in our records."

"This goes beyond paperwork," Claudius replied coldly. "We'll wait for Hortensius to arrive before discussing this further."

The minutes ticked by in a tense silence. The manager fidgeted, occasionally opening his mouth as if to speak, then thinking better of it. Claudius didn't say a word. Just stared at the man and waited, causing him to squirm even more.

Finally, the door burst open, causing the nervous manager to jump in his seat, making a small squeaking sound.

Claudius ignored him and turned to Hortensius. He'd only met the manufacturer a handful of times, but he'd always found him to be genial and reasonable.

Which is why Claudius found himself a little surprised by a much more irritated version of the man.

"This had better be important, Tribune. I was in the middle of …" he said, and then stopped short, taking in the scene before him. "What's going on here?"

"Master Hortensius, thank you for coming so quickly. We have a situation that requires your immediate attention. You're aware, I assume, of the investigation into diverted munitions that were smuggled out of Britannia and ended up in the hands of the Egyptians and the Easterners."

"Wait, I never …" the manager stammered.

"Quiet," Claudius said, his voice making it clear the man would regret interrupting him.

"Yes," Hortensius said, looking to the manager and back to Claudius. "I told the Empress that we would look into it, but that I found it hard to believe any of my people would betray the Empire."

"Well, as part of my investigation, I have been working in this warehouse for the past week, since it seemed that the munitions we recovered could only have come from one of three warehouses in Factorium. Over this week, I've observed a pattern of extra crates being added to shipments at the last minute. These crates do not appear on any official manifest. When I questioned the workers and foreman about this, they all indicated that these additions were made on direct orders from the manager here."

The manager's face paled further, but he remained silent.

"What's more concerning is that these crates are consistently marked with damage in the same spot and in exactly the same way, which I believe is meant to make them identifiable to agents in Devnum. When I asked about it, I was told they were last-minute orders accidentally left off the manifests, and that it was a common occurrence in your operation."

"That isn't true," Hortensius said. "The manifests are set by the factory production office. We keep meticulous records of everything that leaves these facilities."

"Which is why I found the statements both troubling and telling."

The manager finally found his voice. "Master Hortensius, surely you can see this is all a misunderstanding. We're working around the clock to meet the Empire's needs. If there have been some … oversights in our paperwork, it's nothing more than …"

"Silence," Hortensius snapped, as angry as Claudius had ever seen him. "You said you have evidence of this?"

"I have copies of the official manifests for the past week, along with my own observations of what was actually loaded onto the trains. I also have the trains currently in the rail yard held outside with the extra crates sitting in their train carriages at this very moment."

"Then I apologize for my tone. I will admit, I am … shocked this could happen here. How far do you think this goes?"

The manager opened his mouth to speak, but Claudius cut him off. "That's what we intend to find out, sir. Given the gravity of the situation, I believe it would be prudent to take this man in for questioning."

"Agreed. But we can't shut down operations here. The war effort depends on our production."

"Of course. Do you have someone you trust who could temporarily oversee the operations? Not just someone you have no reason to question but actually trust."

Hortensius rubbed his chin thoughtfully. "Yes, my deputy manager. He's been with me for years, is utterly reliable. I'll have him brought up to speed immediately."

The manager, who had been watching this exchange with growing horror, finally exploded. "This is outrageous! Master Hortensius, you can't possibly believe these accusations. I haven't done anything wrong."

Hortensius turned to the man, looking both disappointed and angry. "If that's true, then you have nothing to fear from answering a few questions. Tell them the truth, and if you've done nothing wrong, you'll be fine."

"But … but …" the manager sputtered, his eyes darting wildly around the room.

Claudius nodded to the praetorian guards. "Take him away."

As the guards moved to apprehend him, the manager's composure shattered completely. He leaped to his feet, knocking over his chair as he tried to run past them and out the door.

He did not make it.

"No! You can't do this! Someone help me!" he yelled as the guards grabbed his arms and dragged him out of the room, his shouts fading as they marched him down the corridor.

"I'll also need to bring in anyone involved with loading these crates, as well as those who packed them. We need to determine if they were simply following orders or if they were knowingly complicit."

Hortensius nodded, his face grim. "Of course. Whatever you need to do to get to the bottom of this."

"I apologize for the disruption to your work, Master Hortensius. I assure you, we take no pleasure in this."

Hortensius sighed heavily. "No, no, you're right to investigate. It's just … I can't believe one of my people would be involved in something like this."

"I understand. We'll keep you informed on our progress," Claudius said.

Chapter 19

Eastern Germania

Ky frowned as he read over the latest reports from the observation balloons. While he had been pleased that for the past two weeks, they finally had good weather for the balloons to operate continuously, the news they were getting back was not what Ky would have wanted.

It hadn't stood out at first, because they were being slow and cautious about it, but it seemed clear now that the enemy was reducing the size of their force all along their line. While that might be a cause for celebration, suggesting they were losing men faster than they could replace them or being forced to reinforce faltering sections of the line from this one, Ky's instincts told him that wasn't the reason. There was a deliberate pattern in the way the enemy was pulling men from their line and it suggested they were being driven by something other than desperation.

"You're seeing this too, right?" Ky subvocalized.

"Yes, commander. The troop movements are not a repositioning along this section of the front, most likely a change in strategy."

"To what?"

"There is not enough data currently available to simulate what their desired offensive strategy might be."

"Then guess. Use the other intel we got and run calculations on possible options, even if they are inside the margin of error. Include negative data into the calculations. Let's look at what they're not doing."

As the AI began its calculations, Ky continued to study the maps. The balloon reconnaissance had proven its worth, clearly showing the ebb and flow of the enemy movements.

Of all the things the enemy had yet to copy from them, Ky was surprised they were not flying balloons of their own yet.

Ky's thoughts were derailed as Sophus began displaying the results of its findings, running various scenarios across his vision. While Sophus was right, they didn't have the data to prove any of these true, Ky thought some of the data suggested more than what it showed on the face of it. He was fairly certain his gut feeling was right, but seeing as what wasn't there was not the forte of an artificial intelligence, Ky wanted a second opinion on it before he decided to take action.

"Find General Bomilcar and bring him here," Ky ordered the guard stationed outside his tent.

As he waited, Ky went over the data again, and then a third time. Sophus wouldn't commit to agreeing, but everything he saw kept giving him the same conclusion.

A few minutes later, the tent flap pushed open and Bomilcar entered. "You sent for me?"

Ky nodded, gesturing for Bomilcar to join him at the map table.

"I need your assessment of these latest reports," Ky said, handing them to the general. "The enemy has thinned their forces in these sectors. What do you make of it?"

Bomilcar flipped through the pages and a few hand-drawn maps. "It would say they're redeploying. Maybe moving these men to another position on the front."

"Do you think they're contemplating a strategy change?"

"I don't know. Maybe. They are still making regular attacks along our line, which suggests they're still committed to this front."

"I'm not so sure. I think they're willing to kill their people in order to make it look like they're committed, without any real goal to actually break through. The scale of the attacks has been much smaller recently and they usually only last a wave or two before they give up."

"They do seem to involve fewer men than before," Bomilcar admitted.

"I can't help but think they're diversions. They're meant to keep our attention fixed here while they prepare for something more significant elsewhere."

"With respect, Consul, couldn't this simply be the result of battlefield attrition? They've suffered some very heavy losses in the past few months. Perhaps they're struggling to maintain their previous force levels."

"I've considered that, but I'm not so sure."

"Indeed, so if they are redistributing, where do you think they're going to focus their men? I know we've had increased activity to the north with multiple attempted river crossings."

"It's possible," Ky said, although he couldn't keep the doubt out of his voice.

"If they are planning something, I'm not sure we'll know until they launch their attack. We haven't gotten much from the few prisoner interrogations we've had so far. The information has been … inconsistent. It's difficult to separate fact from misinformation."

"Which might be because the only prisoners we've managed to interrogate are men who were pressed into service. We haven't been able to communicate effectively with any actual Easterners yet. As for the northern incursions, while concerning, they lack the coordination and force that would indicate preparations for a major offensive. These attacks involve forces of only a few thousand men at most. They're not serious attempts to break through our lines. They're diversions, meant to keep us occupied and guessing."

"So if not there, then where?"

"Have you read Modius's reports from Greece?" Ky asked in an apparent non-sequitur.

"I have," Bomilcar said, a little confused, clearly wondering where Ky was going with this. "They detail sporadic skirmishes, but nothing that suggests a major threat. The region has been relatively quiet."

"That's exactly what concerns me. This silence, combined with the timing of these increased attacks along our position and to the north, it doesn't feel coincidental."

"With respect, Consul, you may be reading too much into this. I still think the most likely explanation is that the enemy is simply conserving their strength."

"If conservation was their goal, they wouldn't waste men on these probing attacks. Why continue to sacrifice troops unless they're trying to fix our attention in place?"

"They haven't shown a lot of care for their men's lives so far."

"Or it's to keep us from reinforcing other sections. There's also something else that's been nagging at me. When was the last time we encountered any Egyptian or Greek forces among their troops?"

"For the Greeks, not for several weeks, at least. I'm not sure we've ever seen an Egyptian among them."

"Because they're being held in reserve. The enemy is gathering their forces for something significant. No, the more I think about it, the more convinced I am that Greece is their new target."

"That sounds a lot like speculation."

"It is, but it's the logical move. Greece provides access to the Middle Sea, and if they can secure it, our line will have to bend all the way around to Italia, extending us even further and allowing them to attack Germania from the east and the south."

"Even if you're right, we can't afford to weaken our position here based on suspicion alone."

"It's a risk, I agree, but if I'm right, we can't afford to be caught out, or this whole front will crumble and we'll have to give up most of Eastern Germania. No, I'm convinced. I'm ordering a partial redeployment. We'll thin our defensive line here and move those troops south into Greece."

"Consul, I can't agree with this. If you're wrong, we'll have compromised our strongest defensive position for nothing. The enemy could be trying to bait exactly this kind of response."

"The general's concerns have merit," Sophus interjected in Ky's mind. *"Historical data suggests defensive positions are typically more costly to retake than to maintain."*

"I understand the risk," Ky said aloud, addressing both Bomilcar and Sophus. "But sometimes the greater danger lies in being too cautious."

"At least let me send scouts further south before we commit to this. Maybe make a few probing attacks in that direction. We could get confirmation of enemy movement within days."

"Days we don't have. The enemy has been methodical in their preparation. When they strike, it will be swift and with overwhelming force. No, I'm committed to this. In fact, I'll lead the redeployment personally. I also want us to do most of our redeployment under the cover of night. I don't want them to know we're shifting our forces."

"You're going to Greece?" Bomilcar's eyebrows rose.

"Yes. You will stay here and maintain our defense. Keep enough men to hold the trenches, and hopefully make the enemy think our entire force is still here. We'll replicate their game."

"And if they launch a major offensive here while you're gone?"

"They won't. They've committed too many resources elsewhere, but you should still stay vigilant. I think it's very likely they'll continue their probing attacks to keep us occupied."

"How many men will you take?"

"Three legions, including the Ninth. I know you don't like this, but I am very certain that this is the right course of action. It's the only thing that fits the facts we're seeing."

Bomilcar was clearly still not pleased, but he only nodded and said, "I'll maintain our position here as ordered."

"Good. You're our most capable commander, Bomilcar. That's why I need you here. If I'm wrong about Greece, you'll have our fallback position."

"And if you're right?"

"Then we'll still have a chance to win this thing."

233

Devnum

Hywel could only stare at the brass contraption Hortensius's assistant had set on the workbench in front of him. It was a strange thing, a slender brass tube mounted on a stand with a small platform beneath the long neck-like thing, as if it was peering down at the platform.

"What did you call it again?"

The young man who had delivered it, who to his credit was well known as one of the manufacturer's more intelligent assistants, said, "The Consul's instructions called it a 'microscope.' We've had the base design for almost a year, but there were a lot of issues working with the glass masters to get the new grinding technique right while not making the glass opaque. It is a very difficult process. My master sent along these instructions."

Hywel picked up the stack of pages the young man had brought and began looking over them. He was used to the handwriting by now and knew how the Consul organized his instructions. Considering he was leading an army in a war, Hywel had no idea how the man ever found time to produce the sheer volume of documents he did, but it seemed as if every other written page in the Empire had been produced by him.

"Fascinating," he murmured after reading for a few minutes before setting the pages aside to examine the small glass rectangles that had been delivered alongside the main apparatus. "And these are the 'slides' mentioned in the notes?"

"Yes, sir. They're for holding the samples you wish to examine."

Hywel lifted one of the thin glass rectangles, holding it up to the light. The clarity was remarkable, far superior to even the newest window glass he'd seen produced. "The craftsmanship is exceptional."

"I know. We had to develop an entirely new grinding technique for this, although my understanding is that it has additional uses beyond this project. Actually, getting it clear and maintaining a very specific curvature of the lens was the most challenging part. It had a tendency to deform badly."

Hywel nodded absentmindedly as he returned his attention to the Consul's notes. The concept was surprisingly simple, it was like the spyglasses but in reverse, allowing them to see things that were apparently too small to see with the naked eye.

"Very well," Hywel said, rolling up his sleeves. "Let's see how this works."

Hywel was often distracted by his work and was not the tidiest person in Devnum, at least in his personal workspaces. He reached for a small earthenware bowl that had been sitting on his workbench for several days, containing water that had grown cloudy from disuse. Following the Consul's instructions precisely, Hywel put a tool in the water to extract some and then dripped a single drop of the water on the slide.

"Now, according to these notes, after I've placed the droplet on the first slide I then cover it with a second slide to flatten the sample."

Carefully, he pressed the two pieces of glass together and set them on the small brass stage beneath the tube. He adjusted the height according to the specifications in the Consul's notes and leaned forward to peer through the eyepiece.

"I see nothing but a blur," he said after a moment.

After checking the notes, he looked for and found a small knob on the side of the microscope, and turned it slowly in the direction the diagram suggested.

"How precisely am I to … ah!"

Things started to get clearer as he turned the knob. It was finicky though, requiring the smallest of moves to step it closer to clarity. When he finally got it to the point he wanted, his breath caught in his throat.

Abruptly, Hywel jerked back from the eyepiece, blinking rapidly as if to clear his vision. He looked down at the slide with his naked eye, seeing nothing but a small water droplet sandwiched between glass. Then he leaned forward again, returning his eye to the lens.

"Cac na caorach!" he exclaimed in Caledonian. "This cannot be possible."

"What?" the assistant asked eagerly.

"Tiny creatures. Living, moving creatures swimming through the water. They're translucent, some round, others elongated. I count at least seven distinct types, moving independently of one another," he said, adjusting the focus slightly. "Some appear to be pursuing others, like miniature predators hunting prey. They move with purpose, not randomly as one might expect from mere particles."

"May I look, sir?"

Hywel reluctantly stepped aside, allowing the young man to observe the sample. The assistant's reaction mirrored his own, initial confusion followed by startled amazement.

"They're exactly as the Consul described, although until this moment I'd thought he'd been at least exaggerating, if not just saying things to convince us to do as he directed. No wonder he insists on boiling drinking water in the field."

He tapped a particular paragraph in the notes. "The Consul suggests these invisible organisms might be responsible for the illness spreading through Port Caolros. He's outlined a methodical process for testing infected bodily fluids against various treatments."

"Will this help identify the cause of the outbreak?"

"Potentially. We've already eliminated several causes through conventional methods, but this new tool might help identify which of the remaining candidate pathogens is responsible."

He turned toward the door and shouted, "Celsus! Come here!"

A moment later, one of Hywel's medical assistants appeared, looking somewhat startled by the urgency in his master's voice.

"I need blood samples from the quarantined patients recently transported from Port Caolros. Prepare them exactly as this young man will demonstrate. Ensure you follow the containment protocols I established, we cannot risk spreading whatever affliction these men carry."

As Celsus departed with Hortensius's assistant, Hywel returned to the microscope.

He reached for a small silver case containing his surgical tools and selected a thin, sharp needle. Following the instructions they'd been using for some time to prevent infection, he first cleansed his fingertip with alcohol, then carefully pricked the skin. A small bead of blood welled up, which he transferred to a clean slide before covering it with a second piece of glass.

Positioning his own blood sample under the microscope, Hywel adjusted the focus once more. What he saw precisely matched the anatomical drawings the Consul had included, countless small disk-shaped cells packed tightly together.

"Remarkable," he murmured.

The contrast between the water and blood samples was stunning. While the water contained distinct moving creatures, the blood presented as a field of uniform cells arranged in a consistent pattern. Hywel spent several minutes simply observing the regular arrangement of healthy blood cells, committing their appearance to memory.

He was so engrossed that the sound of the door opening as Celsus returned with Hortensius's assistant caused him to jump. The pair were carrying several sealed glass vials containing blood samples from the quarantined patients.

"We've brought samples from three different patients, sir," Celsus reported. "All exhibiting severe symptoms, high fever, difficulty breathing, and the distinctive skin discoloration you noted in your examination yesterday."

"Excellent," Hywel said, gesturing toward the workbench. "Prepare slides from each sample."

Celsus nodded, carefully handling the vials with cloth-wrapped hands. Under Hywel's supervision, he prepared three separate slides. It was slow, careful work, but with practice, it would probably speed up.

Hywel placed the first slide under the microscope and leaned forward to examine it. Initially, the infected blood appeared similar to his own healthy sample, but he knew that wasn't accurate. The notes had been very clear that there would almost certainly be a sign if the blood came from an infected person.

It took time, but after several minutes of staring at the samples, he finally noticed some differences. Some of the cells, the ones used for transporting air through the body that the Consul had previously described, looked slightly different than his own. They were distorted. Not like the small circles in his sample, but instead elongated and misshapen.

The two assistants watched him, seemingly a little perplexed, but Hywel ignored them as he went back and forth between the

Consul's notes and the microscope, trying to reference what he was seeing against the illustrations.

"Here," he said, tapping the page. "The Consul has documented this exact blood cell deformation. It's characteristic of a specific illness transmitted by mosquito bites. The disease is prevalent in warm, humid regions with standing water, which does fit with what we've been told about Port Caolros. The mosquitoes breed in stagnant water and transmit the pathogen through their bites. The Consul's notes specify a treatment using a plant called 'sweet wormwood' that grows in eastern Germania and northern Greece, among other places."

Celsus leaned closer to examine the detailed botanical illustration. "I'm not familiar with this plant, sir."

"Nor am I," Hywel admitted, "but the Consul has provided detailed identification information and instructions for preparing an effective medication called Artemisinin from its leaves."

Hywel quickly examined the remaining patient samples, confirming the same distinctive blood cell deformation in most, now that he knew what to look for. Satisfied with his diagnosis, he turned to his assistants.

"Celsus, I need you to draft immediate instructions to be sent to Port Caolros. They must implement mosquito control measures. Drain all standing water where possible, place netting over beds, and the like. The Consul also mentioned some kind of salve that can be applied to the skin to repel the creatures. I will write to him and find out how we, or more likely Sorantius, can develop that. Speaking of, we also need to send a formal request to him, so he knows these plants are coming. Once we've managed to collect them, he'll have to process it into this ... Artemisinin, which is supposed to help the infected men."

After Hortensius's assistant was dismissed and his own began working on his assigned task, Hywel returned to the device. It was astounding.

He honestly couldn't wait to put other things under its lenses to find out what the world had been hiding from him for all these years.

Chapter 20

Camp Banwīhraz, Central Germania

Medb settled onto the rough wooden bench in the watchtower just as the sun started to make its way over the horizon. She'd been watching these people for weeks now and she found she'd gotten the most useful information in the morning, before the sun was all the way up and the temperatures started to really rise. It was when they were the busiest, which meant she got to see more interactions between the prisoners, which is where she got her most interesting observations.

The guards had quickly learned not to disturb her. Her reputation had preceded her arrival at Camp Banwīhraz, and a few well-chosen words to those who initially tried to be helpful, or were simply just curious, had ensured her solitude.

She opened her small leather-bound journal, its pages filled with meticulous notes and drawings. She'd developed her own system to track individual prisoners and their movements, creating a detailed map of the camp's social structure, which had quickly expanded into something even she was having trouble following as it got more complex.

She looked at the small book for a moment, appreciating it. A gift from Cormac before she left Carthage, the leather cover bore the marks of constant use, worn at the edges from being carried everywhere, and stained with ink where her pen had leaked during a sudden summer downpour three days prior. The fact that it was worn actually made her like it more, even though it was a gift.

Things were meant to be used. To box them up and save them was to deny them their purpose and remove the meaning behind the gift. The worn edges, the stain, the filled pages, these were the signs of a gift truly appreciated.

She pulled herself out of her reverie as the first prisoners emerged from the rows of tents that were lined up, one after the other, around the huge square field enclosed by wire fences topped with barbed wire and dotted with guard towers. One of dozens at Camp Banwīhraz, each more or less alike, able to hold a thousand prisoners. The camp population overall had passed thirty thousand prisoners. It was not the largest of the prison camps in Germania. There were three medical camps that held seriously injured prisoners who made up the bulk of those they'd captured, and who were only moved here when it was safe for them to maintain themselves on their own.

She found this one the most enlightening of all the sections she'd observed because it was built on a slight hill, the center point of which was more or less in the center of the square. Although it was a square, the inmates had arranged themselves into what she'd started to think of as a set of concentric circles, with the most privileged prisoners occupying the central area situated on slightly higher ground. This elevated position, which was drier and more comfortable, had not been designated by the Britannian guards and she wasn't even sure the designers had noticed the gradations, or counted them as serious enough to account for. The prisoners, however, had noticed and, from what she was told, established this arrangement within days of this section being opened. And they'd maintained the arrangement with remarkable consistency.

She'd noticed the pattern early on and had even tested it to a degree, to get a sense of the camp hierarchy. Three separate times she'd instructed the guards to relocate prisoners randomly throughout the camp. Each time, the original order had reasserted itself within hours, the privileged returning to the center, the lowest ranked banished once again to the periphery. There had been no riots or fights and yet the pattern remained unbroken.

Most revealing was how new prisoners were integrated into this system. Medb had witnessed the arrival of thirty fresh captives the day before yesterday and, within hours, each had been assessed and assigned his place within the concentric rings.

Breakfast had begun and the guards had set up a station for men to come through and get their rations. Each man got a bowl of whatever was being served that morning, each given the same amount, regardless of how they classified themselves. And yet, the distribution did not stay that way.

Certain middle-tier prisoners collected food as the men came through the line, pouring some into an extra bowl or giving additional food from the extra bowl, depending on their place in the hierarchy, apparently. The central elites consistently received the largest portions, sometimes significantly larger, while those in the outer rings survived on much less. Often half of what they'd been given.

The guards had tried to put a stop to this, but without a huge influx of praetorians, it was impossible to stop altogether. She'd put a hold on that when she'd started observing this section, however, so she could observe how it was naturally working for them.

What made this arrangement remarkable was its persistence without overt enforcement. Medb had witnessed few attempts by the lower-ranked prisoners to secure more food for themselves.

She'd divided the camp into five distinct zones, marking the territories claimed by different groups within the prisoner population.

Zone one, the central area, housed what Medb had classified as the administrative elite. There were very few of these, only about thirty men, mostly captured in the early days before the trenches had gone in and the front lines had become static. A few had been recovered from Valdar's actions in Africa.

These men did not seem to be the type that purposefully put themselves in harm's way. Here, they rarely engaged in physical labor and were deferred to by every other group in the section.

Zone two contained what appeared to be higher-ranked military officers. Unlike the central elite, these men participated in work details, although usually in a supervisory way. They also seemed to serve as intermediaries between the central figures and the broader population.

Zone three seemed to be made up of lower-ranked officers, men who led small groups into battle similar to a Britannian Decanus or Optio. Here, they worked mostly as go-betweens for the first two zones and zone four.

Zone four housed the bulk of the prisoners, common soldiers, Medb presumed. Even among them, there was an internal hierarchy that was too complex for her to have worked out yet beyond there being two distinct groups.

Zone five, the outermost ring, presented a puzzle Medb hadn't yet solved. Everyone in the entire section was an Easterner, with the soldiers from subjugated countries held in their own sections. And yet, the Easterners themselves seemed to see a difference between the people in Zone five and those in the other zones. Its inhabitants showed signs of severe malnourishment despite receiving the same initial rations as the others. They occupied the lowest, dampest ground, falling ill more frequently than their counterparts. Yet they made no visible attempt to improve their circumstances, accepting their position with a resignation that suggested permanence.

Medb tapped her pen against her journal thoughtfully. There also seemed to be no way to move from one zone to another. When beds became available in better positions due to prisoner transfers or deaths, lower-ranked captives never attempted to claim them. The system operated as if governed by immutable laws rather than convenience or comfort.

She believed that entire camp operated as a miniature replica of a larger social system that probably existed in their homeland. While it did tell her something about the TianYou, that they were a rigid hierarchical society, more than even the Romans or the Carthaginians were, it did not tell her the kinds of things she actually needed to know.

Not that she hadn't found a way to get what she needed. Among the outer ring prisoners, mostly in Zone four, she had identified several men who didn't fully conform to the established patterns. These individuals, while positioned in the lower ranks, maintained a certain independence from the hierarchy.

They were standoffish. Separate.

These men interested Medb. She had tracked five of the men for the past two weeks, noting their interactions. They operated under the same social rules as everyone else but kept to themselves.

They were loners, which was exactly what she was looking for.

One in particular, a lean, younger-aged man with a distinctive scar across his jaw, had particularly captured Medb's attention. He was from Zone four, and at first glance, he was quiet and abided by all of the unwritten rules the Easterners had put in place.

But the more she watched him, the more she realized he was watching them. During the downtime, and there was a lot of downtime in a prison camp, most occupied themselves with games among their own group, with conversation, or sleeping.

He watched. Not just watched. He studied them.

And she saw no good reason for someone in their ranks to do that. Which intrigued Medb even more.

Medb snapped her journal shut. She'd seen enough. Now it was time to move on to the next stage of her plan.

Descending from the watchtower, she went to the office of the camp commander, a burly Britannian officer named Tiburtius.

"Lady Medb," he said with a short bow. "Have your observations been productive this morning?"

"I've seen enough. I have a list of fourteen prisoners I would like segregated for questioning. I will provide you with their descriptions and which tents they sleep in."

"As you wish," he said, clearly intrigued, but smart enough not to ask questions.

She waited as he dispatched guards to retrieve the prisoners. While she was actually interested in the scar-faced man, for what she needed, she knew that pulling him alone would draw too much attention to what she was hoping to achieve. The others were merely camouflage, some high-ranked, some mid-level, deliberately selected to obscure her true interest.

Within the hour, all fourteen prisoners had been segregated into individual holding cells. Medb did not start with the man she wanted. In fact, she started with a man from Zone five, followed by one from Zone one. The interrogations were, of course, brief due to the language barrier. She would speak, they would stare at her, time would be wasted.

She did just enough that, if they started comparing notes, the men would have enough to guess what she wanted them to think she was doing.

Then she got to her real target.

The cell was sparse, since these cells were for holding problematic prisoners, and not actually meant for interrogation, only containing a chair and a mattress on the floor. The man sat on the chair, his hands resting in his lap. She took the chair sat at a small table one of the guards had carried in for her and sat facing the man, a few steps away, as the guards took up positions against the door, inside of the cell with them.

Medb sat at the table and said nothing. Not a word. She simply watched him as he watched her.

Minutes passed in silent evaluation. Most prisoners she had interrogated grew nervous in such silence, fidgeting or attempting to speak first. This one did not. His breathing remained steady, his gaze direct but not confrontational. The scar along his jaw gave his otherwise youthful face a hardened quality.

She estimated him to be in his mid-twenties, old enough to have seen combat but still a young man with a full life ahead of him.

After fifteen minutes of silence, Medb reached into her pocket and removed a small cloth bundle. She unwrapped it on the table, revealing bread, dried meat, and a small apple, far better fare than he had been getting.

She pushed the bundle toward him without a word.

The prisoner glanced at the food, then back at her. His expression revealed nothing, but she caught the brief flicker in his eyes. Hunger. Not desperation, he was not starving, but definite longing.

Still, he made no move toward the offering.

"Take it," Medb said, knowing he would not understand the words but making her intent clear with a gesture of her hand toward the food.

The prisoner remained motionless for another moment before reaching for the apple. He bit into it without taking his eyes off her, the crunch unnaturally loud in the silent room.

Medb waited until he had finished the fruit before beginning her real work. She pointed to the table.

"Table," she said clearly.

The prisoner stared at her.

She repeated the word, tapping the wooden surface. "Table."

No response.

She pointed to herself. "Medb."

Then she waited, eyebrows raised expectantly.

Nothing.

Medb tried again with the chair, with the same result. The prisoner watched her with those calculating eyes but made no attempt to repeat her words or offer his own.

After twenty minutes of this one-sided language lesson, Medb felt her patience wearing thin. The man was clearly intelligent; his reluctance was not from a lack of comprehension but willful resistance.

Well, she had not expected it to be easy.

There would always be tomorrow.

She stood abruptly, giving him a curt nod, the barest acknowledgment, and turned toward the door. The guards, seeing her approach, moved to open it.

As she reached the threshold, a single word sounded behind her. "Liu."

Medb paused, then slowly turned back. The prisoner sat exactly as before. She raised an eyebrow at him again.

"Liu," he repeated, tapping his chest.

A small victory, but significant. Medb returned to the table and sat down.

"Liu," she repeated, pointing at him then to herself. "Medb."

The man, Liu, nodded once.

Medb pointed to the table again. "Table."

"àn," Liu said.

"Chair." She pointed.

"Jī."

Medb's lips curved into a small, satisfied smile. "Good."

The next hour passed in a basic exchange of words. Medb would point to an object, name it, and Liu would tell her what, she assumed, was his word for it.

She kept the session deliberately simple, focusing on objects in the room and basic body parts, hand, eye, head. When she sensed his attention beginning to flag, she stood.

"Tomorrow," she said, making a gesture for him to stay and eat.

Liu watched her for a moment, then nodded.

"They are all to spend the night in these cells. Have someone occasionally question them with the exception of this one. It does not matter what they say or if they understand. Feed this one the same ration the guards get on the same schedule. He is to remain comfortable but locked in."

This was going to be a long process, she knew. But she had finally made progress toward actually learning about these people, at long last.

The rest would follow.

Mouth of the Nile River

"Signal the fleet to form attack columns," Valdar ordered as the fleet approached the Egyptian coast, one of the mouths of the mighty Nile River opening up in front of them. "Two columns."

"Aye, Admiral," his flag lieutenant responded, turning to dispatch the necessary pennants up the mast.

Sixteen vessels spread out behind the Bellona, eleven caravels and five of the faster schooners, each ready to get some payback for the Egyptians' treachery. After weeks of hunting Egyptian vessels throughout the Middle Sea, it was time to teach the Ptolemies what happened when they betrayed their allies, and Valdar was happy he was the one who got to teach them that lesson.

"Fortifications ahead, sir," reported the lookout from his position in the crow's nest. "Stone walls at both sides of the channel entrance."

Valdar raised his telescope again, focusing on the entry into the river. Sure enough, a pair of large fortifications sat guarding the entry into the river, although not exactly at its mouth. They were maybe a quarter mile in, which was clever. To engage with them, ships would have to be in the river itself, limiting maneuverability. This was new. He'd sailed along this path several times in his life, and these had not been there before.

Worse, he recognized the construction. These were built copying the Britannian fortress designs Valdar had started at Port Vikhavn. Clearly, they'd heard how effective those were and, taking advantage of being an ally at the time, had someone study them up close so they could replicate the structures.

As with Port Vikhavn's forts, each was positioned to provide covering fire for its neighbor with what looked like heavy cannon emplacements crowning the elevated positions. The size of their barrels suggested weapons of significant caliber.

Valdar nodded, considering their options. Taking Alexandria and cutting the Egyptians off from the Middle Sea was critical to keep supplies flowing and the armies on the continent in the fight. But he'd seen how hard it was to break through a position like this firsthand and did not relish being on the other side of it.

"Signal the fleet to maintain maximum velocity and follow close in line with the flagship until within effective firing range," Valdar decided. "And have gunners prepare timed fuses rather than impact detonations. We'll need plunging fire to reach behind those walls."

Going into a river at full sail was usually not a good idea. Even with local pilots, which they did not have, it was best to slow down enough to avoid the shoals and sandbars that could be found on most rivers. At speed, the risk of grounding a ship was very high.

It was also a risk Valdar was going to have to take.

The morning conditions provided optimal visibility, with moderate winds from the northwest, theoretically perfect firing conditions once they reached effective range. Of course, it was also perfect firing conditions for the enemy as well.

"Channel narrows ahead," the navigator, one of the few men in the fleet who'd sailed this stretch in the last year. "We'll need to maintain course within thirty passus on either side."

Valdar nodded. "Helmsman, steady as she goes. Maintain speed."

The minutes ticked down as the fleet sailed toward the land-mass, charging for the mouth of the river.

"Why haven't they opened fire yet?" his first officer wondered.

"Waiting until we're committed to the channel," Valdar replied. "Once we're boxed in ..."

As if to answer the man's question, a massive column of water erupted from the sea ahead of them. The sound reached them a moment later, a deep boom that carried across the water.

His first officer was surprised, but Valdar had expected this. They'd done the same thing at Port Vikhavn, installing larger guns with a longer range than what they could have aboard ships.

A second explosion followed, then a third, the shells falling in a pattern that bracketed the lead column of ships. The Egyptian gunners were finding their range with alarming speed.

Finally, a fourth shell found its mark. The lead caravel in the starboard column took a direct hit amidships, the explosive shell tearing through its hull just above the waterline. The vessel shuddered, wood splinters flying in all directions as smoke billowed from the wound. Within minutes, it began to fall out of formation, listing heavily to port, taking on water.

"Maintain course," Valdar ordered. "Signal pennant seven for evasive maneuvers within channel constraints."

As they entered the channel, two caravels attempted to break formation, but the narrow channel and surrounding shoals limited their options. One veered too close to the shallows, its keel scraping against hidden sandbanks, slowing its progress dangerously.

The Egyptian barrage intensified as the Britannian fleet pushed fully into the channel. Shells rained down on them. Another caravel took a devastating hit to its stern, and a schooner following close behind was forced to veer sharply to avoid colliding with it, nearly running aground.

They were in range for their own cannons, but the river was fairly straight at this point, which is why the forts had been placed there. Ships would have to get parallel for broadsides, which they couldn't do easily, giving the Egyptian gunners free rein for a long time before an enemy could answer.

"How long until we clear the broadsides?" Valdar demanded.

"At current speed, three minutes, sir," the master gunner replied.

"Not acceptable. Signal the schooners to increase speed and break formation. They're to come around us and put those forts under fire as soon as they can."

The faster, more maneuverable schooners surged forward, spreading out to present more difficult targets. In response, the Egyptian gunners shifted their attention, dividing their fire between the advancing schooners and the main caravel formation.

A tremendous impact rocked the Bellona, sending Valdar staggering against the railing. An Egyptian shell had struck the starboard bow, exploding on contact and tearing a jagged hole in the hull. Shouts and screams rose from below decks.

"Damage report!" Valdar called out, steadying himself.

"Hull breach above the waterline," came the response from below. "Fire in the forward hold!"

"Get it under control," Valdar ordered. "Shift men from the port battery if needed."

The schooners he'd sent ahead were faring even worse. One was already listing badly after taking a direct hit amidships, starting to fall behind the others, and another was on fire.

Finally, though, they were at the forts, their broadsides able to take aim.

Valdar watched through the haze of powder smoke as their shells struck the Egyptian fortifications. His hopes faltered as the smoke cleared, revealing minimal damage to the thick stone walls. The Egyptian cannons continued their devastating fire without interruption.

The shells bursting above the fort, at least, seemed to be having an effect with their rate of fire dropping sharply as shrapnel rained down on the defenders.

It, however, wasn't stopping them entirely.

Another caravel took a critical hit to its mainmast, which splintered and collapsed, crushing several crewmen beneath its weight. Fires broke out across its deck, the flames spreading rapidly through pools of spilled tar and cordage.

Smoke began to obscure visibility across the battlefield as guns from both sides continued firing and ships burned in the channel.

Valdar assessed the situation rapidly. The right column was taking the heaviest fire, with one caravel clearly sinking and another struggling to maintain headway with its sails in tatters.

"Sir," an officer said, coming up from the hold. "We're taking on water in compartments three and four. Carpenter's mate says the pumps are keeping pace for now, but another hit in the same area would be problematic."

Valdar nodded grimly. "Tell the carpenter to prepare collision mats and bracing timbers."

Finally, his ships had reached the forts and were able to fire, sending shells crashing into and above the Egyptian forts. Unfortunately, he could see two more forts in the distance that had just started to open fire on the schooners he'd sent forward.

'This isn't going to work,' he thought as another caravel erupted in flames as an Egyptian shell ignited its powder magazine.

The resulting explosion tore the vessel in half, sending debris and bodies tumbling into the water. The ships following were forced to veer sharply to avoid the floating wreckage.

Three more ships damaged or sinking, at least one lost completely, with two more forts ahead. The Egyptians built not merely a defensive position but a gauntlet.

"Signal the fleet; order a withdrawal."

Colored banners climbed the Bellona's masts, whipping in the smoke-laden wind. It was at least done in good order, with the strongest vessels on flanks, damaged ships in the center, staggered withdrawal maintaining covering fire.

The Bellona's hull creaked as it turned, the deck tilting beneath Valdar's feet as it made the tight turn to get around and head back the way they came. The Egyptians saw the retreat for what it was and intensified their fire, apparently determined to exact maximum punishment.

The withdrawal proceeded with agonizing slowness. Ships that had been sailing with prevailing winds now fought against them, giving the enemy more time to shell them.

The enemy was going to have clear shots at them all the way out, and he was going to lose even more ships, and that didn't count the schooners behind him which were trying to catch up to the fleeing column.

If he was going to have any ships left following this debacle, he had to do something.

"Bring us about and reef sail. Hold us parallel to the western fort. Rapid fire on all cannon."

"Admiral …" his shocked first officer said, but Valdar cut him off.

"Do it."

The man swallowed hard and nodded. He knew as well as Valdar did that he'd just signed their death warrants.

The Bellona swung across the channel, shielding the rescue operation, blocking much of the ships from direct fire and posing a threat to the western fort. The Egyptians did as Valdar had wanted them to, their fire shifting to the flagship. Shells splashed into the surrounding water, one striking the bow tearing out the admiral's quarters and half the deck.

Another explosion, while not direct, ripped out a good part of their top sails, which would make it harder to sail out of this channel and back out to sea, except Valdar did not expect that to happen.

At least his barrage on the western fort was having an effect. Several of its gun emplacements were blown off the wall and the air bursts were killing large numbers of the enemy inside the fort.

It wouldn't save them, but it would prolong the confrontation and give his men more time to escape. The Bellona's cannons roared, shells arcing toward the fort. The barrage forced their gunners to seek cover, disrupting their fire long enough for one of the schooners to complete its rescue of men in the water.

For several minutes, the Bellona maintained position, trading fire with Egyptian forts as rescued men were moved to safety.

"Water rising in forward compartments. Pumps struggling to keep pace."

"Shift ballast aft. Get more men on those pumps."

The Bellona wallowed deeper as water flooded forward sections, responding sluggishly to the helm. Another hit would doom them.

Then, unexpectedly, the Egyptian fire from the eastern fort, which had been pounding them the hardest, slackened. Valdar turned around trying to figure out why they'd gotten the sudden reprieve. The reason was one of the schooners that had been catching up had done the unthinkable. It had apparently sailed right at the fort and then turned hard, driving itself onto the shore, with its broadside still facing the fort, its guns fired continuously at point-blank range. That close, even the thickest walls would not stand up to the fire the schooner was putting down.

The schooner itself was taking a massive beating and fire had engulfed its deck. It managed to fire off one final devastating broadside before flames reached its powder magazine. The ship was smaller than a caravel, but it still carried significant amounts of powder and shells, and the resultant explosion sent a wall of fire and destruction over the fort, taking part of its western wall with the doomed ship, silencing many gun positions.

"Brave souls," Valdar murmured, adding the schooner's sacrifice to his mental tally.

The reduced fire gave him an opportunity. His ship was barely afloat and wouldn't have made it out at all, but the remaining two schooners threw tow lines as they passed, pulling the damaged flagship out after the fleet.

It helped that the enemy forts had slowed their fire. Between the pounding he'd given the western fort and the damage done by the exploding schooner to the eastern one, both were in bad shape.

The cost, however, had not been worth that tiny victory. In return for severely damaging two of the enemy forts, he had lost six caravels and three schooners, more than half his fleet, and the ships he had left were all damaged to some degree. The Bellona alone would need weeks in a dock to be truly seaworthy again.

They needed a new strategy if they were going to take Egypt.

Chapter 21

Factorium

"Empress," Hortensius said to Lucilla, as she and her guards were ushered onto the firing range. "Your timing is perfect. We've just completed our final checks."

She could smell the harsh scent of spent powder, suggesting that he'd already been testing the weapon this morning, which was good. The news from the front had not been good lately, and they needed this weapon out of testing and into the hands of the soldiers as quickly as possible.

"I trust this demonstration will prove more successful than our last, Hortensius."

She didn't intend for the statement to come out as caustic as it had, but it was hard to keep her concerns from coloring everything she said.

"Without question, Your Majesty. The problems we encountered were entirely in the cartridge manufacturing, not the weapon itself, and they have been sorted."

"Good. Then let's proceed with the demonstration," Lucilla said.

"Indeed. Manius, if you would."

Several praetorians and assistants had been standing off to the side when she'd arrived. One of them stepped forward to the table. He lifted the rifle, checking its mechanisms briefly before loading cartridges into the magazine and moving to the fire line. Bringing the rifle to his shoulder, feet planted in a stable stance, he took aim at the nearest row of wooden silhouettes positioned thirty paces downrange.

He paused, looking to Hortensius.

"Ready when you are," the manufacturer said.

Turning back, Manius fired the first shot, a loud crack split the air and startled Lucilla, even though she knew it was coming. Without lowering the weapon, he worked the lever mechanism, sending a brass cartridge cartwheeling out of the weapon and landing a few steps away.

A thump could be heard downrange as a hole appeared in the wooden silhouette.

As soon as the lever clicked closed, he fired again. Then he repeated the process, fire and lever, fire and lever, in a steady rhythm. Seven shots, seven holes in the target, all within the span of fifteen seconds.

She'd seen this once before, of course, but that time, the weapon had jammed after a few shots, even after being broken down and reassembled.

This time, there was no such delay.

As with that demonstration, she was impressed by how quickly it fired. Seven shots in fifteen seconds was much faster than the three shots a minute their best legionaries could manage with their current rifles.

"Impressive, although I do remember it firing all seven rounds in one of the last demonstrations as well."

Hortensius smiled. "Watch."

Manius lowered the rifle, reached for the ammunition box, extracted seven fresh cartridges, and fed them into the bottom of the weapon. The entire process took less than twenty seconds.

"From empty to fully loaded in under half a minute," Hortensius said. "In battlefield conditions, perhaps slightly longer, but still remarkably fast compared to our current rifles."

Once more, Manius brought the weapon to his shoulder and fired. Seven more shots rang out in rapid succession. Seven more targets showed impact marks. Not a single misfire or jam interrupted the sequence.

"We've conducted over three thousand test firings with the refined cartridge design," Hortensius said. "The failure rate is less than one in five hundred, which is unfortunately impossible to eliminate entirely, and is about the rate of failures for primers in our current rifles as well."

"Good," Lucilla said.

Hortensius motioned to another praetorian. "I did want to add a bit to the demonstration. Avitus here has never fired this rifle before today. He received basic instruction this morning, fired it once, and that's it. You're aware of how long it takes to teach new recruits to load and fire the current weapon in a reasonable amount of time. I think, beyond the direct benefit on the battlefield, once these are generally in service, it should also help decrease the amount of time needed to train the men. By a bit, at least."

Lucilla nodded thoughtfully. With their manpower consideration and all the conscripts about to enter service, that would be helpful.

The second praetorian took Manius's place at the firing line. His handling of the weapon lacked the grace of his more experienced counterpart, but he loaded more rounds without difficulty.

"The targets at sixty paces, if you please," Hortensius instructed.

Avitus raised the rifle and fired at the more distant row of targets. His first shot missed, but he quickly adjusted his aim. The next six rounds all struck their targets. A little slower and with somewhat less precision than Manius had demonstrated, but hits nonetheless.

"Most importantly," Hortensius continued, "the rifle's operation is intuitive enough that soldiers familiar with our current weapons can quickly master it. A few days of training should suffice for basic proficiency."

Avitus reloaded and fired another series of rounds, this time hitting all seven targets.

"The rate of fire is about four times that of our current rifles."

Avitus finished his demonstration and stepped back from the firing line. Hortensius turned to the third target range, where human-shaped silhouettes stood way in the distance, right up against a high, dirt berm meant to stop missed bullets.

"Those targets are over a thousand paces away. Manius, if you please."

Manius returned to the firing line, loaded more rounds into the weapon, and took aim at the distant targets. It was impossible to tell what happened with the naked eye. Hortensius picked up a spyglass from the table and handed it to her. It took Lucilla a moment to find the target, but when she did, she was able to make out a neat hole in the center of the wooden figure.

Manius continued firing, working the lever with remarkable speed. As she watched, three more found the target. The remaining must have missed, but it was hard to see where they impacted looking through the spyglass.

"The rifle's effective range is about the same as the current rifles, although I'm to understand the new powder Sorantius is working on will greatly extend that," Hortensius said, and then looked at Cynwrig, who'd been standing a few steps behind Lucilla. "Captain, would you care to try the weapon? As someone with no prior experience with this particular design, your assessment would be valuable."

Cynwrig looked to Lucilla, who nodded her approval. He stepped forward, accepting the rifle from Manius with the careful respect of a veteran warrior handling an unfamiliar weapon.

"The loading process is straightforward," Hortensius explained, demonstrating the procedure. "Insert the cartridges here, pointed end forward, and then slide the next one in behind it, and so on."

Cynwrig loaded seven cartridges into the magazine, his fingers hesitating between each round. Unlike the demonstrators, he was much slower in loading the rounds. Even still, he had them all inserted within about thirty seconds.

"The lever serves two purposes," Hortensius explained to him. "When pulled down and forward, it ejects the spent cartridge and cocks the hammer. When returned to the starting position, it chambers a new round."

Cynwrig nodded, then raised the rifle to his shoulder. He squinted down the sights at the closest target and squeezed the trigger. The rifle's recoil jerked his shoulder back. He blinked once, then worked the lever down with a stiff motion. Brass ejected out the side as the mechanism clicked. By his third shot, his hand moved the lever in one smooth motion, the mechanism flowing from fire to reload without pause.

All seven rounds struck their targets. Though half as fast as Manius, Cynwrig was still able to empty the weapon in under thirty seconds, a fraction of the time needed with a muzzle-loading rifle.

"Your impressions, Captain?" Lucilla asked.

Cynwrig hefted the rifle, testing its weight and balance. "I'm impressed. It's lighter than our current rifle, and much easier to use since it's not so long. The balance is good, although being able to use that weapon as a spear in moments of combat was a noticeable advantage."

"And maybe not needed since you can fire the weapon so much more quickly," Hortensius pointed out. "But, we have also developed a new bayonet for it. Yes, it doesn't have the reach of the current rifle, but you also aren't facing phalanx spears any longer."

Cynwrig shrugged and handed the weapon back to Hortensius.

Hortensius offered, holding it out to her as well. "Would you care to try the rifle yourself, Your Majesty?"

Lucilla considered the offer. As Empress, she rarely handled weapons, though over the last several years, Ky had taught her to shoot, just in case she ever found herself in need.

Also, because she enjoyed the experience.

"I would."

Hortensius smiled and checked the mechanism personally, quickly clearing it before loading new rounds into it and presenting the rifle to her.

"Loaded and ready, Your Majesty. Simply aim and squeeze the trigger. Be prepared for the recoil."

Lucilla accepted the weapon, bringing the stock to her shoulder and taking the stance Ky had shown her. She could hear Cynwrig let out a wry chuckle as he did every time she showed how capable she was. She drew a breath, aimed the rifle looking down the barrel as she'd been taught, and squeezed the trigger.

The rifle kicked against her shoulder harder than expected. Through dissipating smoke, she saw her shot had struck the target near its edge.

"Well struck," Hortensius said. "Now work the lever to chamber the next round."

Lucilla pulled the lever down and forward. The mechanism ejected the spent cartridge with a satisfying click. She pushed the lever back, feeling resistance as it chambered a new round.

Her second shot landed closer to the center. By the fifth round, she found her rhythm with the lever action, though each recoil challenged her smaller frame. She hit the target with all seven rounds.

"Remarkable," she said, lowering the weapon.

Her shoulder was a little sore as she handed it back to Hortensius, and she knew she would feel that in the morning, but it had been an exhilarating experience. Lucilla handed the rifle back to Hortensius, who immediately began disassembling it.

"Begin full production immediately. As soon as you have enough to justify it, I want them added onto whatever shipment is headed to frontline units in Germania and Greece. Make sure you send someone along with that shipment to explain how the rifle works. I know Ky should be there, but just in case."

"As you command. We've already got one line set up for them, and I will be adding additional lines within the next week."

"Good. Don't wait on any approvals. Just do what you have to do to get these to the front as quickly as possible. This weapon may determine the outcome of the war."

Devnum

Claudius and three of his praetorians crouched against the wall in the shaded alley as the freight train from Factorium pulled into the station, steam erupting from the locomotive's valves. It was a good position with a clear view of the unloading area, but just far enough away to keep them out of sight of the casual viewers.

He and his men each wore the types of clothes favored by dock workers instead of the uniform he normally took so much pride in.

After stopping the warehouse manager's arrangement for getting military supplies out of Factorium, Claudius had been sure another system would open up. The manager hadn't been nearly smart enough to be behind the smuggling operation himself, which meant whoever was would eventually find another middleman.

Claudius had been right. After a few weeks they'd started noticing more armaments going missing. This time, it was packers who were adding additional pieces into crates that were scheduled to ship before loading them. He and his men had been watching the activity for weeks, had witnessed them being unloaded on the other end, and where the marked crates had the extra pieces removed, were resealed, and then sent on their way.

Last time, he'd stepped in because he thought he could turn the manager and get the identity of his boss. Something Medb had been very good at doing. Sadly, the person behind it was smart enough to use a series of cutouts to pay the manager, so even the names he had given them ended up going nowhere, so he let the thefts continue so he could follow them to their destination.

The men loaded the new containers with the stolen goods into a wagon. As it pulled out, Claudius and his men followed on foot. Devnum was a bustling city with people quite literally everywhere, which made it easy to follow a wagon on foot. It headed toward the western edge of the port.

At the docks, the wagons turned away from the mass of warehouses that sat at the end of the docks and headed toward one of the loading berths at the far edge of the long dock area. It sat on the opposite side from the section that ended against the drydocks and was furthest from any of the warehouses that ships loaded and off-loaded from.

These were the least popular berths a ship could have and most ship's captains complained when they got stuck at one of these, which meant they tended to only be used when the port was particularly busy.

Which it wasn't right now, which meant the Scandi vessel waiting there now was secluded and by itself.

Claudius did not know the ship, whose name painted on its side proclaimed it to be the Njord, but he did recognize the man standing on the dock near its gangplank, supervising its loading.

Tall, with a red beard that was streaked gray, Sten had been one of the ship-owners whose ships Claudius had found were meeting the Egyptian crewed vessels. He and Medb had questioned Sten at the time, and he'd claimed ignorance, blaming the captains for acting without his knowledge.

It had seemed possible, as there had been several ships dealing with the Egyptians, and only one had been his. Now, however, it seemed like maybe that was also a cutout the man had been using, hiring other ships not connected to him to do his dirty work.

Sten was clever; there was no doubt of that. The fact that he was here and put himself where smuggled goods were being loaded suggested maybe things were not going so well for him at the moment.

And they were about to get worse, Claudius thought with a smile.

As Sten directed the goods from the wagon that Claudius had been following personally, a port official came walking up the dock, stopping and talking to the merchant. Claudius was not so naive to think that this was a chance inspection or that Sten would get caught, even though that was the official's job.

Sure enough, after less than two minutes speaking together, Sten handed a small sack, probably full of coin, to the man, who slipped it into his pocket and walked away, never once looking at the crates being carried onto the ship.

Claudius made a mental note to deal with that man later.

"Return to headquarters," he said to one of his men. "Bring twenty praetorians and meet us at that warehouse there, the one with the broken window on the second floor."

The man nodded and slipped away as Claudius made his way to the warehouse that had a view of Sten's ship. He had some time, as there were a lot of crates still left to be loaded. Probably there to help bury the smuggled cargo in the hold. The second floor of the warehouse provided an unobstructed view of the Njord, allowing him to watch everything without having to stand in the open.

The ship probably wouldn't sail until the evening tide, which was a good three hours away.

Praetorians arrived in small groups, filtering into the warehouse. By the time the twenty men were assembled, the loading operation was near completion. Empty wagons departed, and the Njord's crew looked to be preparing to sail.

"Once aboard, we need to move fast to make sure they don't destroy or hide any of the cargo," he ordered, pointing at a group of nine to ten of the men. "I want you lot to secure the deck and round up all the sailors. Bring them to the center of the deck and hold them there for questioning. The rest of you I want down in the hold as soon as we're onboard to make sure no one does anything to the cargo. As soon as we have the sailors there secured, I want you to start going through every single crate down to the very bottom of them. We're looking for controlled goods such as rifles, rifle parts, and artillery shells, although anything that seems out of place from the other goods should be set aside to be examined. Let's go."

The group moved quickly, practically sprinting from the warehouse to the ship, so that they would be on board before Sten and his men had a chance to do anything. A shout went up as they got to the gangplank, but by then, it was too late.

The ship's crew, startled, had only started to look around as his praetorians reached the deck and began rounding the men up.

"This ship is impounded by order of the Empress," Claudius announced. "Any resistance will be met with lethal force."

"What is the meaning of this?" Sten demanded, emerging from the captain's cabin.

"Your vessel is suspected of transporting contraband weapons and military supplies in violation of Imperial export restrictions and is hereby impounded on order of the Praetorian Guard."

"This is absurd! I carry only legitimate trade goods, wool, ceramics, and lumber," he sputtered, turning to the ship's captain. "Show them the manifest."

The second praetorian team had already descended into the cargo hold. The crew must not have done a good job of hiding the goods, because by the time the Njord's captain produced the ship's manifest, one of the praetorians had returned to the deck.

"Tribune, we've found some artillery shells buried beneath other goods. The men are still looking through the rest."

"I know nothing of this! If contraband is aboard, it was loaded without my knowledge. Perhaps ..."

"I didn't just happen to stumble across your ship. I observed you personally directing the loading of crates I knew to contain contraband materials," Claudius interrupted. "You supervised the entire operation, accepted the shipment from wagons, and paid off a port official, who is being detained at this very minute."

Claudius hadn't sent anyone for the official yet, but Sten didn't need to know that.

The merchant's shoulders slumped slightly, but he maintained his facade. "These are baseless accusations. I demand to speak with the Scandian consul."

"You'll have that opportunity after questioning at Praetorian headquarters."

Claudius dispatched two praetorians to secure Sten while he oversaw the search of the captain's cabin. They seized the ship's logs, navigation charts, cargo manifests, and correspondence.

Now, they would need to question the man and see just how far this went.

Chapter 22

Greece

Gundomar pressed against the muddy trench wall as another shell screamed overhead. Thirty yards behind their position, it detonated, hurling dirt and metal fragments in all directions. It was as though Nastrond, the shore of corpses, had been brought from the underworld into this place. They had endured eighteen or maybe even twenty hours under constant fire. He'd lost count by this point as, minute after minute, shells exploded around them, shaking the ground and his nerves alike.

"Down!"

Another shell landed closer. The impact struck ten yards right, percussion hammering his chest as dirt rained down. A young legionary huddled against the opposite wall, hands over his ears, mouth opened in the way that they'd all learned helped equalize the pressure. The young man's eyes, however, told the tale. Vacant, wide things that stared into nothing.

The men were starting to break, enduring things he'd never thought possible until now.

"The tribune said they would pull us from the line soon," a man huddling near Gundomar said, one of the veterans who'd arrived when the Consul repositioned them from Germania to this place.

Blood trickled from a cut above the man's eye.

"The tribune says things. It doesn't matter. Either they'll come or they won't."

The man shrugged in response.

For a moment, the shells began to fall a little further away, pounding a section of the trench to their left. It didn't help his nerves, since he knew they would swing back in his direction, but for now, he used the reprieve to check on his men. He crouched, still staying low to keep from being surprised, scuttling through ankle-deep mud, checking their trench section. Around a corner, he found a partially collapsed wall and three men injured by a very close hit.

One would be gone in the next few minutes, a massive hole torn through his chest. The other two … perhaps. A few years ago, he would say all three would die, but the Britannians had been doing impressive things with medicine these days.

"You four," Gundomar said, pointing at some men who looked mostly together. "Drag them to the aid station, then return to your positions."

As the men moved to obey, another shell landed close by. Close enough that, for a moment, Gundomar thought he would be going with the injured men. But no explosion followed. Looking up at the edge of the trench, he could see something metallic protruding from the packed soil. The shell hadn't exploded. It just … sat there. The men around him, who he'd ordered to pull the injured away, just stood there, all of them staring at the thing, probably wondering if it was going to go off.

"Ignore it and do as you were ordered!" Gundomar said, startling the soldiers out of their fixation and getting them moving, taking the wounded to the rear.

Gundomar turned to see a wild-eyed soldier climbing the trench wall, clawing at the dirt, screaming, "Have to get out! Have to get out!"

Three men dragged him back as another explosion showered them with dirt. The man collapsed sobbing, curled against the trench wall.

Gundomar just shook his head and moved on, both to continue his inspection and to get away from the unexploded shell. He wasn't sure how much longer they could sustain this.

He continued down the trench, stepping over, and sometimes on, men packed into the narrow confines. Some prayed, others stared ahead. Veterans reloaded rifles or just hunkered down, trying to stay sane.

They were in an important section of the miles of trenches dug into a long, zigzagging line. This section held a curve that bent toward a set of low hills, standing out and exposed as one of the furthest east points in the line.

Not a great place to be.

Another impact, followed by the rumbling of a wall collapsing. Screams could be heard coming from down the line. And then suddenly ... silence. It hadn't tapered off or slowed. It had simply stopped.

The men around him looked momentarily relieved, but Gundomar knew what the sudden, complete silence meant.

"Firing positions! Check rifles! Fix bayonets!" He began yelling; pulling men out of the places they'd been hiding and pushing them into position.

Veterans needed no explanation. Coordinated artillery silence like this meant an infantry attack. Men rushed to the firing steps, sticking their weapons above the edge of the trench.

"Movement," someone called from down the way.

Gundomar climbed up on a firing step, peering through a sand-bag gap. As a breeze shifted the smoke, he felt his stomach drop.

The horizon had transformed into a moving mass of men. Eastern troops with their pale skin like ripe wheat, Greeks with their olive complexion and wiry hair, Egyptians with their almost bronzed hue were all part of the first wave, advancing in large masses that stretched beyond sight in both directions.

"Gods of my fathers," Gundomar whispered.

He'd been on this end of many charges against the trenches in Germania. None had rivaled this.

A shot cracked and a man standing beside Gundomar jerked backward, blood spurting from his throat. Gundomar grabbed him, dragging him down as crimson spray patterned their uniforms. The man's eyes rolled back, his final breath gurgling through his neck wound.

"Fire!" he screamed as his men just watched the oncoming horde.

The Britannian line erupted as the enemy closed in. Gundomar sighted an officer leading the first wave, squeezed the trigger, and watched him crumple. Front ranks fell, but the waves of men coming behind pushed forward over fallen comrades without pause.

Where one man fell, three more appeared, with weapons lowered toward the trench. The waves created an illusion of the dead rising again, an endless tide flowing toward their position.

Britannian artillery responded from behind their position. Shells burst among the advancing troops, throwing bodies skyward. One blast opened a twenty-foot gap in the enemy formation, but it closed within seconds as men flowed around the crater.

It was like they had a never-ending supply of bodies to throw at them.

Gundomar dropped below the parapet to reload, measuring powder, ramming the ball down the barrel. Along the line, men fired in a staggered sequence, maintaining pressure while their comrades reloaded.

"They're at the wire!" someone shouted.

Gundomar returned to his position. True enough, the enemy vanguard had reached the barbed obstacles two hundred and fifty paces in front of the trench line. Eastern soldiers pushed sections down with poles, others threw mats over the barbs. Some simply pushed forward, or rather were pushed forward, their falling bodies becoming bridges for those coming behind.

He fired, reloaded, fired again. After his third shot, the enemy closed to one hundred paces or so. Individual faces became visible. Determined, afraid, some shouting unintelligible war cries through the battle noise.

At fifty paces, both sides fired with frantic urgency. No-man's land became a hellscape of cratered mud, discarded weapons, and dismembered bodies. Blood and black powder stench filled the air.

"Grenades!"

All along the line, men grabbed the fin-shaped weapons from belts or small stashes, pulled the priming cords, and heaved them onto the ground above. A ripple of explosions blasted out as they landed, killing men by the dozens. And still, on they came.

"Through on the left!"

Egyptian forces, by the look of them, poured into a section where the defenders had been thinned. Men fired at point-blank range, then fought with bayonets.

An Eastern soldier appeared above Gundomar's position, sliding down the wall with rifle extended. Gundomar lunged, driving his bayonet into the man's chest. Dark eyes widened in shock, then glazed over as Gundomar wrenched the bayonet free.

More followed. Gundomar fired at the next man, the shot taking him in the face. Three more dropped in before he could reload.

"Stand fast!" Gundomar shouted as he swung his rifle like a club.

The wooden stock connected with an attacker's head, sending him sprawling. Single shots, clashing metal, and screams filled the air. The trench became a slaughterhouse. Britannians thrust bayonets, dropping enemy soldiers while others fought hand-to-hand.

A few even pulled swords that they kept on them, returning to the old ways of fighting.

One of the men he'd sent earlier to carry the wounded was a few steps away, grappling with a Greek soldier, locked in a deadly embrace until drawing a knife and plunging it into his opponent's ribs. Blood spurted, coating both men as they fell. His man rose while the Greek remained on the ground.

Hand-to-hand fighting engulfed the entire trench system as the firing line was overwhelmed. Gundomar faced an Egyptian officer who slashed at him with a curved sword, missing his throat by inches. Gundomar countered with his bayonet; the Egyptian parried skillfully.

Gundomar was saved from the man's counter when a grenade landed amidst the handful of Egyptians that had come with the officer and exploded, tearing their bodies apart.

The victory was short-lived as another man tackled him from behind, slamming him into the trench wall. Hands closed around his throat, cutting off his air. Gundomar twisted, trying to turn over, clawing at his attacker's face, fingers finding an eye socket and pressing with desperate strength. The man screamed, releasing his grip.

Few men reloaded rifles now. The fighting was too close for the slow process of powder and ball. They fought with bayonets, knives, entrenching tools, and bare hands.

Bodies littered the trench floor, creating macabre barricades used by both sides. Gundomar grabbed a fallen rifle and vaulted over intertwined corpses to engage an Eastern officer who had killed two Britannians.

The officer thrust his blade toward Gundomar's midsection. Gundomar twisted aside, feeling the blade tear his uniform without touching flesh. Gundomar brought his rifle butt down on the officer's arms, breaking his weapon grip. A follow-up strike dropped the man to his knees, where a Britannian finished him with a bayonet thrust.

The enemy was everywhere and quickly surrounding them.

"Front line collapsing! Fall back! Fall back to the secondary trench."

That was all the men needed to turn and run as if their lives depended on it.

Which they did.

Gundomar led the retreat down a narrow zigzagging trench toward the rear positions. They met Eastern soldiers who had broken through elsewhere, engaging them in short, violent clashes in the confined space.

Men around him fell as the enemy fired into their backs.

Those with loaded rifles provided cover fire, each shot followed by desperate bayonet defense during reloading. Gundomar had managed to load the last round he had on him and fired at an enemy blocking their path, then rushed forward to finish him with his bayonet.

As he started forward again, a young legionary near him stumbled, blood pouring from a thigh wound. Gundomar dropped his rifle and pulled the sword he kept at his side, something most of the men still did. Grabbing the injured man's collar, he dragged him toward the secondary line while fending off attackers. Thankfully, the men who'd been there, mostly recuperating from the daylong shelling, had formed a line at the communication trench and fired over their heads at the pursuers.

Ahead, someone yelled, "Hold fire! Friendlies coming!"

Hands pulled them into the secondary trench and relative safety. Gundomar counted eight men from his original section, plus the wounded soldier. The rest were lost in the attack.

The secondary trench was better constructed, deeper, with comprehensive overhead cover and reinforced firing positions, built for this contingency.

Desperate fighting continued as front-line survivors joined the fallback defenders. Gundomar found himself alongside troops from three different units, all fighting to prevent the enemy from overrunning this final line.

He'd found a rifle someone had dropped and some ammo from a reserve box, putting himself back into the fight. They had a small reprieve when the enemy attack briefly slowed. They still pushed at them, but with less intensity than before.

He knew it was only a reprieve, though. They were reorganizing, reinforcing, and getting ready to go again, and Gundomar didn't have enough men to counterattack and take back the lost stretch of trench, and what men he did have were injured and out of ammo.

Gundomar positioned his remaining men along the thirty yards near the communication trench and waited. Men distributed ammunition and water from the dead to the living. A medical orderly applied hasty bandages to wounds that allowed the men to keep fighting.

The reprieve didn't last long. Within a few minutes, the Easterners and their allies got themselves sorted out and the attack was renewed, just as vigorous as before.

Gundomar fired at the first man he saw, an enemy officer advancing through the zigzag of connecting trenches, dropping him as he came around a corner. But he wasn't alone.

Before Gundomar could reach for another paper cartridge, three Eastern soldiers rounded the same corner, leaping over the dead man. Gundomar thrust with his bayonet, driving the lead man back against his comrades in the narrow passage while Britannian soldiers to either side dealt with his friends.

The ground shook, knocking Gundomar off balance for a moment as Britannian artillery adjusted their fire, shells now landing nearly on top of them, just beyond the captured front line positions, trying to stem the flow of the enemy soldiers pouring into their trenches with a wall of metal and fire.

Gundomar attempted to reload, but the mechanism seized. The rifle he'd grabbed had mud caked with powder clogging the firing hammer, keeping it from evenly striking the primer cap. He discarded the weapon, snatching another from the dozens dropped on the ground around them. This one must have just been used, since the barrel was still warm to the touch.

To his right, there was a sudden commotion: shouts for help as the defenders in that section, which connected to a separate communication trench, began to thin beyond their ability to defend themselves. Gundomar pulled five men from the center section and rushed to the threatened intersection.

"Stand! Stand and fight!"

The Eastern forces had broken through the junction, advancing in single file through the narrow passage. Gundomar thrust his bayonet into the lead soldier's abdomen, twisting the blade before wrenching it free. His men fired a ragged volley past him into the packed communication trench, dropping several attackers who tried to press forward over their fallen comrades.

Men stabbed and slashed at those within arm's reach, unable to properly swing weapons or maneuver. Blood slicked the duckboards underfoot, forcing men to grab at trench walls for balance as they fought. Greek officers shouted orders from the rear, urging more men forward into the bottleneck where Britannian defenders cut them down.

"They're coming through the left passage!" someone shouted from behind him.

Gundomar grimaced. They were about to lose this trench, too, and there was not a third trench line here like there had been in Germania. They hadn't had time to dig out more.

Gundomar pulled two men he'd just brought with him. It might not leave enough men to hold this junction, but they were running out of men and options. They rushed through fifty yards of support trench, arriving at the threatened position as Egyptian soldiers emerged from a connecting passage.

One of his men fell the moment they turned a corner into point-blank fire. Gundomar and the others took cover behind a collapsed section of trench wall, firing whenever Egyptian helmets appeared at the junction. A rifle ball grazed Gundomar's upper arm, slicing out a small gouge of cloth and flesh.

More enemy soldiers pushed into the junction, forcing Gundomar and his men back. Three attackers rushed at once. Gundomar parried a bayonet thrust with his rifle barrel, pivoted to drive his own blade into a second man's throat, then narrowly avoided a knife thrust from the third. The other man with him fought with equal ferocity, knowing that retreating deeper into the trench system only hastened their encirclement.

Finally, he heard something he'd been longing for since the attack started: trumpets. The unmistakable brass notes of Alliance reinforcements sounded from the rear support trenches, stopping where the enemy had pushed forward and firing full volleys into them.

The sudden influx of Western Alliance men caused the momentum of the Easterners to halt, and then to retract. Gundomar and the other survivors joined the counterattack, battling alongside the fresh troops to retake their lost ground.

For the first time since the bombardment began, Gundomar thought he might survive this. The Eastern forces, now caught in the same confined spaces they had used to advantage, fell back through the communication trenches, pressed hard by the now larger allied forces. Their own reinforcements had been stopped by a veritable wall of artillery.

They cleared the trenches yard by bloody yard, stepping over the fallen troops from both sides. Some wounded still lived, pressed against trench walls to avoid being trampled as the counterattack surged past. Men moaned for water, for mercy, for death.

As they approached the original front line, resistance stiffened. Eastern soldiers had fortified key junctions, turning dugouts into strong points. Gundomar directed rifle fire against these positions, then led a rush down a straight section of trench toward a dugout entrance held by Egyptian forces.

As he rounded the final bend, almost back to where he'd started the day, an Egyptian soldier suddenly emerged from the corner, driving his bayonet deep into Gundomar's chest before he could react. White-hot pain exploded through his torso as the blade sunk into him.

His anger was joined by a flood of pain, and Gundomar stabbed out with his own rifle, right into the man's head. As his killer fell, Gundomar collapsed against the trench wall, blood filling his lungs with each labored breath. His rifle slipped from nerveless fingers, clattering onto the duckboards as he slid down into the mud.

The man who'd been with him was grabbing onto his jacket, trying to hold him up, yelling for a medic, but the sound was distant. Far away.

The pain started to fade as the world became fuzzy around him. Gundomar's final thoughts weren't of the war, weren't of victory or defeat, not of armies and the men he commanded. They were of the forests of his childhood and of the wind through its trees, calling him home.

Devnum

Lucilla stood at the window of her private reception chamber, looking out at the bustling main street that led from here all the way to the coliseum. It had been quite the day, every minute of it filled with long, stressful meetings.

But meetings she needed to chair, in order to prepare things for the conversation she was about to have.

She turned from the window as a sharp knock sounded at the door, followed a moment later by Commander Faenius, who entered, trailing a weathered man with broad shoulders and dark hair that set him apart from his countrymen.

"Your Majesty, Captain Kolbeinn, as ordered."

"Your Majesty," the captain said in accented but fluent Latin. "I am honored by your summons, though I confess I am puzzled why someone in your position would wish to speak with a simple ship captain."

Lucilla studied him for a long moment, partially to set the mood and make him just a little more nervous, but also noting how much he resembled his uncle, Bjarki, who was one of the leading merchants in all of Scandi, and the de facto leader of their council.

"You are more than just a simple captain. You are also the nephew of, arguably, the most important person in Scandia."

"I am not my uncle. I am just a simple ship captain."

"True, but you can get in to see your uncle, which makes you exactly who I need. Now, I'm curious. Are you aware, Captain, that Scandi vessels continue to trade openly with Egyptian ports despite Egypt's recent betrayal of Britannia and their alliance with the Eastern forces?"

"I've heard rumors of some independent merchants making such voyages, Your Majesty. But many captains operate without direct oversight from ..."

"These are not rumors, Captain. We have intercepted several Scandi ships coming and going from Egyptian ports in the last several weeks, and the ports of allies who've been invaded and are currently held in Egyptian hands. Some of these ships have been carrying military supplies like gunpowder, which is being used against our people."

"Again, Your Majesty, these are private merchants acting on their own initiative. The Scandi Council has declared neutrality in this conflict."

"Neutrality is buying military supplies from us and selling them to our enemies? This passes as neutrality to you?" Lucilla asked. "That isn't the worst of it, however. One week ago, practorians seized a Scandi vessel called the Njord. Its captain was caught loading military supplies stolen from our factories. Supplies not sold to anyone outside the Western Alliance. Supplies meant for our troops fighting on the eastern front."

"Your Majesty, I know nothing of this. That ship and its captain are unknown to me."

"I am highly doubtful of that, but whether you know him personally is irrelevant. What matters is that your countryman was caught smuggling Britannian artillery shells to Egyptian vessels, which were used to learn how we made the weapons and then produce shells of their own, which are right now killing my people."

"Your Majesty, I cannot speak for the actions of individual captains or ..."

"Then speak for your government. Because I have reason to believe that Scandi leadership is deliberately maintaining commercial relationships with both sides in this conflict while claiming neutrality. A profitable position, to be sure, but hardly a neutral one when those commercial relationships include selling weapons to our enemies."

"I know nothing of any such arrangements and cannot speak for the leaders of my people either."

"I am aware, and I wasn't expecting answers from you. I want you to take what I'm going to say and speak with your uncle. I need him to understand that this pattern of behavior constitutes a serious breach of Scandi's claimed neutrality. One that Britannia will not tolerate. I want you to tell him that, effective immediately, Scandi will be considered a potentially hostile nation by the Britannic Empire. This decision has been reached after consultation with the other Western Alliance nations who share our concerns and they will be treating your people the same way."

The captain's face registered shock. "Potentially hostile? Your Majesty, what exactly does that mean?"

"It means, Captain, that all Scandi vessels are now barred from entering any Britannic port throughout the Empire. Any Scandi ship attempting to dock at a Britannic port will be turned away by naval forces. This blockade extends to all commercial, diplomatic, and private Scandi vessels regardless of their stated purpose. Moreover, our Western Alliance partners have agreed to implement similar restrictions in their territories. Germania, Gaul, Italia, and Hispania will all close their ports to Scandi vessels."

"Your Majesty, surely this is an overreaction to the actions of a few ..."

"I am not finished, Captain. To enforce these rules, any Scandi vessels ignoring this embargo will face military consequences from Britannian naval forces. Ships attempting to get around the restrictions by trying to sail into one of our ports will either be sunk or confiscated as prizes of war, and their crews detained for the duration of the conflict."

"This is tantamount to a declaration of war!"

"No, Captain. This is a measured response to Scandi's breach of neutrality. A declaration of war would involve our navy actively hunting down your vessels on the open sea and sending legionaries into your villages. For now, we are simply protecting our own waters and ports from a nation that has demonstrated it cannot be trusted."

The Captain opened his mouth to protest, but Lucilla continued without pause.

"In addition to the restrictions on our ports, Scandi merchants and government officials are no longer permitted to purchase any military goods or technology from Britannia. All existing agreements for weapons, ammunition, and military equipment are suspended indefinitely. Several pending orders for muskets and powder will be canceled, with deposits forfeited to the Imperial Treasury. Again, this prohibition extends to all Britannian allies who have agreed to honor this military embargo."

"Your Majesty, the economic impact of these measures ..."

"Will be severe, yes. So, perhaps, selling to our enemies wasn't the wise financial decision it once seemed. Furthermore, construction on Scandi ships currently in Britannian shipyards will halt immediately. Any vessels that have already started being built will be sold to another ally, with the money put down for their construction being forfeit. Scandi representatives will not be permitted to place new orders with any Britannian industrial concerns until this matter is resolved to our satisfaction."

"You can't do this. You have limited us from trading with nearly every nation in our reach. This will ruin most of our merchant houses!"

"I am aware of that, Captain. *These are the consequences* for the decisions your people have made. I hope they know that it is within your, or at least your uncle's, power to get these restrictions removed. You are to deliver this message personally to your uncle. It contains the formal written terms for Scandi to end the embargo," she said, handing him an already written and sealed document. "Scandi must cease all trade with Egypt and the Eastern forces immediately. Your vessels will submit to inspections by Britannian naval officers to verify compliance. Additionally, you must turn over any captains who delivered smuggled cargo to enemies of the Western Alliance for trial under Britannian law."

"And if we comply with these demands?"

"Full diplomatic and trade relations will be restored, the embargo will be lifted, and Scandi vessels will once again be welcome in our ports.

"I see," he said, taking the message.

"You are dismissed, Captain. Your ship will be the only Scandi vessel permitted to leave Devnum harbor, to ensure my message reaches Scandi leadership promptly. Every other Scandi vessel in any Britannian port is, as of this moment, impounded until we receive a response."

"I will deliver your message, but I cannot predict how our council will respond to such … demands."

"That is not my concern, Captain. My concern is protecting the lives of my soldiers from weapons *illegally sold to our enemies*. How your government responds will determine whether Scandi prospers or suffers in the months to come."

Chapter 23

Greece

Mud caked their boots in thick, sucking globs as Ky and Modius made their way down the secondary trench. Recent rainfall combined with thousands of men moving through the narrow passages had turned sections of the defensive network into a quagmire and the wooden boards put down to ease the situation had been totally buried in a few days.

Modius looked slightly ill as they pushed through the throng of men moving around the trench. Ky was glad for the control Sophus's nanites gave him to cut off the smells of unwashed bodies and latrine pits.

"Third cohort reports all quiet in their sector, Consul," Modius said.

"That won't last, but I'm glad they have a reprieve. Let's see what we can do about getting some reinforcements into their ranks while we have the chance."

Modius nodded, making a mental note, as they passed a group of soldiers huddled around a small fire, heating tins of beans and salt pork.

Not one of the flashier inventions like artillery and gunpowder, but the ability to can and preserve food in thin metal cans, sealed and then heated to kill bacteria, had been one of the key things that had allowed him to turn their society into a reflection of the post-industrial revolution world.

Less food rotted in the autumn and more food was available in the winter, meaning starvation, once one of the biggest killers in the world, was slowly becoming a thing of the past.

It also made it much easier to feed and supply men who used to rely on foraging for most of their rations. Looking at this place, its trenches where no one wanted to stick their head above ground level, foraging wasn't an option. It made armies of the size they were fielding now possible.

"Sit. Sit," Ky said when the men all jumped up. "How's the food?"

"Better than nothing, Consul," a young soldier replied, his accent marking him as one of the new recruits from Gaul.

"When's the last time your squad rotated to the rear?"

"Three days ago, sir," answered an older soldier with sergeant's marks on his collar. "We're due for relief tomorrow."

"Good. You're doing a fine job, boys. Keep it up."

He continued down the line, stopping occasionally to speak with groups of soldiers. Despite their fatigue, morale remained surprisingly high. The men had confidence in their defenses, in their commanders.

A big change from how soldiers in trenches felt during the first use of the strategy, in that different future.

A distant rumble broke the relative quiet, followed by several more in quick succession. Modius tensed and all the men around them paused, listening, wondering if this was the sign of the next attack.

"Sounds like the northern sector," Ky said. "They've been hitting it hard for the past three days."

They weren't in the line of fire, but it was a sign that a new attack was starting, which meant it was time for the pair to return to the command bunkers. In his heart, Ky wanted to stand and fight with his men, but being ripped apart by a shell wouldn't help them, so he went where he was most needed.

The command bunker was a sturdy structure of timber beams, sandbags, and corrugated metal, built into the reverse slope of a small hill. A young signalman held the canvas door open as they approached, and they ducked inside just as another shell exploded nearby, rattling the lamp that hung from the center beam.

Inside, a dozen officers and signalmen worked at wooden tables covered with maps and telegraph stations.

"Situation report," Ky demanded as he moved to the central table where a large map of the defensive lines was spread out.

A staff optio straightened from where he'd been marking positions. "Eastern batteries opened up across the line thirty minutes ago, Consul. Heaviest concentration in sectors three and four."

"Casualties?"

"Minimal so far. Most men were already in the trenches or shelters when the barrage started."

Ky studied the map, noting the positions of their own artillery batteries and the estimated locations of enemy guns. The Britannian line formed a rough semicircle protecting the approaches to Athens from the north and east. But the northern section bulged outward in a dangerous salient, a vulnerability the enemy had clearly identified.

Another shell landed close enough to shower dust from the ceiling.

"Another attack will be coming soon," Ky said.

"It might work. We've abandoned these forward observation posts as unsustainable. And here we were forced to withdraw to the secondary trench line after they hit us with what must have been fifteen thousand men. We held as long as possible, but they were willing to take massive casualties to force us back."

Ky studied the pattern of withdrawals. Most were minor, tactical retreats to more defensible positions. But the pattern was concerning, a slow, methodical compression of their defensive perimeter, particularly in the northern sector.

"They're creating a breakthrough point. If they punch through here, they can roll up our flanks and compromise the entire defensive position."

"Precisely my concern. The cost for them has been high. My best guess is they're losing five to ten men for every one of ours. I can't believe they're willing to waste so many lives."

"And yet it's working. They're forcing us to expend precious ammunition and wearing down our men. Yes, the enemy may be losing more bodies, but they're inflicting high losses as well. Our veterans are being replaced with green recruits who've barely completed basic training. The worst part is, there's no sign the East is running out of men, especially now that they're throwing Greeks and Egyptians into the fight. This is a war of attrition, Modius, and I think we're losing it."

The artillery fire outside intensified, the impacts coming closer together. The bunker shook continuously now, small streams of dirt trickling from between the ceiling timbers.

"We could reinforce the northern section with reserves from the southern trenches," Modius suggested. "The attacks there have been less frequent and less severe."

"Bring up small groups, but we have to be careful. I saw this tactic in Germania. They hammer one section of the line, wait for us to shift our forces, then strike where we've weakened ourselves."

"Message from the rail depot, Consul," a messenger said, coming into the bunker and handing over a folded paper.

"Finally," Ky said, reading its contents. When Modius raised an eyebrow, Ky added. "New shipment from Devnum."

"Ammunition?" Modius asked hopefully.

"Better. Come on."

Ky led Modius through a series of communication trenches toward the rear area where the rail depot had been established. The narrowness of the trenches forced them to move single-file, Ky in the lead with Modius following closely.

They passed stretcher-bearers carrying wounded men toward the field hospital, soldiers moving ammunition forward to the fighting positions, and messengers running between command posts. Despite the chaos, there was order to the movement, the product of months of training and the hard lessons learned from recent battles.

When they emerged from the trench system, they found themselves in a cleared area a mile behind the front line. A short wagon ride later, they arrived at a rail depot consisting of three parallel tracks with wooden platforms between them. A locomotive stood hissing on the central track, six freight cars behind it. Dozens of men worked to unload crates from the cars, transferring them to wagons for distribution to the front.

"Those crates marked with red bands, are those the special shipments from Factorium?" he asked one of the quartermasters.

"Yes, Consul," the man said, consulting a manifest. "Forty crates of the new rifles and two hundred of ammunition for them."

"Have three crates of each brought to that clearing," Ky ordered, pointing to a flat area thirty yards away. "I want to inspect them before they're distributed."

While they waited, another artillery shell landed close enough to be concerning, though they were well out of immediate danger. The men at the depot barely reacted, continuing their work with the resigned efficiency of soldiers who'd grown accustomed to the danger.

The requested crates arrived on a handcart pushed by two legionaries. At Ky's direction, they set them down and pried open the wooden lids.

Inside the first crate, packed carefully in straw, lay ten lever-action rifles. Ky lifted one out, feeling its weight and balance. It was noticeably shorter than their current model, with a distinctive brass loading mechanism on the right side.

Modius picked up another, examining it with the critical eye of a professional soldier. "These are strange. So much shorter than our current rifles. It's hard to believe this is what we're going to replace our current rifles with."

"The reduced length is by design. It makes them easier and faster to use."

He reached into one of the ammunition crates and removed a small cardboard box. Inside were twenty metal cartridges, each containing powder, primer, and bullet in a single unit. Ky loaded seven cartridges into the rifle's tubular magazine.

"Stand back," he warned, moving to the edge of the clearing where several empty crates were stacked against an earthen berm.

Ky raised the rifle to his shoulder, aimed at the crates, and worked the lever to chamber the first round. He fired, the rifle bucking against his shoulder. Without pausing, he worked the lever again, chambering a new round from the magazine. He fired seven shots in rapid succession, his hands a blur of motion.

The sound of the unexpected gunfire caused men throughout the depot to dive for cover. A few reached for their own weapons before realizing who was firing.

Modius stared at the splintered remains of the target crates, then at the rifle in Ky's hands. His normal stoic expression gave way to undisguised amazement.

"That's ... incredible," he said finally. "Seven shots just like that, without reloading."

Modius accepted the rifle Ky handed him and tried the loading procedure himself. Though he was not as quick as Ky, he managed to load the seven rounds without difficulty.

"This changes everything," Modius said, working the lever to feel the action's smoothness. "One man becomes the equivalent of a dozen."

"That's the plan," Ky confirmed, watching as Modius took aim at the remains of the target and fired three quick shots. "They've matched us in artillery. They've copied our basic rifle designs. But they don't have this, yet. It took them years to replicate our rifles. I hope it takes just as much time to figure out these."

Ky put the two rifles back into the crate and called over the quartermaster who'd been standing just a few steps away, watching his commanders talk.

"I want these rifles distributed immediately, with priority to the front-line units in the northern sector."

The officer saluted and began barking orders to his men. Within minutes, the crates were being loaded onto wagons for transport to the front.

Ky felt the first wave of relief he had in months. Finally, they had an edge again.

Devnum

Lucilla wiped Titus's chin, getting the bits of mashed-up vegetable that hadn't made it into his mouth. He gurgled at her, smiling and giving a little laugh.

That sight never failed to warm her heart, and she was thankful again for being able to be here in Devnum with him. No matter what setbacks they'd had to deal with, she always had this little refuge to return to, escaping the pressures of her office.

A soft knock at the door interrupted her as she lifted him out of the small, enclosed stool she used for feeding him. Part of her wanted to shout and tell the person to go away, but she knew that wasn't an option.

With a frown, she turned and handed Titus to the nurse who was hovering a few steps away and said, "Enter."

"I'm sorry to bother you," the guard said, knowing as well as anyone how much she valued this time. "But a group of Scandi officials just arrived in port and are being escorted here to the palace. They're demanding an immediate audience."

Lucilla sighed. She'd been expecting this; she just wished they'd had better timing.

"Have them shown to the Small Audience Chamber. I'll receive them in twenty minutes." After the man bowed and exited, she went back to little Titus. "I'm sorry to leave you so soon. Be good for your nurses."

She leaned down and kissed his little head before giving a tired but warm smile to the woman holding him and going to her dressing room. This meeting required proper attire, not the full Imperial regalia, which would suggest defensiveness, but something that projected authority without ostentation. She selected a deep purple stola over a white tunic, with gold clasps at the shoulders bearing the Britannian Eagle, and a simple gold diadem to complete the ensemble.

She preferred the pants and tunics that had become common wear in the last several years, even for official functions, but something like this, it was better to lean on tradition. It added weight to the statement she was making.

The Small Audience Chamber was aptly named, a room designed for more intimate diplomatic meetings rather than full state functions. Marble columns supported a ceiling painted with scenes from Britannian history, including the near burning of the palace during her brother's revolt.

Lucilla entered through a side door, the guards snapping to attention as she passed. She took her seat, arranging herself on the high-backed but otherwise simple chair, and waited, gaming out the conversation that was about to happen in her head, preparing herself.

After several minutes, the double doors opened to reveal four men in heavy woolen tunics with intricate embroidery. Warm but as much their leaning into tradition as she was. Hrolfson, who she'd negotiated with several times before, was at their front. The other three were unknown to her. Two older men who had both clearly spent a long life at sea, and a younger man who seemed much too green to be at a meeting like this.

"Empress," he said, skipping the normal formalities. "By what right does Britannia seize Scandi vessels? By what right do you close every Western port to our ships? We are a neutral nation, free to trade with whom we choose. This embargo is nothing short of piracy. After a lifetime of peace between our peoples, including our joining you in your war against Carthage, and now you treat us as enemies. We will not be bullied by Britannian imperialism. We demand the immediate release of all vessels and crews you are holding and compensation for lost trade."

Lucille had waited, keeping any emotion or thoughts off her face, just watching him passively as he vented his anger. When he finally wound down, breathing slightly from the lather he worked himself into, she didn't reply right away. She continued to stare at him, calmly, causing him to squirm slightly.

"Are you finished, Commander?" she finally said.

"For now."

"Then let me explain why those ships were seized." Lucilla rose from her seat, stepping down from the dais to stand on equal footing with the delegation. "The Evrinna was found with four tons of gunpowder in barrels marked as salt. The Hammerskjold, docked in one of our harbors, was holding three hundred rifle barrels and firing mechanisms. I could go on, listing the prohibited items smuggled out of Britannian ports. Or I could mention that most of these ships had Egyptian crew members, which is something I found to be very interesting. It has always been my understanding that the Scandi think poorly of the Egyptians as sailors, which makes finding so many of them aboard Scandi ships involved in smuggling military supplies interesting. To say the least."

"I wouldn't ..."

"Neutrality, Commander, does not extend to smuggling weapons that will be used to kill Britannian soldiers," she said, rolling over him. "It does not cover espionage or the transport of enemy agents. These are acts of war."

"The actions of individual captains do not represent the policy of the Scandi Confederation," he said. "These men are independent merchants seeking profit, not representatives of our government. We maintain our neutrality in this conflict."

"Your captains carry weapons that will be used against our citizens. The distinction between private action and state policy becomes meaningless when the result is the same."

That seemed to pause him for a moment, before he seemed to shake himself and get back to his points.

"Release our ships and lift this embargo immediately, or Scandi will have no choice but to seek stronger ties with the Eastern forces. Perhaps they would value our friendship more than Britannia seems to."

"We should do that anyway," the younger man said. "They would welcome us, unlike how we are treated here."

"I'm certain they would, yet you're here in Devnum, not in the East. Why is that, I wonder? Consider what ports you are close to, which ones you trade with often, and what your options are if you could only trade with Egypt. Also consider this; if Scandi allies with the East, you become our enemy in truth. Every Scandi vessel, not just those carrying contraband, becomes a legitimate target for our navy. Every Scandi citizen in Britannian or Western Alliance territory becomes an enemy national, subject to detention. You would be isolated, cut off from your new 'allies' by geography and by our fleets. Your ships would never reach Eastern ports."

"You dare threaten us," Hrolfson said, going red in the face.

"I am simply explaining the realities of the situation, another of which includes the fact that the Easterners are not looking for trade partners. They're looking for subjects. The Macedonians thought the same as you and sided with them. My understanding is that many of their cities have begun being integrated as protectorates of the Eastern Empire. Does that sound familiar?"

She did not have to directly remind them of how the Carthaginians acted to get her point across. She could see Hrolfson's understanding on his face.

"And here you are, dictating who we may or may not trade with. How are you any different?"

"There is a significant difference between limiting trade with one group among dozens you regularly deal with and having soldiers in your towns dictating every aspect of your lives. The Eastern Empire has demonstrated its intent to conquer all of Europe. They've secured Greece and Egypt. They will not stop there."

"However ..."

"Say all you want, but from our point of view, you are no different, forcing us into submission ..."

"However," Lucilla continued, cutting his tirade short again. "There is an alternative to the full embargo."

"What alternative?" He said, suspicious.

"Scandi joins the Western Alliance in a limited capacity. You would not be required to commit ground troops to the conflict. Instead, you would provide material resources for the war effort, timber, iron, and other raw materials at preferential rates. Your vessels would participate in blockading Egyptian ports but would not be required to engage Eastern fleets directly. Your merchant ships would transport Western Alliance supplies, maintaining our supply lines across the Middle Sea. In return, all Western Alliance ports would reopen to Scandi trade. Your commerce would resume, your captains freed, your seized vessels returned, minus the contraband, of course."

For a moment, the four men looked at each other. Many of the things she was offering were limitations she'd asked for in previous conversations. Then, she'd held the line, demanding participation in the fighting itself.

The older men seemed to be seriously considering it. The younger man, however, remained defensive.

"Why should we accept any deal when we could simply continue trading with both sides?

"Because that is not an option. You will either trade with every Western nation save Egypt and certain Greek ports, or you will face the same fate as Egyptian vessels in the Middle Sea. One or the other, gentlemen. It's up to you to choose."

"You still ask us to put our people in danger. Any formal alliance would make us a target for Eastern retaliation."

"I am not saying it's without risk, but consider your actual exposure. You are so far north, you represent a low-priority target for Eastern forces, who have almost no naval presence this far north. Also consider that, if the West loses this war, Scandi will become a target regardless of its current stance."

The men looked to each other.

"Excuse us a moment," he said, pulling the other men with him several steps back.

The quartet leaned in, speaking in hushed voices. Even though she couldn't hear what they were saying, it wasn't hard to see they were not all agreeing, especially the younger man.

After several minutes of intense debate, which the younger man clearly lost and was unhappy about, the delegation separated and came forward again.

"We have several conditions. First, Scandi vessels must have greater autonomy in choosing which ports to help blockade. We will not commit our entire merchant fleet to military operations."

"Half your seaworthy vessels. With your captains selecting which ships participate on a rotating basis."

Hrolfson nodded reluctantly. "Second, we require a formal guarantee that no Scandi citizens will be conscripted into Western Alliance forces. Our people will not die for Britannia."

"Fine."

"Lastly, we require immediate compensation for the twenty-three vessels already seized, regardless of their cargo."

"The ships will be returned. The contraband will not. Nor will there be any compensation for the seized contraband. Those vessels violated existing trade agreements by carrying war materials to our enemies."

"Half-value compensation for the contraband."

"No compensation. The return of the vessels themselves is concession enough."

Hrolfson looked to the three other men. The two older gave short nods, while the young man gave nothing.

"We accept your terms. Scandi will join the Western Alliance under these conditions."

"Good. A formal treaty will be drawn up by tomorrow. Your ships will be released upon its signing, and Western Alliance ports will reopen to Scandi vessels immediately thereafter."

"And the captains found to be carrying contraband?"

"Those without Egyptian connections will be released with their vessels, with a formal warning. Those who transported enemy agents will be held as any hostile spy would."

Hrolfson didn't seem pleased with this, but he nodded all the same. Turning, he led his men out, having to half drag the youngest of his party with him.

She would have to find out who that boy was, and how he'd come to be included in this group. If he had high enough connections, or if he had some kind of connections to the Easterners, they would have to keep an eye on him.

Chapter 24

Alexandria, Egypt

Valdar watched Alexandria grow in size as his fleet approached the city, holding onto the low ceiling of the heavily armored riverboat that wasn't meant to operate in open seas, even one as calm as the Middle Sea.

The trip here from Britannia had been harrowing. Worse, he'd started with eight ironclads, but one had been lost to the waves just before they'd crossed from Oceanus into the Middle Sea. Thankfully, it had been one of the ships refitted as a transport and it had yet to be loaded with legionaries, but the loss had required a readjustment to the plan that Valdar hoped wouldn't result in another devastating loss.

"There goes the fleet," someone said.

Valdar turned to look out one of the side viewing ports to see the two dozen wooden-hulled vessels slowing down, made up mostly of commandeered merchant ships with a few armed caravels mixed in, separating themselves from the seven squat figures that continued to steam toward the port, black columns of smoke pouring from each of their smokestacks as they shoveled in the coal, pushing the boilers to their max.

Alexandria had changed since his last time there. At the mouth of the harbor, on either side of the breakwater, stood a large stone fort, again copied from the designs used by Valdar at Port Vikhavn.

Valdar shook his head in wry amusement. He knew impersonation was the height of flattery, but he wished that his development there hadn't been so popular.

It turned out that facing heavily gunned forts like this was much less satisfying than hiding behind them.

The Western Fort was much larger than its eastern twin and dominated the harbor approach, its curved walls bristling with cannon emplacements. The Eastern Fort, though smaller, was well placed on a rocky promontory sticking farther out, allowing for interlocking fields of fire across the harbor mouth. Together, they mounted at least fifty heavy guns, more than sufficient to destroy any conventional fleet attempting entrance to the port.

"Ships are trying to flee the harbor," someone else said.

A dangerous move. If his people hadn't been so thorough in sinking every Egyptian ship that had been out of range of forts like these, down to the smallest fishing trawler, the now fleeing ships would have had warning and been able to escape before his ships were almost in the mouth of the harbor.

Instead, they had to try to make a run for it before the shells started falling, even if it meant sailing past the broadsides of the enemy.

Or maybe they didn't recognize these as warships. They hadn't been seen outside of the continent, so most ship masters would have no idea what the long, slope-sided things coming toward them were.

They were probably more concerned with the masts of the more traditional ships sitting just off the coast.

"Let them pass," Valdar ordered. "The caravels outside will deal with them."

Their hasty departure did create an unexpected complication, however. The fleeing merchant vessels choked the already narrow approach channel, forcing his ships to push closer together, lest one of the panicked ships collide with them in their haste to leave.

One passed within a few dozen paces of his ship, close enough to see its sailors staring with open dismay at the squat, smoke-belching monsters.

The wake of the ships caused his ships to pitch and roll.

"The eastern position appears less heavily manned. Perhaps ..." Aelius, who had been assigned to take the port and establish a foothold on Egyptian soil, started to say something while standing next to him when he was cut short by a thunderous boom from the Western Fort.

A fraction of a second later, a waterspout erupted fifty yards off their port bow.

"And so it begins," Valdar said. "Signal the gunships to begin the attack on their assigned forts."

The ironclad fleet had split in two when they got into the harbor, with three holding back just outside of the harbor as the other four came all the way in, putting themselves in line with the guns of the forts. Now, those four separated again, two heading to the Eastern Fort while Valdar and the other ship headed for its western sibling.

The Egyptian gunners found their range quickly. More cannon opened fire from both forts, a mix of solid shot and explosive shells arcing toward the ironclad formation. Valdar's ship shuddered as the helmsman threw her into a zigzag pattern, steam engines protesting the sudden directional changes.

The ironclad trembled as her cannon replied, firing each time the ship's wild turning brought a broadside into range.

An Egyptian shell struck the water ten yards from the flagship's bow, drenching the forward deck with spray. Two more followed in quick succession, bracketing the vessel but failing to score a direct hit.

The same could not be said for the other ship with his, steaming along to the starboard. An Egyptian round smashed through her forward observation port, ripping through the thinner metal in the protrusion. The lookout stationed there simply vanished as the entire housing was smashed flat.

The ironclad engines labored at full capacity, pushing the ungainly vessels through the increasingly turbulent waters. From both shoreline fortifications, Egyptian cannon maintained a punishing rate of fire. Across the bay, three shells struck the water directly beside one of the vessels attacking the Eastern Fort, lifting her starboard side partially from the water and throwing crewmen against the bulkheads.

Aelius braced himself against the pilothouse wall as the flagship executed another evasive maneuver. "This is madness."

Valdar smiled to himself. Aelius was used to open field battles and hiding in trenches. Navy men were used to riding into withering fire, with ships pounding each other with cannon fire, ripping the very ground out from under you.

"Welcome to the navy, Legate," Valdar replied, smiling.

Not that he didn't harbor concerns of his own. This was very different from facing land forces with a handful of cannon.

A tremendous impact rocked his flagship, the sound of tearing metal reverberating through her hull. Valdar steadied himself against the chart table as reports flooded in from below.

"Direct hit forward armor plate!" shouted the damage control officer. "Outer layer buckled but holding!"

The Egyptian shell had struck the vessel's forward armor square on, denting the reinforced plating but failing to penetrate. The impact transmitted through the entire vessel, rattling men's teeth and loosening fittings throughout the ship.

"Helmsman, bring us to five hundred paces and closing."

"Sir," the helmsman glanced back in surprise but did as he was commanded.

The flagship turned toward the Western Fort, exposing less of the ship but briefly taking her guns out of the fight as it closed on the fort. The other combat ironclads maintained their zigzag approach, drawing fire from both fortifications.

As they got close, the helmsman turned the ship again, bringing its guns very close to the walls, which opened up as soon as the broadside cleared. It also put them closer to the enemies' guns, which now pounded his ship, with each hit sending fragments of scale and rust raining down from the ceiling. But the iron armor continued to hold.

This close, they could clearly see the effects as the Britannian shells struck the stone fortifications with devastating effect, each impact sending chunks of masonry flying. Several Egyptian gun emplacements had already fallen silent, their crews either dead or driven from their positions by the continuous barrage.

"We're hurting them," Aelius noted.

A tremendous impact against the vessel's superstructure cut short any reply. The pilothouse filled with acrid smoke as alarms sounded throughout the ship.

"Forward smokestack hit! Stack collapsed, boiler pressure dropping!"

Smoke poured across the deck as the damaged ventilation system failed, reducing visibility to near zero. The flagship's speed dropped noticeably as reduced steam pressure affected her engines.

The battle had raged for nearly thirty minutes, and casualties were mounting. A messenger arrived from below decks, his face blackened with powder.

"Gun three crew reports five wounded from fragment penetration through gun port, sir. Two serious."

"Tell them to bring in replacements and keep firing."

Things were going much worse with the Eastern Fort. One ironclad had taken serious hits to its pilothouse and had stopped putting up signal flags, which suggested its captain might be dead. It didn't stop fighting, so that was a problem for later.

The other ship had fared worse, in practical terms. From here it looked as if it had suffered damage to her steering or propulsion. She had stopped maneuvering entirely, although she still had her broadside pointed at the Eastern Fort, that position put her in serious danger, as most of the Eastern Fort's guns were now concentrated on the lamed vessel.

This was war and there would be setbacks. In spite of the damage his ships had taken, they were doing their job. Aelius was right. They were hurting the forts. The rate of fire from both Egyptian forts had diminished significantly, one side of the Western Fort seemed to be down to only two guns.

The battle continued for another ten minutes, the ironclads maintaining position despite accumulating damage as they pounded the forts.

The lamed ship's luck, or lack of luck, continued as an Egyptian shell found the vulnerable seam where two armor plates joined near her waterline. The impact tore through the weaker connection, breaching her hull and causing her to start listing.

Valdar watched as the stricken ironclad began to drift, black smoke pouring from her damaged hull. He knew it was bad when the guns were retraced from two of the gun ports facing him and buckets of water began to be tossed out of them, as the men tried to keep her from going under.

There was nothing to be done for it now. The other ship on that side was in no condition to come to their aid, and they couldn't stop the fight now. The battle had raged for forty minutes and the tide was turning.

They just needed a little more time and luck.

"Look there," Aelius said, pointing to the Western Fort's lower wall section where concentrated Britannian fire had taken its toll. "The wall structure is failing."

Through the smoke, Valdar could see that the legate was correct. The stone facing of the fort had begun to crack under the relentless pounding, one bastion showing signs of imminent collapse.

"Helmsman, close to two hundred paces. Signal all guns to fire at that section of wall."

"Two hundred, Sir?" The helmsman's voice betrayed his concern. "The charts show shallow rocks that close to the breakwater."

"The gods take you, do it or step aside for a man with a spine."

The man paled and did as he was told.

The flagship pushed forward, closed the distance to the Western Fort until he could have thrown a rock and hit the fort's masonry walls. At such a close range, the ironclad's guns could hit its target easily. The Egyptians must have thought he'd gone insane, since his ship was as easy of a target, and they redoubled their efforts.

The ironclad's keel scraped against submerged rocks with a horrific shriek of metal on stone. The impact threw men off their feet throughout the vessel, but her shallow draft allowed her to continue where a deeper-keeled warship would have foundered.

"Concentrate all fire on the lower wall section. Maximum elevation."

They were close enough now that a few of the handful of legionaries he had on board, sharpshooters assigned to the navy, popped open hatches along the top of the ship. It was wildly dangerous for them, with all the shrapnel in the air, but at this range they could target individual Egyptian gunners visible through the fort's embrasures. Rifle fire began to crack, sending Egyptian soldiers falling off the wall here and there.

The flagship's guns maintained a punishing rate of fire, each heavy shell striking the already weakened wall structure. Valdar watched as the cracks in the stonework widened with each impact, mortar and facing stone crumbling under the assault.

A shell struck the flagship's upper works, tearing away a section of railing and killing four of his sharpshooters. Another impacted directly against the pilothouse armor, the sound inside deafening as the metal held but buckled inward several inches.

Time and pressure, however, proved that rock wall wasn't invulnerable as the damaged lower section of the fort wall gave way with a tremendous roar, tons of stone collapsing in a billowing cloud of dust and debris. Egyptian defenders caught in the collapse disappeared beneath the avalanche, while others abandoned their positions in the sudden chaos.

Through the swirling dust, Valdar could see that the breach was substantial, at least thirty feet wide at the base, and expanding as weakened sections above continued to collapse.

"Signal the transports to begin their approach," Valdar ordered.

A signalman rapidly worked the flags on the remaining signal post, relaying the command to the ironclad transports waiting beyond the harbor entrance. Through billowing smoke, Valdar watched the three blocky vessels begin to move forward.

In spite of the brutal beating his four ships had just taken, this was the riskiest part of the operation. The three ironclads fitted out as transport ships were much more vulnerable than the assault ironclads. To allow them as shallow of a draft as possible, they were not fitted out with the additional armor plating for added protection. Seeing how badly his ships had been maimed, a few good shots on the transports and hundreds of men would be dead in an instant, and their assault would be in real jeopardy.

Thankfully, the forts did not seem to realize these new vessels, which did not open their gunports and were not firing, were the real danger to them. Instead, they continued to attack his combat vessels.

"We need to maintain suppression fire," Valdar said, turning to the damage control officer. "What's our ammunition status?"

"Thirty percent remaining, Admiral. More than we expected at this point. The gunners report reduced rate due to ventilation damage."

"Tell them to push through. I don't care how hard it gets to breathe down there. We need to keep hitting them. Back us up to about three hundred paces and prioritize the gun placements that are still firing."

Black smoke poured from the flagship's damaged stack, mixing with powder smoke to create a miasma across the battlefield. The heat inside the pilothouse had become nearly unbearable as the ventilation systems failed.

The first transport ironclad pushed through the waves, its modified bow riding higher than the combat vessels. The flat-bottomed hull had been designed specifically for this purpose to run aground and disgorge troops directly onto the rocky shore.

Two of the transport vessels were headed toward this fort, while one turned to the smaller Eastern Fort. Unfortunately, that fort had somehow become a bigger problem than its larger sibling.

While one of his ironclads continued to pound the Eastern Fort, the other lay practically dead in the water, listing heavily to port. The Eastern Fort's remaining guns continued to fire with alarming accuracy.

The first transport had reached its destination, its bow grinding onto the narrow seawall leading to the Western Fort. With a tremendous bang, the specially designed bow crashed down onto the rocks, forming a bridge from ship to shore.

Valdar watched as the first century and a half of legionaries charged down the ramp. There was no attempt to form up and make firing lines. They charged the breach, knowing how vulnerable they were out in the open.

The second transport was close behind, positioning itself alongside the first to create a continuous landing platform. More legionaries poured onto the beach, joining their brothers in the charge.

Egyptian defenders appeared along the walls, using rifles to fire down at the exposed troops. Men fell on the open breakwater, but the legionaries didn't let that slow them down, charging hard for the wall, occasionally stopping to fire at an exposed man on the wall.

"Movement in the city," one of his officers said.

Valdar turned to see a column of Egyptian soldiers, perhaps three hundred men, running toward the Western Fort. Reinforcements for the beleaguered defenders.

"Helmsman, bring us ninety degrees to port. Gunnery officer, prepare broadside for ground targets, six hundred paces."

The ironclad pivoted slowly, bringing her starboard battery to bear on the approaching column. At Valdar's command, twelve guns roared in unison, shells arcing across the water to explode among the Egyptian ranks. Men disappeared in clouds of dust and smoke. Those not directly hit scattered or were sliced down by shrapnel, their neat formation disintegrating under the unexpected bombardment.

Three more salvos transformed the reinforcement attempt into a rout, the survivors fleeing back toward the city's protective walls.

"They're almost at the breach," Aelius said, having kept his attention on his men in action.

Indeed, the first wave of legionaries reached the fallen wall section, charging through the gap into the fort's interior. Others set up firing positions behind whatever cover they could find, providing cover for their comrades as they stormed inside.

Valdar directed his attention across the harbor, where the situation had deteriorated. The third transport struggled to approach the Eastern Fort, weaving through water churned by shell impacts. The fort's guns concentrated their fire on the approaching vessel, probably having seen the other two land and guessing its intent.

"Take us to that Eastern Fort. We need to draw their fire from the transport."

He wasn't the only one who saw the problem. The damaged ironclad seemed to have gotten some propulsion restored and pushed closer to the Eastern Fort despite the heavy damage to her hull. Her remaining operational guns fired continuously, attempting to suppress the Egyptian batteries.

"Captain Tulon is asking if they are to join us," the signalman said.

The captain of his partnership on the Western Fort had managed to get a makeshift signal pole up and had restored some communication.

"No. Tell him to maintain position and continue suppression fire on the Western Fort and any reinforcements from the city."

The third transport took a direct hit to its upper works as it neared its landing position. Smoke billowed from the struck section, flames visible even at this distance. A second hit struck near the waterline, though the vessel continued its approach.

"Make it to shore," Valdar muttered to himself, watching the transport push through despite the punishment it was taking.

The transport finally reached its intended position, grounding firmly on the narrow strand below the Eastern Fort. Her ramp descended under fire, legionaries disembarking into a maelstrom of rifle and cannon fire. There wasn't a large breach in the walls of this fort and the rocky shore offered minimal cover.

Valdar and his other two ships spent the next hour pounding the Eastern Fort's gun placements, trying to keep them suppressed as much as they could. Most of the legionaries on this assault had retreated, using the hull of the transport ship as protection from the constant onslaught, unable to get to the fort walls. Their losses had been costly.

Thankfully, the Western Fort assault had fared much better, with Aelius' men pushing through the breach and securing the outer works. Almost all of the guns on its walls had been silenced and they had begun to push deeper into the fortification.

"Signal Captain Tulon to join us here. All fire is to shift to the Eastern Fort. But keep an eye on the western position, in case we need to return."

Another hour passed as they tried to silence the Eastern Fort's guns and had little success.

He had miscalculated in thinking the Eastern Fort would be the softer of the two targets. It had turned out to be a tenacious beast that shrugged off everything he was throwing at it.

"Captain," one of his assistants said.

Turning, Valdar saw a red signal flare arcing from the Western Fort's central tower.

"Finally, some luck," Aelius said. "Signal the tribune. Half his men are to reboard the transport and reposition to this side of the bay to join the assault."

The signal had barely started to go out when more bad news came in.

"Sir, Captain Kenaz signals critical damage. They've had another hull breach below the waterline. Pumps engaged but losing ground."

The already listing ironclad was dropping lower in the water as Valdar watched.

"Tell them to beach her if necessary. Preserve the crew and guns; keep firing."

It was almost a death sentence for the men aboard, but they could not let this attack fail. The added fire power was having an effect and the legionaries had finally managed to push forward, establishing positions at the base of the walls but struggled to scale the shortest of the walls.

Valdar was surprised when a series of very large explosions smashed into the western side of the fort. Looking back at the Western Fort, he could see its much larger cannons firing again, but this time across the bay at the Eastern Fort.

Chaos seemed to be reigning in the Eastern Fort as they tried to figure out why their countrymen were firing on them, not realizing the fort had been lost, and trying to deal with the damage caused by the larger cannons.

"Pull the legionaries back and signal all vessels to coordinate fire with the Western Fort batteries," Valdar ordered. "Concentrate all of it. Blow a hole in that damn thing."

The combined firepower of Valdar's remaining vessels and the captured guns of the Western Fort hammered the Eastern Fort relentlessly for almost twenty minutes. Multiple breaches appeared in its walls as the concentrated bombardment took its toll on the stone fortification.

Aelius had been busy during that time, and ten smaller boats, dinghies and lifeboats, probably found inside the fort, were coming across from the fort with even more legionaries, who appeared to want to join their countrymen in taking the Eastern Fort.

Part of the Eastern Fort wall began to crumble under the intense fire, as most of its cannons fell silent.

"Move your fire to the northern side. It's time for my boys to go to work," Aelius said.

Valdar agreed and the orders were sent. In a few minutes, the firing shifted, freeing up the land side of the fort for the legionaries, now almost two hundred men strong, charging at the broken structure.

Their assault was much easier than before. Easier even than the assault on the Western Fort, as most of the defenders were hunkering down inside or dead from the long, direct bombardment. Whatever defenders were there to protect the breaches were quickly overwhelmed by the seething mass of Britannian men.

It still took almost an hour for the battle inside the fort to be settled, but finally, a Britannian battle flag appeared on the parapet, announcing the fort's fall.

Not that they were without losses. The injured assault ironclad had finally beached itself to avoid sinking, and its men had abandoned ship. The rest of his ships were all damaged in one way or another.

Not that it mattered. The ships could be repaired. They had achieved their goal. The forts were down, the forces inside Alexandria had been discouraged in their attempts to retake the forts, and the vast majority of Aelius's legion was healthy and ready to fight, sitting on transports just offshore.

"Signal the rest of the fleet to join us. Let's finish this," Valdar ordered.

Alexandria was theirs.

Chapter 25

Greece

Ky moved through the muddy forward trench that still hadn't dried in spite of the lack of rain for the past week and the relatively warm temperatures. The dampness was affecting everything, from the men's morale to the construction of the very trench itself.

The planking, laid down to provide stable footing, had rotted away in places, creating treacherous spots that could be dangerous to men running through the trench in the heat of combat.

He made a note to have the officers check the wood frames of the trench and the planking and to replace them as needed.

The trench followed the natural contour of the hillside, cutting a jagged line across the Greek landscape that had probably once been lush farmland but now looked like the moons of Jupiter that he'd flown patrols around in a life long ago.

Or, rather, a long time from now.

"Excuse us, sir," a voice called from behind.

He turned to see a decanus, leading a squad of eight men carrying crates of ammunition, waiting to get past Ky and his party, who were partially blocking the narrow path through the trench.

"Good thinking, Decanus. You're going to find that your men will go through this ammunition much faster than the older stuff. Make sure you keep a lot of spares around and that your men keep their pockets full for when the enemy tries another push."

"Yes, sir, we'll do that. We got training with these things two days ago, and by the gods do they shoot fast. Those bastards are going to be in for a hard day when they try and push us again."

"Better them than us," Ky said, slapping the man on the shoulder as he stood aside to let him and his squad through.

The men laughed as they went by. The conditions may still be horrendous, but from what he'd seen so far on this tour, their spirits were up now that they'd had a chance to try out the new rifles for themselves and saw just what they could do.

He continued forward, passing a group of veterans who were showing several new recruits how to brace a rifle against the front wall of the trench. An older soldier demonstrated placing the weapon in a notch carved precisely into the earth, explaining how to aim at specific points across No Man's Land and to recognize the range markers they used to tell the distance and how to adjust their sights. Ky paused, listening to the man give his instructions.

"This notch is for two hundred paces, where they usually form their first line. You'll see when they pass that big crater with the fallen tree there, they should line up just right. And this one's for one-fifty, when they're halfway to us. You'll want to wait until they reach the old crater there with the sleeping man on the rim before you start firing."

It was a macabre sort of marker, using the body of a fallen Easterner who did indeed look like he'd just curled up for a nap, as a visual guide to the distance of the enemy. The recruits, however, took the instructions seriously, nodding along with each word, their faces intent.

"It's the Consul!" one of the younger ones, a boy still in his teens, said.

The teenager jumped to attention, just as a drill instructor at the training grounds had probably taught him. The veterans, on the other hand, sort of turned around or stood up, but otherwise kept slouched and relaxed.

They knew Ky from his frequent visits to the line, and his preference to not stand on ceremony.

"As you were," Ky said, stepping closer to inspect the notches cut into the trench. "Replacements?"

"Yes, sir," the veteran answered. "Straight off the train from the training camp. Arrived this morning."

"Listen to your officers and the seasoned men; remember your training, and you'll do fine," he said, putting a hand on the younger man's shoulder.

"Yes, Consul," the boy replied, seeming like he was about to swoon.

Ky smiled at him, mostly to keep the grimace off his face. The kid had to be a Roman. The allied men or even Caledonians could be bad enough, but true Romans were the worst when it came to the pedestal they liked to put him on. In spite of his best efforts, the story of the sword had become all but universal in Rome, and every man who followed the Roman gods believed it with his whole heart.

It could be tiring to deal with. Not that Ky held it against the young man. He knew what he knew, and he was out here putting his life on the line. The least Ky could do was play his part.

He moved on, stopping at intervals to check defensive positions and speak with the soldiers. Britannian troops lined the trenches as far as he could see, most wearing the standard dark grey tunics of the legion, now covered with mud and worn from weeks in the field. Although clean-shaven was the standard in Rome, most had joined their Germanic brethren in growing beards.

At a widened section of trench that served as a squad post, a centurion sat on an ammunition crate, cleaning his rifle. Six of his men were eating a cold breakfast of hardtack and dried beef. All were veterans and remained where they were when Ky spoke.

"How are you all doing?" Ky asked, gesturing for them to continue their meal.

"Good, sir. It was quiet through the night. Their patrols were active until about three hours before dawn, then they withdrew. We've spotted increased movement behind their lines since first light. Probably gonna have a fight today."

"How are your men holding up?"

"Tired but ready. The new rifles have lifted spirits considerably."

"Where are you from, soldier?" he asked one who appeared older than the others, with deep lines etched around his eyes.

"Londinium."

"What did you do in Londinium, before the war?"

"Fish merchant before I enlisted."

"Family?"

"Wife and three children, sir. Youngest was born after I left for the front."

"And you?"

"Linnglas in Ulaid. Raised sheep."

"Good farming country there."

The soldier smiled slightly. "That it is, sir."

Ky continued down the line, asking each man about his home and family. It was a small thing, but he'd learned over years of command that such personal connections mattered, especially before battle. Men fought harder for leaders who saw them as individuals rather than interchangeable parts in a military machine.

One of the soldiers was trying to balance his rifle and a small package. That was one of the things that Ky had worked with Lucilla to set up. A way for men to send letters on the supply trains back home, and for their families to send things to them.

Besides knowing their loved ones were alive, hearing about the front gave the people at home incentive to keep it at the forefront of their minds, instead of thinking of it as something separate and far away.

"Mail from home, sir," he explained when he saw Ky looking at him. "Just arrived this morning."

"I hope it's something good," Ky said.

Before the soldier could share his treat with his friends, there was the sound of a distant boom, followed by the distinctive whine of an incoming shell.

"**Incoming!**" someone screamed.

The shell impacted thirty paces behind the trench, sending dirt and rock fragments showering over them. Moments later, dozens more explosions erupted along the line as the enemy artillery opened up in full force.

Ky pressed himself against the forward wall of the trench as more shells screamed overhead. The ground shook with each impact, dislodging dirt from the trench walls. Men crouched low, protecting their rifles from the debris raining down.

A shell landed directly on the trench twenty yards down the line, sending bodies and equipment flying. Screams of wounded men cut through the din of the bombardment. Medics rushed forward, dragging casualties toward a reinforced dugout that served as an aid station.

"We need to get to the command bunker," Modius insisted, grabbing Ky's arm. "You can't direct the defense from here."

Another shell landed nearby, closer this time, the concussion slamming them against the trench wall. Ky shrugged Modius off and moved toward the impact site where soldiers were already digging to free buried comrades.

"I'm staying," Ky said as he started pulling rubble off the buried men.

Modius frowned but, to his credit, did not argue. Probably due to the long years of dealing with Lucilla and seeing how stubborn she could be. Instead, he joined Ky, helping rescue the buried men.

Another shell flew overhead, wailing its death song before striking somewhere behind their position. Ky ignored it and continued digging through the collapsed trench section, finally pulling the last young soldier from the rubble. The man's face was covered in mud, but his eyes fluttered open as he gasped for breath.

"Can you stand?" Ky asked.

Three more shells struck in quick succession along the forward line, causing the ground to buckle beneath them.

"Into the dugout!" Modius pointed to a reinforced shelter twenty paces away.

"Get him to the aid station first."

"We'll handle him, Consul. You need to get under cover," a centurion said.

A shell hit ten yards to their left, flinging dirt and splintered planking upward. The blast slammed them against the trench wall as Modius took Ky's arm and pulled him toward the dugout entrance.

"Now, sir."

They entered the reinforced shelter just as another shell landed above. The dugout quivered, and dirt filtered down between the timber supports. Inside, soldiers crouched along the walls with their rifles held above the floor to keep them from the dirt falling with each impact. Outside, the men pressed themselves against the trench walls for protection.

The bombardment intensified. Shells hit in patterns along their front line, smashing the Britannian line in rapid succession.

A medic stumbled in dragging a wounded man whose trouser leg was drenched with blood where shrapnel had carved through muscle. Two soldiers helped apply a tourniquet above the wound.

"Medical dugouts filling fast," the medic said. "Stretcher-bearers can't keep up."

Outside, officers shouted for men to hold positions despite the pounding. Ky heard trench sections collapsing and water splashing as the artillery found one of their storage cisterns.

"Flood! Water's coming through!"

Ky stepped toward the entrance, but Modius blocked his path.

"Please, Consul. Wait until this barrage lifts."

Ky hated hiding in here while his men died, and wanted to be doing something, but Modius was right. Even with all of his enhancements, there was little he could do, either about the flooding or the shells. Muddy water flowed past the dugout, carrying broken equipment and needed supplies. A quick-thinking soldier grabbed floating canteens, securing them for the thirst that would follow once the fighting began.

On and on it went. The men with him, in the relative safety of the dugout, were handling it well, but Ky knew the men unlucky enough not to have a place to hide would be feeling the full effects with each bone-rattling explosion. After twenty minutes of constant shelling, the shells slowed.

No, they didn't slow, just shifted, moving from the front line to the secondary line and even a little beyond.

"They're shifting to the rear areas," Ky said. "Cutting off our reinforcement routes."

"They learned from last time. Our second line reinforcements kept their breakthrough from succeeding."

"Which means they're planning another major push."

"Sir, the tribune reports heavy damage to the communication trenches. Second and third-line reinforcements will have difficulty reaching us when the attack comes."

"They will find a way. Tell him to identify alternate routes now, before the infantry assault begins and he's ordered to send in reinforcements as soon as the attack starts. As long as he can do so effectively. Tell him to use his own initiative," Ky said, before turning to Modius. "I'm going to check the line."

This time Modius followed without argument as Ky went into what remained of their forward trench. The destruction was extensive, with whole sections collapsed, creating gaps in their line. Soldiers cleared debris and rebuilt firing positions while others collected weapons and ammunition from the dead.

In one section, water from the destroyed cistern had turned the trench into knee-deep mud where soldiers stood on makeshift platforms, keeping rifles and ammunition dry.

Ky stopped at a badly damaged section where men struggled to rebuild a firing step.

"Use the support beams from the collapsed section," he said, lifting a timber into place. "Pack dirt behind them and reinforce with whatever you can find."

The soldiers worked quickly at his direction as a young optio approached.

When they finished, he ordered, "Redistribute from the dead and wounded. Then, send men to retrieve more from the supply depot if they can get to it. You'll need every round when they come."

For nearly thirty more minutes, enemy shells fell on their rear positions. It was strange in the front trenches, where the relative quiet allowed the men to prepare for the coming assault. The enemy had definitely learned from past attempts and was trying something new.

"Forward observer reports movement in the enemy trenches. They're forming up for an assault," a runner said.

Ky nodded. "Alert all positions. Have them hold their fire until they reach the range markers."

The runner left, relaying the orders down the line. Soldiers adjusted positions and checked their rifles while those who had been repairing trenches took up their weapons and moved to firing positions.

"We really should withdraw to the command bunker, sir," Modius said.

"No. Not this time," he said, taking a rifle that was lying next to an ammunition crate, checking the action and lever before filling his pockets with cartridges.

"Sir," Modius began, but stopped when he saw Ky's expression.

"They need to see that their commanders stand with them." Ky took position at a firing step. "We have the weapons now. We can finally turn things around."

Modius was still not happy but found a rifle of his own, following his leader's example.

Ky could tell that the word was spreading quickly that the Consul himself was manning the forward trench. More men came running up, joining them on the line. Even some who looked pretty seriously injured had come back into position, ready to keep fighting.

"Here they come," someone called out.

Through a periscope mounted on the trench wall, Ky studied the approaching enemy as they emerged in what looked like a continuous wave. Their numbers were terrifying, but they still had to cross nearly half a mile of exposed ground.

"Remember your training," Ky called out. "Wait for the order to fire. Make every shot count."

The enemy advanced across No Man's Land. Through the periscope, Ky saw officers urging them forward, knowing they would be fired on any minute.

"They're approaching the first marker. Six hundred paces."

"Remain steady. Wait for my command," a centurion said, watching the range markers.

"Five hundred paces."

Ky didn't interfere. He let the officers do their job. It was their right to give the order. Ky was just a visitor in their world.

"Four hundred paces."

Men gripped their rifles tightly, focused on the approaching enemy as the lead elements became clearly visible through the smoke and dust left behind by the artillery barrage.

"Three hundred paces."

Ky joined the other men in lifting his weapon, preparing to fire.

"Two hundred paces! Fire!"

The trench erupted with hundreds of rifles firing simultaneously. The front enemy rank staggered as bullets tore through them. Unlike previous engagements where defenders would now be frantically reloading single-shot rifles, giving the enemy a chance to close more ground to the trench line, a second barrage followed. And then a third. And then a fourth.

Ky was already empty, having worked his rifle's lever mechanism with inhuman speed. Seven shots found marks among the advancing troops before the men around him had fired their fifth shot. By the time they emptied their rifles, he was sliding his last reload into the rifle and lifting the weapon again.

The effect on the enemy was devastating as their front ranks fell under the unprecedented volume of fire, creating obstacles for the following waves of men. Officers tried to maintain momentum, but the continuous fire tore their formations apart faster than they could reorganize.

At one hundred fifty meters, the enemy advance faltered. Men dropped to the ground, seeking cover from the literal hail of bullets while officers moved among them with drawn swords, making threats. Some troops resumed advancing, but others stayed in place, unwilling to face the wall of lead cutting through their ranks.

"They're breaking on the left!" a soldier called out.

Ky shifted attention to the left flank, where enemy troops were falling back. The rest of the attack, however, continued in spite of their losses, with men reaching the hundred-meter mark.

"Concentrate fire on the right flank," Ky ordered.

Enemy officers had found the weak point in the Britannian line where a collapsed trench section had reduced the number of men able to fight, and they directed their men toward this gap, accepting casualties to exploit the vulnerability.

Ky aimed at officers directing the assault. Sophus's targeting assist tracked and highlighted people for him to kill. His rifle never stopped firing as he eliminated targets. Every single bullet was a kill shot.

The men around him cheered as Ky mowed down the enemy.

At seventy-five meters, the enemy force began to waver as their losses mounted beyond what was sustainable, even for troops threatened with execution for retreating. Officers struggled to maintain the momentum as men sought cover or fell back.

The enemy, however, wasn't without their own surprises. A group rose from a shell hole to the right, throwing objects toward the Britannian line.

"Grenades!"

Most fell short, exploding harmlessly, but several landed on the trench parapet. Soldiers kicked them away or flattened themselves as the devices detonated, sending shrapnel outward.

He shouldn't have been surprised. As weapons go, the grenade was not a terribly difficult weapon to copy once it was seen in combat. The Easterners probably didn't even need to steal examples to achieve the feat.

Just seeing them in combat was enough.

Despite these attacks, the Britannian line held as their continuous fire prevented the enemy from closing to effective grenade range. For every grenade that reached their position, dozens of attackers fell trying to get close enough to throw them.

Numbers, however, had a power all of their own.

At fifty meters, enemy commanders committed their reserves for a final push. Thousands of fresh troops surged forward, hoping to overwhelm the defenders before they could reload.

"Grenades forward. Prepare for close combat," an officer near Ky ordered.

Soldiers passed grenade crates down the line.

The enemy reached forty meters, then thirty, men charging with fixed bayonets, accepting casualties to close the distance. Their officers drove them forward with threats, creating a human wave meant to overwhelm the Britannian defenses.

"Throw!"

Britannian grenades arced through the air, landing among the densely packed attackers. Explosions tore through their ranks. Still, they pressed forward as survivors regrouped, pushing on with the attack.

No amount of sustained fire was going to stop them from reaching the trench, although the losses they suffered here were probably the worst they'd sustained in a single attack in the war.

"Fix bayonets!" someone ordered as the distance closed to fifteen meters.

The first wave of Eastern troops topped the lip of the trench with bayonets leading, plunging into the Britannian line and splitting the defenders. A squad of Easterners drove forward through the initial breach, shoving aside the bodies of their comrades.

Ky's rifle swung toward them as he worked the lever to chamber the first round. The rifle bucked against his shoulder in rapid succession. Three Easterners toppled backward with red holes in their gray tunics.

"Break on the left! They're through!" a voice called out somewhere ahead of him.

More Eastern troops poured into the gap, widening the breach. Beyond them, infantry pressed forward across No Man's Land, feeding the breakthrough now that the Britannian fire had slackened.

"The line's compromised," Modius shouted next to him.

"I can see that." Ky ejected his spent cartridges and slid in fresh rounds. "Get reserves from the right section. I'll handle this breach."

Ky ran along the trench toward the breakthrough, dodging around men and even hurdling them at times. Britannian soldiers fought hand-to-hand in the open section of the trench.

An Eastern soldier appeared at a junction with his rifle raised. Ky fired without stopping. The man fell backward with a hole between his eyes, Ky stepped on his body as it fell, working the lever as he rounded the corner and finally reached the breach.

A group of Eastern soldiers had established a foothold in the trench and were tossing grenades around corners before advancing. Their backs were to Ky as they prepared to take out the Britannian line.

Ky raised his rifle and fired. The first man pitched forward, dead before he hit the ground. Ky worked the lever, aimed, and fired again. The second man fell. Five more shots, five more bodies, all before they had a chance to react. Seven shots in less than four seconds.

Two more Easterners jumped down into the trench. Ky didn't have time to reload and charged them instead, hitting one with the butt of his rifle hard enough to crack his skull open before putting his bayonet into the chest of the other.

More Easterners dropped into the trench, pressing forward despite their losses. Several climbed onto the parapet, firing down into the Britannian positions while their comrades advanced below them. Ky dropped to one knee grabbing a dropped rifle and hoping like hell it was loaded. It was. Three shots, three bodies tumbled from the edge.

An Eastern officer with gold braid on his collar directed the assault, pointing units toward weak spots in the line. Ky's rifle barked once. The officer's head snapped back as he collapsed.

Britannian soldiers responded to his sudden appearance. Eastern troops, accustomed to facing single-shot weapons, found themselves caught in a storm of lead as his men redoubled their efforts, overwhelming the enemy's numerical advantage.

An Eastern grenade landed at Ky's feet. In a single motion, he scooped it up and tossed it back over the parapet. The explosion sent dirt raining down as screams erupted from beyond the trench.

Ky pressed forward into the thickest part of the fighting. An Eastern soldier lunged with his bayonet. Ky sidestepped, grabbed the man by his tunic, and hauled him in front of his body to be used as a shield. Two Eastern rifles discharged, the rounds punching into their comrade's body. Ky felt the impacts through the corpse, then shoved the dead man forward into one of the men while thrusting his bayonet into the nearest attacker's chest.

The trench had become a charnel house with bodies piled atop each other, creating barriers that channeled the fighting into confined spaces. The longer Eastern rifles proved unwieldy in the tight quarters, forcing many to resort to bayonets, knives, or improvised weapons. Britannia's new, shorter rifles remained effective, spitting death at the enemy.

Ky ran into a group just as they entered a section of trench, dropping onto the Britannians there, he fired into them at point-blank range. Muzzle flashes ignited clothing, creating small fires on the dead men. The air filled with the stench of burned wool and flesh.

A group of Britannian reinforcements arrived with Modius, pushing through the communication trenches from the right flank. Ky directed them to secure the initial breach point while he pressed forward.

The Eastern forces had established a foothold and were expanding outward, trying to cut the Britannian line in two.

Ky reloaded, sliding fresh rounds into his rifle before vaulting over a barricade of broken timber and bodies, landing amid an Eastern squad. His rifle spoke seven times in rapid succession, killing a handful of men. He was too close for the enemy to shoot him with their long rifles. Ky parried a thrust from a bayonet with his rifle, then reversed his motion, driving his own bayonet into the attacker's throat. He pivoted, firing point-blank into another man's chest.

More Britannians came in behind him, finally sealing the breach.

"Hold this position," Ky ordered a nearby centurion. "Reinforcements are coming through the second communication trench."

The centurion nodded, dispatching runners to adjacent sections with orders to consolidate their line.

Ky moved forward through the muddy warren of trenches. The sounds of battle intensified ahead, confirming he was moving in the right direction.

Eastern troops had captured a fifty-yard section and were forcing Britannian soldiers back with coordinated volleys from their muzzle-loaded rifles.

Ky diverted, going down a communication trench and then running parallel down a secondary trench before coming back up another communication trench that led behind the captured section. Four Eastern soldiers appeared, blocking his path. Ky's rifle barked twice and two men fell. The others raised their weapons, but Ky was already upon them. He drove his bayonet into one man's chest, then reversed his grip and smashed the butt into the fourth man's face.

Reaching the contested section, Ky found himself behind a squad of Eastern troops preparing to fire another volley. He grabbed the nearest soldier and hurled him into his comrades. The man collided with three others and knocked them off balance, Ky then quickly finished them off with his bayonet and a well-placed stomp, saving his rapidly dwindling ammunition.

The remaining Eastern troops turned to face this new threat, their rifles unwieldy in the confined space. Ky moved among them, firing at point-blank range, using his bayonet when enemies pressed too close. His genetically enhanced strength and speed gave him an overwhelming advantage. He broke one man's neck, drove his fist through another's ribcage, and ripped out a third's windpipe.

Britannian troops, seeing the massacre conducted by their Consul, surged forward behind him, cutting down the now panicking Eastern forces. The section was secured in minutes.

Ky reloaded, counting his remaining ammunition before waving on his growing, patchwork squad that had started following him from fight to fight.

"Push forward to the next junction. We need to close the gap."

The intensity of the fighting began to diminish as Eastern casualties mounted beyond sustainable levels. Their assault had fractured into isolated pockets of resistance as communication broke down and their officers fell.

Ky reloaded with his last rounds as he continued fighting alongside the increasingly confident Britannian troops, eliminating one threat after another.

An Eastern officer attempted to rally his men for one final push. Ky's rifle cracked once and the officer dropped. He seemed to be the last officer in this section. Without leadership, the remaining attackers faltered. Some sought cover in shell holes, while others turned and fled toward their own lines.

The retreat began in small groups, then spread through the Eastern ranks. Panic replaced discipline as soldiers abandoned their positions, their wounded, their weapons.

Ky grabbed two handfuls of rounds from an open ammunition crate nearby and stood, watching the rout in progress.

"They're breaking!" Ky shouted. "Counterattack! Now! Over the top!"

One of the centurions with him pulled out a whistle and blew it. A moment later, more whistles blew, signaling the general advance. The Britannians hadn't been asked to do this before and were exhausted, but they could sense victory.

The men didn't even hesitate. They poured out of their trenches in pursuit of the retreating enemy.

Ky vaulted over the trench parapet with them, firing from the hip at the fleeing soldiers. He waved his men forward. No Man's Land lay open before them. In a few places, the retreating enemy attempted to establish defensive positions in shell craters, but Britannian soldiers were on their heels and quickly eliminated these pockets of resistance before they were established.

The Britannian counterattack gained momentum across the entire sector. The men were in a near frenzy as they charged, ready to take revenge for all of the attacks they'd been forced to endure.

The retreating Eastern soldiers, exhausted from their earlier assault and demoralized by their heavy losses, offered increasingly disorganized resistance. Some surrendered, others fled.

Ky drove forward relentlessly, firing his rifle and reloading with inhuman speed. The Eastern front-line trenches appeared ahead, largely abandoned.

Ky spotted the opportunity to seize the opposing defenses. Emptying his rifle into the nearest Easterners, he cleared the immediate approach before leaping into the enemy trench with dozens of Britannian soldiers following him.

The surprised defenders never stood a chance. Ky bayoneted his way along the trench line, Britannian rifles spitting death at any Eastern soldier who stood his ground.

The breach of the enemy line widened as Western soldiers poured into the enemy positions from multiple entry points. The rifles proved devastating in the confined space, allowing small groups of Britannians to outgun much larger Eastern units.

An Egyptian rearguard attempted to slow the Britannian advance from a trench junction. Ky gathered a group of soldiers who had become separated from their unit.

"On my signal," he said, loading fresh rounds in his rifle.

Ky burst around the corner, firing as he moved. His first shots eliminated the two Egyptian officers. More rifles fired behind him. The three remaining enemy soldiers broke and ran.

Ky pressed on, clearing trench after trench. Eastern resistance collapsed. In an hour, it was all over and the entire front-line position had been secured. Britannian forces pushed further, capturing the enemy's reserve trenches and support positions.

His men seemed ready to chase the runners all the way into Sarmatia. Ky reluctantly had to stop them to keep his own line from becoming dangerously overextended.

Hundreds of prisoners sat in groups under guard, their weapons stacked nearby. Britannian soldiers moved through the captured trenches, collecting abandoned equipment and tending to the wounded from both sides.

The war wasn't over, but they'd finally managed to get ahead of the Easterners. It felt like this might be the beginning of a new stage of the war.

Chapter 26

Camp Banwīhraz, Central Germania

Medb walked quickly toward the door to the walled prison building from her carriage. She had too much dignity to run, but the rain that had started the previous night had intensified and was coming down in thick sheets.

She was happy to be out of it, inside the brick building that was used as administration, barracks, and interrogation rooms for the large prison camp. After her first week here, she'd given up staying with the guards and had found more comfortable accommodations in a nearby village.

What she was doing took time, and she also had a standard she was used to, and she needed to be at her best for this. It was her thirty-first session with the Eastern prisoner. So far it had been mostly language lessons, with nothing beyond that learned. An important step, to be sure, but today she planned to move beyond that.

The two Britannian guards straightened as she approached.

"Lady Medb," the taller one said. "The prisoner is inside. Been waiting about ten minutes."

"Good. I'll need at least two hours. No interruptions unless the camp's being overrun."

The guards exchanged glances, uncertain if she was joking. The room was the same one they'd been using for these sessions. Familiarity, even hostile familiarity like a prison camp, made people let down their guard.

It, and a hundred other small actions, were all designed to one end. To get the man sitting at the small table inside to talk.

Fa Jian, although for these people, the second name was their given one, and the first was their surname, sat as he always did. Comfortable but aloof at the same time, hands folded on the table.

"Again today, we speak," Medb said, using the words in his language, which she found exceptionally difficult to master.

She set down a small basket containing a small bundle of dried meat, bread, and other additional rations that were his payment for doing these lessons, and took the seat across from him.

"Again today. More words, yes?" he asked in Latin.

After thirty-one sessions, she'd learned to read the minute shifts in his expression, the slight tightening around his eyes when he was actively engaged in something she said. The slight downturn of his mouth when he was frustrated.

The man was exceptional at controlling his features, which again spoke to his intelligence and self-control, but everyone showed something eventually.

"More words, yes. But different today. I think you understand more than you show."

His face remained impassive, but something stirred behind his eyes.

"Small understanding," he replied.

"No," she said, switching to Latin. "You understand far more than you admit. You like to hide it, but you are very intelligent and understand more than you let on. You've been pretending to learn slowly, but you listen very closely when I talk to the guards. You've been watching and listening. I'm honestly impressed. I would do the same."

Jian tilted his head slightly, reassessing her.

"What questions today?" He asked, not dropping the charade.

"First, I want to understand something I've observed. You avoid the high-ranking prisoners, the officers and administrators at the center of the camp who've secured better food and sleeping arrangements. Why?"

"Not understand."

"I think you do understand. I have watched you for weeks. You deliberately keep your distance from them. When food is distributed, you position yourself away from them. Them, I understand. Such men are typically the same in every empire. Those who order conquests while remaining safely distant from bloodshed, and demanding tribute without labor. They impose their will on common people without suffering any consequences. I've known their type my whole life."

The prisoner's eyes narrowed fractionally.

"If I had to guess, these were the men that control your empire, just as their type once controlled mine. Perhaps we share a common disdain for such men, despite fighting on opposite sides."

"How say 'season change' in your tongue?"

Medb ignored his deflection. Her instincts told her she'd struck a nerve, and thirty years of political intrigue had honed those instincts well.

"I haven't always done this job. Before this, I was a queen of my own people, until Carthage came to my island and convinced us to fight for them. And then abandoned us. I didn't see it at the time, but I think even in defeat, we were liberated. Freed of the yoke the Carthaginians put on everyone, friend and foe alike. I know what it means to hate those kinds of men, and I recognize the look of a man who holds such feelings hidden."

Again, he didn't answer, but she could see the understanding in his eyes. He was getting what she was saying.

"I'm sure you've figured this out, but prisoners who provide valuable intelligence receive considerations, better quarters, additional food, potential freedom. The more valuable the information, the greater the consideration. But I don't think that's what you want. You don't want better rations. You have purpose beyond survival. Men like you always do."

His eyes met hers directly now, calculated passivity momentarily set aside.

"Someone with the right information could ask for more than mere comforts," she offered. "They could name their true desire, however ambitious."

"What promise would person have? Words between enemies mean little," Jian said, the sudden stilted version of Latin gone.

There were still small errors, but this was the real man, at last. At least a taste of him.

"True. But some enemies share greater enemies. Some conflicts mask opportunities. A man I know once told me, 'the enemy of my enemy is my friend.' Perhaps we are friends, after a fashion."

"That kind friend is dangerous."

"Indeed. You know, I think there are moments for some people when they see an opportunity, but fear takes hold and they let it slip away. Other people, though, they see the opportunity for what it is and do not let the fear control them. These people are the people who get things done. I think maybe you are the second type of person. For people like that, these moments create possibilities. But only if they're willing to risk something of value in exchange."

He didn't say anything, but she could see he was very interested in what she was saying.

"The time for dancing around each other has ended. I need information about your empire. You need something from me. Let us speak plainly."

Jian sat motionless, weighing his options. Outside, rain pounded against the roof.

"Ask your questions. Why have you pulled me from sleep thirty-two days in line?"

"Part of it was the language lessons. We needed to communicate to get this far, after all. But you're right, my interest goes beyond vocabulary. I want to know about your people. We know next to nothing about you, except your homeland lies to the east."

"It does."

"Where?"

"The main part of our country is very far. It took weeks and weeks to get here. Many week groups. Something ..."

"Months," she offered.

"Yes. Months. It takes more than two months to get here from the capital, although the edges of the empire are only a few weeks travel."

"It extends that far?" she asked, surprised.

"It does."

"Show me the area your empire covers," she said, pulling a paper out of her pocket and unfolding it, showing a hand-drawn map messaged to her by the Consul.

She had been shocked when she'd seen what the world actually looked like, not that she doubted him. But comparing the areas she did know, such as Britannia and Germania, to the parts to the east, beyond Sarmatia, she hadn't known how vast that land could be.

"Where did you get this?" he asked, showing true surprise for the first time.

"That question is for another time. First, show me the extent of your people's lands."

Jian hesitated before placing his finger on the eastern coast at the far end of the land mass and then tracing a boundary that stretched all the way to Sarmatia and the far edges of Alexander's empire. From the north of the land mass all the way to the south. They essentially controlled everything east of Anatolia, Sarmatia, and Persia.

A truly terrifying amount of land, vast beyond anything they had estimated, easily triple the lands once controlled by Carthage. Maybe even more.

"How can any single authority administer such a vast territory?" she asked, astonishment breaking through her control.

"We have many people like you. The empire is five rings? Levels? Parts may be the right word. The center part is Nei Du, the region of capital at Chang'an. It is ruled by the emperor and his people personally."

He put his finger on a part of the map to the far east, not at the coast, but close to it. He then circled a wider area, although still much smaller than the area they controlled as a whole.

"Second part is eighteen pieces, the Zhong Zhou, where big men, I do not know the word for them in your language, but important men maintain rigid control in emperor's name. Third part is thirty-two army sections, again not right word but close, called Bian Jun. It is where people and army combine to control the area. Those are the three main parts of empire, controlled directly by the emperor's men. Beyond these are the ... I don't know the word, but places ruled by men not of the emperor called Feng Guo. Although other people rule these areas, they do so with the emperor's men at their elbows. The last part, farthest out, is the An Di. They give honor to the emperor, and money, but do not have the emperor's men at their elbow. Although the emperor's men are only a short time away if they do not pay with the men and gold they owe."

The language barrier was becoming something of a problem here. She thought she understood what he meant, but there was almost certainly nuance in the system of administration that was being lost.

"There must be tensions between these farther out places and those places with the emperor's men telling people what to do. I assume, like the Carthaginians, the things provided by these outer parts all flow into the ... you called it Nei Du."

"Yes. All goes to the emperor. All comes from the people."

"It must take a large army to control all of this, yes? Are they all conscripts?"

"Most yes, but not all. There are ... Qi Jun, I do not know how to explain. Soldiers trained to be soldiers, yes?"

"Professionals."

"If that is word. Good training. Good arms. They stay in the central areas. They protect, and most of the men in them come from those areas directly controlled by the emperor's men. The Nei Du, Zhong Zhou, and Bian Jun. Each area controls and gives things to the Qi Jun from this area."

"So the central parts provide professional armies made up of, I'm guessing, citizens."

"That sounds correct, if I understand words."

"You said the other parts had to pay money and men. Men I assume means soldiers."

"Untrained soldiers. Farmers given swords."

"Conscripts," she offered.

"We call them Yi Jun. They make up most of our armies and are sent to die first. Every man in every region except the Nei Du must put name on list, although names from the outer areas are chosen much more than those from the inner two areas."

"And you were a member of this Yi Jun?"

"Originally, yes. As a boy, I was taken from family farm to serve Yi Jun, but I did well and was from a Zhong Zhou, so they make me Qi Jun, the professional as you say, and pay me to fight."

"Can you tell me about what your army can do? How you get your new weapons?"

"I am just soldier, and our leaders do not tell us these things. Until three years ago, I used spear and bow. Three years ago, our spears and swords were taken and we were given rifles, like ones your people use. I do not know where they came from or how they were made."

"I thought that might be your answer, but I wanted to ask. And what about the man who rules you. I assume he's the emperor."

"Yes. Emperor. Zhengdi, the Son of Heaven, latest in an unbroken line of divine rulers."

"Tell me about him."

"He is Zhengdi. What is there to tell?"

"Anything. What he looks like."

"No one knows. No one sees him. No one hears him except for most important men. His word like word from gods. Only trusted nameless men put his voice to words and spread them."

While she got the gist of that, it was one of the most confusing sentences he'd uttered.

"A convenient arrangement for those who might wish to rule in his name."

Jian didn't contradict her.

"You have told me a lot, for which I'm grateful, but you still haven't told me what you really want."

"Maybe I just want food."

"I don't think so. The way you speak of your empire doesn't suggest loyalty to its cause. You don't strike me as a man hoping for TianYou's victory."

"Words that would take my head."

"And yet I still think they are true. You have no love for those people from Nei Du, at the center of your empire."

"I do not."

"I told you that our people once suffered under similar arrangements."

"The Carthaginians you mentioned."

"Yes. Near the end of Carthaginian rule, before we overthrew them, they were working with your masters from the east. Did you know that?"

"That is often how they work. Let a people defeat themself."

"Is that what you want? To remove your overlords as we removed the Carthaginians?"

For over a full minute, Jian didn't answer. He only stared into Medb's eyes. Studying her. She stared back in silence. If she pushed, he would retreat.

"Yes," he finally answered.

"We could help with that."

"I don't seek to replace one overlord with another. Eastern lands have no want to become western."

"We don't want that. You know, we didn't come east. We've only defended our territories against your empire's expansion."

"True. And no, not everyone in the empire wants to conquer forever. Not everyone thinks that giving up young men to make our lands bigger is right. But it is as it is. Zhengdi will not be full until he eats the world."

"Unless he's stopped," she said.

"Unless he's stopped," he agreed.

"These people who don't want the empire to be at endless war, are there those among them who are trying to stop him?"

"Yes."

"An organized group of such people?"

"Yes."

The revelation sent Medb's mind racing through potential implications. If dissidents existed within TianYou's structure, especially those with military connections like Jian clearly had, then there was a real chance to do more than just gather intelligence.

"That's very interesting. Tell me more."

Greece

Ky sat on a small folding chair inside his command tent and took a moment to close his eyes and center himself. After so long in the trenches, it was good to be on the move in open fields again. The army had set up a fortified camp for the night and had scouts out, and he could smell the wood smoke from cooking fires as men enjoyed a break from the long days of marching and fighting.

The last eleven days had moved increasingly fast, ever since the breakthrough that had collapsed the Easterners' trench line. They had pushed the enemy back nearly eighty miles. Every time the Easterners had tried to stiffen their resistance, the volume of their firepower and the ability to load quickly from cover allowed his men to push through them before a new trench line could emerge.

He knew it wouldn't last, but for now, they had the upper hand.

Ky waited for the camp to settle into its nighttime routine. Sentries posted, watches set, men in their tents. Privacy was rare in war, but these quiet after-dark moments sufficed.

"Lucilla? Are you there?"

"I'm here." Her voice came through clearly despite thousands of miles between them. "I was beginning to think you'd forgotten about me."

"Never. Just needed to wait until things quieted down. How are you holding up?"

"Well enough, all things considered. The Senate continues to be a collection of petulant children, but they're at least cooperating with the conscription efforts now. Titus asked about you today."

Ky smiled. This was a game she liked to play. Their son had said a few words, but mostly, he still only babbled. She had done this since he was a baby, filling in his side of the conversation when Ky was away.

"Did he? What did he say?"

"He wanted to know when Father would come home to play horses with him. He says he misses being carried on your shoulders."

"Tell him his Father misses him just as much, and I can't wait to see him. Did he get the legion figures I sent?"

A gift made by one of the more talented men in the army. Ten little legionaries carved from wood with a surprising amount of detail.

"He sleeps with one in his crib and cries when he's not allowed to have it. Pretty soon, he will have them all out, lined up for battle," she said, before her voice turned serious as she got to business. "How does the breakthrough progress? Sophus was light on details when I asked."

"Probably because things are changing rapidly. Right now, the advance has stalled a bit as we've outrun our supply lines and are starting to spread thin. The initial push went well, thanks in no small part to the new rifles. They were completely unprepared for the rate of fire. We're entering a new phase of the war, I think. At least until the Easterners copy the design."

"It seems that way. I received an update from Germania, where they've just had a breakthrough themselves, after getting their first shipment of rifles."

"I saw that. I think Bomilcar's going to have a bigger issue as he starts to push them back than we did. We're in a compressed area, but most of his line is protected by riverboats. He's going to have problems once he moves past the river system. Even with the better rifles, their larger armies will flank us. I trust Bomilcar to not let that happen, but it means we will only advance so far. I think that will be what ends our advance here as well. Once we swing up and hit the Black Sea, we will have to pause until we have the manpower to continue beyond. We'll need to consolidate our position, bring up reinforcements."

"The new conscripts should be out of training in a few months. That should give you the manpower you need to push further."

"I hope so. Although by then the Easterners may have copied our weapons and we will be back where we started, held at trench lines. It's bothering me how fast the Easterners have been copying our designs. From when they got the smuggled shells to when they had their own version was only a few months. Our rifles, our cannons, they're replicating everything at an alarming rate."

"It is an unexplained complication. A civilization without direct access to the knowledge base I possess should not be able to look at a finished product and then reverse engineer it in less than a year," Sophus interjected. *"Even accounting for captured examples and espionage, the speed of technological adoption suggests outside assistance or pre-existing knowledge."*

"I know, but that has always been an unexplained issue," Lucilla said. "We might have some movement there as well. I received a telegram from Medb yesterday. She says she's starting to make headway with one Eastern prisoner. She's learned some things about their empire and she believes he's part of some internal resistance movement within it. If that's true, we might finally find out what we're actually facing."

"We might."

"But?" She asked, hearing something in his voice he couldn't mask.

"But it still bothers me that there's a Chinese kingdom that stretches as far as this man says it does. In my history, China remained fragmented for centuries during this period. Even when it unified, it never projected power like this."

"You always said this time was different from the one you knew. So that could be different too, couldn't it?"

"Yes, but there are a lot of reasons they never got that large in my time, and those reasons should still remain true. Geography hasn't changed. The logistics of maintaining an empire across Central Asia are almost insurmountable with pre-industrial technology. Even with later technologies, it wasn't possible. The fact that they also had cannons seven years ago, even crude ones, has always bothered me. None of it makes sense."

"What are you suggesting?"

"I don't know exactly. But there's more going on here, and until we find the answer, there's still a chance there's something out there that will be an issue. Possibly a fatal one."

"You are too much of a pessimist. We'll deal with that when it comes just as we always have," Lucilla said. "For now, the war goes well and we are winning. You've pushed them back in Greece, Bomilcar has them retreating almost to Sarmatia, and Valdar controls the Middle Sea and has taken Alexandria. We are winning."

"Yes," Ky admitted. "For now."

To Be Continued ...

About the author

Travis writes science fiction, fantasy, and thriller novels (and the occasional coming-of-age story), with the hope of transporting and enthralling readers. Publishing novels since 2015, Travis's passion is creating worlds and characters that live and breathe, and experiencing the joy of those stories with his readers. When not writing, Travis enjoys connecting with readers and other writers, managing the popular Complete Marvel Reading Order website, where he works on his other passion for comics and graphic novels, and spending time with his family. If you have enjoyed this book, please consider taking a moment to rate or review it wherever you found your copy, as it helps new readers find my works and ensures I can continue writing book into the future.

Find out more at:
amazon.com/TravisStarnes/e/B072YBDC3S/

Or visit
https://tstarnes.com

Maps available at
https://tstarnes.com/book-series/imperium/

Signup to get free previews and notifications of upcoming books at
http://tstarnes.com/preview-notification-newsletter/

Also by

John Taylor Stories

Rebirth
False Signs
The Wrong Girl
Burying the Past
Family Ties
Election Day
Danger Close
Extraction
Designated Target
Border Crossed
Desperate Rendition

Country Roads Series

Playing by Ear
Fanfare
Dissonance
Elegy
From the Top
Center Stage

Imperium Series

Volume 1
The Sword of Jupiter
The Trumpets of Mars
The Sands of Saturn
The Depths of Neptune
The Fires of Vulcan
The Triumph of Venus
Volume 2
The Wings of Mercury
The Plains of Pluto

Shattered Lands Series

In the Shadow of Lions
An Ending of Oaths
The Barons' War

False Start Series

Second Down
Scramble

The Veilguard Saga

Threads of Destiny
The Blackstar Legacy

Stand Alone

Going Home

www.ingramcontent.com/pod-product-compliance
Lightning Source LLC
Chambersburg PA
CBHW070627260626
47161CB00007B/2616